Thorns of Malice

WILTED KINGDOM DUET
BOOK 2

MAGGIE COLE

Pulse Press Inc.

Dear Reader,

This duet is a dark romance, which may be unsettling for some readers. My characters Dax Carrington and Ivy Ford both evolve through this duet; however, this is not for the faint of heart.

Book one begins when they are in college. This first part of the duet is a college bully, dark billionaire romance. Book two takes place ten years later and continues as a dark billionaire, second chance romance where Ivy is determined to get revenge for all Dax did to her.

Please note I said dark.

Expect substance abuse, addiction, sexual manipulation, graphic and taboo sexual scenes including multiple partners, dub con, humiliation, bullying, revenge, and heart-wrenching chapters.

If you don't like dark romance, or any of these elements, then I advise you not to read. I have faith you know your triggers.

I promise you that if you decide to read, Dax and Ivy will have their happily ever after. And both of them will redeem themselves in the end.

Thank you for reading (or not if it's not your thing).

XOXO

Maggie Cole

Contents

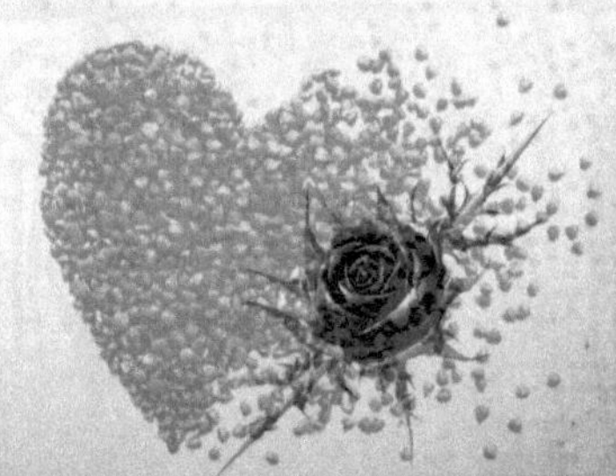

Contents

Contents

Ivy 1

THAT'S MY GIRL

Jaxon Savoia presses me closer against the dirty, white, peeling wall, his hot breath against my ear, ordering, "Come now, Ivy." He thrusts harder, over and over, until adrenaline finally releases throughout me.

It's a teaser, giving me only a moment of relief. The high I'm desperate to experience—the one that should have faded into a mere memory by now but is stronger than ever—stays buried deep.

"That's my girl," he grits, pumping everything he has into me until he's spent.

His ragged breathing is fiercer than mine. He stays planted, his chest filling with air against my spine until it's almost back to normal. "We have to stop doing this," he reminds me, spinning me to face him and stepping back to pull up his pants.

"Spoken to the choir," I mumble, grabbing wet wipes from my purse and cleaning myself up. I tug the hem of my dress down over my hips.

He secures his belt and reaches into his sports coat. He takes a swig of whiskey from a flask and then hands it to me.

I take a sip, barely grimacing as the hot liquid warms my throat.

"You wore that dress on purpose today, didn't you?" he accuses, his eyes narrowing in a bizarre ironic state of disapproval and approval.

My insides quiver, my pussy throbbing once again in need. Jaxon's expression briefly reminds me of the only man I ever loved.

I'd do anything to forget Dax Carrington, yet nothing will let me. And every time I see that look in Jaxon's eyes, no matter how quickly it comes and goes, Dax's face lights up all the memories I crave to relive and hate to remember, torturing me further.

Jaxon steps closer, tilting my face toward the ceiling, demanding, "Admit it. You planned on derailing me again."

"Did you expect any different?" I question.

His lips twist, and it's probably another reason I allowed myself to get into this situation with him. There's something sadistic about his mouth, reminding me again of Dax.

I have to stop thinking about him.

He destroyed me.

Jaxon's phone buzzes, and he releases me. He pulls it out of his pocket, taps the screen, and motions for me to go first.

"You're such a party killer," I whine.

He grunts. "Last week, you were the one who insisted we attend the meeting."

I begrudgingly open the door, carefully step out into the alley, and get slapped with a gust of wind. I hustle around the building and up the steps of the church, brushing past the smokers and hating myself even more.

"Ivy," Ben greets me, giving me his welcoming smile.

"Hi, Ben," I say, then sit on the cold metal chair.

Several of the smokers come inside, and Jaxon follows. He plops in a chair across from me, avoiding my gaze, and makes small talk with the woman beside him.

"Welcome to Sex Addicts Anonymous. It's good to see all of you. It looks like we don't have anyone new today, so let's get started," Ben states, then sips his coffee and sits inside the small circle. As if he knows what I've been up to, he directs, "Ivy, why don't you start today."

Guilt fills me like it does at every meeting. Most of the time, I wonder why I allow Jaxon to force me to attend. I've never abstained for more than four days, and I confess my last encounter in every meeting. No matter how I attempt to do better, I can't. And over time, my addiction has only gotten worse.

Jaxon nods in encouragement, and I want to slap him. We met in this room years ago, the first day I attempted to rid myself of my impulsive behavior. We sat side by side. I quickly learned he was the CEO of Blooming Gardens, a national wholesale floral corporation, and it led to a long conversation about botany. By the end of the month, we had not only formed a friendship, but he offered me a job and a scholarship to finish my schooling.

It felt too good to be true, like when my father told me the Carringtons would put me through Clifton University. So I resisted at first, but Jaxon finally won.

My father was barely making ends meet, and we needed extra income. It was my fault he lost his high-paying job with the Carringtons. What Jaxon offered for my monthly wage was more than Dad made in six months, so I wanted to do whatever I could to help out.

It's another thing that torments me. My father's never gotten a decent job since Dax fired him. He won't even apply for one. It's as if his spirit was broken the day Dax demanded we leave the estate.

The only thing I could do to help my father was accept Jaxon's job and be grateful. I knew it didn't change anything. It's my fault Dad was in the position he was in. Yet it gave me a small amount of relief to contribute to the household.

Over the years, Jaxon's been a great mentor, boss, and friend. But our weaknesses run deep.

Maybe it's because we know the other's demons, but it didn't take long until we were feeding each other's addictions. No matter how much we try to stop, we can't.

At first, I thought he needed it more than I did. He constantly tempted me until I caved, which didn't take a lot of persuasion.

Lately, I can't stop pulling him down the rabbit hole with me. Every move I make centers around getting my next fix. And the fact I keep coming back to this church tosses my hypocrisy in my face once a week.

I wouldn't have come today if it weren't for Jaxon's one rule. I have to show up to every meeting or I lose my job. It's his nonnegotiable.

The one time I didn't take his threat seriously and skipped, he suspended me for a week with a final warning. Then he sat me down, and we had a long discussion about the importance of beating our addictions.

After I signed a form promising to attend future meetings, I batted my eyes how Avery Carrington used to, seduced Jaxon, and he pinned me down on his desk and fucked me hard.

When we finished, we once again said it was the last time and went off to our meeting.

"Ivy," Ben repeats.

Anxiety floods me as it always does, mixing with my shame. I'm a twenty-eight-year-old woman who can't let go of the past. I pay for it daily, as does my father, who never forgets. He may not speak about what happened, but anytime he looks at me, it's always with pity. He tries to hide it, but I see it.

Jaxon nods at me again.

I swallow hard, then admit, "I'm Ivy, and I'm a sex addict. It's been..." I glance at my watch and cringe internally, continuing, "...six, maybe seven minutes since I've indulged in my addiction."

"Hi, Ivy," the room offers in unison, with no judgment.

Ben asks, "How did it make you feel?"

I bite my lip, fidgeting with my fingers, trying to think of something more creative than my typical answer, especially with Jaxon, who's been so good to me, sitting across from me.

I can't think of anything but the blinding truth. So I take a deep breath, lock eyes with Jaxon, and admit, "Empty. Disappointed."

He gives me the same look he always does. It's full of compassion and understanding, which somehow makes me feel worse today.

"What else?" Ben asks.

Without thinking, I keep my gaze on Jaxon and blurt out, "Unable to attain the high I crave but ready to try again."

His eyes turn to fire. He licks his lips, his chest slowly rising higher, and his fingers dig into his knees.

"Ivy, look at me," Ben orders.

I wait a calculated moment, knowing what it does to Jaxon, pretending I'm Avery and hating myself for it. She's another person I want to forget but can't. The fact that I replicate so much of what she does makes zero sense. Yet I can't help myself.

Jaxon shifts in his seat, and I finally turn toward Ben. He questions, "Do you believe you'll find what you desperately want if you indulge in your addiction?"

I shake my head, knowing I won't. It doesn't matter who I fuck, where, or how. There's no recreating what I felt with Dax. Or that night...

I squeeze my eyes shut as a flashback torments me. Bobby's pushing my head into Lilly's pussy while Dax's and Bobby's cocks thrust in and out of me in tandem, my body violently convulsing with pleasure. Then Dax is pushing everyone off me, caging his warm, hard body over me and creating another hit of adrenaline so intense I blackout for a brief moment.

"Ivy, come back to us," Ben firmly orders, tearing me out of my flashback.

I blink hard and swipe at my cheek, realizing I'm crying. I sniffle. "Sorry."

"It's okay. Everything you're feeling is okay," he reassures.

But it's not. It never will be, and I know it.

I stay silent for several moments, and Ben finally says, "Carrie, why don't you go next."

I barely hear her or any of the others. When the meeting ends, I rush out of the building with Jaxon on my heels.

"Ivy," he calls out, grabbing my arm at the bottom of the steps.

"Not now," I warn, not looking at him.

"Ivy—"

"I said not now," I shriek, spinning to face him, full of another emotion I never escape—raging anger.

He slowly lifts his hands in the air. "I'm here if you need me."

I say nothing, hightail it down the street, and jump on the

bus before it pulls away. I find a seat toward the back and get lost in my self-loathing.

It's dark by the time the bus driver stops in my neighborhood. I keep alert, rushing past anyone I encounter, relieved when I enter my front door. I lock it and call over the TV, "Dad, I'm home."

He doesn't reply, which is unusual.

The hairs on my neck rise, and I call out again, turning the corner into the family room.

A choking sound fills the air. Dad's in his armchair, holding his chest.

I rush over to him, fretting, "Dad!"

Sweat covers his purple cheeks. His widened blue eyes glisten.

"Dad!" I cry out, grabbing his cold hand.

His eyes roll, and foam spills past his lips.

My insides quiver. "Dad!" I pull my phone out of my purse and try to turn it on, but my gut dives when I realize the battery's dead.

"No, no, no!" I sob, glancing at the table and patting Dad's empty pockets.

The purple deepens, more foam falls, and I tug him into me, weeping.

He freezes, his eyes wide open.

"Dad," I shriek, my hands on his cheeks. "Dad! Breathe!"

He doesn't take in any more oxygen. The warmth leaves his body, and his face goes slack.

I tug him into me, sobbing until I have no more tears. Feeling numb, it takes a few moments for the sound of loud music to register.

I slowly turn, and then paralysis hits me.

The TV shows Avery Carrington, sitting with her legs

crossed and perfectly manicured hands in her lap, beaming at talk show host Winter Sophia.

"Welcome back. If you're just joining us, we've been discussing the newest scent developed by Avery Carrington. Tell us more about how you created Seducing Ivy," Winters asks, holding up a bottle of perfume in the shape of the letter I. It has whore-red garnets and diamonds encrusted on it. A vine of gold ivy leaves wraps around the pendant with more garnets etching the vine.

Whore red.

My stomach churns. It's the same design as the necklace she gave me the night of my demise. The color of the I matches the nail polish and lipstick Dax used to insist I wear.

Avery chirps, *"Well—"*

"I think it's best if I explain, don't you, dear sister?" a voice calls out, and my insides tremble harder.

The camera turns, and an older, sexier, more filled-out Dax Carrington appears. He leans down, kisses a surprised Winter on the cheek, then does the same to his sister and sits on the sofa beside her.

Avery quickly gets over her surprise, and her smile reappears. *"Dax."*

"Well, isn't this a treat! If you don't already know, this is Dax Carrington, CEO of Carrington Enterprises and Avery's oldest brother," Winter gushes.

Dax grins, and my world continues to fall apart. That grin has haunted me for ten years, never fading from my memory. He states, *"I wanted to support my sister's latest venture. I hope it's okay to join you."*

"Of course!" Winter exclaims.

Avery's expression never changes, and I can feel her seething underneath, but it's something the rest of the world wouldn't pick up on.

Dax nods. *"Great. I think you asked how we created Seducing Ivy?"*

"She meant how Avery Carrington Scents created it," Avery corrects.

Dax nods at her and grins wider. *"That's right."* He repositions his gaze on Winter, stating, *"As a subsidiary of Carrington Enterprises, we allowed Avery Carrington Scents to incorporate in their latest perfume our newest, and soon-to-be highly-sought-after, hybrid flower."*

Winter arches her eyebrows. *"Love your confidence for your new flower."*

Dax grins confidently. *"Yes, well, I don't ever make statements I can't back up."*

"Fair enough. So tell me, what's so important about this new flower?" Winter questions.

Dax continues, *"A lot, Winter."*

"Like?"

"The—" Avery starts to answer.

"For starters, the new hybrid creates a vibrant red blooming flower. The scent is incredible and the blooms stay alive 80% longer once they're unattached from the plant. I anticipate it'll cut the demand for roses in half before the end of the year," Dax interjects, speaking over her.

Winter gapes.

"What my brother means—" Avery tries say but is once again interrupted by Dax.

"I mean, every floral shop in the world will want the new hybrid," he declares.

"So you have a new million-dollar product," Winter gushes.

Dax chuckles. *"Try over a billion dollars."*

Winter's shocked expression appears again, but she recovers faster this time, stating, *"Sounds like we should show our viewers what this newest craze-to-be looks like!"*

The sound of applause floats from the TV.

A pop-up screen shows ivy crawling up a wall with gorgeous red flowers dancing around it.

"How did you create this new hybrid?" Winters asks.

"I—" Dax starts.

"He's always had a knack for knowing how to take the winners to the patent table, haven't you, Dax?" Avery interjects.

Something passes over Dax's expression, but it fades almost as soon as it appears. He nods, claiming, *"It's why my grandfather chose me to run Carrington Enterprises. He knew I'd continue to grow it."*

Hatred fills Avery's expression, but she quickly recovers, and her sugar-laced voice adds, *"And my grandfather saw how my enterprising ideas would take the assets Carrington Enterprises have and expand them into billions of dollars' worth of profits."*

Winter beams. *"Such brains between you two."*

Avery leans closer to the camera and lowers her voice, as if she's letting me in on a secret, keeping my trance fixated on her, claiming, *"Seducing Ivy is the most important project we've ever worked on, isn't it, Dax?"* She slowly glances at him.

A look of disgust briefly flashes on his face and then it morphs into agreement. He pulls me in just as Avery did, answering, *"If I'm telling the truth, Ivy's the only thing that's ever mattered to me."*

My insides crumble. A new wave of heartache, rage, and grief hits. I grab the rose paperweight on the table and hurl it at the TV.

Glass shards land several feet in front of me. I wrap my arms around my father's cooling corpse, wailing.

I don't know how much time passes before I calm down. I take my phone to my bedroom, put it on my charger, and look around the house for my father's cell so I can call 9-1-1, unsure what I'm supposed to do with his body.

I can't find it anywhere. I grab my charger and phone, return to the living room, and plug it into the outlet. I set my cell on the table and sit beside Dad, still in shock.

Several moments pass. I turn to see if I can make a call, then I freeze.

Dad's worn, tattered, leather-bound notebook sits next to my phone. He's used it for as long as I can remember to write down all his ideas. I pick it up, stroking the leather, tearing up again.

I wipe my face, open it, and cry harder at seeing his hand-writing. After a few moments pass, I calm down. I review each page, remembering how excited he'd get when he thought he was on to something new.

Halfway through the notebook, I turn the page and discover a white, folded piece of paper. I open it, muttering, "What is this, Dad?"

It's a printed page from the United States Patent and Trademark Office. As I read it, four words cause bile to creep up my throat.

Seducing Ivy.

Patent granted to Daxton Everett Carrington V.

My pulse skyrockets.

Why is this in my father's notebook?

In a new state of shock, I read the paper again, then stare at Dad's notes, focusing on several words.

Red blooming ivy.

$10,000 patent attorney.

My eyes dart between the printout and my father's hand-writing of a date from fifteen years ago, until the truth becomes clear.

How did Dax get Dad's notebook?

This is my fault.

Dad knew what he did.

I stare at the broken TV, an onslaught of new guilt soaking my entire being until I'm drowning in grief and self-hatred.

There are no tears this time. A snowball of something new rolls at lightning speed, growing bigger until I can't see straight.

It's the need for revenge.

I put my head on Dad's chest, squeezing his freezing hands, muttering over and over, "I'm sorry. I'll make him pay. I'll make all of them pay."

How?

There's no room to be weak or feel sorry for yourself, Ivy.

I straighten up, squeeze Dad's hand, and pick up my phone. I take several deep breaths and dial 9-1-1.

A woman answers. "911. What's your emergency?"

My voice cracks. New tears fall. I state, "My father's dead."

Dax 2

EARN HER TRUST

Winter holds up the perfume bottle, deeply inhales, and groans. She looks at the audience and beams, "Seducing Ivy is my new go-to scent! But if you're in the audience, you don't have to rush out to the store to purchase your own bottle! Avery's been kind enough to give everyone in this room a special gift!"

The audience goes wild, and my sister beams.

Enjoy your moment while you can, Avery. I'll take you down soon.

Winter's staff appears in the aisles, passing out travel kits with Seducing Ivy body wash, lotion, and perfume.

When things calm, Winter declares, "Let's give a huge round of applause for Avery and the wonderful surprise visit from Dax!"

The room erupts into more ear-shattering applause.

My grin widens, seeing my sister's fake smile stay planted on her face and knowing she's beyond pissed.

I stole her moment. I knew I would before I decided to step on stage, and any chance she attempted to speak, I shot her down.

Serves the bitch right.

We rise, and I kiss Winter on the cheek, then leave the stage as she announces her next guest.

Avery's quick on my heels. She waits until the staff takes our mics off and we're in the elevator. She's seething. "You piece of shit."

A giddiness I rarely experience anymore warms my insides. It almost makes me feel drunk.

Getting under my sister's skin has gotten harder over the years. She gets better at her games, and I can't seem to beat her like I used to. I haven't for ten years.

She ruined my life.

Ever since Avery slept with Ivy and released the sex video at Clifton University, my hatred for her hasn't diminished. If anything, it grows stronger by the day.

She's continued to claim innocence around that event, even though I know she did it. The only other person who could have done it was Bobby. Somehow, one of them tapped into my phone and computer and stole my footage of Ivy.

After I kicked her and her father off the estate, Bobby soon showed up at my doorstep, seething about how I ruined our ability to extort the senator since Lilly was all over the video.

My rage lasted months, and I didn't know if Bobby or Avery was to blame, but I finally realized it had to be Avery. Bobby was right. The video eliminated our ability to gain power via the senator.

The realization didn't make my relationship with Bobby return to normal. To this day, it still hasn't. He drugged Ivy the night of our foursome without me knowing, as did Avery, and for that, they'll both pay.

So I don't want to participate in her or Bobby's warped world. I've kept them close because that's what you do with your enemies—you don't let them out of your sight until you're ready to destroy them.

The last thing I wanted to do was give Avery access to Seducing Ivy for the company she set up with her trust money. I wanted nothing to do with it, but Avery has a knack for pulling me into most of her twisted projects, even when I don't know it's happening.

After years of secretly testing the hybrid while my attorney researched if any other patents were close to John Ford's creation, I finally filed for Seducing Ivy.

Once the patent office awarded it to me, I got drunk.

I thought I had kept my project a secret, yet somehow, my sister knew about it. She turned up in my home office while I was celebrating by myself, but also going down the dark hole I can't seem to escape, wondering what could have been between Ivy and me.

If only she hadn't slept with my sister.

My housing situation is another thing that I'm biding my time on. The day I graduated, per my trust stipulations, I fired my father and kicked him and my mother out of the main house.

They argued with me, but I pointed out how the trust clearly stated they could live on the estate but it didn't say where. I transferred their belongings to one of the more outdated workers' cottages and moved his family to a newly updated one.

My parents tried to legally fight me, but ultimately, I won.

Unfortunately, the trust doesn't give me the power to do that with Avery or my little brother Cooper. It clearly states we all own the estate and have the right to live in the main house.

So, no matter how much Avery or Cooper annoy me, I can't get rid of them.

Yet.

I have faith in my abilities to eventually figure out how to get them out of my house. But right now, I have to deal with my sister's twisted soul and Cooper breathing down my neck, trying to prove he's a valuable asset to Carrington Enterprises.

He's not.

And Avery showed up at the exact moment I was fighting my demons, loathing myself for ever letting Bobby near Ivy and not stopping the game before rush night.

I hate how he drugged her.

I hate how Avery, or he, drugged her again at the induction brunch. I'm still unsure which of them did it, but the amount she had, sent her into a deep sleep for too long. And I know what happens if you take too much or too many doses in a short time span. Bobby's father was always clear that the drug he created could turn goats into nymphomaniacs.

To this day, I wonder if my sister drugged Ivy again the night she slept with her or if Ivy willingly fell for Avery's charm. Either way, when I let myself go down the Ivy rabbit hole, I can't get the images of my sister and her kissing out of my mind.

So when Avery barged into my office with a folder, I was already three sheets to the wind and reliving my nightmares. I told her to get out, but she waved a piece of paper in my face, claiming if I was going to steal John Ford's hybrid, then didn't I want to rub it in his face?

I was too drunk to know how she knew it was John Ford's, but after I sobered up, it reconfirmed she had to have been the one who leaked the video on campus. Avery must have seen the photos I took of John's notebook.

Avery continued to wave the paper in my face with his address. Instead of realizing I could get a private investigator and find him myself, I let my intoxicated emotions take over and fell for Avery's trap. I would have let things be as they were, knowing it was for the best.

Over the years, I thought about finding Ivy. To this day, she's the only woman who's ever captivated me. But anytime I contemplate finding her, the scene with Avery's hand on her pussy and their lips locked stops me.

So Avery caught me at the perfect time, and the temptation was too much. Her plan to throw Seducing Ivy into John Ford's face suddenly seemed like I had to do it.

He hated me before he laid eyes on me. It was my father's fault, but he never would have given me a fair chance. There were even times Ivy stayed away from me because of him.

So I became desperate for Avery to give me information I could have found myself.

She conveniently had a contract ready for me to make her company a subsidiary of Carrington Enterprises. She'd wanted it for a long time, and I never understood why. However, I wouldn't give it to her just because she wanted it.

Until that night.

There was a clause stating she got to utilize Seducing Ivy for a new fragrance line, but I was too drunk and drooling over the information she had in her hand.

Once I signed and she gave me the paper with John Ford's address, I kicked her out of my office.

I went to the patent website where it stated Seducing Ivy was awarded to me, printed it off, then stuck it in an envelope.

I contemplated driving to Georgia and hand-delivering it so I could see his face when he opened it.

But I knew deep down I wanted to see Ivy more.

And then the vision of her and Avery filled my mind once again.

I addressed the envelope, put it in the outgoing mail, and burned the paper my sister gave me, knowing it was too dangerous for me to keep.

But my actions for being weak that night created deeper consequences, and I curse myself for the millionth time.

Avery's company is part of Carrington Enterprises. The necklace she gave to Ivy that I designed, which my sister took credit for, is the one my little slut wore so proudly with her matching whore-red lipstick and nail polish. And now it's for the entire world to see.

I tried to forget about that necklace. It represents everything about the night I wish never happened.

Now, it'll forever be in my face. Seducing Ivy is a game changer in the floral business, and Avery's surely created a best-seller.

So I hate my sister more than ever. Stealing her moment of glory gave me satisfaction, but it's only the start of what I'm about to unleash.

The elevator dings and the doors open. I motion with my hand, stating, "After you, dear sister."

She glares at me harder and struts out of the elevator, and I follow. We turn the corner, and everything I planned turns to reality.

A crowd fills the lobby, along with a small stage with a microphone and podium. Cameras flash, and too many reporters yell at us.

Avery thinks they're for her. She steps onto the stage. Her smile widens, and she puts her hands in the air. She instructs, "One at a time. I'll answer all your questions about Avery

Carrington Scent's newest creation, Seducing Ivy, but please, be polite and ask one at a time." She winks.

Giddy once again, I step beside my sister and boast, "They aren't here for you."

She snaps her face toward me with a rarely seen expression on her face.

Avery always thinks she knows what's coming. It's rare she doesn't. This is the start of her demise.

I lean into her ear and mutter, "Checkmate."

She freezes, holding her breath.

I glance at the crowd and point to a reporter from the biggest news station in the country. "Tommy, what's your question?"

His cameraman turns a light on him, and another guy points a brighter one toward me.

Tommy asks, "Trademark paperwork and several patents have been filed for Hybrid Pharmaceuticals. Dax, you're listed as the CEO and 100% shareholder. Is this correct?"

I nod. "Yes."

"And the rumor on the street is one billion dollars has been transferred into the new company?"

Avery's body stiffens next to mine.

"It's a private company. I'm going to keep that in my secret vault for now," I answer, then give my sister a look to confirm it's true.

The color begins to fade from her cheeks.

I point at another reporter. "Sally, what's your question?"

A bleach-blonde woman steps forward. "Is it true you've created several breakthrough drugs to deal with the after-effects of what's known on the streets as Trance?"

I glance at Avery with more endorphins soaring through me. She grows paler. I stand taller, replying, "Yes."

"And Trance is legally called Ecliptamine, a drug Winston Pharmaceuticals created for the meat industry?"

"Yes. Danny, you're next," I say, pointing at a former Texan who works for the *Global Times*. I'm loving how this is going exactly as planned.

He drawls, "Winston Pharmaceuticals' main shareholder is Robert Winston, Jr., the father of Robert Winston, III, who most people refer to as Bobby, correct?"

Hook, line, and sinker.

I put my most somber face on. "Yes, that's correct."

"Does your interest in Trance have anything to do with Bobby's legal issues?" Danny continues.

"Can you expand on that question, please?" I ask, letting Danny play right into my hand.

He arches his eyebrows and adds, "Over the years, several lawsuits against Bobby Winston disappeared quickly after they were filed. Claims in these lawsuits all stated he used his father's drug, Ecliptamine, known on the street as a date rape drug called Trance. The women and men claimed in the initial filings they were drugged without their knowledge, and they not only did things they would never do, but they had ongoing issues controlling their sexual urges afterward."

"I can't comment on Bobby's legal issues," I state. I point to a redhead. "Karen. You're next."

Avery shifts next to me.

Karen declares, "Two patents were filed on behalf of Hybrid Pharmaceuticals."

"That's correct. My attorney filed a third"—I glance at my watch—"about ten minutes ago."

Avery grips the podium so tight her knuckles turn white.

Karen says, "My understanding is that one of your new drugs is to stop the sexual urges from getting worse. Is this correct?"

I reply, "You're referring to our drug CogniShift. What we've concluded is if a male or female—or any animal, I should point out—is given too much or too many doses of Trance in a short time span, they'll have increased sexual urges that only get worse over time. So this particular drug we created will stop them from worsening."

"But it won't eliminate them?" Karen questions.

I shake my head. "No. That's why we created our second drug, NeuroZap, for when CogniShift doesn't give enough relief to the victim."

"NeuroZap is the drug that eliminates all addictive urges?" Karen asks.

"Yes."

"So why don't you give everyone NeuroZap? What's the point of only giving them CogniShift?"

"That's a good question, Karen."

"Well?" she urges.

I admit, "NeuroZap comes with a side effect the patient may not want to experience. It should be taken with extreme caution."

"What is the side effect?"

My chest tightens. I confess, "I wish we could eliminate this issue, but so far, my research and development team hasn't found a way. For some patients, they'll want to take it no matter what. For others, they won't want to take it if given the information and choice."

"Why?"

"There's a risk they won't ever have any sexual desire again. So some people won't want to take that risk. For others, they're willing to do it because the addiction has gotten so overwhelming it's destroying their everyday life. So even taking CogniShift to stop the progression isn't enough."

The reporters all raise their hands.

"Alex," I direct, pointing to a dweeby twenty-something man who works for a national radio syndicate.

He clears his throat. "What's the third drug?"

I keep my gaze off Avery, too afraid I'll be unable to handle my glee. I answer, "TimeMarker. It's a drug used in conjunction with our proprietary software. The patent for the technology was filed ten minutes ago as well. Through our research and development, we discovered that Trance leaves an imprint on DNA. TimeMarker pinpoints any exposure down to the date and hour a victim was drugged, as well as the amount of the drug ingested."

A reporter calls out, "Will it hold up in court?"

"I expect the head of my research team to be in court often, until the precedent is sent that TimeMarker is admissible in legal cases. In addition, I've already sent thorough data to several senators who are on board with pushing this agenda through the courts. And that's our hope. To help victims find justice against their predators. Isn't that right, Avery?" I turn toward her.

She takes a deep breath and recovers, putting on her sympathetic expression. "Yes."

Another reporter calls out, "Aren't you afraid this might cause a rift in your friendship with Bobby Winston?"

Avery slightly flinches.

I refocus on the press. "As you mentioned, lawsuits filed against Bobby were all dropped. I can't comment on legal things, as I'm not an attorney, but if he's as innocent as he claims, my drug would also prove it." My stomach flips, knowing he's far from it.

He deserves what's coming to him.

"If you'll excuse us, my sister and I have more meetings to attend today," I state, whisking my sister off the stage and through the yelling press.

We step out into the cold air, and I breathe deeply, feeling alive for the first time in years. I escort Avery to my SUV and the driver opens the door.

She slides in, and I follow, putting the divider wall up and hitting the record button I had installed. The last thing I'm going to be is unprepared for this conversation.

When it's shut, she fumes, "What have you done, Dax?"

"Created a trillion-dollar empire," I state.

She hisses, "You snake!"

"Snake? I'm not the snake, Avery. I don't have to drug up my sexual partners."

She stares at me and then her expression slowly turns into a smirk.

My chest tightens. I hate it when she acts like she has one over on me. She usually does, but I won't give her the satisfaction. I keep my haughty gaze pinned on her.

She breaks the silence first, claiming, "You know damn well Bobby slipped Ivy Trance the night of your foursome."

"Yeah. He admitted it to me in a text the day after. I had no idea. I'm not to blame," I declare, but guilt still hits me.

Avery scoffs. "You're not to blame? You manipulated Ivy just like the rest of us."

Regret tries to annihilate me, but I push past it, claiming, "I didn't drug her. Bobby did, and I didn't know, or I'd have never let her do anything."

"Don't act so high and mighty, Dax," Avery seethes.

"What's wrong, little sister? Worried some of your actions might come back to bite you?" I taunt.

Red anger flares on her cheeks. Her eyes turn to slits. She shakes her head. "Destroy the drugs, Dax."

I chuckle. "You wish."

"I mean it. You're taking things too far. At least destroy TimeMarker," she orders.

All the time and money to develop the drugs were worth this moment. And more wins are coming.

I lean closer and study my sister, wanting to hold on to this rare occasion.

Avery's never scared. Right now, there's fear swirling with her rage.

My grin grows until my cheeks hurt.

"I mean it!" she snarls.

A high I've not felt in a long time hits me. It's the rush of the game I've refused to play with Avery for ten years. It's the same game I mastered and then regretted teaching my sister.

Now, I'm all in again.

There's no way I'm tapping out.

She accuses, "You've let Ivy turn you soft. All these years and you still can't get her out from under your skin."

"Keep thinking that," I state, but I know my sister is right.

"You're letting her win!" Avery scolds.

Maybe so, but I don't care. Ivy can win all day if Avery goes down. So I chuckle.

"This isn't funny! Destroy it," Avery repeats.

I've never felt so happy as I threaten, "Don't worry, Avery. I'm sure you'll look great in an orange jumpsuit."

Ivy 3

NOTHING LOOKS BEAUTIFUL TODAY

One Week Later

"Ivy, I think it's time to go," Jaxon gently states, readjusting the umbrella.

I don't take my eyes off the casket.

The rain pours harder, but it seems like something my father would appreciate.

He loved the rain. He said it's what makes flowers bloom, and without it, there wouldn't be beauty in the world.

Nothing looks beautiful today. I wonder if it ever will again.

If it hadn't been for Jaxon, I wouldn't have known what to do. The day after my father died, I called him, too distraught to attend work, semi-hysterical, and unsure how to even start planning Dad's burial.

Jaxon took over, making all the arrangements and even paying for it. When he asked me who I needed to notify about Dad's death, it hit me harder how much I ruined my father's life.

I unknowingly allowed Dax Carrington to destroy it.

Dad kept to himself when we moved to Georgia, not making any friends. Anybody we did know in West Virginia is long gone. So the only people who attended were people from my Sex Anonymous Group.

It's ironic. If my father knew how far I'd fallen, how I'm addicted to the thing I'm most ashamed about, I wouldn't have been able to ever look him in the eye. Yet the only people to stand next to me and bury him all suffer from my same demons. But they've all left now, and there's no one at the grave site except Jaxon and me.

The burning for revenge simmers under all my grief. I keep telling myself to get through today. Then I'll figure out how to get back at Dax and Avery for stealing my father's idea, patenting it, then announcing to the world my father's hybrid as theirs.

And I know they named it Seducing Ivy to torture Dad and me. They had to have known we'd find out. So it just solidifies that all I ever was to Dax was a sick, twisted game; something for him to conquer and destroy.

My grief and revenge aren't helping my demons. I've been more hypersexual than normal, going from crying my eyes out to being obsessed with getting my next orgasm.

A bolt of lightning streaks across the sky, followed by a loud explosion of thunder.

"Ivy, it's time," Jaxon asserts.

I stare another moment at the casket, then nod.

Jaxon puts his arm around my waist, leading me through the storm and to his car.

I slide inside.

He goes to the other side, tosses his umbrella in the back seat, and gets into the driver's seat. He turns on the engine and wipers, then the heat to defog the windows. He turns toward me, and raindrops roll down his face.

I reach for him, needing to feel anything but my pain. I want so badly to forget everything I've done. The decisions I made—choices my father warned me about, but I refused to heed—all brought me to this point.

I blurt out, "He should have had people at his funeral."

"He did," Jaxon claims.

I huff, sniffling. "No one he knew came except you, and he barely met you."

"Ivy—"

"It's true."

Jaxon takes my hand off his face and squeezes it. "The only person your dad cared about was you, and you were there. It's all that matters."

I turn toward the window, unable to see past the water running down the glass.

I need to feel anything but this.

"Take me to your place," I order.

Jaxon's voice turns darker than normal. "I don't know if that's a good idea."

My voice cracks. "Please."

He hesitates, and I think he's going to, but then he slowly shakes his head. "No, we have to stop this. This past week of all weeks, I shouldn't have let this go on."

A new anger fills me. It feels like the same rejection I experienced when Dax fired my father and wouldn't even listen to me when he kicked us off his property. It mixes with all my grief, making me feel hollower inside than ever before. But I'm not accepting Jaxon's answer. I question, "Are you going to make me beg?"

Jaxon sighs. "I won't let you do this."

"Do what?"

"I'm not going to take advantage of you while you're grieving your father's death."

I scoff. "Take advantage of me by doing the same things we've been doing for years?"

Guilt fills Jaxon's face, and I hate myself for making him feel that way, but I can't help it.

There's only one thing I know to do. Deep down, I know it'll only momentarily make me forget and feel something different, yet I'm desperate for it.

"It's not what you really need right now," Jaxon claims.

I reach for the door. "If you're not going to—"

He reaches over and grabs my arm, ordering, "Ivy, stop."

Fresh tears fall, turning into another sob. I accuse, "This isn't the time for you to be all moral."

"Ivy—"

"It's not! You've come to me before. I've never denied you. I've never rejected you."

"I'm not rejecting you." He hits the lock button.

I huff through my tears. "That's a lie." I attempt to open the door, but he must have put the child lock on. I seethe, "If you don't want to fuck me, then let me out."

"No."

My entire body trembles. I blurt out, "So you're going to drop me off at my house so I can be all alone?"

He sighs. "You can stay at my place, but we're not having sex."

I tilt my head. "I'm coming to your place, but you're not going to fuck me?"

Determination fills his expression, and he shakes his head.

But I know Jaxon. His demons are just like mine. And I need what I need. So I add, "Okay. If you want to do it before we get to your place so you feel better, we can."

"Ivy, I'm bringing you to my place as a friend. That's it."

"You can't resist it, Jaxon, just like I can't. You know it," I declare, putting my hand on his thigh, feeling so desperate to have sex that I think I might explode.

He clenches his jaw, pulling out of the cemetery.

No matter how much he tried to not fuck me this last week, he didn't win. And I always know that the threat to find somebody else to go fuck will get him to do what I want.

That's the thing about Jaxon and me. If I'm with him, then he knows I'm safe.

It's not a jealousy or control thing. If I found someone to date who treated me well, he'd be happy for me.

But I don't date. I'm only interested in getting what I need and moving on. Dax taught me a lesson I'll never forget.

Your heart is yours, so keep it. Giving it to anyone will only end up with it broken. And it's not worth the pain.

So I'm never allowing anyone to have my heart again. But that doesn't stop me from having frequent sexual encounters with different partners.

One time, I admitted in Sex Addicts Anonymous that I was frequenting a sex club and participating in anything I could, including some masochistic things I never want to do again. Those scared me, so I switched to random hookups online, which was even more unpredictable.

Jaxon didn't like it. He warned me I wasn't staying safe. We got into it, and I ignored his warning.

Then a girl choked to death at the club. It was all over the news, and I decided he was right. So we came to an agreement.

If either of us needed to go on a bender, we'd discuss it. Whatever we needed—threesomes, foursomes, guys, girls, whatever—Jaxon would ensure whoever we were fucking was safe. And we'd do everything at a high-end hotel he'd pay for so after we fed our demons, we could go back to our normal life.

I've stuck to our agreement...most of the time. There have been a few lapses, but I didn't feel safe like when I was with Jaxon. So it's been a long time since I deviated from our agreement. But I'm desperate and will do it if needed. I threaten, "I guess I'll go to the club tonight."

He doesn't say anything, gripping the steering wheel, his knuckles turning white, eyelids lowering into slits.

I settle in next to him, telling myself it'll be fine. As soon as we get to his place, he won't have a choice, and we'll both get what we need, just like we always do.

He pulls into his garage and unlocks my door. We get out of the car and go into his house.

It's large, but it's nothing like the main house on the Carrington estate. Jaxon has money, but I assume it's way less than anything Dax's family has.

Jaxon leads me through his house to the kitchen. He pulls out a chair. "Sit down, Ivy."

I don't obey. Instead, I slide my ass on the table and put my feet on the chair, moving my dress up and widening my legs. "Is this what you want? Me to sit here so you can stare at my pussy, and I can be a good little slut for you?"

He closes his eyes, and a frustrated breath comes out. He mutters, "Don't talk like that."

"You know I'm a dirty whore you can't resist," I continue, feeling the same rush of adrenaline I used to get when I'd say these things for Dax.

"Stop calling yourself that," he orders, clenching his jaw.

"Come here, Jaxon." I curl my finger and bat my lashes like Avery always did.

He doesn't move, his chest rising and falling faster.

I get off the table and take two steps toward him. I put my fingers on his chest, crawling them until I reach his lips. I murmur, "One more time, Jaxon. That's all."

He grabs my wrist. His eyes fling open. "Ivy, you just buried your father. This isn't the way we're going to handle this."

Rage fills me. "Who are you to act all moral? Don't you dare judge me, Jaxon. You, of all people, don't get to do that!" I begin sobbing, and grief, shame, and guilt hit me so hard I can't handle it. I'm soon wailing with Jaxon's arms around me.

He holds my head to his chest. "Shh. Ivy, it's okay. Everything's going to be okay."

"It's not. It'll never be okay. I destroyed my father's life." I sob, and another storm of tears erupts.

"No, you didn't. You couldn't have," Jaxon claims.

"I did. You know what happened ten years ago. You know I got him fired."

Jaxon was in the Sex Addicts Anonymous meeting when I finally confessed how I got there, what had happened to me, and how those sexual encounters I had on the Carrington estate and at the sorority house somehow changed me. I don't know how, but they did. Since then, there's been no going back, and Jaxon knows all about it.

"Shh, Ivy, that was a long time ago. You didn't ruin your father's life."

"I killed him!" I cry out, admitting what's been running through my mind the last week but never saying it aloud.

Jaxon holds me tighter. "Stop it, Ivy. You did no such thing."

"I did. I didn't obey him. And then everything he worked for... They took it! They took it, and he saw it, and that's why he had his heart attack," I admit, sobbing harder.

Jaxon holds me tighter. "Ivy, I don't know what you're talking about, but you didn't do anything."

"I did. I did. They took it. They took everything."

Jaxon shushes me. "Shh. You're hysterical right now. Calm down and tell me what you're talking about. What did they take?"

I break down, wailing so much my knees give out, emotions overwhelming me. The sorrow, the grief, the guilt, all of it hits me harder than ever before.

Jaxon somehow leads me through the kitchen and to the couch. He tugs me onto his lap, and I continue wailing.

I don't know how long my hysteria lasts. I finally calm, barely able to breathe.

"Take deep breaths," Jaxon instructs, then practices breathing with me until I'm finally just sniffling.

My face, dress, and his shirt are covered in tears.

I wipe my cheek and stare at the mascara on my hand.

"Ivy, I want you to stay calm. Okay?"

I look at Jaxon through blurry eyes.

He asks, "Why would you say you killed your father? You didn't have anything to do with it. He had a heart attack."

I nod, insisting, "I did. If they hadn't stolen from him..."

"Who stole from him?"

"*They* did."

"Who's *they*?" Jaxon asks.

In our meetings, I only used D for Dax. Avery was A. Bobby was B. Lilly was L. Marcey was M, and Cindy was C. I never used their real first or last names. I didn't even tell them it actually happened in Connecticut. I told them it happened in Rhode Island. I don't know why I lied about that detail as well. Perhaps I was afraid that saying their names out loud would somehow bring them back into my life. I don't know. But that's how I told my story.

Jaxon strokes my hair, firmly asserting, "I want to know who you're talking about."

"The people I talked about in the meetings. The ones who destroyed us—destroyed me and my father. They stole from him, and he learned about it. That's what was on TV when he was having his heart attack, and I saw the patent paperwork in his notebook. They stole his hybrid."

Jaxon's eyes widen. "Ivy, who are they?"

I turned my head, squeezing my eyes shut.

Dax's face appears in my mind, first when we were younger and then how he looked on TV. All the feelings I've ever had for him swirl faster inside me, then Avery's face appears.

I curse myself for being so stupid to have trusted them. I shouldn't have thought they would accept me. I should have listened to my father, who knew they weren't good.

Well, he knew Dax wasn't. Avery also had him fooled, which is another thing he used to beat himself up about.

Jaxon demands, "Tell me. Who are they?"

I can't say their names. I don't know why I can't say their names, but I can't. So I reply, "Can I see your phone?"

Jaxon pulls it out, swipes the screen to unlock it, and hands it to me.

I pull up his Google search and then insist, "You can't tell anyone. Please. This has to stay between us."

He nods. "Okay. You have my word," he promises. "Whoever these people are, are they threatening you?"

"No, they've had nothing to do with me since the day we were kicked off their estate."

Jaxon exhales a deep breath, continuing to stroke my head. "What they did was horrible based on what you discussed in our meeting, but I only know pieces, Ivy. I know it's hard for you to talk about it, but I need to know who they are so I can understand why you believe you killed your father."

"Promise me this stays between us," I repeat once again, worried about anyone knowing who they really are. Though, I don't know why I have that fear.

He vows, "I promise."

I slowly type into his phone "Seducing Ivy." I click on the link. The new website with the fragrance I've looked at way too many times over the last week pops up.

Jaxon's eyes widen the moment he sees it. "You're talking about the Carringtons?"

I sniffle harder, trying not to cry, but I can't help it. New tears fall. "Yes."

"We just placed a huge order for the Seducing Ivy flower," he says.

I start to cry harder.

"You're Ivy. They named it after you," he states, putting two and two together.

"Yes."

The color drains from his face. "They stole the hybrid from your dad?"

I nod.

"Who did it? Dax or Avery?"

I shrug. "I don't know, but it doesn't matter."

"The patent's in Dax's name. It would've been him."

"Not necessarily. You don't know them. You don't know what Avery's capable of...what either of them are capable of," I admit.

Moments pass, and the tension grows.

"Please say something," I plead.

Jaxon strokes the side of my head. "Ivy, how do you know this was your dad's hybrid?"

"The night he died, I found all his notes."

"Where?"

"His leather notebook, where he kept all his creations. It

was on the table. For some reason, I opened it. Avery and Dax had been on TV talking about her perfume. A printout of the patent was folded up inside his book."

Jaxon questions, "Did he create it when he worked for the Carringtons?"

"No."

"How do you know?"

"He didn't," I snap.

Jaxon holds his hands in the air. "I'm on your side. Just tell me how you know."

"Because it was dated. My father had dates on every page. The notebook's in chronological order. He even had written he needed $10,000 for a patent. It's all in his notebook." I start to cry again.

Jaxon pulls me to him and lets me sob on him for a while.

When I finally calm down, I retreat. "I'm sorry, your shirt's destroyed," I say, cringing at the black streaks of mascara all over his white button-down.

"Who gives a shit?"

I sniffle again. "I shouldn't have said anything to you, but you see why it's my fault that my dad died? You understand, right?"

He firmly asserts, "No, Ivy. You didn't kill your dad."

"I did. It's my fault."

"No. If it's anyone's fault, it's theirs."

I insist, "It's mine. I let them into our lives. They would've only gotten that notebook information because of me...because Dax was in my house. I let him in there."

"You don't know when he came in contact with the notebook and stole that information," Jaxon argues.

I look away, staring into the blackness through the window. I'm not sure what to believe or think anymore.

"The Carringtons are powerful," Jaxon says in a low voice.

I turn toward him. "Yes. Maybe that's why I'd never said their names out loud."

Something changes in Jaxon's eyes. A determination, a hatred, a darkness that I've seen at times while we've had sex or while he's talking at Sex Addicts Anonymous.

A chill runs down my spine. "I shouldn't have said anything. Forget we had this conversation."

He shakes his head. "No, Ivy, I'm not going to forget this. And I know I told you we wouldn't talk about this with anyone, but tomorrow we're meeting with my attorney."

"What? No, you can't tell anyone!"

"They can't get away with this!"

I cry out, "They won't! I'm not going to let them!"

"How?"

"I-I don't know. But no attorney is powerful enough to fight them. They're the Carringtons. I-I'll have to figure out how to beat them at their own game."

Jaxon's voice fills with more determination than I've ever heard. He says, "Ivy, they will pay for this. This is your dad's hybrid, and I'll be damned if I'm going to sit back while they make billions of dollars from it. This is your fortune to reap, not theirs. Tomorrow, we're meeting with my attorney."

Dax 4

WERE YOU LYING ALL THOSE YEARS?

"Michelle, where are those numbers I asked you for?" I bark at my assistant.

"Check your email. I sent it to you."

I hit refresh on the computer. "It's still not here."

"I know I sent— Oh, shoot. I forgot to hit the send button again," she claims.

I groan and shake my head. "Well, hit the send button. I don't have all day," I demand and hang up. I make another note to figure out how to get my normal assistant, Katrina, to return from maternity leave early.

Michelle's the biggest ditz ever, but I don't have time to train anyone. Katrina assured me Michelle was ready, but the girl has serious common-sense issues.

My phone beeps, and I pick it up. Michelle boasts, "I hit send. It should be there."

"You want a bonus check for that?" I mutter and hang up.

I hit refresh again, and her email pops up. I open it, download the attached spreadsheet, then scan the numbers.

It's the first week that Seducing Ivy perfume has been out, and Avery's company's done well. It's not a surprise. The new hybrid's a winner in so many different ways.

So far, the perfume has grossed $15 million in sales. It cost Avery more than that to develop it, so she's still in the hole. I made her fund the company with her personal money, refusing to give her any of Carrington Enterprises' funds. She wanted to get a loan, but I once again vetoed that idea, quickly showing her who has the power.

Avery had a fit. Yet there was nothing she could do. For reasons I have yet to figure out, Avery wanted it under Carrington Enterprises. It was her mistake. I control Carrington Enterprises and all entities under it. So she couldn't get funding without my approval. Her perfume deal would only happen if she used her own money, so that's what she did.

It's my sister's dumbest move ever.

I have her by the balls, and she's going to experience the pain.

I type in the web address for another business I created a few years ago, Carrington Banking and Securities.

The website login page appears, and I type in the username *Seducing Ivy*. Then I type in my password, MyForeverLove.

The Ivy Ford Trust account pops up. Below that are the Carrington Enterprises, Avery Carrington Scents, and all my other business accounts.

I sweep $14 million from the Avery Carrington Scents account into the Carrington Enterprises main account. I leave Avery $1 million to keep running the operation.

For now, at least.

I continue looking through the spreadsheet at all of my

businesses, but there are only two other companies I'm interested in. It's the orders for Seducing Ivy flowers.

Our entire stock sold out within minutes. It was $42 million worth of flowers. I increased the price, and pre-orders are coming in for the next season. It's already at $87 million, proving that they'll sell as fast as we can grow them.

I tap my finger on the table, staring at the sheet, then glance at the pharmaceutical numbers.

I'm not interested in the profits on that. That was created for other reasons, and I'll be in the hole for a while based on all the money I've pumped into research and development.

Plus, unlike Avery, I utilized the bank and risked very little of my personal funds.

Michelle's voice tears me away from studying the numbers. "Mr. Winston, you can't go in there."

"Fuck if I can't," Bobby shouts, and my door flies open.

I sit back in my chair, press the pads of my fingers together, and arch my eyebrows. "No need to be rude to Michelle."

"What the fuck have you done, Dax?"

"Mr. Carrington, I'm so sorry. I tried to stop him. I did. I really did," Michelle frets.

I briefly look at her. "It's fine. Shut the door."

"I really am sorry."

"He said, shut the door. Now get the fuck out," Bobby orders.

"Don't talk to my assistant like that," I reprimand.

He turns back toward me, seething.

Michelle glares at him, then shuts the door.

Bobby lunges toward my desk. He slams his hand on it. "What the fuck do you think you're doing?"

"Whatever are you talking about?" I question, just to piss him off further.

He roars, "You know damn well what I'm talking about, Dax!"

I innocently ask, "Oh, do you mean all the drugs that counteract the drug you've been giving women for over a decade?"

His eyes turn to slits. "You don't know what the fuck you're talking about."

"Don't I?"

"No, you don't."

I keep my cool, replying, "Oh, I'm sorry. Were you lying all those years about all the women you've drugged?"

"Since when are you the fucking moral police?"

I slowly grin. "Oh, I'm not, but I told you numerous times that you went too far. You didn't listen to me, Bobby. By the way, how was the French Riviera or wherever you were?"

He scowls. "Better than this fucking place. But thanks to you, I had to come back."

A wave of satisfaction hits me. Bobby spends as much time as possible in the South of France. The fact my little announcement interrupted his six month, or however long it is this time, trip, only makes me mentally high-five myself. Bobby's as lazy now as he was in high school, and all he does is live off his trust fund.

I taunt, "Why? Is the DA's office already after you?"

He leans closer to me. "Why would you decide to come after the Winstons?"

I grunt. "Your family name doesn't scare me. You must have been in the sun too long and forgot I'm a Carrington."

He stares at me a moment, then laughs.

"What's so funny?" I ask.

"This is a joke, right? You did this to get me back in the States. You're ready to get back into the game?" he questions.

I chuckle too, asking, "You think I'd go on national television and announce I filed for patents just to get you to return to Connecticut?"

Red burns his cheeks, and his anger returns. "Are you seriously for real doing this? You're going to release those drugs?"

"Yeah, of course I am. I've spent billions developing them."

"Since when are you in the pharmaceutical business?"

I tsk. "Bobby, Bobby, Bobby. Didn't your daddy explain to you that when you have money, you can go into any business you want? It's all about hiring smart people. You would know that if you ever started to work."

He stares at me a moment longer. He once again finds a way to calm himself. I have to give him credit. The Bobby I remember didn't know how to do that when he thought someone wronged him. He sits across from me, puts his ankle over his knee, and positions his fingers like mine. "Okay, Dax. What do you want?"

"What do you mean what do I want?" I question, enjoying watching him squirm and beg for something I'll never give him.

He blows out a frustrated breath. "What do you want in exchange for those drugs? Sell them to Winston Pharmaceuticals."

"Now, why would I do that?"

He flips back to anger. "You motherfucker. You tell me what the price is. You know those drugs shouldn't be out on the street."

I scoff. "*My* drugs shouldn't be on the street? Don't you mean *your* drugs? You know, the ones your father gave you access to that are now all over the street for the sole purpose of raping women?"

"Shut the fuck up. I've never raped a woman in my life," he claims.

"You don't call drugging a woman so she'll do anything you want while having sex with you, rape?" I hurl.

"They don't do anything they don't want to," he retorts.

Rage fills me. I point at him. "You've always been a sick bastard, Bobby."

"Didn't take you as a goody-two-shoes, Dax. Seems like you forgot a lot of our childhood," he threatens.

"I never drugged anyone to sleep with me."

He clenches his jaw, and tense silence fills the air.

I wait him out.

He finally says, "You partook in an event that I believe neither of us will ever forget. That West Virginia whore was more than eager to have us both, along with Lilly. Or do you have a selective memory?"

My stomach turns. I hate the fact that I was part of that foursome. I loathe the fact that I manipulated Ivy into doing what she did and didn't stop it. I'll always detest myself. I was more concerned about winning the game and having leverage over Lilly's father than stopping what should have been stopped. And I hate that I allowed Bobby to ever lay a finger on Ivy.

She was *my* Ivy.

Not his.

"Ah, so you didn't forget," he smugly states, as if he has one over on me.

Don't show him any weakness.

I keep my calm demeanor and shrug. "I may have been part of it, but I had no knowledge of the drugs. If I knew you'd drugged her, I never would have partaken in it, and I would have gotten her out of that room."

"That's convenient. If I go down for anything, you're coming with me, Dax," he threatens.

"You think so?"

His eyes turn darker and his lips curve. "I know so."

I grunt. "You admitted to me in writing what you did and that I had no knowledge. My attorney's already seen the texts and has copies. If you think I would've released any of this if I was at risk of going to jail, you'd be wrong. You know I'm smarter than that. Oh, but then again, I've always been the smart one between us, haven't I?"

"You motherfucker," he snarls.

I point to the door. "Get the fuck out of my office, Bobby. Go back to the South of France or wherever it is you want to go."

He doesn't move, accusing, "Since when the fuck have you turned on me? We've been friends forever."

I start to laugh, and I can't stop for some reason.

He furrows his eyebrows. "What the fuck is so funny?"

I stop laughing and rise. I glare down at him, admitting, "I've not been friends with you since you did what you did."

He jerks his head back and then studies me. He recovers from his shock and states, "You've never gotten over her, have you?"

I don't say anything.

"You let that West Virginia piece of trash, slutty, dirty, fucking whore ruin our friendship? What? Did she come back and ask to suck your dick?" he bellows.

I lunge across the desk and grab him. I take my fist and slam it into his face. Blood spurts everywhere. I push him back. He tries to come toward me, but I hit him again. He falls over the desk.

"Get out!" I order.

He slowly looks up, cupping his hand under his bloody nose. "Jesus Christ, Dax. What the fuck is your problem?"

I huff. "What the fuck is my problem? My problem is you. It's been you for years. And you know what, Bobby?

I've been waiting for this moment. Your days are numbered, and there's nothing you can do to stop it. So go enjoy whatever exotic destination you want. You'll be locked up soon."

He grabs a tissue off my desk and wipes blood from his face. He lowers his voice, gritting out, "You've been waiting for this moment to accomplish what?"

"To watch you get what's coming to you," I admit.

"What's coming to me? What, are you a thug now?" he asks.

I scowl. "Call me what you want, Bobby, but I guarantee you, your fun days are over. Enjoy them while you can. And you might want to stop drugging women now. You're a bit in the spotlight at the moment."

He rises, lifts his chin, and curls his fists at his sides. "If you want a war, Dax, you have one."

I laugh. "We've already been at war. All of us have, and you know it. Avery. Cindy. Marcey. Lilly. You. Me. All of us. So, like I said, go back to the South of France, because any moment you spend in this town, I'll make hell for you."

He studies me another minute and then raises a finger and points it at me. "You're going to pay for this. All of this. And when my father and I get done with you, there'll be nothing left of Carrington Enterprises."

I smile. It's twisted, and I know it. I reply, "I welcome it. Tell your father to bring everything you got at me because you're fucking going to need it. The lawsuits coming your way after all the women you've been with take TimeMarker will be icing on the cake."

He scowls again and shoves a paperweight off my desk, and a bunch of papers fly into the air and flutter to the floor. He spins on his heel and leaves.

I pick up the phone and hit the button for security.

The head of my security teams for the estate and my corporation answers, "Mr. Carrington."

"Chad, I need you to ensure Bobby Winston's escorted out of here. Don't let him in my building ever again. Understand?"

"Yes, sir," Chad says with confusion in his voice.

I don't blame him. Bobby's had the run of the office for years, just like he did with our estate.

I add, "Make sure you contact the estate security. He never steps foot there again either. Understand?

"Yes, sir," Chad answers and hangs up.

I pace the office and stare out my window at the water, wishing it was warm and I was on a boat with Ivy. I squeeze my eyes shut and curse myself.

I have to stop wishing these things. I have to figure out how to let it go—how to let *her* go.

I know I can't. I've never been able to. And all this unveiling of Seducing Ivy perfume, the flowers, and the drugs seems to have made it even worse.

My need—my craving—to have her as mine once again, but for real this time, only grows with time. Yet there's no way to make what I've done right.

She slept with Avery.

I grind my molars, my stomach churning, trying to use that little fact to remind myself that she never was mine. Anyone who sleeps with Avery can't be mine.

It could have been from the drugs.

No, she wanted it. She fell for Avery.

I don't know that.

She did.

My debate continues until it drives me crazy. I finally sit back at my desk and pull up my spreadsheets again, looking at the numbers.

I grab my pen and write in my notebook.

$14 million from Avery.

$20 million in profits from Seducing Ivy blooms delivered.

$38 million from Seducing Ivy bloom pre-order profits.

I stare at the numbers and all the zeros and then add them together.

$72 million.

I take a deep breath and call my private investigator, Hank Tallywind.

"Dax. Long time since I've heard from you," he says.

"Yep," I reply.

"How have you been?"

"Fine. Let's avoid the niceties," I state.

He chuckles. "Same old Dax Carrington, I see. Who do you want me to find?"

My heart aches. My chest tightens. I open and close my fists. I've made this call to him before but have yet to have him do it. I've always told him, "Never mind."

This time, the words come out of my mouth. "I need you to find a woman. She'd be about twenty-eight now. Her name's Ivy Ford. Her father's name is John."

"John Ford? Pretty common name."

"They're somewhere in Georgia, near the Savannah area."

"How do you know that?"

"Because I had their address."

"Then why do you need me?"

Because I burned it like a fucking moron.

"None of your business. All you need to know is that I no longer have the address, but I need you to get it."

"Sure. Ivy is spelled I-V-Y?" he asks.

"Yes."

"Is John J-O-H-N or J-O-N?"

I grit my teeth, thinking about how much John Ford hates me. Can't say I have any good feelings for the man either.

Although, as bad as a father as I think he was to Ivy by not supporting her as well as he should have, he was smart. He created the hybrid.

His daughter gets to profit from the hybrid, not him. Besides, he never would've done anything with it if it had stayed in his little leather notebook.

I reply, "It's J-O-H-N."

"Okay. On it," Hank declares and hangs up.

I turn back to my piece of paper with my handwritten $72 million, staring at the numbers.

Time to do it.

I click on the Carrington Enterprises account and go to the transfer button. From the dropdown menu, I select the Ivy Ford Trust. Then, I transfer $72 million into it.

Ivy 5

TORMENTED AND TORTURED

"Jaxon, you're not being fair. You promised me it would stay between us," I remind him.

He scrubs his hand over his face, groaning. "Ivy, we've been over this. We need to take legal action and quickly. The sooner we move on this, the better."

I shake my head. "I don't think that's the right way to handle this."

"Then how will you gain control of your dad's patent that Dax Carrington stole?" Jaxon questions.

I stare at him with no answers. I haven't had any solutions any of the other times he's asked me this question.

There's a knock on his door. Jaxon calls out, "Come in."

His assistant, Kay, chirps, "Your attorneys are in conference room A."

"Thank you. We'll be right in," he replies.

My stomach flips. I don't know why I'm opposed to this,

but everything in my gut tells me it's not the right way to beat Dax and get my father's patent.

Jaxon pushes, "Ivy, let's go talk to them. Everything we say is confidential."

"You don't understand how powerful the Carringtons are," I say for the millionth time. I can't get Jaxon to understand how much money they have. I know he does well, but the Carringtons are uber-wealthy. They could bankrupt Jaxon if they wanted to, and I wouldn't put it past them to do so.

He claims, "Yes, I do."

"No, you don't," I argue.

"Ivy, I know who the Carringtons are, and I'm not scared of them. Now, let's go meet with the legal team. I won't force you to do anything you don't want to, but at least talk with them and hear what they have to say," he insists.

I'm exhausted from our argument. We've been fighting about this since last night. Maybe I should give in, but instead, I ask, "Why does there have to be a team of people?"

Jaxon crosses his arms. "Because we're dealing with Dax Carrington. We need the biggest number of legal brains possible."

I groan. "This is what I was talking about. We're never going to beat him. They could financially destroy you or destroy you some other way," I warn, wishing he'd listen to me.

"Ivy, I'm not scared of them, and I'm not backing down. Now, go see what your options are before you lose the ability to get your father's patent back," Jaxon advises.

I sigh. "Fine."

He leads me to the conference room. Several men in suits have their backs toward us, selecting plates of baked goods. One sits at the table sipping coffee.

I sit down and tap my finger on the table, staring at it and biting my lip, wondering how this will do any good. The Carringtons have more money than God. The last thing I want to see is Jaxon go down.

"Ivy?" a familiar voice says in surprise.

My heart beats faster, and my pulse increases. I glance up and stare at a familiar face.

No way.

He's older, more filled out, and still has the same type of glasses. He pushes them up on his nose, exclaiming, "It is you!"

"Matt?" I question, then gape at him.

He shifts on his feet, nodding. "Yeah. Long time no see. It's been..." His face falls. He goes quiet, and we exchange glances.

It's been since he saw me fucking everyone on the video.

My face heats with embarrassment and shame.

A tense moment passes.

Jaxon asks, "You guys know each other?"

I slowly turn my gaze from Matt and nod. "Yes. Matt went to Clifton University with me." My cheeks burn hotter, and I stare back at Matt.

He quietly mumbles, "I wondered what happened to you."

Panic hits me. Matt was always nice to me but was under Avery's spell. Who knows how loyal he'll be to the Carringtons. He might still be in contact with them, for all I know.

I snap my face toward Jaxon, gripping his arm and shaking my head, declaring, "I don't think I want to talk anymore."

He arches his eyebrows, then glances at Matt and then back at me. "Why not?"

"Can we talk in private?" Matt interjects.

The room turns silent again, and tension floods the space.

My heart beats faster.

"I can stay," Jaxon states.

"No, we need to talk alone," Matt insists.

I glance up at him.

"Please," he says, with desperation in his voice and eyes.

I open my mouth, but nothing comes out.

He leans down into my ear. "I believe our enemy is common. Please, let's talk, just you and me."

"Matt, what's going on?" an older gentleman in an expensive suit questions.

Matt doesn't take his eyes off me.

"Ivy?" Jaxon says.

"Can I use your office?" I ask, turning toward him.

His eyes turn to slits. He claims, "I think it's better if we stay in here. Whatever Matt has to say to you, he can do in front of all of us."

I shake my head. "No, I want to talk to him in private. He's right."

Jaxon doesn't reply. He gazes suspiciously at Matt and then back at me with concern.

I put my hand on his thigh. "It's fine. I'll be right back."

He doesn't say anything, and I get up.

Matt follows.

We say nothing until we get into Jaxon's office.

I shut the door, and we sit at the desk on the same side. I blurt out, "Why are you in Georgia?"

He nervously laughs, repeating, "How are you in Georgia?"

I admit, "My father got a job here. He felt it was best to get as far away from Connecticut as possible. He didn't feel like we could return to West Virginia either."

My chest tightens, thinking about my father, and I tear up. I blink hard and look away.

Matt puts his hand on my arm. "Ivy, are you okay?"

I wipe my wet face and sniffle. "I'm sorry, my father died last week. I buried him yesterday. I..."

"Oh my God, Ivy. Are you okay?"

I take a deep breath and then raise my chin. "I'm as good as I can be, but... Well, that's why Jaxon wanted me to meet with attorneys."

Matt stays silent.

"Why are you in Georgia?" I question again.

He licks his lips. "I work for a national law firm. There was a position open in Georgia, and I too thought it was best to get away. I thought it might help me eliminate the bad memories," he confesses.

"Bad memories?" I inquire.

His jaw clenches. He breathes a few times and slowly nods. "Yeah, you weren't the only one they tormented and tortured."

My heart sinks. "Matt, I'm sorry. What did they do to you?"

He glances at the ceiling, sniffs hard, and shakes his head. He meets my eye. "Nothing worse than they did to you."

"Who hurt you?" I question.

He scoffs. "The Carringtons. Avery, mostly. Bobby. Professor Dyer. All of them."

"Dyer? What did Professor Dyer do?" I blurt out.

His expression grows dark. "All you need to know is he's scum, just like the rest of them. And he's all part of their game."

I take a deep breath. "I'm so sorry, Matt. You didn't deserve whatever they did to you."

An understanding passes in his expression. He swallows hard. "You didn't deserve any of it either. What they did to you was horrible. Is that why we're here, to discuss some sort of lawsuit for what they did?"

I blink a few times and shake my head. "No, that was a long time ago."

"You could still sue them," Matt states.

I roll my eyes. "I don't think suing the Carringtons is a good plan. Not with all the money they have at their disposal. They'll bankrupt anybody who tries, I assume. Don't you think?"

Matt's face falls. He nods. "Yeah, I think you're right. But if that's not why I'm here, then why?"

My stomach dives, and my chest tightens. The air in my lungs turns stale. I open my mouth, but once again, no words come out.

Matt waits, continuing to stare at me.

For some reason, I trust him. He wasn't one of them. I know he wasn't. He was just like me. He wanted to be accepted and fell under the Carringtons' spell.

I don't know what they did to him, but I have a feeling it left just as many scars. Since he saw the video, I should be embarrassed to be around him, but he was always kind. So far, he hasn't said or done anything to show me differently. So, for some reason, I trust him just like I trust Jaxon. I finally admit, "Dax stole something from my father."

Hatred fills Matt's face. "What did he steal?"

My mouth turns dry. My voice cracks. "He stole..." I lick my lips and swallow. Then, I clear my throat. "He stole my dad's hybrid, the new Seducing Ivy flower that was used for Avery's perfume."

Matt gapes at me.

I continue, "The patents... That hybrid is my dad's."

Matt peers at me closer. "How do you know it's your dad's?"

"Hold on," I say. I leave the room and go into my office. I unlock the drawer and pull out my dad's notebook.

The worn leather in my hands makes me tear up. I force myself not to get emotional. I return to Jaxon's office, shut the door, and sit beside Matt. I put the book on my lap and state, "My dad died while watching Avery on TV. She was promoting the new Seducing Ivy perfume. It was before Dax came on. I came home, and my dad was having a heart attack. His notebook was on the table next to him. After he died, I was in shock. For some reason, I picked it up and started reading everything. As you can see, everything in here is dated."

Matt stares at the notebook.

I open it and point to different dates spanning decades of my father's work. Then, I get to the page with the Seducing Ivy flower hybrid. I hand Matt the folded piece of paper and point to the date. "You can see when my dad created this. He even wrote he needed $10,000 for a patent."

Matt glances at it, then opens the piece of paper, reads it, and mutters, "Motherfucker."

My pulse quickens again. My heart aches thinking about how Dax took the only thing that was worth any money in my father's life and stole it from him.

"Jaxon wants me to go after Dax, but I don't think the legal way is the way to do it. You know how they are, Matt. The worst thing I can do is go after him with a legal team."

"So you don't want the patent?"

I release a frustrated breath. "No, I do want the patent. But if Dax is going to pay, we have to make him pay so it hurts. It's not about the money. He could give me the patent and then some, and he'd still have tons of money. It's not going to hurt him. So this is...it's about...*everything*," I confess for the first time, fully understanding what I want.

Matt stays quiet for a moment, then asks, "Can I look at that?" He points to the notebook.

I hand it to him.

He flips through it carefully, going through the entire book. Then he takes the piece of paper, folds it, and puts it back in the same spot. He closes the book and hands it back to me. "I know the law really well, Ivy. I graduated top of my class. I aced the bar exam in five states. I've been promoted very quickly. I've seen a lot in the eight years since I graduated law school."

"Matt, you know how they are. It doesn't matter how good you are. They'll win in a legal battle," I insist.

He holds his hand in the air.

I wait.

He collects his thoughts. His eyes turn to slits. "The law will never provide justice for anything the Carringtons have done. You're right. If it's not money you're after, and you really want revenge so it hurts Dax, then a legal battle isn't the way."

Relief fills me. Matt gets it. Finally, someone gets it!

I nod. "I know."

"So how are you going to do it?" he questions.

I shake my head, admitting, "I'm not sure yet, but I know I have to think like them to make them pay."

Matt warns, "They could damage you further, Ivy."

I consider his statement, then shrug. "I have nothing else to lose. My father died with his life's work stolen. And after he saw that video of me..." I turn, the tears spilling down my cheeks.

Matt's gentle voice turns dark. "All I thought about was getting back at the Carringtons, Bobby, and Dyer."

"You could help me," I state.

At first, I think Matt will agree, but then he shakes his head. "No, Ivy. If you want to pursue something legally, I'll help you, but I have a family now. I have a wife who loves me and a baby on the way. The last thing I want to do is get within an inch of them."

I take a deep breath and release it. I can't argue with him.

So instead, I say, "Congrats on your baby and wife. I hope you're happy."

Matt smiles, and it's genuine. "I am. I have a good life, Ivy. And you know what?"

"What?" I ask.

"You can too. What happened in the past doesn't define who you are."

"So I hear," I say, having heard that phrase a thousand times in Sex Addicts Anonymous. And it makes me curious.

Matt goes to rise, but I grab his arm. "Matt, wait."

He sits back down.

I take a deep breath. "I don't mean to pry, but did they mess with you sexually?"

Matt's face hardens. He nods and doesn't say anything.

My stomach flips faster. I shouldn't ask him, but I have to know. "And do you get sexual urges that you can't control? Are..." I take a deep breath. "Are you a nymphomaniac?"

He gapes at me.

"I'm sorry. I didn't mean to pry."

He puts his hand on mine. "No, I'm not. But is that what you're experiencing?"

Shame fills me, and I curse myself for asking him about his personal life. Of course he's not a nympho like me. There's something deep inside of me, something internal, that's making me the addict I am.

Maybe it's time I stopped blaming Dax for what I've become.

I quickly add, "Forget I said anything. I'm sorry. I didn't mean to insult you."

"Ivy, Dax just created three new drugs you need to research."

I freeze. "What kind of drugs?"

"Drugs to counteract Bobby's father's date rape drug."

The walls start to close in on me. I barely choke out, "Date rape drug?"

"Yeah, it's called Trance. Well, that's the street name for it. When it's given to people too many times or in too high of a dose, they become sex addicts. They can't help themselves. And Dax created some drugs to counteract it. My guess is all the lawsuits Bobby had against him weren't lies, and he had been using it on his prey."

The room spins. I put my hand over my stomach, swallowing down bile, trying to understand what Matt's saying.

He continues, "Ivy, if you're experiencing problems, Dax has a drug to stop it getting worse. There's even one to reverse it, but it has some side effects. But they can test you now to see if you were given the drug and even pinpoint the dates or if it was more than once."

My insides quiver. I can barely look at Matt, claiming, "I couldn't have been raped. I couldn't have. I remember it all. I-I-I wanted it," I admit, tears of shame filling my eyes and falling down my cheeks. I look away, wiping my face.

Matt puts his hand on my arm. "Ivy, that doesn't mean they didn't drug you. The drug does that. You should get tested for it. If they gave it to you, it makes you do things you would never do. And the urges you have only get worse with time."

My lips quiver harder. I stare at Matt in shock.

He insists, "Ivy, promise me you'll go get tested. At least you'll know either way."

I don't say anything, trying to comprehend it. Then I run into Jaxon's bathroom and throw up.

Would Dax have really done that to me?

When I return to Jaxon's office, Matt asks, "You okay?"

I nod. "Yeah."

Matt stares at me a moment, then his face hardens.

"You're making me nervous," I admit.

He blurts out, "If you want to piss Dax off, use the others."

I furrow my eyebrows. "I don't understand."

"They used you. So use everyone. None of them like or trust the others. So use it to your advantage. Figure out how to hit them where it hurts, and do it. But, Ivy?"

"Yeah?"

Matt's eyes narrow. "Promise me you won't let them play you again. Hit them hard, then get the hell out of there."

Dax 6

YOU STOLE MY MONEY

"Where's my money, Dax?" Avery seethes, glaring daggers at me.

"Your money? Don't you mean Carrington Enterprises', money?" I taunt.

Her eyes light with more fire. She demands, "Give it back!"

I try to hold in my glee, but I can't. I grin. "There are seven figures in your account."

"You know I can't run my company off a million dollars. The operating costs alone—"

"I don't care, Avery. Put your own money in if you've mismanaged the funds," I interject.

"You know I haven't mismanaged the funds. You stole my money," she accuses.

I chuckle. "It's not your money. Or did you forget that you wanted your company to be part of the family business?"

"That wasn't your money to take," Avery snarls.

"It's the company's money."

"It's money to be paid back into my trust fund, and you know it!"

I cross my arms and sit back in my chair. "I'm the CEO of Carrington Enterprises. You signed a contract for your company to become a subsidiary. You begged me to allow it. I did. Now you want to dictate where the funds will go? Sorry, but the money isn't yours to take. It's the corporation's."

"You bastard! If you don't give me my money—"

"What are you going to do about it, Avery? Cry?" I mock.

More anger fills her expression. She lowers her voice, asserting, "Transfer my money back."

I scoff. "Once again, it's not your money. Now, get the fuck out of my office before I have you thrown out."

She stays planted, her rage only growing stronger.

"I mean it, Avery. Get out, or you'll be sorry," I warn.

"You can't throw me out. I have every right to this house just like you and Cooper do."

I grunt. "You have access to your wing, and that's it. Don't forget your place in this family. And speaking of our brother, why don't you go tell him to get off social media and learn to work."

She doesn't move.

I point to the door. "Last warning, Avery. Get out of my office, or I'll add debt to your company and take every penny out of it. Be grateful you have a million for operations."

Her face drains of color, and I love it. I've never had my sister in such a compromising position before. She thought she was going to outsmart me? Well, she's not.

And I'll be damned if I let her use the Seducing Ivy hybrid to build her fortune.

She had no right to it.

She had no right to Ivy.

Avery will finally get what's coming to her, and it'll hit her where it hurts her the most—in her pocket. Without money, Avery will be nothing.

She finally storms out of the room and slams the door.

I sit back, feeling giddy, for only a few minutes. Then, my eyes return to the folder on my desk.

I open it up and study dozens of pictures that Hank collected.

My Ivy's just as beautiful as ever. She's older, slightly curvier, and those fucking C-cups are perkier than ever.

Jesus, even in pictures, they're giving me an erection.

She's always given me one.

I read about the town she lives in a few miles from Savannah and all she's been up to since I kicked her off the estate.

How stupid was I?

She slept with Avery. It would never have worked out.

I could have figured out how to get past it.

Not true. Avery would always have her hooks in Ivy.

I thumb to the next page, and a surge of pride sweeps through me. She still got her degree in botany.

That's my girl.

Ivy's always been smart. I'm glad that what happened to her at Clifton didn't destroy her.

There's a picture of her and another man, which makes me uncomfortable.

I scan the report and learn his name is Jaxon Savoia. According to my PI, he owns the largest wholesale floral company in the country. It's an impressive feat, but it's still small potatoes next to the Carrington fortune. And I don't like how close he looks to Ivy.

She has a decent position in his company, but I can tell by the photos that it's not just a working relationship. They're definitely friends.

I swallow hard, wondering if it's more than that. I flip the page and my gut drops. I reread it several times to make sure it's true, but over and over, I read Sex Addicts Anonymous too many times to count.

Sex addicts.

She got hurt.

The drug stayed in her system.

All the guilt I felt over the last ten years worsens. I curve my fingers into a fist, squeezing as hard as possible, to the point I feel like my knuckles might break.

I reaffirm my vow to take Bobby down, no matter what. He, his father, and anybody associated with their company.

Just like I'm going to take Avery down.

The words Sex Addicts Anonymous glare at me on the paper, and I shake my head. I read the report the PI added about what Ivy talked about when he pretended to be a new member. Then I read up on Jaxon Savoia and all of his demons.

The report states they sat across from each other, but there were multiple times when they exchanged glances. According to Hank, Ivy had had sex thirty-some minutes prior to the meeting. Jaxon had last had it about thirty minutes before as well, and it doesn't take me long to put two and two together.

Bile rises in my throat. My stomach flips faster. I didn't expect her to not have anyone in her life. She's too amazing not to, but, Jesus—two sex addicts going at it? Plus, this guy's at least ten years older than me.

Does he give her what she needs? What I used to give her?

Does she even think about me anymore?

She's chasing the high.
Is she in love with him?
I need to get her on the medication.
But which one?

The thought of Ivy experiencing the side effects that could destroy any enjoyment she could ever have again regarding a sexual relationship makes me feel ill. I've already done so much to her. She doesn't deserve more disappointment.

I pick up the phone and call the head scientist working at Hybrid Pharmaceuticals.

Craig answers, "Mr. Carrington?"

I ask, "Where are we at on NeuroZap? Did you figure out how to eliminate the side effects?"

His voice drops. "I don't have any good news. There haven't been any breakthroughs. We can't seem to eliminate the possibilities of the risks."

"You need to figure it out," I order.

"Mr. Carrington, it's not that easy. We've discussed this. All drugs have possible side effects."

"Not good enough," I declare.

"Mr. Carrington—"

"I'm paying you to eliminate it. Figure it out," I interject, then hang up the phone, pissed off.

I've come so far with these drugs, but it's not good enough. I want to be able to completely eliminate the addictions of people who have been harmed by Trance—who have been harmed by Bobby and his family. So Craig's statement isn't going to fly with me.

I beat myself up a little bit more and then my phone rings.

I answer, "Michelle," wishing again that my other assistant was back from maternity leave.

She chirps, "I wanted to remind you that it's time to get ready for tonight's Clifton charity event."

I glance at my watch, groaning inside. The last thing I want to do is go to Clifton University or their charity event, nor do I want to give that fucking place any money. My life was destroyed because of that school and all the people associated with it. I hate everything about the university, including its fraternities and sororities.

It's a necessary evil to take Avery and Bobby down.

I have to play the game.

"Thanks," I say and disconnect the call. I go to my room, shower, and put on my tux. I secure my gold cuff links and then leave the estate. I race through the gates and over to Clifton.

It's a route I've taken too many times. I glance to the passenger seat, wishing Ivy was next to me.

If only I hadn't fucked everything up.

I should have realized I had the best thing ever in front of me. Instead, I was dumb and had to worry about getting one over on Avery and Bobby. Ultimately, I lost the only thing that ever mattered to me.

By the time I pull into my reserved parking spot, I'm once again traveling down memory lane. I take a few deep breaths, not wanting to go in but forcing myself to get out of the car.

I step inside, bypassing everyone, barely greeting those who offer me hellos. I go right up to the bar.

The bartender asks, "What can I get you?"

"Scotch. Neat," I order.

He pours three fingers and hands it to me.

I drink it, trying to enjoy the warm liquid sliding down my throat, and set the glass down. I point. "One more."

The bartender refills it.

I take another large mouthful, turn, then freeze. My heart beats so fast I think I'm going to have a heart attack. I blink, wondering if I'm seeing things or if my drink is laced and I'm already drunk.

"What's wrong, Dax? Didn't expect to ever see me again?" Ivy asks, then licks her whore-red lips. She traces the outline of her matching satin spaghetti-straps on her dress.

My dick goes hard. My balls ache, reminding me of ten years ago.

She's even more beautiful in person than in the pictures. Her long, dark hair is in curls. Her profound curves make my mouth water. And those fucking C-cups... She's showing just enough cleavage to be classy, yet it tortures me, bringing me back to everything I used to have and no longer do.

I step forward, reaching for her. "Ivy—"

"Hands off my date, Dax," Professor Dyer's voice interjects.

Once again, I'm taken off guard. All my red flags go up. My pulse skyrockets, and my insides churn. Dyer steps up next to Ivy and slides his arm around her waist.

She giggles, puts her palm on his chest, and glances up at him. "I was wondering when you were going to get here."

"Sorry, doll. Didn't mean to keep you waiting. You know how it is with all these people here." He leans down and kisses her on her lips.

"What are you doing?" I seethe.

She slides her tongue into his mouth and tightens her fingers around his neck for another brief moment, then barely moves her face, just enough to catch my eye. "Sorry. Did you have something you wanted to say, Dax?"

Something in her eyes lights up, and my gut sinks lower. I know that look. I perfected that look. I taught my sister how to give that look even better than me.

That look is trouble.

It's a devious wild card, and I realize Ivy's no longer innocent.

She has something up her sleeve.

Why else would she be here with Dyer?

But what is it?

She can't be with Dyer!

My heart tightens, giving me pain.

She knows about the patent.

She knows about the medication.

I tell myself that must be it, but I feel like it's only the tip of the iceberg.

"Ivy—" I start.

"Didn't know if you would remember me, Dax. How have you been?" she questions.

"Yeah, Dax. How have you been?" Dyer asks, giving me an arrogant look I want to smack off his face.

He knows she's off-limits. I warned him ten years ago.

What the fuck is he doing with her?

"Oh, maybe you don't remember me?" Ivy asks, tilting her head, her lips twisting in a smile. She bats her eyelashes and then steps closer.

Dyer releases her and she slides her fingers along my hip, slowly stroking it. She rises up on her tiptoes, leaning into my ear. Her breath taunts my lobe, sending tingles down my spine. She flirts, "It'd be a shame if you told me you forgot about me."

I stand there, for a rare moment in my life unable to speak, my dick hardening even more as she presses against me and softly laughs.

"That's the Dax I remember," she whispers. "Your dick still remembers its dirty little whore."

My cock throbs. I clench my jaw, staring at her, my chest tightening, unsure how to respond.

She turns and steps away from me.

Dyer slides his arm back around her waist, his arrogance growing.

She puts her palm back on his chest. "Do you think there'll be dancing tonight? You know I really like to dance."

"Yeah, doll. I know you do."

"I'm not your doll. Remember?" she says, giving him a seductive look.

He lowers his voice, but it's loud enough so I can hear him state, "That's right, my little slut. Maybe we should go to the bathroom before we go to the table? I can fuck that wet pussy of yours."

"You're not fucking Ivy in the bathroom!" I warn, louder than I should.

Several people turn to stare at me.

Ivy's eyes widen. "Dax. Why would you raise your voice in such an aggressive tone?" she innocently asks, acting shocked.

I stay quiet, unsure of what's happening and how this is possible.

I'm having a nightmare.

Yes, that must be it.

I pinch the side of my leg, but I feel it and realize this is real life. This is reality—Ivy standing in front of me with Dyer, of all people.

And I can't decide if Dyer or Bobby would've been worse to stand next to Ivy.

I need to figure out what's going on here.

I grab Ivy's bicep and try to pull her away from Dyer, but he holds on tight.

She cries, "Ow, you're hurting me, Dax."

"Don't bruise her," Dyer accuses, and people's shocked gasps fill the air.

Stay calm, I tell myself, but my insides rage with anger so hot, I don't know how to contain it.

"You're hurting me," Ivy states again, staring at her arm and then pinning her blues to mine.

I slowly release her, but I step closer, inhaling her scent, remembering how it felt for her to be mine, waking up in my arms and just being with me. My voice comes out desperate. "Can I talk to you, please?"

"Not tonight. At least not in private, if that's what you're asking," she answers.

"We have to get to our table," Dyer states.

I snap my head toward him, snarling, "Shut up."

He arches his eyebrows, but his grin gets bigger. "Settle down, Dax. I didn't know you'd be so upset if I showed up with Ivy. After all, you did say you were done with her ten years ago, didn't you?"

"He did," Ivy affirms with a smile.

"Didn't you say you didn't want the dirty whore anymore?" Dyer taunts.

"Don't you talk about her like that!" I seethe.

Ivy reaches out and brushes at my tux, as if there's a piece of lint on it. Her soft voice fills the air. "Don't get upset, Dax. A lot of time has passed. Let's just let bygones be bygones. Right?" She smiles at me, and it reminds me of Avery's fake smile.

As much as I hate Avery, Ivy's smile sucks me in.

A new realization smacks me upside the head.

This isn't the Ivy I knew. This is a new and different Ivy. An Ivy who's confident and no longer naive. And she's not here for any good reason. She's here for only one thing. It sure as hell isn't Professor Dyer.

Please don't let it be for Dyer.

She smiles at me, asking, "William, should we take our seats?"

And that's when I know why she's here.

She's here for revenge.

THEY'LL NEVER SEE IT COMING

Walking away from Dax is one of the hardest things I've ever done. No matter how much time has passed, the chemistry between us is just as potent.

I wanted to step aside with him and hear him out, but I reminded myself that's what I would have done in the past.

Dax is a game player. I'm not going to be his pawn again. This time, he's going to be *my* pawn, just like the others.

Professor Dyer was shocked when I showed up in my evening gown at his office. I didn't even have to remind him who I was. He knew.

I sat on his lap, kissed him, and asked, "Wouldn't it be fun if you took me to the charity event tonight?"

His eyes turned dark, and a chill went up my spine. It was then I knew Matt was right. He's no good. He's scum, just like the others. But using him will get at Dax. I know it will. Heck, it might even get at Avery and Bobby. Who knows? But I'm sure they'll all be in attendance.

One thing I've realized: no one's on anyone's side. So, like Matt said, I'm going to use everyone against each other. They'll never see it coming.

Professor Dyer's going to be my pawn as well. Matt might be unable to seek revenge, but I'll do it for him. Besides, now that I know Dyer's part of their game, I'm sure he could have stopped the video from releasing that day if he'd really wanted to.

Shortly after my father's death, a life insurance check arrived in the mail for $250,000. I found the policy in a folder he kept in his nightstand. Jaxon helped me fill out the paperwork.

When it arrived a week ago, I still didn't know how to get my revenge against Dax and the rest of them. I was researching Dax Carrington online when the charity event popped up.

It didn't take long to realize this was my opportunity to insert myself back into their lives. So I deposited the check and went shopping for a dress.

I could have asked Jaxon for money, but he wouldn't have given it to me without me telling him what I needed it for. And he would never approve of this plan.

I don't have all the answers, but Dax probably doesn't either. One thing he, along with the others, is great at, is making decisions on his feet. And if I'm going to beat them, I have to be as well.

So I found the whore-red lipstick and nail polish that I used to wear every day. It's the color Dax insisted I wear—the same shade I proudly wore for him but haven't worn for years. Then I went to a boutique and found the matching red satin dress, knowing it would be perfect.

When I arrived at Dyer's office, his assistant wouldn't let me in. I finally walked past her desk and opened the door.

He was in with another coed, unbuttoning her blouse. Dyer took one look at me and was too happy to let her go.

I told him I'd meet him at the event, thinking it would be better for me to scope out the landscape before he entered the scene. My heart almost stopped when I saw Dax. But I reminded myself, just like now, that he's the enemy.

It's not helping that my urges are taking over. My pussy's pulsing with an intensity I loathe right now. So, as much as I hate Dax, all I've wanted to do since Professor Dyer mentioned it is take him into the bathroom.

My urges are increasing every day, but I have to fight them. I tap into everything they preach to do at Sex Addicts Anonymous, but nothing could have prepared me for this situation.

Dyer pulls out a chair at a table in the second row.

Dax calls out, "Don't sit there. You two come sit at my table."

I freeze, my heart beating faster.

Dyer puts his hand on my waist, creeping me out again.

It's a necessary evil, I remind myself and don't brush off his touch.

Dyer arrogantly states, "I thought you'd never ask."

What happened between Matt and Dyer?

A new panic hits me.

I shouldn't be here.

Stop being scared.

Put on Avery's face.

I coyly smile at Dax, inquiring, "Isn't your table full?"

"Not anymore. Come." He steps in front of his table. It's right in the center, at the front of the room. He pulls out a chair. "Sit, Ivy."

I obey.

Dyer tries to sit on my left side, and Dax orders, "That's not your seat."

"I'm sitting next to my date or we'll stay at the other table," Dyer threatens.

Dax points to the other side of me. "That's your seat."

Dyer glances at it and back at Dax.

Dax gives him an equally arrogant, challenging stare.

Professor Dyer finally caves and sits on my right side. Dax sits on my left, facing the stage, so we're both centered.

Dyer puts his arm around me, and I try not to cringe. He murmurs in my ear, "The slit in your dress is convenient, you fucking slut. I want that pussy of yours right now."

I turn to look at him, playing the game, and smirk.

Dax puts his hand on my thigh, and tingles race over my skin. I turn to him.

"Ivy, we have to talk," he insists.

"Go ahead and talk. I'm listening," I state, smiling and gazing down at his hand.

When I glance up, there's a fire in Dax's eyes, and I know there's a matching one in mine. The air's electric between us. It's always been that way. Nothing has changed in that area.

At least, I feel it. I don't know if Dax always pretended or if our chemistry was real for him, but I didn't realize my hatred for Dax wouldn't squash my attraction toward him.

Unless Matt was right, and I was drugged. Maybe that's what's forcing me to feel this way.

No, I felt that the moment I saw Dax.

I wasn't drugged. I couldn't have been.

I was.

No, I wasn't.

As much as Matt urged me to take TimeMarker, I haven't. He even sent me an email with information on it. Yet I can't.

Something about knowing the truth is stopping me. It seems like another cruel slap in the face.

Maybe it wouldn't be. Perhaps it'd give me a reason to understand why I am the way I am. But it would make me their victim on another level, and I don't know if I can handle another blow.

A young woman comes up to the table. She's dressed to the nines, dripping in diamonds. A man's next to her. She politely states, "Excuse me, I think you're in our seats."

"Fuck off," Dax barks.

Shock erupts on her expression.

The man states, "Dax—"

"Go away," he orders, giving the man a threatening glare.

Unhappiness fills the man's expression.

Dax nods to Dyer's table. "Your seats are there, under Dyer's name."

The woman huffs.

The man turns her, and they go to the other table.

Dyer runs his hand under the slit in my dress so it grazes my thigh.

I want to close my eyes and scream, but I don't.

Suck it up, I tell myself, remembering the end game.

Dax stares at Dyer's hand and then leans across me, warning, "If you don't remove your hand from Ivy, I'm having you escorted out of here."

Dyer chuckles but doesn't remove his hand. "Is that so?"

"You want to test me?" Dax challenges.

"She's my date, aren't you, Ivy?" Dyer taunts.

I glance at Dax, offer a tiny smile, and then turn to Dyer, pretending I'm Avery, assuring him, "Of course you're my date."

He cockily questions, "Do you want my hand off you?"

"Don't answer that, Ivy. Take your hand off of her. You have three seconds. Three, two, one." Dax picks up his phone.

Dyer slowly removes his hand, muttering, "Jesus, Dax, get a fucking grip."

Dax points his phone at Dyer. "I'm warning you."

"Why don't we all calm down?" I suggest, putting one hand on Dax's thigh and one on Dyer's.

Dax looks down and takes a deep breath.

I look toward the stage, knowing he and Dyer are staring at me. And it's funny. I never realized it in the past, but they're practically drooling. It gives me more confidence, a feeling of power I've never known.

It almost makes me feel sorry for Dax.

Almost.

Then I remind myself of everything he's done.

"Ivy?" I hear Avery slur from behind me.

My insides quiver, and I slowly swivel to face her.

She looks shocked to see me. "Ivy? Oh my God. Ivy, is that you?" She puts her hand on my shoulder.

"Go away," Dax orders her.

I look up.

She's drunk, and I'm not used to seeing Avery past a buzzed state. Her eyes are red, and the scent of stale tequila hangs around her.

"Jesus, Avery. You might want to lay off the booze," Dyer states under his breath.

She doesn't tear her gaze off mine. "Ivy, you're back."

I lift my chin and square my shoulders, turning more toward her. "I am."

She opens her mouth, and I put my hand on her arm.

Dax shifts in his seat.

I ask, "Are you okay?"

"Yeah, w-why wouldn't I b-be okay?" she stutters and wobbles.

Dyer puts his hand on her hip. "Avery, you're drunk. You need to sit down."

She snaps her head toward him. "I don't need to sit down. I don't need you to tell me what to do. You're a little peon. Remember that."

Dyer's face hardens.

Horror fills me, but also amusement. This is the Avery I know.

She turns back to me and softens her voice. "Where have you been all these years, Ivy?"

"Oh, you know, here and there," I reply.

"Well, besides Georgia," Avery adds.

My head rears back in shock and my mouth goes dry.

How did she know I was in Georgia?

She leans into my ear and says louder than I believe she intends, "You didn't think I'd forget about you all these years, did you? I looked you up. I wanted to come find you. I didn't think you wanted me to."

Dax puts his arm between Avery and me. "Get away from her. You're drunk." He pushes her away.

"Don't you—"

"It's okay, Avery. Nothing's wrong. Dax is just a little off right now," I interject.

"Seeing Ivy, I'm sure he is," Bobby says, stepping up next to Avery and steadying her with his arm around her waist.

She turns her gaze off me, glancing at Bobby.

Bobby nods at me. "Ivy. It's been a long time."

My insides quiver harder. I hate everything about Bobby, especially after what Matt told me.

Not only did I research everyone's names online, but I also

spent too many hours on Bobby's legal issues. They all quietly went away, but it made me sick.

I force myself to stand up, put my hand on his chest, and rise on my tiptoes. I go to kiss him on the cheek, but he turns his head and meets my lips.

I want to hurl.

Don't mess this up, I scold myself when I almost flinch.

He puts his hand on my ass. "Ivy, you're looking as hot as ever. Isn't she, Avery?" He glances at her.

Avery puts her hand on my bicep to steady herself, and she nods as if in a trance. "Yeah. You look amazing."

It seems genuine, but I know nothing about her and Bobby is. I remind myself that it's all a game to them. Nothing they say is true.

I pretend I'm Avery when she's not drunk. Putting on a smile and batting my eyelashes, I reply, "Thank you, and you two look..." I run my fingers down both of their chests, stopping right in the middle of Avery's cleavage.

She inhales sharply and holds her breath.

I lower my voice. "Just as amazing." I let my gaze linger on Avery's breasts, then slowly pull it up to meet hers.

The same heat I saw when she tried to seduce me multiple times erupts within me.

I lean in, but I no longer smell the same scent she used to wear. It's a new one, and it hits me that it has to be the Seducing Ivy perfume. It's intoxicating, just like her old one used to be.

Once again, I resist the urge to run away. All the memories of what used to be hit me. Things I tried to force out of my head but never could.

My lower body throbs, adrenaline pools in my cells, and the urge to do things I shouldn't gets stronger, making me loathe myself.

I have to get out of here.

But I can't.

"Well, well. Looks like I'm missing the party," another familiar voice interjects.

I freeze, my heart beating faster. The smell of arousal bursts in my nose, making me dizzy.

I grasp Dax's arm to steady myself and realize it's a memory. I slowly turn to stare at Lilly.

She gives me a friendly look. It's the same one she always gave me when I thought she was my friend.

Was she a victim like me or part of their game?

Lilly was on that tape as well. And there was a blowout afterward, I'm sure, with her father, the senator. Yet I don't know what happened.

My father wouldn't let me turn on the TV after everything went down. And I don't know if she was truly friends with them, but I assume she was also embarrassed to be on that video.

I remind myself that everyone's the enemy, and force myself to be as friendly as I used to be with her. "Lilly, it's good to see you."

She reaches for me, and I hug her. It's just as warm as it always was. There's nothing sexual about it. But once again, I don't know the truth about her.

"My table's right there." She points to the one next to Dax's, then adds, "But it seems like I'm not sitting at the right one."

"We can make room here, right, Dax?" I shoot him a pleading look.

His face hardens. He suspiciously states, "It's been a long time, Lilly."

"Thought it was time to show my face again," she chirps,

then glances at me, adding, "But I see I definitely came at the right time if Ivy's here."

His eyes narrow.

I put my hand on his shoulder. "Come on, Dax. Let's have everybody sit at the table. You can kick these other people out, can't you?" I gaze over at the strangers who've started to take their seats.

They shoot me dirty looks. I don't know who they are. They're obviously people with money, but I don't care.

Dax stays silent, studying Lilly.

I lean down into his ear. "Let everybody sit at the table. Please." I put my face in front of his.

He swallows hard, not breaking our gaze.

"Dax is too big of a pussy to let us all sit here," Bobby mutters.

Dax's face hardens. I put my hand on his cheek and then lean over to his other ear, murmuring, "After the event, we can get together and talk, but let everybody sit here. Please? For me?" I beg gently and then graze my lips against his lobe.

He stays frozen for a moment, as if contemplating what to do.

"You don't want to talk to me?" I push.

He glances at the other people at the table, ordering, "Go to other tables."

Their gasps fill the air and anger heats their faces.

An older gentleman hisses, "What's gotten into you, Dax?"

He points to Lilly's table and another table next to him. "There's room at those tables. It's still the front row. Now get the fuck out."

They begrudgingly all get up and leave.

Lilly beams. "Thanks, Dax. It'll be so nice to catch up with Ivy and all of you."

Instead of sitting back down next to Dyer, I select the seat on the other side of Dax and pat the chair next to me. "Lilly, sit here. We have so much to catch up on," I say, knowing I can't take a whole evening of Professor Dyer's hands all over me.

"What are you doing? This is your seat," Dyer states.

I chirp, "It's okay. Bobby can have it. Right, Dax?"

There's a mix of emotions on Dax's face, but it comes and goes so quickly, I'm unsure if I saw it. Then his lips curve. It's twisted, and it sends tingles straight to my pussy. It's a look that always turned me on in the past.

He pulls the chair out. "Yeah, Bobby, sit down."

I point to the other side of Lilly. "Avery, you sit there."

She studies the table.

I turn around and grab her arm. "Come on, Avery. Sit down."

She gives Dax a haughty look.

He gives her one of disgust in return.

I'd forgotten how much they don't like each other. At least when they aren't pretending to be on the same team.

She takes a few unbalanced steps and safely makes it to her chair, plopping down on it.

A waiter comes by. "More champagne?" He hands me one and then passes out glasses to the others.

I almost take a sip, but then set it down. I point to another waiter two tables over and curl my finger.

He approaches and questions, "Can I help you, ma'am?"

I hand him the glass. "This is chipped. Can I get another one?"

He glances at the glass. "Where is it chipped?"

"It is. Can I get another one?" I ask, unsure if I was drugged or not years ago, but knowing I'm not taking any chances.

He exchanges my glass, and I smile. "Thank you." I turn back to the table and put my hand on Dax's thigh. "Such service. Although I prefer the frat boys with the thongs and bow ties, don't you, ladies?"

Lilly giggles. It's the same one I heard so many times when we friends; the same one from *that* night.

Lilly's a wild card.

I'm unsure what side she's on, but I need to find out.

Quickly.

Dax 8

I'VE MISSED THAT LAUGH

At least I wasn't the only one shocked, I think, looking at my sister in disgust.

She's drunk. She was already drinking when she came into my office earlier, demanding her money. But now she's hit it way too hard.

It's a rare occasion to see Avery this wasted, especially in public. She can't play her game well if she's intoxicated. So it's a position she doesn't put herself in often, but everything's falling apart around her. If I get my way, in no time at all, she'll be nothing but a poor alcoholic living on the streets.

Why is Lilly here?

It's been years since I last saw her. She's stayed away from everyone, so why did she choose now to reappear?

The looks on everyone else's faces are a priceless bonus to my evening. I may not have expected Ivy to be here, but neither did anyone else.

Bobby demands, "Ivy, tell us what you've been doing all these years."

I want to smack him. I can't stand the sight of him. But I also know he can't be happy she's here, knowing what he did and that I have a drug to pinpoint his crime. Yet Bobby doesn't show his cards, maintaining his confident façade.

Ivy waves her hand. "Oh, my life's boring compared to all of yours. Bobby, I hear you've been in the South of France?"

He freezes, but it's just momentarily, and I want to laugh out loud. He doesn't like that she's looked him up.

To get under his skin, I state the obvious. "Someone's done their homework."

Ivy bats her lashes. "I did. Looks like you're having a really good time in life."

Bobby chuckles. "That I am." He bypasses the champagne and takes a large swig of his scotch.

Ivy turns. "And, Lilly, what have you been up to?"

She shrugs. "Not much. I'm living out in California now."

Ivy leans closer. "Are you married?"

She scoffs. "No, marriage is for the birds. Besides, how much fun would I be able to have if I were married?" She winks and takes a large sip of champagne.

Ivy laughs.

My heart aches at the sound. I've missed that laugh.

Ivy lowers her voice, putting her hand on Lilly's arm. "So, what are you doing for fun?"

Lilly's lips twitch. "Anything that pisses my father off."

Ivy bites her lip, studying Lilly, then commands, "Tell me more about what that entails."

Lilly leans into her ear and whispers something I can't hear.

Ivy's face turns red, and she inhales sharply, then stares at Lilly.

I hate the look they exchange.

Avery must too because she shoves her arm over Lilly and puts her hand on Ivy's thigh. "Ivy, how have you liked Georgia?"

Lilly leans back in her chair.

Ivy shrugs. "It's fine. Nothing special."

"Well, you're there," Avery says, but it's not with her normal elegant charm. She's too drunk.

"Don't embarrass yourself," I scold.

Avery shoots daggers at me with her glare, snarling, "Shut up, Dax."

Somebody gets on stage, taps on the microphone, and says, "If you'd all take your seats, please."

The room quiets down. "Our MC tonight will be Dean Bramwell, but we'll serve dinner now. After we're done, get out those checkbooks for our annual live auction. Enjoy your-selves," the no-name says from the stage.

A filet mignon and lobster tail get placed in front of Ivy, Lilly, Avery, and then the rest of us.

The server comes up to me. "Mr. Carrington, are your other guests late?"

"No."

"Okay," the server replies. He picks up the other covered plates, sets them on his tray, and takes them away.

Bobby picks up his fork and knife and cuts a piece of meat. "I'm freaking starving."

I wonder how he can eat at a time like this, knowing one of his rape victims is two seats over.

Does he not realize she's here for revenge?

No, he underestimates her.

Dyer pulls out the chair next to him. "Ivy, why don't you come sit next to me?"

"She's talking to the ladies. Leave her alone," I warn.

Ivy turns toward Dyer, licks her whore-red lips, and coos, "I haven't seen the girls in so long. I'll be with you later tonight. Don't worry." She pins a seductive look on him, and I curl my fist at my side.

"What's wrong, Dax?" Bobby mocks, tapping my knuckles.

"Fuck off," I mutter under my breath.

Ivy puts her hand on my thigh and leans into my ear. "Don't worry, we'll still have our conversation."

I turn my head. Her lips are inches from mine, taunting me. All I want to do is run away with her. It's what I should have done years ago. I should have gotten her as far away from these people as possible.

"Let's go have our talk now," I urge.

She purses her lips and shakes her head. "No, Dax. We're at a charity event. Let's honor the occasion."

Honor the occasion? Like I give a shit about this occasion. I doubt Ivy does either.

"Yeah, Dax, we need to make sure that there's money raised for this wonderful university," Lilly chimes in, then rolls her eyes and finishes her champagne. She motions to a server across the room, and he brings another tray over. He hands her a full glass and takes her empty one.

Avery reaches for another.

"Haven't you had enough?"

"Shut up, dickhead," she says, then takes one from the server and grabs another one off the tray. She downs the glass and hands it back to him. "Thank you." She pats him on the ass as he leaves.

He jumps.

"You're so crude," I state.

"Avery, do you want to join Ivy and me tonight? You too, Lilly," Dyer adds.

"Shut the fuck up," I threaten again.

His cockiness shows on his face. I have to stop myself from reaching over Bobby and punching him.

Dyer and I have had a bad relationship since everything went down with Ivy. To this day, I don't know if anything was going on between them. Ivy had insisted nothing happened when I caught her in his arms after the sex video streamed all over campus.

I tend to believe her. But Dyer? He's always gone back and forth on it. So I don't know what to believe.

I've never played a game with him since. I've stayed far away from him and everyone else, only going into his office if I needed something. And because he's an employee of the university, I've always had him by the balls. Yet Ivy is one thing he's always held over my head, one time telling me they did nothing, and another tormenting me and claiming he's had her.

I don't know the truth, and it drives me nuts. Yet part of me doesn't want to know because if he really did sleep with Ivy...

My insides quiver.

Dyer, Bobby, Avery, Lilly... All of them need to keep their paws off of my Ivy.

"You can play too, Dax," Dyer says.

"What about me?" Bobby asks, with a twisted excitement in his voice.

It's all too much. The air in my lungs turns stale, the toxicity suffocating me.

"Maybe we'll see what the night brings," Ivy suggests, and my heart sinks further.

I slide my arm around her and lean into her ear, murmuring so only she can hear, "Stop playing this game. This isn't you."

She looks at me in surprise. "I don't know what you're talking about."

"You do. And this isn't how to get back at me."

"Get back at you? What's she going to get back at you for? She said let bygones be bygones," Dyer states.

I realize I spoke too loudly. I don't tear my gaze off Ivy's, silently begging her to end whatever she's trying to accomplish.

She says, "Dax, I hold no hard feelings. I told you that."

"Eat your food and shut up," Bobby says, shoving another forkful of meat into his mouth.

"Yeah, eat your dinner," Ivy agrees, sliding her hand up my inner thigh and grazing my erection.

I shudder. My chest grows heavy, rising and falling slowly, as I try to pull it together, staring at the lobster and filet on my plate.

Everyone begins to eat. I barely hear the conversation. I take another swig of scotch, my appetite gone.

The no-name steps back on stage when dinner is finally over and dessert is served. He booms, "Everyone please welcome our MC tonight, Dean Bramwell."

The room erupts in polite applause, and Dean Bramwell steps on stage. He's gotten fat over the years, and his shiny bald head has larger sunspots. The alcohol's turned his cheeks redder, and he grips the podium. He begins, "Thank you all for being here tonight. The funds that come to our university are important for our future students. The research we do here at Clifton University—"

Ivy leans into my ear. "We did a lot of research, didn't we, Dax?"

I stare at her, uneasy, blocking out Bramwell's voice.

She slides her hand on my thigh again, revealing, "Lots of

research on how to make me your good little slut, right, Dax?" Her lips twitch.

My mouth waters. I've dreamed about those lips for over a decade. I'd do anything to have them against mine again. And those words coming out of her mouth...

She slowly licks her lips, tormenting me, and then the room erupts in applause. She winks and rises.

I grab her wrist. "Where are you going?"

She points to the stage. "The stage. Dean Bramwell just called me up."

I don't release her. My pulse skyrockets, unsure of what's happening and hating every minute.

She giggles. "You have to release me, Dax."

"Yeah, release her," Bobby orders.

I nudge him in the chest with my elbow.

"Fucker," he barks, then takes another swig of scotch.

"Don't make a scene," I advise him.

Ivy pats me on the shoulder. "I have to go, Dax."

I finally release her, unsure what else I can do.

She struts across the room with all eyes on her, our table in a trance, swaying her whore-red, satin-covered ass, making my cock throb harder.

A student holds her hand to help her up the steps of the stage.

Dean Bramwell hugs her as she approaches him. He retreats and says into the microphone, "It's my pleasure—"

Ivy covers it and leans into Dean Bramwell's ear.

He chuckles and steps back, opening his arm.

"Okay, then, all yours."

Ivy waits until he sits down. Then she takes a deep breath and states, "Most of you probably remember me. Some of you might not. I'm Ivy Ford. You know...the sex video girl." She beams.

Gasps and a few lewd comments echo around the room.

I cringe and tighten my fist, wanting to pull her off the stage.

"Well, this is interesting," Bobby voices.

"Shut up, fucker," I warn under my breath.

She waits and then confidently stares at everyone at our table before locking her eyes on me. She continues, "As some of you might recall, I had a very special relationship with the Carringtons, as well as Bobby Winston and Lilly McBean." She points at our table.

The room turns so silent you can hear a pin drop.

She giggles. "Well, anyway, we had, like I said, a very special relationship. It all started the night that I rushed my sorority, Gamma Sigma Phi. I was given a very special gift. Wasn't I, Avery?"

I glance at my sister.

She tries to sit up straighter, her face turning maroon, in a daze, unable to tear her eyes off Ivy, the same as the rest of us.

Ivy reaches under the podium and pulls out a whore-red satin box. She opens it and dangles a gold necklace in front of her. The camera zooms in, and the screen behind her focuses on the pendant.

My gut drops.

Ivy chirps, "I'm sure you're all familiar with this symbol...or should I say trademark now? Many of you probably have bottles of Seducing Ivy in your bedrooms. Can we get a round of applause for how successful Avery's new perfume is doing?"

The room erupts in applause.

My chest tightens, and Avery grips the table.

Ivy coos, "And Dax... Wow. How smart of him to create the Seducing Ivy flower and file for the patent. You were always one step ahead of everyone, weren't you, Dax?"

My mouth turns dry.

Ivy smiles, adding, "We should all be proud of the quality students Clifton University creates." Ivy begins clapping.

The room follows suit until it's loud with applause, and bile rises in my throat. It takes everything I have to swallow it down.

Avery glances over at me, and I've never seen her so uncomfortable.

But I don't remember ever being that way either.

Ivy holds the necklace higher. "Avery made this for me. She designed it. Who would've known that ten years ago, such talent would have morphed into the company she's created today?" Ivy claps again.

More applause fills the room.

Ivy lets it die down and announces, "I'd like to auction this necklace off so the university can help more young students become the people that we've become. You know...contributing to society and all." Her lips twist, and she refocuses on me.

More applause.

The auctioneer steps toward her.

Ivy holds the necklace in front of him, adding, "Please ensure this goes for a high price. It doesn't deserve anything less. It's very..." She puts her hand around the symbol and then stares at Avery. "It's very special to me."

Avery's chest rises and falls faster.

Ivy gazes at the rest of the crowd. "You know how it is when special people give you special gifts. Every day was a unique experience for me at Clifton University. So please bid accordingly."

The camera zooms out, and Ivy releases the pendant to the auctioneer and gets escorted off the stage.

She grabs a glass of champagne from a server's tray, saunters across the room, and sits beside me.

The auctioneer starts, "Do I hear a hundred thousand?"

Before I know it, the attendees are bidding on the necklace I designed for Ivy—the one Avery took credit for.

It's another thing I regret. I allowed my sister to give it to Ivy the night everything went down. It was a gift I put a lot of thought into and genuinely wanted to give her. Avery found it and challenged me to let her give it to Ivy the night of the party. I couldn't let Avery win, so I let her.

It was another dumb move on my part.

The bid quickly gets up to two million.

Ivy reaches across the table to Avery and grabs her hand, smirking. "It was the nicest gift anyone's given me. I will truly miss it."

Avery arches her brows, unsure what to say, speechless in a rare moment.

The bidding continues to go on. Bobby gets into the game, holding up his paddle. "Five million."

Murmurs are heard from around the room.

Dyer takes a swig of his drink, meeting my eye.

"Too bad you can't bid on it, you poor bastard," I taunt.

Lilly giggles. She holds up her paddle. "Ten million."

Gasps fill the air.

Avery holds up her paddle. She calls out, "Twenty million."

"That's it. Spend all your money," I encourage her.

Avery snaps her head toward me, glaring.

I finish my scotch, letting all of them fight for it for a while.

The bid gets up to fifty million between Bobby, Avery, and Lilly.

I finally hold up my paddle, calling out, "A hundred million."

Everyone in the room claps.

Bobby glares at me and holds his paddle up. "One hundred ten million."

"One hundred twenty," Lilly follows, then puts her hand on Ivy's thigh.

Ivy inhales sharply, then gives Lilly a look I can't decipher.

What the fuck is going on?

More panic hits me.

Avery moves her paddle up and then freezes.

"Come on, Avery. You know you want it," Dyer taunts, even though he doesn't know that she'll be broke if she does.

She stares at her empty champagne glass, breathing hard.

"Do I hear 130?" the auctioneer questions.

I hold my paddle up. "Two hundred million."

The room fills with louder gasps than before.

Ivy gapes at me.

I glance at Bobby. "You might want to save your money for your legal fees."

He grinds his molars, and I know he's reached his end. His trust fund's smaller than mine. He's been wasting it in France while I've been growing my empire.

"Lilly, outbid him," Avery encourages.

I don't look at her. I doubt she's going to. Her trust fund doesn't run that deep either.

Lilly shakes her head. "Sorry, I'm out. Although it always looked beautiful on you, Ivy."

"Thanks," Ivy replies, confusing me on their relationship status.

They were friends, yet Lilly set her up too.

They're not friends.

No one is anyone's friend.

Ivy was a friend to me.

She was the only person who was ever genuinely good to me.

I hate myself more.

"Congratulations to our winner, Dax Carrington, for 200 million," the auctioneer booms.

Deafening applause breaks out, and I go up on the stage and hold my hand out, demanding, "Give it to me."

The auctioneer's eyes widen. He hands it to me.

I exit the stage, open the clasp, and put it around Ivy's neck. I lean down. "Avery didn't design this for you. I did. And it's yours."

Ivy 9

HERE FOR REVENGE

I CAN'T HIDE my shock. I don't know if I should believe Dax or not. "Don't lie to me," I scoff.

"*I* designed it," Avery insists.

"You're the liar. I spent a month designing that, and you know it," he barks, scowling at her.

I glance toward her.

She's intoxicated, drunker than when she arrived. Her arm's on the table, her head near it, as if she can barely keep it up. She starts to laugh, slurring, "You did design a good one." Then she glances at me. "That necklace does look good on you. Then again, you can wear anything and everyone will want a piece of you."

My insides quiver.

Dax places his palm on my shoulder and gently says my name.

I swallow hard, then meet his eye.

"Let's get out of here, please." There's a plea in his voice, and it tugs at my heart.

Don't fall for him again.

"Yeah, I think it's time to get out of here," Bobby says, rising.

"Agreed. We could have way more fun than this," Lilly suggests, trailing her fingers over my thigh, giggling.

Dax glares daggers at Bobby, snarling, "Go wherever you want, Bobby. I'm not coming with you."

Why doesn't Dax like Bobby anymore?

Is it because of me?

No.

Play the game, I tell myself.

Dyer challenges, "What are you scared of, Dax?"

He stays quiet.

Dyer adds, "Are you scared Ivy's interested in Bobby and me?"

I glance at Dyer, feeling ill. I find nothing attractive about the man. I would have a different opinion if Matt hadn't told me he's like the others. Now, he's gross to me.

He's a weapon to utilize.

I coyly suggest, "It depends on what position you put me in." I put on my best Avery expression, darting my eyes between him and Bobby.

Dax's hand grips my shoulder tighter. "Ivy, let's go. You promised me you'd talk with me."

I put my hand over his. "Let's have an after-party."

Hope fills his expression. "Okay, you and I will have one. Let's go."

It's what I really want. Yet I'm not here to rekindle my one-sided romance with Dax.

I'm here for revenge.

I wave my finger in front of Dax's face. "No you don't."

"Don't what?" he questions.

"Get to have all the fun."

His face hardens.

I add, "Everyone at the table is invited to the after-party."

Lilly claps, singing, "Yay!" and I want to laugh. It's the same Lilly I remember.

"Where are we going?" Dyer asks, and my insides crawl.

Dax snaps his head toward him. "You're not going anywhere with us."

"Dax, it's not an after-party without others," I whine, grazing my thumb over the front of his wrist.

The color slowly drains from his cheeks.

My heart beats so hard I'm sure he can hear it.

Avery slurs, "Yeah, Dax. Let's have an after-party at Dyer's."

"My place is ready," Dyer offers.

"Of course it's ready, you eager fuck," Dax seethes, then quietly pleads, "Ivy, please. Let's go talk."

I rise. It's now or never. Even though I hate Dax, nothing sounds better than being alone with him. I can't help it. I'm a sex junkie who wants the high I've been craving for ten years. The electricity between us hasn't faded over the years.

So I don't want to be around any of the others. I don't trust them, except maybe Lilly. I still can't tell what her part was in all this.

Play the game.

I slide my hands up Dax's torso as I rise, and then wrap them around his neck. "We can talk on the way to the after-party. Let's have it at your place."

His eyes turn to slits. "My place?"

I nod. "Yeah. Do you still live in the cottage? Or are you in the main house now?"

Avery chimes in, "We're all in the main house. Cooper, Dax, me. He can't kick us out."

Dax clenches his jaw. He puts his arms around my waist, tugging me closer, begging, "Ivy, please. Let's go talk. Alone."

"We will, but everybody has to come to the after-party," I declare, smiling.

Dax's expression hardens.

I lean into his ear. "Do you want to talk to me in the car, or do you want me to leave with Dyer?"

It's enough for me to get my way. "Let's go," he replies, leading me away.

Dyer steps up next to us. "Where are you taking my date, Dax?"

I put my hand on Dyer's. "We're going to Dax's. I'll meet you there."

"No, I'll drive you. You're my date," Dyer insists.

Dax moves me to the other side of him and jabs his finger in Dyer's chest. "She's not going with you. You're lucky you have an invite, but I advise you not to show up."

"Dax, don't be like that," I chide, putting my hand on his cheek.

He doesn't say anything. He swiftly moves me through the crowd, and everyone stares at us.

I can only imagine what's going through their minds.

No one at Clifton University is unaware of what happened ten years ago. I'm sure everyone in the room's seen the sex video.

After the scene I created on stage, everyone at the table bidding on the necklace, and Dax putting it back around my neck after paying $200 million, I can't imagine what they must think.

Why did he design it for me?

We get out into the cold air, and Dax silently leads me to his car. It's right at the front in his reserved parking spot. It suddenly seems funny to me and I laugh. He opens the passenger's door. "What's so funny, gorgeous?"

My heart soars.

Gorgeous. *How long has it been since I've heard that word from his mouth?*

It doesn't mean anything, I remind myself.

I point at the sign. "Of course you have a reserved parking spot in this lot." He had one for school, but it was in another area.

"And?" he questions, confused, as if having reserved parking spots all over campus is normal.

It is in his world.

I shake my head and shrug my shoulders, admitting, "It's just Dax Carrington." I get into the car.

He pauses a moment and then shuts the door.

The others step out of the building, and Dax scurries around the front of the car, then slides into the driver's seat. He revs the engine and peels out, driving the same way as when we were younger.

Another rush of adrenaline hits me, just like it used to. I state, "Some things never change."

"Some things do," he declares and glances at me in disapproval.

I raise a brow. "Such as?"

He scowls. "You."

"Spoken from the chameleon," I accuse.

He sighs, then grabs my hand and kisses it.

I have to fight those feelings I wish I could erase. I realize this is harder than I thought it would be, even though I knew it wouldn't be easy.

"I'm sorry, baby girl. I didn't mean to snap at you."

"Didn't you?"

"No, I didn't. I know none of this is your fault."

"None of what?" I question, curious about what part of this toxic evening he's referring to.

He glances over at me and then back at the road.

"This isn't you, Ivy. Whatever you're trying to do here, it isn't you. You're better than this...than all of us."

I snort, laughing. "That's rich coming from you."

"I mean it," he insists, stroking his thumb over my hand and sending surges of need straight to my core.

Stay in control.

I take my hand out of his and move it to his thigh, slowly crawling my fingers toward his erection until my pointer finger grazes it. I move it up and down.

A low groan comes out of him. "Jesus, Ivy."

I quietly ask, "How much of everything between us was a game to you?"

He grinds his molars.

My pulse quickens. "It's okay. You can admit it. It was a long time ago, Dax. I'm just curious when you decided I would be used and manipulated."

Dax turns a corner, steps on the accelerator, and shakes his head. "It was all a mistake, Ivy."

"Oh? What part was a mistake?" I challenge.

He swallows hard.

"The part where you posted the video all over campus or something else?"

"I didn't post that video. I swear to you it was not me," he insists.

I almost want to believe him, but I can't. I reply, "Sure you didn't. But it's okay. It was a long time ago. You can admit it."

He shakes his head, his voice raising. "I didn't do it. Avery did."

I scoff. "Not very nice to blame your sister. After all, she was so nice to me."

Anger fills him. He seethes, "Oh, sorry, Ivy. Maybe your allegiance is to her since you slept with her."

"I didn't sleep with her!" I hurl before I can stop myself. Maybe he should think I did.

He turns his blazing eyes on me. "So you claimed."

"I claimed I didn't sleep with her because I never did. She tried, and I stopped her."

He snarls, "With her fingers up your pussy?"

Rage fills me, along with embarrassment. It wasn't my fault what Avery did to me, but I still hate it happened. "You know what, Dax? You don't get to judge me. But I didn't do anything with Avery."

"Sure."

My voice shakes when I say, "I never did anything with anyone you didn't encourage me to do."

Guilt fills his expression, but then it turns hard again.

I continue, "I'm telling you, I didn't do anything with your sister. I pushed her off me. I would have told you what happened if you had been at your house that night. And if you had the balls to ask me about it when you saw the video, I would've told you then."

He grips the steering wheel so tight I can see his knuckles turn white even through the darkness.

My voice gets louder. "Why would you think I would sleep with her? I loved you! Only you!" It's more than I should give him, even though he already knows how I felt about him.

He turns toward me, pain evident in his features. "Her fingers were up your pussy. I saw it on the video."

"And I shoved her off me. You, of all people, should know that things aren't always what they seem, now are they?" I point out.

His face falls. He turns back to the road.

Silence fills the air.

I finally ask, "What did you want to talk to me about anyway?"

"Fuck it," he mutters. He pulls over to the side of the road and parks the car.

"Why are you stopping?"

He turns toward me and grabs my hand. He grinds his molars and then blurts out, "Ivy, the worst thing I ever did was what I did to you. I should never have let you do any of those things that night. I should have treated you better. I shouldn't have kicked you off the property."

"And fired my dad?" I blurt out, my eyes welling with tears. I blink hard to stop them, willing myself not to show any emotion to Dax, and pissed that I already am.

He clenches his jaw.

Tense silence fills the air.

"Or do you regret stealing my father's invention and patenting it?"

The accusation hangs between us, but he doesn't look surprised to know I'm aware of what he did.

He also doesn't look remorseful. He chooses his words carefully, claiming, "Your father would never have done anything with it. It sat there for years and years, and not once did he do anything with it."

I cry out, "So you stole it from him?"

Something passes over his expression. I can't say it's regret. I don't know what it is, but it makes me uneasy.

"Things will soon come to light, Ivy."

"Come to light? What the fuck is that code for, Dax?"

"You have to trust me," he declares.

Enraged, I snatch my hand away from his. "Trust you? You want me to trust you after everything that's happened?"

He scrubs his palm on his forehead. "I shouldn't ask you to, but I am."

I huff. "And why should I trust you?"

He sighs. "Because I'm the only one who cares about you around here."

I sarcastically laugh. "You care about me? Is that what you'd call it?"

"I loved you, Ivy. I still love you," he voices.

Shock fills me once again. My butterflies explode the same way they always did when he would make that claim. I gape at him, yet I'm not naive anymore. I know it's not true.

He puts his hand on my cheek, softening his tone. "I do. Not a day's gone by that I don't regret what I've done. I love you. Please, you have to believe me. I'd do anything to get you back. Anything."

A war erupts within me. My heart flutters harder, mixing with an uneasy feeling in my chest. I want to believe him, but I scold myself. I can't be that same girl anymore—the one who's naive and gullible.

This is Dax Carrington. He stole my father's patent. He created products that will make him a billionaire over and over again. And ultimately, he and his sister are responsible for killing my father.

I won't ever forgive him.

"I love you. I always have," he insists.

"You don't love me."

"I do."

The more he insists he does, the more I want to believe him, but my anger continues to build, my pulse throbbing out of control.

Stay calm.

Play the game.

He's my pawn. I'm no longer his.

"Ivy—"

"If you love me, then prove it," I demand.

He freezes and then asks, "Okay. How?"

"What will you do for me, Dax?"

Hope fills his expression. "Anything, Ivy. I'll do anything for you."

"Really? I don't think you will," I challenge, my insides full of adrenaline, my pussy aching, and my heart beating faster with lust and rage.

I'm at an uncontrollable point with my addiction. I need what I need, and I'm going to get it and hurt Dax and everyone else in the process.

He slides his thumb over my lips, asserting, "Ivy, whatever I need to do to prove to you I love you and I'm sorry, I will."

It sounds so genuine, I want to believe him, but I remind myself there's nothing genuine about Dax Carrington. He used me, abused me, and threw me away like I was a piece of garbage not even worthy of his trash can.

Don't let him win this time.

I study him as the tension builds.

"You have to give me another chance," he demands.

I pretend to give in. "Okay."

"Okay? What does that mean?" he cautiously asks.

I lean over to him and put my hand on his head, pulling him closer to me. I brush his lips with mine while ordering, "You'll start proving it to me tonight."

His breathing picks up. He reaches for my head and pulls me into him, kissing me and sliding his tongue against mine.

It only takes seconds before I'm back into the bliss that I remember, the world of Dax Carrington and me, his tongue thrashing against mine, his palm holding me firmly, making me feel alive.

It's the first time I've really felt it in ten years. No matter what I've done to find it again, I never could.

A high hits me, but it also intensifies my cravings for everything else the demons deep inside me need.

I force myself to retreat. "We have an after-party to get to."

The color drains from his face. "Ivy—"

"You told me you'd do anything for me. I did everything for you. Then you stole the only thing my father had. The only thing that wasn't taken from him, you took," I accuse, unable to stop myself from spewing my thoughts.

"I told you, things will soon come to light about that," he argues.

"I don't know how to follow the labyrinth you're creating about my father's work, but I'm not interested in figuring it out. There's only one thing I'm interested in right now."

His eyes turn to slits. He questions, "What's that?"

I sit back in my seat and point out the window. "Drive. We have an after-party to get to."

He warns, "Ivy, you can't trust the others."

I almost laugh out loud, but I hold it in. I turn to him. "I'm supposed to trust you, but not them?"

"Yes," he insists.

"And what did you do that was any better than what they did?" I ask.

He squeezes his eyes shut and slowly shakes his head. "Ivy, you don't understand."

I can't help it, I laugh. "Well, fill me in."

He opens his eyes and leans his head back against the headrest, continuing to shake it, staring at the ceiling.

I put my hand on his erection and lean back toward him.

He rolls his head toward me.

"Dax, you just told me you love me. Is it really true?"

His eyes glisten. He blinks hard. "Yes."

I smile. "Then let's go to the after-party. It's time you prove it to me."

He stares at me in confusion.

This isn't the conversation I thought we'd have. I didn't expect him to go this route to play the game, but I should have anticipated it.

I thought he would try to run me out of town, but if he's going to willingly embrace me in this game, then that's fine.

Let him claim his love for me. I'll have to play my strategy differently. Either way, Dax Carrington's going down.

No matter what he, or any of the others, says, it'll never be true. They'll always see me as a hillbilly girl from West Virginia, one to be manipulated, used, and abused.

But the tide's turning. They're the ones who will get what's coming to them.

I'll die making sure of it.

Dax 10

UNZIP ME

Ivy HAS something up her sleeve, but I can't figure it out. I'm walking into a trap. I can feel it, yet I can't stop myself.

I'll do anything to get another shot with her. It's been too many years of pain without her, and now that she's back, it's glaring at me in the face.

So I have to get her back into my life. There's no way I'm not going to right the wrongs I did and let her go again.

All the years of wondering how she was and beating myself up about what I should have done differently come crashing together. It's now or never. This is the only chance I'll ever have to make her mine again, and I know it. And if she disappears again, it's over.

I'm over.

One touch from her and life sprung back inside me, reiterating what I've known all these years.

I've been dead without her.

It's on the tip of my tongue to tell her that I have money in a trust for her, that it's more than her father would've ever done with that patent.

If she wants to give it to him, she can. But it's hers to do with what she wants.

Yet I know Ivy's not only here because of the patent. This is about more than money. It has to do with everything that happened the night of the sorority rush and after.

More than anything, I want to believe that nothing happened between Avery and her, and that Ivy rejected my sister, but I can't get the video footage out of my mind. I haven't been able to for ten years.

If she didn't fuck Avery...

What if she did?

What if she didn't?

Can I forgive her if she did?

My gut tells me I've been a fool. Ivy never wanted Avery. If I had given her a chance to explain, things could have been saved between us.

My entire life would be different.

I pull up to the estate and the gates open.

Ivy takes a slow breath.

I glance over at her and put my hand on her thigh. "I assume it's hard for you to come back here."

She turns her head and smiles once again. It's a look Avery would give. But everything about that look on Ivy is intoxicating, drawing me more into her. She claims, "Not at all. I love this place. It's where I learned to become a little slut. Your dirty, pussy-dripping whore, right, Dax?"

"Don't say that," I order, and more regret hits me.

She puts her hand on mine. "Well, Dax Carrington, have you suddenly become a prude?"

It's the first time I've ever been called that. And I hate it. It's a dose of reality of how she must've felt when I would use that tactic on her or the others.

"Ivy, you don't have to do this."

"Do what?" she asks as I drive up the long path to the main house.

I answer, "You don't have to do whatever you think you have to do right now."

She gives me an innocent look. "What do you think I need to do, Dax?"

I stay quiet, unsure how to answer, continuing up the driveway and catching a glimpse of the lighted windows.

She states, "You know, I've never been inside this house."

"It's because I hated it," I admit.

"Why did you hate it so much?" she questions.

I park the car and shake my head. "Lots of reasons." I go to get out.

"Stop," she commands.

I freeze and then look at her, waiting.

She declares, "I want to know why you hated it. I've always wondered what was so bad that made you not want to live in this grand house. So tell me."

My gut flips. "Let's talk about it a different night."

"No, let's talk about it now," she firmly asserts.

The tables have turned, and I hate it, but I'm too desperate to keep her in my life. So I swallow my pride, admitting, "My father hated me. But you knew that. My mother couldn't stand me much either. She preferred Cooper. My dad preferred Avery. I was the kid they didn't really want."

I can see compassion in her eyes as her voice softens. "What do you mean they didn't want you?"

I pull my thoughts together, shoving my emotions down, confessing, "They didn't want me. My mom got pregnant. My grandfather hated my father, but my father tricked my mother into marrying him."

Ivy continues to push, asking, "Why didn't your grandfather like him?"

I sniff hard and stare at her, knowing the answer will sound horrible.

"What is it? Go on. You can tell me," she encourages.

All the trust I had in her reappears. I try to collect my thoughts.

She softly demands, "Don't lie to me, Dax. Just tell me the truth. For once, tell me the truth."

I cave. "Okay. My father was poor. According to my grandfather, he grew up on the wrong side of the tracks. So he didn't like him."

Ivy's eyes turn to slits, but then she starts to laugh, asserting, "So he was like me."

I shake my head. "No. My father was nothing like you."

"No? I'm poor. It's just a reverse situation, isn't it?"

I hate that it looks that way on paper. I claim, "You don't understand my father. He was conniving. He's a horrible person. He used to hit me," I blurt out and then turn my head in shame, staring out the window.

Tense silence fills the car.

Ivy puts her hand on my leg, and tingles go right to my cock once again. "Look at me, Dax."

I slowly turn and face her.

"Your father used to hit you?"

I must be drunk from being in her presence. Things I've never told anyone roll out of my mouth. "Yeah. When I was five, he took a belt and beat me so badly, I had welts on my ass for a week. But that's how I grew up. And Avery and Cooper, they could do no wrong. I was the whipping boy."

Pity fills Ivy's expression.

I hate it. I insist, "It's water under the bridge. He's dead and my mother's in Europe. So I no longer have to see them. You don't have to feel sorry for me."

"Well, that explains a lot, if it's true," Ivy says.

"You think I'd make something like that up?" I accuse.

She narrows her eyes. "Can you blame me?"

I sigh. "Ivy, I know I've done a lot of bad shit to you, but I'm not lying about this...not that it matters. It is what it is. You asked me a question, and I told you the truth. I'm done lying to you."

She tilts her head. "Really? You're never going to lie to me again?"

"Yeah, I'm not going to lie to you."

"Good to know." She gets out of the car.

Once again, I'm confused. I'm unsure what her next move is, so I get out of the car and follow her.

I slide my arm around her waist, then lead her up the stairs and into the house.

She glances around the large foyer. "Love the tufts," she says, staring at the circular bench wrapped in navy leather.

"Thanks."

"Kind of looks like your style."

"I had it redone when I moved back in," I admit.

She puts her hand on my cheek and then pecks me on the lips. I try to pull her closer, but she pulls away. She takes my hand. "Show me around."

I give her a tour of the first floor.

We reach my office, and she chirps, "Well, this is an interesting room."

I question cautiously, "Yeah? Why is that?"

She struts over to the desk, her whore-red, satin-clad ass swaying, and orders, "Unzip me, Dax."

Unzip her?

Is she serious?

I don't move.

She turns her head, giving me a coy look. "Are you shy all of a sudden? I thought you said you love me. Unzip me."

In a trance, I walk toward her. I unzip her, move her hair over her shoulder, and kiss it the way I used to.

She moves her hands to her straps and shoves them down her arms. Her dress falls to the floor, unveiling a matching whore-red strapless bra and thong. She spins to face me. "Step back, Dax."

My heart pumps harder. Adrenaline hits me to the point I feel dizzy. I drag my eyes down her body and rest them on her C cups that have tortured me since the moment I first laid eyes on her.

She giggles and pushes me. "I said step back."

I do.

She hops onto the desk, crosses her legs, and puts her hands behind her.

"Jesus, that's quite the scene," Dyer's voice interjects, pulling me out of our private moment.

I step in front of Ivy to cover her. "Get out of here."

"Oh, don't be such a party pooper, Dax. Come on in," Ivy welcomes in a confident tone.

I thrust my head toward her, glaring. "What are you doing?"

"Time for you to prove some things to me, Dax."

My gut churns.

She's trapped me.

"This isn't the way—"

She puts her finger over my lips. "I'm not the one trying to prove something to somebody. You are. Remember?"

My chest tightens. A war continues to rage within me. I suddenly feel like that kid again, the one who got caught in too many lies and manipulative situations. Scenarios I shouldn't have let happen but did, now demand I pay the price.

Ivy's in control, and I'm owed every bit of pain she wants to unleash upon me.

Dyer steps next to us and places his hand on Ivy's spine. She trembles, and a momentary flash of disgust fills her expression, then disappears. I wonder if I imagined it—if I'm only seeing what I want to see.

She turns toward him and smiles. "Hey there, handsome. I thought you'd never get here."

"Looks like we have a party," Lilly says, beaming as she walks in.

Avery, who's hanging on Lilly's arm, giggles and then slurs, "Don't start without us."

"Yeah. Don't leave us out," Lilly adds, then asks, "Where's Bobby?"

My gut dives.

No, no, no.

This is not happening.

Ivy turns my chin and leans forward. I think she's going to kiss me, but at the last minute, she moves her face and plays tongue tag with Dyer.

My world collapses. I snap out of it and push him away. "Get off of her."

"Dax," Ivy scolds, jumping off the desk.

I turn toward her. "This isn't you."

She laughs. "You don't know who I am anymore." Then she turns her head toward my sister. "Hey, Avery."

"What?" Avery asks.

"Come here." Ivy curls her finger.

My sister smirks at me and tries to saunter over, but it's sloppy from her intoxication.

My stomach churns.

Ivy orders, "Avery, kiss Professor Dyer."

Relief fills me.

Avery drunkenly slides her arms around Dyer and looks up.

He bends down willingly, and they make out for a few minutes.

"All right, enough," I say, hating watching my sister do any sexual act. I slide my arm around Ivy again, declaring, "We're all over this game. Come on, Ivy. Let me show you the rest of the house."

"Nope," she says, shaking her head and wiggling her finger at me. "I'm not done in your office yet."

"Meaning?" I question, then regret it.

She pushes me, sits on the desk again, then takes her foot and gently kicks me in the torso so I move backward. She puts her heels on the edge of the desk, commanding, "Lilly, come here."

In horror, I watch Lilly walk over.

Ivy's thong is crotchless. Her pussy's as pink as ever, glistening. My mouth waters as my chest pains intensify.

Ivy leans back on her elbows and locks eyes with Lilly. "Have you missed me?"

Lilly giggles and puts her hand on Ivy's inner thigh. "I have."

"That's enough," I say.

Ivy refocuses on me, pouting. "You don't want to prove to me what you claimed in the car?"

My blood boils hotter.

"This is what I want, Dax. Or is it still about what you want?"

Bobby booms, "Yep. Dax is selfish as fuck. Nothing's ever changed." He walks through the door.

The last thing I want to do is spend a night with Bobby, especially with Ivy here and her pussy on display. And he shouldn't be here anyway. I blurt out, "How did you get past security?"

Avery answers, "I lifted your stupid ban."

My chest tightens.

I'm going to kill Chad for following Avery's orders.

Ivy threatens, "I'm only going to warn you once, Dax. Go with the flow tonight, or all you'll do is prove I'm right and you didn't mean a word you said in the car."

"What did he say?" Bobby inquires.

"None of your business," I snap.

"I mean it, Dax. Either prove it or get the fuck out," Ivy orders.

Avery erupts in laughter, cooing, "Oh, Ivy, I've missed you so much."

"Shut up," I grit through my teeth, scowling at her.

"Dax, either get in line and return to who you used to be, or that's it," Ivy says, shrugging.

That's it?

Meaning we're done and over and I'll never have another chance with her.

No, this isn't what she wants. She's just trying to hurt me.

"Lilly, hold on a minute," Ivy says and slides off the desk. She walks toward me, grabs my arm, and steers me into the bathroom. She shuts the door.

I push her against it and put my hands on her cheeks. "Baby girl, what are you doing?"

Her lips twitch. "I'm doing what I need to do."

"You don't need to do this," I reiterate.

"Oh, but I do. You have no idea what I need to do... What I need to do every day of my life. And you know why, don't you?" she accuses.

Everything becomes clear.

She knows what Bobby did.

My hands tremble against her cheeks.

Her eyes glisten, and she blinks. "Ah. So it's true. You did do it."

"I didn't do it. Bobby did. I had zero knowledge until after the fact," I insist.

She stares at me and blinks. A tear rolls down her cheek.

I swipe at it. "Ivy, listen to me. I created drugs."

"I know all about your drugs."

"I wouldn't have created them if I had been part of it. Do you think I'm that stupid? I even have proof that I didn't know about it."

She huffs. "Sure you do, Dax. How could you?"

"I swear I didn't know. I never would've let that happen. I have it in text messages from my phone years ago. It's in my safe. I'll show you right now."

Ivy scoffs, shaking her head. "I don't want to see it tonight, Dax. All I want to do is do what I want. Not what *you* want. What *I* want. And you're going to participate. If you love me, you'll participate."

I grind my molars.

She adds, "And you better change your attitude right now. Do you understand me?"

"Baby girl."

"Don't call me that."

I freeze, trying to figure out what to say.

She continues, "I'm your dirty little whore. I'm your slut. That's who I am. That's what you made me into—you, Bobby, Avery, even Lilly."

I blurt out, "Avery drugged you too! I didn't know! I swear I didn't know!"

Ivy looks away and blinks hard, then turns back to me. Her lips twitch. "It doesn't matter, does it?"

"Of course it matters. I didn't do that. And I do love you.

Let's not do this, please. I'll take you out of here, and we can leave this place!"

She shakes her head. "No, this is my game tonight, and you're in it. But I expect you to play your part with enthusiasm. Because if you don't give me what I want, all the words you said in the car mean nothing. You've proven nothing. Is that what you want? Me to prove myself right that you don't love me?" Ivy threatens.

I rarely feel threatened. It's only happened a few times in my life. Avery is usually behind it, but it's rare.

"What's it going to be, Dax? Are you going to prove to me you love me and give me what I want? Or are you going to be a prude? Because this dirty whore that you created has needs, lots of them, and you have to decide. So make your choice. Do you love me or not?"

"Of course I love you. I'm not lying. I do. You're the only person I've ever loved," I declare.

The same look I used to see on Ivy's face when I told her I loved her emerges. But it quickly disappears.

"I do love you. I've never stopped," I firmly assert.

Her eyes glisten. She strokes my cheek and lowers her voice. "Yeah? Then prove it to me."

Ivy 11

PLAY THE GAME

Dax gapes at me.

I've never seen him speechless before. I'm starting to appreciate it. For once, I have power over him.

Every time he says he loves me, my heart bleeds, but I know it can't be true. What he did wasn't love. When he used me, there was nothing but maliciousness attached to it.

I step out of the bathroom, leaving him behind.

Lilly and Avery sit next to each other, making out. Bobby's kneeling next to them, his hands on their thighs, drooling. Professor Dyer's sitting in a chair, sipping his drink, playing with his cock while watching them.

"Same Bobby as always," I say.

He stills and turns his head.

Avery and Lilly part, their lips twitching.

"You've never seen us make out before," Lilly states, then giggles and adds, "Are you going to join us?"

Avery grabs her glass from the table, takes a swig, and sets it down. She stumbles up and saunters over to me.

My heart beats faster.

Did she really drug me?

I was prepared for Bobby but not Avery. Even though I knew it was possible, I think I was in denial since I thought she was my friend ten years ago. And I know now it was all an act, but I still gave her the benefit of the doubt.

I have to stop being stupid. All of them are evil.

Is Lilly?

I also thought Dax was the love of my life.

I beat myself up a little more. How could I have been so naive to think Dax was my love story? I was a fool back then. I had no business believing Dax Carrington was my soul mate and we would be together forever. I was the girl from the wrong side of the tracks. I should have listened to my father instead of believing Dax would always worship and adore me.

We weren't real.

He says he loves me.

He doesn't.

Avery puts her hand on my breast, but all I feel is disgust. She slurs, "Ivy, do you want to play?"

She's not who I remember. The Avery I knew was confident and intoxicating, not a slurring drunk. She was always in control, even when she drank, and I wonder how she's gotten like this.

Dax snarls behind me, "You're drunk."

Play the game.

Play the game.

Play the game.

I turn and wiggle my finger. "Uh-uh-uh. That's not the attitude we need this evening."

His face hardens.

Bobby snickers, taunting, "Yeah, Dax, change your attitude."

Hatred erupts in Dax's eyes.

I resist the urge to run away.

Am I really going to let Bobby touch me after what he's done?

My heart beats faster. The churning in my gut worsens.

Dax gives me another pleading look. It doesn't deter me, giving me the courage to follow my plan.

"Bobby, when's the last time you had three women?"

A sinister expression fills his face.

Dax grits out, "What the fuck, Ivy?"

"Why don't you just leave?" Avery suggests.

Panic hits me. "No, he's staying," I declare, looking at him again. "Aren't you?"

Tense silence looms around us.

"He's gotten soft," Bobby taunts.

Rage overtakes Dax's features. He curls his fist at his side, focused on Bobby. His eyes turn to slits.

I put my hand on his chest, trying to calm the situation. I lean into his ear. "You made me into who I am. I have needs, Dax. Are you going to let me have what I need?"

More guilt floods him. He squeezes his eyes shut, shaking his head, mumbling, "This isn't the way, Ivy."

I kiss him just under his lobe. "Oh, but it is. I'm your dirty whore. Don't you want me to be your dripping-wet slut?" I move my hand to his cock. It hardens in my palm.

His breathing turns shallow.

I lick his lobe, teasing, "You don't want me anymore, Dax?"

He moves my face in front of his, adamantly stating, "Of course I want you. I've always wanted you."

Avery mocks, "Yeah. He's always wanted you. It's all he's obsessed about."

"Shut up," Dax snarls.

"It's true. He's done a lot of stupid things over the last ten years because of you," she says.

My pulse skyrockets.

What is she talking about?

Dax scowls at her.

I'd love to know what she means by her accusation, but I decide not to ask her right now. Avery catches me off guard, sliding her hand on my spine, and I shudder, hating myself.

It's true. I'm an addict. I have needs. One touch from anyone can ignite the demons within me, even if it's from my enemy. My disgust can turn into lust with nothing but one suggestive touch.

Stop being weak.

Dax could satisfy me on his own. I have no doubt, now that we're back in the same room together, but that won't pay him back. It's clear that letting him be the only one who gets me won't hurt him.

He needs to pay, I remind myself.

Avery traces the top of my thong, breathlessly praising, "You've always looked good in whore red."

My core burns with the urges I can't control.

Don't get played.

Stay focused.

I turn and smile at Avery, running my hand over her tit the same way she did it to me.

She inhales sharply, holding her breath, her intoxicated gaze filling with the same look I saw when I was her pawn.

For the first time ever, I realize it's hope.

She recovers, reaches toward me, and grazes her fingers along my cleavage, creating a burst of tingles. She coos, "You've waited a long time for me, haven't you, Ivy? You came back here in whore red to tease us all, didn't you?"

"Fuck off, Avery!" Dax booms.

My butterflies kick off. I state, "Dax is the one who decided this was my color. Didn't you, babe?" I glance back at him.

He studies me, assessing the situation, confusion all over his expression.

I almost laugh. I've not seen Dax like this before. He's always been the one in control, calling the shots. Not this time.

And it feels good.

Bobby strolls over to the bar and pours drinks. He comes over and hands Dax and me a glass, ordering. "Drink up."

"Don't drink that, Ivy," Dax states.

My chest tightens. I force a playful laugh. "Why? Do you think Bobby laced it again?"

Bobby freezes and the color drains from his face.

"Aww." I step forward, put my fingers on his chest, and drag them downward. I turn on my innocent Avery stare, asking, "You didn't think I didn't know, did you?"

"I don't know what you're talking about," he denies.

"It's okay, Bobby. I'm glad you drugged me."

"I don't know what you're insinuating, but I assure you you're misinformed," he insists.

Dax snarls, "You know exactly what she's insinuating, and she isn't misinformed. We all know it, so stop lying."

I take a sip of the drink.

"Don't drink that!" Dax frets.

"Shut up, Dax," Bobby orders.

My heart beats faster.

Did he lace my drink again?

So what? It's already in me and destroying my life.

What's the worst it can do?

If anything, it'll make me go through with this plan, giving me the courage to do what's repulsing me.

I go to take another sip.

Dax grabs the glass out of my hand. Alcohol splashes on

the floor. He declares, "You're not drinking anything he or Avery gives you. "

Avery objects, "Why am I included in this?"

"Like you don't know," Dax hurls.

Anger fills me. "You don't get to tell me what to do, Dax."

"Yeah, Dax. You don't get to tell her what to do," Bobby echoes.

I laugh.

Bobby arches his eyebrows. "What's so funny?"

"Are you a parrot, Bobby?"

"Huh?" he questions, wrinkling his forehead.

I put my hand on his cheek. "Aww, you were never very smart, were you?"

His gaze narrows.

"Nope! That's no-brains Bobby!" Avery chirps.

"A parrot!" Lilly cracks up.

Bobby scowls at her. "What the fuck are you all talking about?"

I try to stop laughing and state, "Parrots repeat things. Is that what you are? A parrot?"

He stares at me.

I stop smiling, asserting, "No one gets to talk for me, so stop repeating what I say."

"Bravo!" Lilly cheers, clapping.

Avery follows suit.

"Shut up," Bobby seethes.

I wiggle my finger in front of his face. "Uh-uh-uh. That's not how this is going to work tonight."

He scrubs his face, spouting, "What are you talking about, Ivy?"

"Have some manners," I reprimand.

"Yeah, Bobby. Have some manners," Avery ridicules, sliding her hand on my ass.

"Get your hand off of her," Dax warns.

I turn my head toward him, giving him a sultry Avery expression.

The fire burns hotter in his eyes, a mix of anger and lust.

My pussy clenches. After all these years, Dax still does it for me.

I hate him more for it.

I order, "You, go sit on the couch and stop ordering people around. It's not very nice."

Lilly giggles louder and pats the sofa, seductively suggesting, "Come sit down next to me, Dax."

He doesn't move. "Ivy—"

"Go," I say more forcefully.

There's a war raging inside him. I see it in his eyes.

I arch my eyebrows in a challenge.

He sighs, shakes his head, then moves to the couch. He sits one seat over from Lilly.

"Move closer to Lilly," I demand.

He shakes his head, grinding his molars, but finally moves.

My gut flips as I say, "Good boy. Now, Lilly, kiss Dax."

"I don't want to kiss Lilly," he objects.

"Aww, you don't like me?" Lilly whines, pouting and batting her lashes at him.

Stay the course.

I saunter over to them like Avery would, straddle his left thigh, and unbutton his shirt.

He clenches his jaw. His voice turns dark. "What are you doing, Ivy?"

In a hurt voice, I ask, "You don't like me touching you?"

He stays quiet, taking deep breaths.

"Help me out, Lilly," I order.

Lilly doesn't hesitate. She straddles his other leg, then

grabs Dax's chin. She tries to kiss him on the lips, but he snaps his head toward me, pinning his gaze to mine.

It doesn't derail her. She slides her hand in my hair, tugs on it, and presses her lips to mine. Her tongue flicks into my mouth, and flashbacks of the night at the sorority house hit me.

Avery whines, "No fair. I wanted to kiss Ivy first."

"Get your mouth off her," Dax orders.

Lilly kisses me harder, and I relax, returning her affection, half of me wanting it to kill my craving for sex and the other half doing it to hurt Dax.

"Ivy!" he bellows.

I slide my hand over Dax's cock, stroking it, still kissing Lilly, then I retreat.

She's breathless, with the same greedy look in her eyes from years ago.

I ask her, "Have you thought of me and that night?"

She grins, reaching for Dax's balls, squeezing them while I stroke his cock, lowering her voice and answering, "All the time. You have one of the best pussies I've ever eaten."

My heart races faster.

Dax's erection hardens even more.

Lilly's perfume, the same one Avery used to wear, intoxicates me further.

I softly laugh and motion with my eyes toward Dax.

Lilly smirks, and we move our faces toward his. She dips to the curve of his neck.

He tugs my head, and the intensity of Lilly's kiss disappears. It's Dax and me, two kids in college, adrenaline racing and hearts beating wildly, even though Lilly's hot body is right next to mine.

He tugs me closer to him, and I retreat from our kiss, slightly breathless, asking, "Are you feeling better now?"

His lips twitch.

I move my hand above his belt buckle, asking, "Dax, does Avery like Bobby?"

The devil appears in his expression, mixing with caution. He studies me.

"Does she?" I goad.

He admits, "Depends on what they're trying to accomplish. Isn't that right?"

Lilly laughs and tries to kiss Dax on the lips again, but he moves his chin.

"Aww, you're not being very fun, Dax," she whines.

"Don't worry, Lilly. We'll still have our fun tonight," I declare and wink.

Dax's disapproval is clear.

"Strip, Lilly. Avery, you too, but keep your bras and panties on," I command.

"Ivy—"

I cover Dax's mouth with my finger. I'm in charge tonight, not him.

Their dresses fall to the floor. Avery saunters over and strokes my hair. "What's next, my sexy slut?"

Dax roars, "Get away from her."

"Shush!" I scold.

"Don't touch her!" Dax warns.

"Learn to share, Dax. Ivy isn't yours to keep to yourself. She wasn't ten years ago and she isn't now," Avery hurls.

I wasn't ever his.

My heart hurts, but I force myself to stay in the game. I ask, "Avery, have you ever fucked Bobby?"

She wrinkles her nose and rolls her eyes. "Yep."

"You don't like it though?" I question.

"It's Bobby," she claims.

"Jesus. What the fuck are both of your problems?" he

accuses. Then he turns to Lilly, asking, "I'm a good lay, aren't I? Tell them."

Lilly smiles at him and shrugs. "I don't know, Bobby. It's been a while."

"Please. Like you don't remember."

"Do I?" she questions, putting her finger on her cheek and tilting her head.

Avery erupts in giggles.

I continue, "So you'd rather have sex with Lilly?"

Avery looks at Lilly and then back at me. "She's a fantastic fuck. But you know you're the one I want, Ivy."

Ten years ago, I always fought Avery's attempts to seduce me. She tried anything she could to coax me into sleeping with her. The perfume she wore intoxicated me. I always assumed I was tempted because of her confidence and personality, but now I know she just knew how to play me.

Tonight, she smells like Seducing Ivy perfume. The only thing intoxicating about her is from all the alcohol she's consumed.

Avery Carrington is no longer attractive.

I let that thought sit for a moment, shocked that the impossible has happened.

Maybe I know too much, but she no longer has a spell over me. And I wonder how that's possible when I'm a sex addict due to Trance.

They drugged me.

It's okay. I survived.

It's not.

I'll live. It was a long time ago.

I wouldn't be like this if it weren't for them.

Keep it together. Now's not the time to get emotional.

Time to make her pay.

I go on a hunch, remembering some of the comments she made in the past. So I ask, "Do you like anal sex, Avery?"

She shrugs.

"No?"

"It's okay. I guess I'm more into..." Her eyes dart down my body. She breathlessly confesses, "Pussy."

The throbbing I used to feel when she'd look at me like that returns, and I realize I'm not immune to her and her charm.

"Fuck off, Avery," Dax snarls.

"I love anal sex," Lilly volunteers.

I refocus on Bobby, ordering, "Put Trance in Avery's drink so she can enjoy herself tonight."

He jerks his head backward.

Avery's eyes widen.

The room goes silent.

Dax arches his eyebrows.

I ask, "Bobby, is there a problem?"

He feigns confusion. "What are you talking about, Ivy?"

I scoff. "Let's stop playing games, Bobby. Give it to Avery, and she'll enjoy it when you take her up the ass."

"I'm not taking that drug," Avery states.

I put my fingers over her cheeks. "No? You won't do it for me, even if you get..." I pause, dragging my eyes down her body and then meet her eye, looking at her like she used to look at me, continuing, "Even if you get everything you want tonight?"

She says nothing, her chest rising and falling faster.

I step closer, murmuring in her ear, "Isn't that what you want, Avery? Something you've never had? *Me?*"

She swallows hard.

Hurt fills Dax's voice. He seethes, "She's already had you."

I snap my gaze at him, protesting, "No, she hasn't!"

Avery smirks at him.

"She hasn't," I repeat.

Dax bellows, "What's the truth, Avery? It's time to stop playing games. Ivy says you didn't sleep with her that day. Fess up."

"I didn't," I insist, maintaining my innocence, glaring at her.

Avery opens her mouth.

"Don't lie," I warn.

She shuts her mouth.

Dax snarls, "Tell the truth, Avery."

She blows out a breath of air. "Fine. We've never slept together."

"You bitch!" Dax shouts, pain mixing with relief and anger so fiercely in his expression it makes me almost run over to him and tug him into my arms.

Almost.

Stay in control.

I step closer, run my fingers down her arm, and question, "But I know you want to fuck me. Don't you?"

Goose bumps break out on her skin.

"If you want me, you have to admit it," I declare.

She nods. "Yeah, Ivy. You know I've always wanted to sleep with you."

"Well, now's your chance, but only if you take Trance and let Bobby fuck you in the ass."

"You really didn't sleep together?" Dax mutters, still not quite believing me.

I refocus my glare on him. "No. I told you we didn't. But that doesn't mean we won't tonight."

His face falls. He turns pale and begs, "Ivy, don't. It's not what you want."

I laugh. "How do you know what I want? I'm a dirty slut, remember?" I turn and demand, "Bobby, make Avery a drink. She's going to lick my pussy while you pound her in the ass."

Bobby's lips tip up in a sinister smile. "Are you serious right now?"

"What about me? Was I drugged?" Lilly pipes in.

Bobby snaps out of his brief, happy daze, returning to denial, claiming, "I don't know what any of you are talking about."

"Yeah, you do. Go on. Make Avery a drink."

Lilly repeats, "Bobby, was I drugged?"

Bobby scoffs, blurting out, "Like you would need to be drugged. You do whatever anybody suggests."

Lilly's eyes widen, then she giggles again, and shrugs. "So I like sex with beautiful people. Sue me."

I pet Avery's head, lick my lips, and ask, "What'll it be? Do you want to enjoy Bobby fucking you in the ass while you lick my pussy, or not? There's only one chance."

She looks between Bobby and me, then answers, "What the hell. Give it to me, Bobby."

"Enough. This is over," Dax calls out, then grabs my arm and maneuvers me through the room.

"Let go of me, Dax!"

"Get back here," Avery calls out.

Lilly adds, "Yeah, you can't take Ivy away."

Avery runs after us.

Dax spins, pushing me out the door. "You three do whatever the fuck you want. Stay away from Ivy. I'm not going to warn you again."

"Dax," I object.

He slams the door and shoves me down the hall, manhandling me.

I fight, shouting, "Dax, stop."

"No, Ivy. This is enough."

"Goddammit, Dax, stop!"

He doesn't obey, pulling me up the stairs and down another hallway.

"Dax, you don't have the authority to make decisions for me."

He pushes me into a bedroom, then slams the door and pins me against it. His eyes burn with anger, his shallow breaths quicken, and he cages his body against mine.

Fear assaults me.

This is the Dax I know. The Dax with hate in his eyes, the one in control, the one who can make me crumble into pieces, doing whatever it is he wants, and enjoying every minute of it.

He's the Dax I've craved for ten years.

He's the Dax I don't know how to resist.

Dax 12

DON'T GET A CONSCIOUS NOW

Rage fills me.

Ivy's lips quiver. Her voice wavers as she cries out, "Dax, what are you doing?"

I press closer to her. "That's not what you want. You know that's not what you want."

"You don't know shit about what I want!" she spouts, her eyes glistening. She blinks harder.

"You don't want them. This isn't you," I claim.

Anger erupts, and she fumes, "You don't know who I am."

I shake my head. "I do know who you are."

"You don't! You made me into everything I am, and you have no clue who that is anymore."

I stare at her for a minute.

She glares harder. "You don't get to judge me. Now, let me go, Dax."

I press my lips against hers, sliding my hand into her hair and kissing her.

She fights me, trying to pull away.

I press closer.

Within seconds, she kisses me back, and I quietly lock the door next to her hip, not willing to risk anyone interrupting us.

Lust boils my blood, rushing through my veins. It's a high I've not felt in years until tonight. Everything I've craved and remembered is still there. Only everything between us is more potent now. And there's more on the line than ever before.

Back then, I didn't need to worry about losing Ivy. It was my game. I was in control. I told myself she was merely a pawn I could let go at any time.

I've never been so wrong in my life.

So everything that happens now counts. I'm fully aware of what the prize is this time.

It's her.

Forever.

But the tables have turned, and she holds the wild cards.

All of them.

Unlike the past, my moves are uncalculated, and I have no room for error. If I've learned anything over the last ten years, it's that it only takes one fucked-up moment to destroy every-thing—to create a situation that'll haunt you for the rest of your life, over and over, until you're broken into pieces you can never mend.

She thrashes her tongue around mine. Her hands grip my hair.

We kiss for a while, and I pin her wrists above her head against the wall, lowering my mouth to the curve of her neck, muttering, "This is what you want—what you need."

She whimpers.

"Tell me you want me and only me. I want to hear it," I order.

"I need it," she mutters.

She needs it?

What is it?

My heart stutters.

I put my face in front of hers, keeping her wrists pinned to the door. "No. Tell me you want me. Not just sex. *Me.*"

Her expression changes. I hate it. There's hatred meant only for me, something so deep and profound I feel it in my soul. It mixes with lust, flaunting her cravings, tugging at my heart.

Is it the drugs, or does she hurt as badly as I do and wants to get back what we had?

"I need it," she says again.

I squeeze my eyes shut.

"Don't get a conscience now, Dax."

I open my eyes. "Don't you get it?"

She nods. "Yeah. I'm your dirty whore. Your sexy little slut with a pulsing, wet cunt, standing in front of you, needing your warm cock inside me. Is there anything you think I don't understand?" She glares at me.

My dick hardens. I loathe myself for it, but it does. This defiant Ivy is so different from the naive, innocent girl she used to be. The new Ivy heats my blood just as hot though.

She threatens, "Either fuck me, or I'm going back downstairs."

"No, you're not."

She scoffs. "So I'm your prisoner? Is that what you're going to do? Keep me locked in here? Will I be your sex slave to use whenever you want?"

I clench my jaw.

"Let me go. You lost your right to boss me around," she hurls.

I don't move.

"I said let me go," she orders more forcefully.

I release her wrists.

She pushes against my chest.

I don't budge, sliding my hands over her cheeks and kissing her again, unable to stop myself or let her walk away.

She's definitely not going back into the office with the others.

I'll kill all of them if they touch her ever again.

Her whore-red lips that tortured me for ten years, consuming all my thoughts, press against mine. Her tongue urgently flicks with a need deeper than anything I've felt from her before.

It's the drugs.

No, it's her.

It's us and our chemistry.

But is it?

The debate rages in my mind, but she kisses me until they fade away, and all I can do is fall prey to her.

Ivy tugs my hair, pushing her stomach into my erection. She reaches for my belt, unbuckles it, and unzips my pants.

A loud clank fills the air. Her warm hands palm my ass, and everything feels like we're right back where we left off.

"Did you miss your dirty slut?" she mumbles against my lips.

My cock throbs, but it pulls me out of my musings.

This isn't back then. It's now. I'm older and wiser, no longer caring about what anyone thinks or a sordid game with no point other than toxic destruction. I retreat from her mouth. "Ivy—"

"Shut up and fuck me, Dax. Fuck your whore in every hole possible," she says, her eyes wild.

"Stop saying that," I order, but the devil in me feels more alive.

My erection throbs against her stomach, and she notices. She glances down, her lips twisting, asserting, "Yeah. That's what you like, Dax. You like little sluts. Now, call me your little slut."

I stay quiet, fighting my demons, wanting to give in, hating myself for it.

Ivy was never a slut or a whore. But every time she called herself my slut or whore, I loved it. It fed my ego. It gave me points on the imaginary game board. But it's wrong. She was pure and good.

I should have treasured every ounce of her.

Her eyes narrow. She hisses, "Say it."

"No, gorgeous. I'm not saying it."

"Say it," she bellows.

I stare at her. My blood boiling, erection pulsing, breath ragged.

She pushes against my chest. "Then get off me. I'm going downstairs to the people who understand what I need."

She spins to open the door. I push her against it. Once again, I cage my body against hers.

"Oh fuck," she breathes, the excitement in her voice, that I've missed hearing so much, creating a burst of adrenaline in all my cells.

I tug her hair back so her face is toward the ceiling.

She looks at me from the corner of her eye, breathing hard.

I put my lips near her ear, unable to stop myself. "Is this what you want, my little whore? You want that slutty, wet pussy of yours filled with my cum?"

"Yes," she breathes.

"You want me to fuck you so hard you can't walk for a week?"

Her voice shakes. "Y-yes."

I push past the thin whore-red thong, slide my finger inside her, and she shudders, moaning. "Your greedy little cunt's missed me, hasn't it?"

"Yes," she breathes.

"You want to be my naughty slut, don't you?"

"Yes."

What am I doing?

She loves it.

I made her this way.

"I'll be the best dirty whore you've ever had, Dax. Now, fuck me everywhere," she demands.

Endorphins hit me hard, crashing through my cells, making me feel so alive I get dizzy. I battle my role from years ago, wanting everything we had but to still do better. I blurt out, "No. You're not a slut or whore, baby girl."

"No. Don't play with me. I-I need it."

"What do you think I need, Ivy?"

"The same thing my body has to have," she claims.

I palm her ass with my other hand.

She closes her eyes.

I pull my finger out of her and trace around the thin material. "You still look good in this color, gorgeous."

She breathes as if in relief.

I slide my finger between her legs, grazing the wet lace, letting my demons win again. "Ah, good little slut. So fucking wet for me, aren't you?"

"Yes. Always."

"You've been wanting it all night, haven't you? You and this greedy little cunt of yours."

"Yes, Dax. I... Fuck me in my pussy, then my ass. Fuck your dirty little whore every way."

"No," I say, my pulse skyrocketing.

"Please," she begs.

I spin her and move her quickly over to the bed. "Get on your knees. Show me what your beautiful slutty lips are dying for," I order, pushing her down.

She doesn't resist, and I don't have to tell her what to do. Her tongue flicks my cock just like I taught her, until it's soaking wet, and then she's sucking it.

I grip her hair in my hand, pushing her toward me, controlling the speed, barely able to contain myself. I grit out, "Fuck, you little whore. Your mouth's gotten better, not worse, over the years."

She digs her nails into my hips just like she used to.

I glance down at the whore-red lipstick smearing around her mouth and my cock, the stain deepening every time I move in and out of her.

Her eyes water. Tears roll down her flushed cheeks.

I move her faster and faster over me until I'm about to come. Then I push her off.

She wipes her mouth, breathing hard. The whore-red lipstick smears on the back of her hand. Blue fire glows hotter in her eyes.

It's a look that's haunted my dreams.

It's one I never thought I'd see again.

I can't wait any longer. I move toward her and pull her up. I press my mouth against hers, unclasp her bra, and push it off. It hangs between us. I move my hands to her hips, sliding her panties down so they fall on the floor. I spin her to face the bed.

Ivy's hands fly to the mattress. Her bra falls with the movement. I kiss her back, trailing down her spine as she quivers. I pause at her ass cheeks, inhaling deeply before pulling back and smacking it.

"Fuck, Dax!" she yells.

I hold her with my forearm and then smack it several more times. "You fucking dirty whore, disobeying me down there. What the fuck were you thinking, Ivy?" I accuse, continuing to smack her ass.

She screams, "Yes! Oh God, yes!"

I rub the sting out and press my lips back to her spine, moving them up until my lips are near her ear. I murmur, "You're mine, Ivy. You've always been mine. You don't get anyone else but me. Do you understand that?"

She stays quiet.

"Be a good little slut, and tell me this greedy pussy's mine and only mine," I demand.

"If it's yours, you better take it," she threatens.

A tidal wave of testosterone courses through me, burning right to my soul. I toss her onto the bed, pinning her body against the mattress.

She sharply inhales.

I raise her leg, entering her in one thrust.

"Oh fuck, Dax. Oh God!" she screams as I thrust fast, not showing any mercy or giving her body any time to get used to mine.

"Harder. My slutty cunt needs it harder," she cries out.

I groan. It's all too much. Her scent, her body against mine, and her voice desperately declaring all the things I've been dying to hear after all these years.

She whimpers, trembling.

I slow down and dip my head to her breasts, muttering, "Fucking C cups," then sucking on her puckered nipple.

She arches her back, slides her hand in my hair, and presses me closer to her.

I suck hard and don't let up, wanting to mark her like I used to.

She thrusts her hips faster, trying to get me to increase my pace.

I release her breasts, brushing my lips against hers, taunting, "Fucking greedy cunt."

"Yes. Yours," she barely gets out before her eyes roll and her orgasm hits. Her body violently shakes.

I continue thrusting, knowing how I used to keep her high for a long time, not willing to let myself come and end the moment. I grunt. "Is this what you want?"

"Yes! I'm your dirty whore!"

"Is this what you need?"

"Y-yes!"

"Say you need me," I demand.

"I need you, Dax," she cries, another violent orgasm hitting her as she trembles beneath me.

"Whose little slut are you?" I demand.

"Yours. I'm your slut, Dax!"

I'm about to come, so I pull out of her, sliding down her body, pressing her legs wider. I flick my tongue on her clit.

She moans.

"You taste the same, baby girl," I mutter, eating her out with a new wave of intensity.

"Dax!"

I shove a finger into her, and she spasms around it. I mumble against her pussy, "Greedy fucking cunt," and suck it harder.

Sweat explodes on her skin. She continues quivering, and I'm in heaven and hell. It's everything I've missed. Yet I promised myself I would never say those things to her again, but I can't help myself.

I flip her over, slide my arm under her waist, and tug her ass in the air, ordering, "Tell me what my whore wants."

"Fuck my greedy ass, Dax!"

I thrust into her once again in one movement.

"Oh God!" she screams.

"Is this what you want, my sexy slut?"

"Oh! Oh!"

"Tell me it's what you want!"

"Yes. Harder," she cries out.

I groan. It's all too much. I move in and out of her with a force of adrenaline hitting me harder than I've felt in years. Euphoria sets in, overwhelming with dizziness and emotions. I cry out, "I fucking love you."

She doesn't say anything.

"I fucking love you," I say again, on the verge of coming.

She doesn't reply.

"Say it back! Be a good whore and say it back," I demand.

"Your whore loves you fucking her," she pants.

"That's not what I said to say," I bark, my cock thickening.

"My greedy ass loves your cock in it," she says, and then her body erupts into another orgasm, clenching my erection.

It's too much. I can't handle it. I come with her. It's violent and explosive, giving me the high that's haunted me for ten years.

I momentarily black out from the power of it, collapsing over her, breathing hard, our sweat mingling.

She continues shaking underneath me, her eyes closed, whore-red lipstick smeared everywhere.

The gorgeous vision of what's underneath me gives me comfort and induces fear.

I can't lose her again.

I slowly pull out of her and flop onto my back, tugging her into me.

Both of us continue breathing hard.

When I finally get enough oxygen in my lungs, I kiss her

forehead and push her hair behind her ear. I confess, "I fucking missed you so much."

She doesn't say anything.

"I mean it, Ivy. You don't understand how much I've missed you."

She maintains her silence. Several moments pass, and I hold her tight.

She moves her head off my chest and pushes against me.

I release my grip on her and palm her ass, asking, "What's wrong, baby girl?"

Her expression sends a chill down my spine. She announces, "I'm going back downstairs now."

Panic hits me. I question, "For what?"

"I told you, Dax. I'm not the same woman you knew. I'm no longer naive and gullible. Everything I am is because of you. And I need more. I'll never stop needing more."

My insides quiver. "You don't need them. You need *me*."

She blinks hard. "Is that what you think?"

"It's what I know," I insist.

She laughs, then a tear falls, and she swipes at it. She turns toward the wall.

I turn her chin back so she can't avoid me. "Ivy, we're going to get through this. I'm going to right my wrongs against you."

She tosses her head back and sarcastically laughs. Then she sniffles and narrows her eyes, pinning them on me, asking, "Do you think a couple of orgasms from you will erase all you did to me? Or that one person to fuck will ever be enough for me?"

My chest tightens, and the air in my lungs turns stale. Bile rises in my throat.

She gives me a look that reminds me of Avery, stating, "I can assure you that anything you're romanticizing in your head right now is a fantasy."

"Ivy—"

"You disappoint me, Dax. You're the one who made me into a filthy whore. Yet, you seem to have forgotten what your role is, as well as the others'."

"Ivy—"

"It's time you remember what dirty sluts are for, Dax Carrington."

Ivy 13

THEY ALL HAVE TO PAY

Everything I felt years ago with Dax comes flooding back, and the high I've been unable to attain since the last time we were together has finally returned.

I can't stay here. It's too intense. The feeling I sought for over a decade is all I yearned for, urging me to do things that don't make me proud.

Yet here I finally am, getting exactly what I wanted.

But I no longer want it.

It's too much.

He's too much.

The rug's been pulled out from under me, and I'm falling back under Dax's control. The more he gives me—the more we sync like we used to—the more I want from him.

It's way too dangerous of a position.

"You're not a filthy whore," he claims.

He's trying to confuse me so he can destroy me again.

Dax's the pawn this time. Not me, I remind myself.

I push the shame away, insisting, "I am, and I have needs."

"Then I'll give you whatever you need," he says, with a confidence that I've missed.

There's no doubt he can fulfill every warped desire I have. But if I stay...

I close my eyes, grappling with my longing to be with him and the sordid impulses allowing me to even fathom what needs to be done.

I can't fuck Bobby or Avery. Hell, even Lilly.

I have to.

My mouth goes dry. I try to convince myself once again that it's the only way.

They all have to pay.

He pins his body over mine, kissing me, making every ache I have for him come back to life.

Our hunger only grows, creating a thirst deep in my soul until I can't resist him anymore.

My resilience dies, decimated by his tongue, erased by one touch.

I'm a slave to Dax Carrington, a servant to his body, too wrapped up in the demons of the past that laugh at the wreckage I've become.

I have to stop doing this.

I can't. I need him.

Stay in control.

So I lie to him. "You can't give me what I need, Dax."

He narrows his eyes, tugging my hair so I'm facing the ceiling.

My breath catches.

He studies me, muttering against my lips, "My fucking whore. Fucking good, sexy, wet little slut."

Endorphins drown every inch of my body.

What am I doing?

How did I get here?

It's his fault my father's dead.

He stole from him.

He drugged me.

No, he didn't. Bobby did.

Dax could be lying.

I know in my heart he didn't.

I freeze.

Dax does as well, worry growing in his expression. "Baby girl, what's wrong?"

Grief fills me. I blink hard, trying to stop the onslaught of pain, willing myself not to cry.

It's a losing battle. Tears spill down my cheeks.

He rolls off me, tugs me into his arms, and holds my head against his chest.

I release an uncontrollable sob.

"Shhh. Baby girl, what's going on?" he gently asks, stroking my head and holding me tight.

I can't fight him. I know I should push him away, but I'm too weak.

Too many things hit me all at once. I wish it was grief only for my father. Instead, the years Dax and I lost, the ever-present agony, and my shattered heart that's impossible to mend, drill deeper into my wounds.

There's too much broken trust, too many dreams that will never come to fruition. And it ruins me over and over.

I wail harder, unable to stop.

"Shh, it's okay, baby girl. Everything's okay," Dax says, tightening his hold and attempting to reassure me.

"It's never going to be okay," I say on a sob.

"It is. I promise you it is," he declares.

I shake my head, insisting, "No, it's not."

The shame I've felt over the years regarding what happened and my addiction, along with the desperate urges that never stop, take their sharp edges, slicing me until I'm raw.

Dax continues to console me, but it only makes it worse.

I don't know how long I cry on his chest. When I finally retreat, my tears are everywhere, mixing with the whore-red lipstick on his body and sheets.

I force myself to pull it together, getting to a point where I'm only sniffling.

He kisses my forehead. "I promise you I'm going to make everything right."

He promises.

Dax made one vow after another to me ten years ago. I know what happens when he makes a promise—the exact opposite.

Anger replaces everything else I'm feeling. I push away from him. "How are you going to make anything right? Are you going to bring back my father?"

IIis eyes widen in shock. "Bring him back? What do you mean?"

My lips tremble. "You killed him."

His head jerks backward, pressing into the pillow. "Ivy, why would you ever believe that? I didn't kill your father."

"You did. You and your sister killed him," I insist, my voice growing firmer.

"Ivy, I'm lost. Fill me in on why you're claiming something so horrible," he says, sitting up and pulling me with him.

I shake my head in disgust, hating myself and once again blaming myself for my father's death. But Dax and Avery aren't getting off the hook either.

No one is. Everyone in this house is responsible. They all played a role in my father's demise.

"You killed him," I seethe.

"I didn't even know your father was dead."

I scoff. "You didn't know he was dead? How is that? You seem to know everything else. You knew I was in Georgia."

"I didn't know until Avery told me a couple months ago."

"Yeah, well, you still got to my father, and he's dead now," I reiterate.

"I'm so sorry. When did this happen?" he asks and tries to tighten his hold on me.

Blood boils in my veins, and a trembling rage overpowers me. I shove him away. "You're sorry? Are you sorry enough to bring him back from the dead? Can you go back in time and redo the day you were on TV, bragging about the patent you stole from him in front of his face? Are you going to reverse the heart attack you caused him to have? What are you going to do, Dax?"

Dax shakes his head, "I-I..."

"There's nothing you can do. My father's death is on you."

"Ivy, I didn't—"

"You didn't what, Dax? How are you innocent?" I shout.

He puts his hands in the air. "I know I've done a lot—"

"You've done a lot? Should we talk about all the things that you've done?" I huff.

He closes his eyes, and his face falls.

My pulse pounds harder between my ears.

Tense silence fills the air.

Dax opens his eyes and looks genuinely remorseful, but I remind myself it's a farce. There is no trusting Dax Carrington. I won't be a fool twice.

He softly says, "Ivy, I'm so sorry about your dad."

"No, you're not. You hated him."

He clenches his jaw.

"You did everything you could to destroy my relationship with him and make him ashamed of me."

"That part isn't true," Dax claims.

I sarcastically laugh. "What part isn't true?"

"I didn't want him to be ashamed of you."

"But you wanted to drive a wedge between us?"

He sighs, admitting, "Yeah, I did, because I wanted you."

"And that's the only reason?" I ask, crossing my arms.

He opens his mouth and shuts it.

"Don't you fucking lie to me, Dax Carrington! For once, stop lying to me!"

He grinds his molars, glancing at the ceiling, then pins his gaze back on mine. It tugs at my heartstrings, but I won't be his village idiot anymore. He doesn't get my sympathy.

He confesses, "Fine. I'll admit it. Causing a rift between you and your dad was part of the game, and I know that was wrong of me."

"And why was I in this game, Dax?" I demand, my voice shaking, hoping to get some insight into the one question I've always wanted the answer to.

He slowly shrugs his shoulders. "I don't know."

"You don't know?" I hurl, the rage building within me.

He hesitates. "Ivy, what I did was fucked-up. I know it was fucked-up, but if you'll just—"

"If I'll just what, Dax? Pretend like nothing ever happened? Like you didn't destroy my entire life and my father's? That you didn't steal from him and then cause his heart attack?"

"Ivy, I didn't cause his heart attack."

"You did."

"How many heart attacks has your dad had over the years?"

I stay quiet, my insides quivering.

Dax orders, "Answer me."

But I don't. I'm not going to admit to him my dad had six heart attacks before his final one.

Dax sighs. "Ivy, your dad had heart issues."

"How do you know?"

"You told me."

"I told you he had one heart attack, that's it."

He tilts his head. "Ivy, your dad had heart issues ten years ago. I'm sorry he's dead. Truly, I am."

"Just say you're sorry you killed him," I demand.

Dax looks at me, insisting, "I didn't kill him, Ivy. He had a heart attack."

"Do you ever take responsibility for what you've done?"

"Ivy..." He tries to pull me toward him.

I push him away. "Don't touch me." I get off of the bed and grab my bra and underwear.

"Ivy," he says, following me.

I reach the door and try to open it, but it's locked.

He puts his hand on the door, turns me to face him, and presses closer. "Ivy, I fucked up on a lot of levels."

I sarcastically laugh. "You think?"

"I know I did. But I'm not here to hurt you. All I want is you."

Once again, I can only laugh, and I shake my head with more tears falling down my cheeks. "You'll never have me again, Dax. Now, let me out."

His face falls. "You don't mean that."

"I do. Let me out."

"Ivy, you know it's still there between us. It's always been there between us. It's always going to be there between us. Let's get past this and figure it out," he urges.

"There is no figuring it out. Now, move," I demand.

He hesitates.

"Now," I warn.

He takes a step back.

I unlock the door and fling it open.

He follows me. "Ivy."

I walk faster down the hall, trying to remember which way the staircase is until it comes into sight.

"Ivy," he repeats, but I'm not giving him any more of my time.

I shouldn't have slept with him. Then again, now he'll understand what it feels like to have someone you want, someone you love—even if he's lying again about his feelings toward me—walk out on you.

"Ivy!" he shouts.

I tromp down the stairs and turn at the bottom. "Which way is the office?"

He shuts his mouth, giving me a challenging stare.

"Now, Dax. Which way? Or I'm walking out of here naked."

He points. "That way."

I race down the hall, enter the office, and step inside. I freeze.

Lilly and Avery are playing tongue tag out on the couch.

Bobby's watching them as if they're his prey, drinking his scotch.

Bile climbs up my esophagus.

Everything about Bobby makes me nauseous. Flashbacks of him taking me from behind only worsen my reaction.

He sees me and rises. His gaze darts across my body, his lips curving. "Well, look who's back for some fun."

"Fuck off, Bobby," I fume, still pissed at Dax and forgetting I'm supposed to be playing the game. I glance around the room and find my dress. I go over to it, reach down, pick it up off the floor, and step into it. I don't bother to put on my bra and underwear. I grab my clutch off the table.

"What's the attitude for?" Bobby asks, coming closer until he's blocking my ability to move.

I reach back and slap him as hard as possible.

His face turns toward the wall. He slowly looks back at me, his eyes full of rage.

My insides tremble.

"Looks like I'm missing the fun," Professor Dyer interjects.

I don't tear my eyes off Bobby.

Dax steps between us, putting one hand on my hip and his other on Bobby's chest, pushing him away, warning, "Stay away from her."

"She just fucking hit me," Bobby whines.

"You're lucky she didn't do more than that. Stay the fuck away from her," Dax repeats.

Avery and Lilly gape at me from the couch.

"What the fuck's your problem?" Bobby snarls, his eyes pinned on me, his fists clenching at his sides.

Suddenly, it's all too much. My world feels like it's collapsing again, and I have to get out of here.

Panicked, I glance around the room, run to the side table, and grab Dax's keys. I skedaddle out of the house with Dax on my heels.

He calls out, "Ivy, wait!"

I get into his car, shutting and locking the doors.

He pounds on the window. "Ivy!"

I start the car, rev the engine, and peel out of the driveway.

"Ivy," he yells, running after me.

I drive as fast as I can, but I don't go to the gate for some reason.

I park in front of Dax's old cottage.

I walk up to it and reach for the door. It's unlocked. I go inside and shut the door, then turn on the light.

Nothing has changed.

It's as if Dax left everything in it and moved out. I bypass the family room and go into the bedroom. I open the closet and freeze.

My heart bleeds at the sight. Dax's clothes hang next to mine. All the outfits he bought me the day I lost my virginity in the dressing room—the ones I was so proud to wear—fill the space.

It was the first time he made me call myself his little slut and whore so others could hear. Flashbacks of those images across Professor Dyer's big classroom screen create more tears. I grab one of Dax's shirts and smell it, crying harder when his scent flares in my nostrils.

I shut the closet door and go into the bathroom. I open the medicine cabinet and stare at the whore-red nail polish and lipstick Dax always had on hand for me to wear.

I shut the cabinet, then stare at the necklace Dax bought for me to continue to wear.

Did he really design it and not Avery?

It doesn't matter.

I take my dress off but leave the necklace on, unable to remove it even though I should. I trace the ivy leaves over the I, remembering how much I loved this necklace.

I haven't worn it in years. I only took it out of hiding to auction off tonight.

I step into the shower, picking up the half-empty bottle of liquid soap I used ten years ago, sobbing when the lavender scent swirls around me.

It's like being in a time warp. I wash myself, trying to scrub everyone off me, including Dax.

As if I ever could.

I realize he'll always be part of me, which only makes me sob harder.

I stay in the shower for a long time. When I finally get out, I dry off and go to bed. I slide under the covers and inhale deeply, still breathing Dax's scent. I hug the pillow, feeling more broken than ever, wondering how I'll be strong enough to get through this.

I have to get vengeance for my father. For myself. For Matt and all the other people they've ever hurt.

And one thing I loathe to admit is way too clear.

No matter how much I don't want to be, I'm still in love with Dax Carrington.

Day 14

BE PATIENT

"Don't let my car past the gates. Call me when she arrives," I order security over the phone, then hang up and run to the garage.

My phone rings when I open the door. "Chad. Is she there?"

"No. Your car's at your old cottage," he informs me.

She doesn't want to leave.

Not yet.

My heart beats faster. "Did she get out of the car?"

"Yeah. She got out and went inside."

"Thanks." I hang up the phone, debating what to do, and then get into a golf cart.

The full moon illuminates the lawn, but I know the yard like the back of my hand. It could be pitch-black and I'd still get wherever I needed to go. So I cross the estate and park in front of my old cottage.

A wave of nostalgia hits me. I stare at the lighted window, the hairs on my arms rising.

The cottage represents the only thing I yearned for as a child.

Freedom.

For as long as I could remember, I wanted to sever the connection to my family—except when my grandfather died and his trust stipulations became known.

After that, it was merely a waiting game; I was biding my time until I could implement all the changes I carefully crafted to put everyone in my family in their place.

Ultimately, that meant disappearing from my life forever.

I've achieved my goal for my parents. The only people left are Avery and Cooper. And although Avery's got it coming to her, Cooper is just a lazy waste of space. In a lot of ways, he reminds me of Bobby. And it doesn't surprise me.

Once I distanced myself from Bobby, he made it his mission to take my brother under his wing. I warned Cooper to stay away from Bobby, but he wouldn't listen. So he's made his own bed. Eventually, I'll also figure out how to get him off the estate.

As of now, I have no reason to speed up the trajectory of his future. The way he spends money, he'll deplete his entire trust fund before he's thirty. And he can deal with the consequences of his irresponsibility.

He's capable of working like everyone else, but he spends a ton of time with Bobby in the South of France. So he's out of my hair a lot, unlike Avery.

The light goes out, the cottage turns dark, and my stomach twists into knots. If this were ten years ago, I'd be giddy over everything that happened tonight.

Yet I'm not that same bored kid. There's nothing fun or joyous about Ivy's grief or need for revenge.

I need to see her.

Be patient.

I wait an hour and then I quietly go inside. I creep through the main area and enter the bedroom.

I stop in the doorway. The moonlight shines through the window, creating an angelic glow around Ivy, in the same way it used to. Her pouty, faded whore-red lips make my dick just as hard as ever.

I sit in the chair in my old room, watching her sleep, wondering how everything between us could be so fucked-up.

She still loves me. I know she does.

She doesn't. She made it clear.

She does.

She didn't sleep with Avery or Dyer. The only people she slept with were Bobby and Lilly during the foursome when Bobby drugged her.

And I pressured her to take part in that.

That's on me.

How could I have been so misinformed and not even given her a chance to explain?

Why did I believe them and not her?

I beat myself up over and over, staring at my baby girl. The memories of waking up next to her and how alive I felt just being with her pummel me, and I regret ever putting her in the game.

She never belonged in it.

I reach for my phone and pull up my search engine, typing in *John Ford, Georgia.*

Several hits pop up, but then I see a death notice.

My chest tightens, and I click on it.

I didn't know Ivy's father had died. Hank should have found that out, and I wonder how he missed such important information.

I read the obituary. It doesn't say much other than John was a botanist, his daughter was Ivy, and where the funeral services were being held.

I reread it several times and then search his name some more. I'm unsure what I'm looking for, but there isn't anything else about him.

It doesn't surprise me. John Ford was an average person, just like most people.

In my world of getting things done, that was his fault. He had the ability in his hands. All of the things he created were in his notebook, sitting there doing nothing.

For a man like me, who knows how to create things and take opportunities to make the most of them, I can't figure out why anyone wouldn't do the same. John was smart and talented. It's unfathomable to me why he would just sit on things instead of making his life better, especially when he had Ivy to provide for.

The same anger I felt back then reappears. He should have done better for her. Then, my guilt shifts back to me.

I *should have done better for her.*

I vow for the millionth time that I *will* do better for Ivy, and somehow, I'll figure out how to make her forgive me.

She thinks I killed her dad.

The air in my lungs turns stale, thickening with every breath. I stare at her, wondering how I'll ever get her to forgive me if that's what she really believes.

I tap my finger on the armchair, wondering over and over what to do. Then I pick up my phone again, pull up my text messages, scroll down, and click on Hank's name.

> Me: I need the medical records and coroner's report for John Ford.

> Hank: He's dead?

Me: Yeah. I'm not sure how you missed that.

Hank: You didn't tell me to find information about him. You said you wanted everything on her.

Me: Since when are you literal?

Hank: You don't like it when I go off track.

Me: And you didn't think her father was important?

Hank: You weren't specific, Dax. You've always told me to stay with what you want.

Hank's right. I didn't ask him to dig into John. And I usually do have little patience for nonsense extra details. But this isn't one of the times, nor is it unimportant.

Me: I expect more from you. Don't fuck up next time. Now, get me those reports.

Hank: Sure, boss.

That's always Hank's response when I've pissed him off. I can imagine his disgruntled expression, and I hold in my chuckle. I like getting under Hank's skin.

My amusement is short-lived though. He did fuck up. That information should have been reported to me. I make a note to watch him closer in case I need to replace him.

Ivy slides her hands under the pillow, and I hold myself back from going over and slipping into bed with her. It's been an intense night. The last thing I want to do is have her leave the estate or my eyesight.

Instead, I revisit all the events of the night, and my rage flares again, taunting me until I make a decision.

It's time for Dyer to go down. I made it clear to him years ago that Ivy was off-limits. He disobeyed me, and now he's going to pay.

I pull up the Clifton University site and stare at his photo, reading his credentials and the decades he's been with them.

He's only still there because of me. I've made it so he can do whatever he wants without getting fired. Anytime he's been close to it, I've intervened with the dean because I run the school. That's what happens when you're their largest donor. Anything you want comes to fruition. But Dyer's time is up.

I glance at my watch and then back at Ivy. The nighttime sky is turning lighter as the sun tries to break through. I return to my phone and text Kristen, one of our longstanding and best household employees.

> Me: I need you to bring a full breakfast to my cottage as soon as possible. Include everything.

> Kristen: Anything else, sir?

> Me: I want a bouquet of Seducing Ivy flowers.

> Kristen: Okay, but we're running low. You said no one was to touch the remaining ones.

> Me: Just do it. And make it a large arrangement.

> Kristen: Yes, sir.

> Me: Bring my two sets of cottage keys. When you get here, text me. Don't knock.

> Kristen: Yes, sir.

Another hour passes before she texts.

Kristen: I'm here.

I quietly go to the door, open it, and take a tray from her. I set it on the table and return to the front porch twice to grab the other trays.

I shut the front door, keep the lids on the food, and stare at the Seducing Ivy blooms.

I hope Ivy loves them.

I go to the drawer, pull out a pad of paper and a pen, and sit at the table, thinking about what I should say.

She wants honesty. Be completely honest with her.

The ache in my chest intensifies, and I fight the demons that usually stop me from speaking from the heart.

Ivy,

I really did patent Seducing Ivy for you. It'll all soon come to light. I promise you, on my life and yours, it was all for you.

And I love you. Don't ever forget that, and you have to believe me when I say it. You're the only woman I've ever loved. That's never going to change.

Stay here, or in the main house with me—preferably with me—but I understand if you can't right now. Your code to get into the main house is 0820. The staff will bring you prepared meals, groceries, whatever you want, baby girl. I've assigned Kristen to be at your beck and call. Just dial 0 on the landline. She'll also give you her information so you can text her anytime.

My phone number's the same. I assume you remember it.

I love you.

We're going to get through this.

Dax

I stare at the note, tear it off the pad, and push the paper next to the flowers. I open the side table drawer and pull out my spare credit card. I grab a set of cottage keys and the car fob Ivy tossed on the counter. I place them next to the letter.

I sneak back into the bedroom, staring at my gorgeous girl, forcing myself not to touch her.

It's time for them to pay.

I leave the cottage, lock the door behind me, get on my golf cart, and drive to the garage.

I slide into my Hennessey Venom F5 and leave the estate, gripping the steering wheel so tightly my knuckles turn white.

It's time for Dyer to go down. He made his bed when he merely spoke to Ivy, not to mention touching her. His days are over. He's going to regret ever getting between my baby girl and me.

The parking garage and my office building are mostly empty since it's Saturday. I get into the elevator and go up to my office on the top floor. Then I open my safe and pull out the hard drive with Dyer's name on the label. I start to shut my safe, then stop, staring at Avery's and Bobby's names.

No time like the present.

I grab their hard drives as well, then spend hours reviewing footage of the three of them doing unfathomable things to coeds over the last ten to fifteen years.

I black out the coeds' faces, but I leave Avery's, Bobby's, and Dyer's on full display. I make sure that I'm not on any of them. Everything incriminating they've done that I've documented stays in my video.

I upload a copy of my reel to a secure cloud. It's over ninety minutes of shock and horror, filled with illegal activities. It's the largest video I've ever created, and I watch it one last time, ensuring no one is identifiable except Avery, Bobby, and Dyer.

Satisfied, I download a copy to my hard drive and save another copy to my personal secure cloud. I unplug it from my computer and return it to my safe.

I hit play again, then pick up the phone and call my tech guy, Shadow. He's the best of the best when it comes to hacking, and he's on my payroll. He's done so many jobs for me over the years, I can't count.

He answers, "Dax. Got a job for me?"

I chuckle. "You know me well."

"What's it this time?" he questions.

I stare at the footage running across my screen. "I need you to log in to the Clifton University system."

He whistles. "That's pretty secure."

"Aren't they all?" I ask.

He grunts. "It's going to cost you."

"It always does," I reply.

"Fifteen million," he quotes.

"Do it in the next hour, and I'll give you twenty," I state.

I hear the grin in his voice. "It'll be done in an hour."

"Good. It's in our cloud."

"I'm already looking at it."

"Let me know when the job's done." I hang up and pace my

office, wondering how I'll make everything right between Ivy and me.

She has to forgive me.

How can she though?

She sees me as the enemy.

I have to prove otherwise to her.

The only thing I'm certain of, whether she forgives me or not, is that everyone's going down. Somehow, I have to prove to her I didn't kill her dad. And I don't know what it'll take, but everything in my gut tells me it'll be her sticking point.

My phone rings, and I glance at it.

> Unknown: You think you can buy me off?

My pulse quickens. It has to be Ivy.

> Me: I'm not buying you off.

> Unknown: It looks like it. You left your credit card. I guess I am your whore now, huh?

I squeeze my eyes shut and shake my head, regretting too many things.

Why did I call her that last night?

I couldn't help it.

She wanted me to.

But did she?

> Me: You've never been a whore, and deep down, you know that.

> Unknown: That's convenient for you to say now.

> Me: Did you read my letter?

A few moments pass with the dots bouncing on the screen, then they disappear. More time passes, and my pulse rises as I stare at the screen, waiting.

A message finally comes across.

> Unknown: Yeah, I read your letter. Then I threw the flowers in the trash where they belong.

My gut drops.

> Me: Those flowers are your legacy.

> Unknown: The flowers you stole that Carrington Enterprises is profiting from? Sure they are.

> Me: I told you everything will come to light soon. You have to trust me.

> Unknown: There's that trust word again. So convenient how you use that and think that anybody could trust you. Is there anyone in the world you haven't fucked over?

I grind my molars, pondering her question. I hate that I can't claim I didn't fuck her over. So I answer honestly.

> Me: Not many.

> Unknown: Just stay away from me. I don't want anything from you except my father's patent.

> Me: Everything will come to light soon.

> Unknown: You're the same Dax, I see.

> Me: I assure you, I'm not.

Unknown: Sure, you aren't. Give me my father's patent, then leave me alone.

I sigh, staring at the messages, and decide maybe I need to follow part of her orders—at least for a little while. I know I won't last long, but maybe a little time will soften her a bit.

I stare out the window with my arms crossed, focusing on the waves crashing against the shore.

My phone buzzes.

Shadow: It's done.

My heart beats faster. I sit down and go to the Clifton University web page.

A pop-up appears with the long video I created, and giddiness erupts within me. Then I check my email. Sure enough, the same thing is in my inbox. I log in to several of my other accounts, and the same email from Clifton University sits in each box.

I text Shadow.

Me: Students and staff?

Shadow: Of course.

Me: Donors too?

Shadow: Do you think I'm slipping or something?

I grin and then I log in to my untraceable offshore account. I transfer twenty million dollars to Shadow.

My phone vibrates on the desk.

Shadow: It's always good doing business with you. I wiped the metadata as well.

Me: Good man. Stay tuned. I'll have another project for you soon.

Shadow: Looking forward to it.

I sit back in my chair, watching the video again, feeling dizzy with excitement. I've waited years for the day I would unleash my wrath upon them.

My phone rings, and my day only gets better. "William," I boom into the phone.

"You fucking bastard. Take it down, now."

"Take what down?" I innocently ask.

"You know damn well what I'm talking about," Dyer seethes.

"I don't. Do you want to fill me in? If something's wrong, I might be able to help you."

"You fucking bastard. You're ruining my life," he declares.

I chuckle, and it gets louder and louder. I can't contain myself as he screams obscenities at me. I finally gain control of myself and state, "Have a nice life, Dyer. I hope you get to keep your freedom." I hang up, thinking it would be awesome if he, Bobby, and Avery were all locked up in the same cell.

There's no way he's walking away from this. The university will have more lawsuits against it than it knows what to do with. I'll conveniently come in and help clean up the mess just to maintain my power.

But I'll never help Dyer again. He's done. He'll never have another teaching job in this country. His pension and everything he's saved will go down the drain from lawsuits. It's all going to be gone. And based on the incriminating evidence on the video, it won't be long before he's in handcuffs.

My phone beeps with another message.

Bobby: You did it, didn't you?

Bobby: You fucking bastard.

Me: What are you referring to?

Bobby: You know damn well what you did.
Take that fucking down, now.

Another message pops in.

Avery: What the fuck, Dax?

I reply to her.

Me: What did I do now?

My phone continues to blow up with messages from her and Bobby. I read the messages, no longer replying, full of giddiness.

I spin my chair, cross my ankle over my knee, and press the pads of my fingers together, staring at the water, suddenly hopeful.

The end is near. Crimes of the past will haunt people for the rest of their lives. Then Ivy and I will be free. We can move forward.

I'll take down anyone who ever hurt her, and somehow, I'm going to make up for what I've done to her.

I'm going to enjoy every minute of watching everyone go up in flames.

Ivy 15

DESTROY ALL OF THEM

My insides quiver. I turn the phone off so Dax can't contact me anymore.

What am I doing here?

I need to leave. But as much as I tell myself to go, I can't move. I'm paralyzed, staring at silver-covered plates, Dax's note with two sets of keys, and a credit card.

He thinks he can buy me.

Same old Dax.

He's trying to be kind to me.

No, this is another form of his control.

Don't fall for it.

My eyes dart to the corner. Seducing Ivy flowers fill the trash can. I study them, blinking until they become blurry.

Dad created those flowers.

Why did I toss them in the garbage?

Because Dax gave them to me.

They're still my dad's creation.

I swipe at my tears and rise. I pull the brilliant flowers out of the trash.

It's ironic. They match the whore-red lipstick and nail polish perfectly. I'd think it was something Dax did, but I know it's not. My father loved red flowers.

I put them back in the vase, one stem at a time, relieved I didn't destroy any. Then I lean down and smell them.

I can't deny the scent's beautiful. And while I smelled the same fragrance in Avery's perfume, it's clear she has other scents in it.

I may not like her creation, but the flowers are pure. There's nothing else in them. They're exactly what Dad created.

I convince myself it's okay to enjoy the aroma around me. Then I sit back down, and more grief hits.

Dad would've been so proud to know that the flowers are a huge success.

Dax's statement from last night interrupts the thoughts in my head. *"Your father would never have done anything with it. It sat there for years and years, and not once did he do anything with it."*

I swallow hard, staring at the flowers, wondering why my dad didn't ever file for a patent.

Don't listen to Dax.

But why didn't he?

Besides the life insurance, I was shocked to learn my father had several retirement accounts from previous employers. They had over half a million dollars in them. I'm sure he just let this money sit and accumulate for years. Maybe I shouldn't be surprised. My father was a talented botanist. Before my mother left, he had a high-paying job at a great corporation. But he never liked to spend money.

After my mom devastated us by running off with another man, my father didn't work for a few years until Dax's father hired him. Even after that ended in disaster, he never went without a job again. But the period he was between jobs was rough. Some nights, he barely scraped dinner together for us.

He always acted like we were poor, so I was shocked when his bank account alone had over $200,000 in cash sitting in it.

Why didn't he take ten grand out and file for the patent?

My stomach churns. His notebook sat there for years. I close my eyes, thinking of all the times I saw my father spend hours hovering over that notebook.

Did he not believe in himself?

Was he just too cheap to spend any money?

All the things Dax said to me ten years ago about my father not providing for me creep into my mind. I would stick up for my father, stating that he always gave me what I needed. But why did he act like we were living paycheck to paycheck if he had money?

Too many questions perplex me, things I'd never thought about until after his death. No matter how much I try to decipher it, I can't figure it out.

My father was always cautious with money, but I assumed it was because we had none. Now I don't know what to think.

I can't let Dax get into my head.

He stole Dad's patent.

My father did nothing with it. Years and years passed, and he didn't do anything.

He had the resources but still did nothing. Why?

Don't let Dax turn you. He stole from him, I remind myself again.

My stomach growls, tearing me out of my debate. I stare at the silver plates and slowly lift the lids, revealing scrambled eggs, poached eggs, eggs over easy, rye toast, wheat toast, white toast, pancakes, chocolate chip pancakes, pecan pancakes, and blueberry pancakes. There are duplicate choices of everything except the waffles.

"What the heck?" I mutter, then reveal more platters.

French toast, strips of bacon, Canadian bacon, sausage links, sausage patties, and ham. Smaller bowls hold whipped cream, berries, and jam. Glass containers of orange juice, pineapple juice, apple juice, whole milk, 2% milk, and skim milk sit on the counter next to sparkling and still water, dishes of regular butter and honey butter, and a bottle of maple syrup.

I stare at the overwhelming amount of food, then suddenly become amused. I can't help myself, laughing until I cry.

This is so Dax Carrington.

In my house, we didn't waste food. Now that I know my father had all that money, I once again question why he was so worried about not wasting anything. His voice in my head warns me, *"Don't be ungrateful and waste things, Ivy. The devil loves excessiveness."*

My face falls. I stare at the food again.

There's no way I can eat all this. I study everything, then select a blueberry pancake. I set it on my plate, add butter, and pour syrup over it. Then I top it with berries. I cut the pancake and take a bite.

The blueberries are still warm with a hint of sweetness, and they melt in my mouth along with the buttery, sugary concoction. And I realize I'm starving.

I didn't eat at the event the night before. There was too much going on, and I was too nervous.

I eat half the pancake, grab a forkful of scrambled eggs, chew and swallow, then take a sip of water.

I pour a mug of coffee, stir in some cream and sugar, and drink half of it, continuing to stare at the abundance of food.

Why am I still here? I should have left the estate.

I glance around the cottage, shaking my head. "What am I doing?"

I eat more food.

I'm here to pay everyone back.

I'm not like these people.

I need to go. I don't know how to play the game the way they do.

I'm capable.

Am I?

Another internal debate continues, and I can't shake the fear that my enemies are too powerful. They have years of screwing people over, and I've never once done anything to intentionally harm anyone.

I push my plate away, unable to eat anymore, wondering if I'm crazy. I came here for a reason. I purposely reinserted myself into their lives, so now, there's no going back. I have to finish what I started.

I stare at the flowers, vowing not to let my fear dictate my decisions.

I mumble, "I will destroy them, all of them, even Dax."

My heart bleeds thinking of hurting him. I hate that I still love him and loathe that he claims he loves me. It makes it worse. Just like that girl ten years ago, the one who was gullible and believed him when he said he loved her, I want it to be true. I still want him to be my love story—my soul mate for eternity. And I still yearn for us to be together forever and for my father to love Dax too.

He'll never get the opportunity.

Dax killed Dad.

It was all fantasy. Nothing between Dax and me was real—at least not for him.

I hate myself for thinking those thoughts. They're danger-ous. And I beat myself up some more thinking about how I contemplated sleeping with the others last night so I could piss Dax off.

They raped me.

They didn't.

They did.

How could I have let Bobby or Avery touch me?

Play the game.

Tears well in my eyes again. I glance at the ceiling, shaking my head, once more asking, "What am I doing here?"

It would've hurt Dax if I slept with the others.

I should have done it.

There's no way I could have.

Yes, I could have, and it would've hurt him.

My head spins to the point I decide I need fresh air. So I put my plate in the sink, go into the bathroom, shower, and brush my teeth with my old toothbrush.

I wonder again why Dax left everything here and why he didn't throw out my stuff.

I bypass my old makeup bag sitting in the drawer, remove my comb, and get the knots out of my hair. I pull the old hairdryer from under the cabinet and plug it in.

When my locks are no longer wet, I return to the bedroom and open the closet.

I pull out my old designer jeans Dax bought me, remembering how I couldn't believe he spent $400 on a pair of denim. It was exciting, especially since my father never let me have anything expensive and a lot of my clothes had been bought secondhand.

I put on an old bra and tank top. I grab Dax's Clifton University hooded sweatshirt and sniff it.

Butterflies erupt in my stomach. It still smells like him. I stand for a few minutes, leaning against the wall, eyes closed, inhaling his scent.

Don't fall for him again.

How can I not?

I can't.

"I have to get out of here," I blurt out. I tug his sweatshirt over my head, find a pair of socks, and put them on. I stare at several pairs of tennis shoes Dax had also bought me.

Once again, they're designer.

Dax's face appears in my mind. He wiggles his eyebrows, stating, *"Nothing but the best for my little slut."*

The same surge of adrenaline that shot through me each time he gave me a gift and said it, hits me. I pick up each pair, reliving the moments and berating myself for my naivety.

It was all for his game.

It wasn't.

It was.

As much as I protested when he gave me gifts, it always made me feel special. I thought it meant he loved me.

I was so stupid.

I select a whore-red pair, grab the keys to the cottage, and step outside, locking the door.

I don't know why I lock it. Dax had it unlocked, so I don't understand why he decided to give me the keys. I'm not staying on the estate. Yet, for some reason, I want the cottage secure. I don't want anyone else inside it.

I stroll through the estate, feeling nostalgic as I approach our old cottage. I climb the two steps to the porch and cautiously reach for the door handle, but it's locked.

I look through the windows. The place also looks the same, but Dad and I didn't have any decorations, minus flowers Dax would give me or that my father would bring home from one of the gardens. In all reality, we had very little, so I can't tell if anyone's living in it.

I force myself to leave, and I pass several of the greenhouses my father managed, tearing up again. I don't go inside any of them. Part of me wants to, but I can't.

I get to the trail leading to the lake and head down it, remembering all the times Dax and I took this path. The first time he took me to the lake was magical, and the same nervous butterflies erupt that I felt back then.

Memories of nighttime swims, making out on the beach, and sailing on sunny days make me smile. I stop moving, close my eyes, and enjoy a minute of the sun on my face and the good memories.

"Homophobe! Homophobe! Homophobe!" Marcey's voice pops up in my mind.

I groan.

Why am I thinking about her?

"Or is she a prude and homophobic?" Marcey asks, not leaving my thoughts.

The same defensive twist in my chest occurs.

Dax's voice interjects, *"Every man wants a slut, Ivy. They don't want a tease. They want a woman who knows she's a woman, not a prude. So you want to be my slut, right?"*

I cringe, knowing those moments formed who I am today. They were the catalyst of manipulation, lies, and, ultimately, my addiction.

I shake my head, continuing through the woods, barely noticing anything, with a reel going through my mind of nightmares I've tried to forget but can't. I step out of the woods and freeze.

The docks have been pulled out. There are no signs of sailboats or other watercraft. The season's over, and everything's gone except for several bright-red buoys in the water, sand lining the edge of the grass, and the boathouse.

My stomach flips. I remember the night Dax and I spent in the boathouse. The footage leaked onto Professor Dyer's big screen, causing my life to fall apart. Yet I can't help myself. I go into the run-down building and turn on the light.

It's the same musty smell and wooden tongue-and-groove walls. The boats hang stacked just as perfectly as ever.

I step into the bedroom, sit on the bed, look around, then turn and stare at the corner of the ceiling.

The red light's on. I shake my head, wondering if I'm being recorded or not. A violent wave of anger slaps me. I rise and throw my hands in the air, yelling, "Are you watching me?"

Silence fills the air, and more rage hits me. I scream, "Are you recording me? Are you getting more footage for whatever sinister thing you have planned next to destroy me?"

I stare at it, as if there's going to somehow be a response, and then get pissed at myself. I shouldn't show these emotions to Dax or anyone else who could be watching.

I force myself to leave the boathouse and sit on the sandy shore with my knees pulled tight to my chest, hugging myself. The never-ending battle with too many emotions plagues me while the horror of my past torments me. It all mixes with the same lingering questions about how to beat these people once and for all.

One by one, images of my enemies pop up in my mind, along with one nagging question I can't answer: What part did Lilly play in all this?

Was she ever my friend, or was she in on their game too?

Dax and the others seemed shocked to see her last night. It sounded like she hadn't returned to Greenwich in a long time. But why?

It could be another trap.

They didn't know I was coming.

Professor Dyer could have called them and told them I was in town. He had over an hour.

Dax was surprised to see me. So were the others.

I stare at the glassy water for several more minutes and then take a deep breath. I reach for my phone, hoping she has the same number, and pull up my text messages.

Me: Can we meet up?

Lilly: I thought you'd never ask.

Me: When?

Lilly: Tomorrow night at eight.

Me: Where?

Lilly: My hotel.

My pulse increases.
What if she tries something?
I can say no.
She's never done anything without my permission.
I don't have any self-control.
I do.
It'll be too long since I've had sex. I won't be able to stop myself.
I will.
I stare at the screen, my mouth dry, hating all my demons.

Me: Which one?

Lilly: Harbor Inn. And come alone.

Dax 16

THE END IS NEAR

Dean Bramwell's been losing his shit all day. He called an emergency meeting, and I was more than happy to go to his office.

"The board's up my ass," he frets.

"What do you want me to do about it?" I question, sitting back in the chair and keeping a solemn look on my face.

Bramwell's cheeks turn redder than normal. He picks up his crystal tumbler of bourbon, takes a swig, and refills it from the decanter. He claims, "This isn't the same as all your other antics, Dax."

I act insulted. "*My* antics? Why am I being blamed for this?"

He points at me. "Your group's always been responsible for these atrocities that happen at my university."

I arch my eyebrows. "*Your* university? Last time I checked, it was a public institution."

He snarls, "Stop playing games! You've gone too far this time!"

I maintain my innocence. "If you're trying to accuse me of something, you better have some proof."

He shuts his mouth and taps his fingers on the desk, shaking his head. He releases an angry breath and leans closer to me. "You really didn't do this?"

"No."

He studies me, then says, "Okay, then who did?"

"How the hell should I know?"

He sighs.

"I'm sorry, but I don't have any information for you on the culprit."

He sits back and drinks his bourbon. He swallows and states, "Okay. Assuming you didn't do it, did you see it? All of it?"

"No, I couldn't get past the first few seconds. Once Avery appeared, I turned it off," I lie.

"It's horrible," he whines. He scrubs his face and then finishes the liquor.

I sit back and cross my ankle over my knee.

He glares at me and points again. "You have to clean this up."

I grunt. "How am I supposed to clean it up?"

"You always clean things up. I know how it works around here."

"You're misinformed."

"Bullshit!"

I let a few tense moments pass, then claim, "I don't have the ability to make this go away. If I could, I would."

"The board could get rid of me for this. It can destroy the university. It's already..." He glances at his watch. "It's been up for over five hours. Do you know how much damage that can do in five hours?"

I casually say, "Since it was sent to everyone's email, I'm sure it'll be viral worldwide within no time. It's already hit the national news."

He scoots the chair back and rises. His belly jiggles when he starts pacing. "This isn't one of your games, Dax."

"Dean, you're starting to sound like a broken record. And I'll remind you again that you better have some proof before you accuse me of things," I warn.

He turns the computer screen toward me and clicks on the video, stating, "Your sister's in it."

"Yes, we've already discussed that," I remind him.

He fast-forwards the video and then pauses it. He points out, "That's Avery."

I don't have to pretend when I shake my head in disgust. "Yeah, it is."

"Look." He pushes the pause button.

Avery's sniffing lines of coke off some coed's ass. Then, the camera changes to her with another coed. She has a badly implemented butterfly tattoo on her stomach meant to cover a large birthmark.

"She sniffs coke off that girl's—" He cuts off his whine.

I arch my eyebrow. To taunt him further, I ask, "Off her what?"

He keeps his mouth shut and hits pause so Avery's nose is right on the girl's clit.

I don't say anything or give any outward reaction.

Bramwell continues to stare at me, distraught.

I offer, "I think the word you're looking for is pussy."

"Jesus, Dax. I'm going to lose my job," he cries.

"Calm down. You're not going to lose your job. The board's

not going to do shit unless I approve it, and you know it," I remind him.

"This will destroy the university."

"Worse things have happened."

"Worse things? That poor girl was only fourteen! She was here visiting her sister at Gamma Sigma Phi! Her father is extremely prominent in Washington, DC!"

I pretend to be shocked, but I knew who it was and her age when I added it to the video. I blurt out, "She was only fourteen? Wow! That's illegal, isn't it?"

"Her father's already called me. He said they're going to be suing the university."

"How do they know it's her? Whoever created the video blurred her face out."

Dean Bramwell shouts, "It's pretty hard not to know it's her when she has that birthmark and tattoo right next to her —" He shuts his mouth again.

"Her pussy?" I offer once again.

"Ugh." He pours another glass of bourbon and swigs it back.

I point to the tumbler. "You might want to slow down on that stuff."

"I'm going to lose my job," he repeats.

"And I told you you're not."

Bramwell shakes his head. He hits fast-forward again and then stops.

A young man's body appears. His face is blurred, but you can still see the blindfold. Ropes attached to the ceiling bind his wrists.

Avery kisses him and giggles, saying seductively, *"Are you ready for your gift?"*

"Yes!" he exclaims, his dick hard and pointing straight in the air.

"Okay, baby. Hold on one second. I want to take my clothes off to do this."

"You're so fucking sexy," he mutters.

Avery steps back, disappears from the screen, and reappears with a frat pledge from years ago. She motions at the restrained guy's cock.

The pledge kneels and begins sucking him off.

"Oh God, Avery. Oh God," he moans. Avery holds the frat boy's head down, thrusting him over and over, faster and faster, until cum leaks out of his mouth and the restrained man is shouting obscenities. Bramwell pauses the screen with no color in his cheeks. "That's Matt Montague."

"Matt Montague? The attorney?"

"Yes, Matt Montague, the attorney," Dean Bramwell repeats, as if I'm deaf.

I peer closer. "How do you know it's Matt? I don't see any birthmarks or tattoos."

"It's him," Bramwell insists.

I'm curious how Bramwell knows it's Matt. I blurred his face really well. So I push, "But how do you know it's him?"

Bramwell explodes, "I play golf with his father every Sunday! He grew up on the course with us and at my house! That's Matt Montague, no doubt about it. And there's another scene with him."

"Is there?" I innocently ask.

"How could you not have watched this before you came over?" Bramwell reprimands.

"Would you want to see your sister naked, doing horrible things to people?" I question.

Bramwell shakes his head, fast-forwards a little bit, and then stops. "Look at what they did to him!"

Matt's blindfolded and tied up again, only this time, he's on all fours, his wrists restrained to the headboard.

Avery's back on the screen, cooing, *"I want to do this with you, Matt. You're the only person I fantasize about doing anything with anymore."*

"I am?"

"Yeah, baby. I-I love you."

"You do?"

"Yes! So much!" she claims.

"I-I love you too, Avery," he replies.

She shimmies her naked breasts over his back, murmuring in his ear, *"Please do this with me. It's all I've been fantasizing about for months."*

Matt hesitates. *"I don't know, Avery. It's not my thing."*

She drags her hand down his spine.

He shivers.

"How do you know it's not your thing if you've not done it before?" she argues.

My gut churns. I feel horrible for the bastard. I never cared much for Matt. He was another nerd after my sister. But what Avery and Dyer did to him was disgusting.

"Please, Matt, just once. If you don't like it, I'll never do it again," she begs.

He stays silent.

"I need it, Matt. Just give me one little gift. Please," she whines, then leans forward and licks his lips.

He hesitates and then sighs. *"Okay, Avery, but if I don't like it—"*

She puts her fingers over his lips. *"Then I'll stop, I promise."*

There's a beat of silence, then, *"Tell me I can peg you, baby,"* she begs in her sultry voice.

He takes a deep breath, grappling with himself.

"Please," she pleads, then adds, *"After we do it, I'm going to fuck you all night, baby. I'll make you come harder than you ever have, I promise."*

He caves. *"Okay. If this is what you really want, we can try it."*

She claps. *"I do. It's going to be great. Let me strap it on, okay?"*

He has second thoughts, asking, *"Are you sure this is necessary?"*

In her most sugary voice, she says, *"Yeah, baby. I've always wanted to peg someone. I promise you're going to get hard and then you can fuck me all night, okay?"*

He hesitates again but finally nods. *"Okay, Avery, can you take the blindfold off though? Maybe untie my hands?"*

She puts her hand on his cheek. *"Remember when you told me you'd let me do anything I wanted to you, that you would fulfill all my fantasies?"*

He swallows hard and releases an anxious breath, admitting, *"Yeah, I said that."*

"This is my fantasy. Just this one time."

"Okay, Avery," he says, nervousness apparent in his tone.

"I promise I'll use a lot of lube, and it won't hurt."

He clenches his jaw.

She orders, *"Now, be a good boy and relax."*

His body remains stiff. He releases a stress-filled breath.

She demands, *"Widen your legs a bit more,"* while dragging her fingers down his inner thighs.

He does it and then his body stiffens again. *"Avery, I don't know if this is really what we should be doing."*

"Are you not going to give me what I need?" she pouts.

Another moment of silence.

She adds, *"Okay, that's fine. I knew you'd disappoint me eventually, just like everyone else. You promised me you'd be different from them, but—"*

"No, it's fine, Avery. Go ahead," he says, grimacing.

Avery kisses him on the cheek and pats his ass. *"Good boy. You make me so happy."* She steps back, looks toward the door, and disappears from the camera.

Professor Dyer appears, his dick hard, ready to go.

"Turn it off," I tell Bramwell. I've seen it too many times and don't want to see it again. Every time I do, I feel ill.

Matt may not have been my friend, but he didn't deserve what they did to him.

Bramwell pauses the video.

I reach across his desk and turn the screen away so I don't have to see it anymore.

Bramwell insists, "That's Matt Montague. I know it's him."

"What are you going to do, tell the whole world and ruin his career? Embarrass him with his family?" I question, genuinely not wanting anything else to happen to Matt.

I wouldn't have put it on there if I knew Bramwell would know it was Matt. I assumed I was doing Matt a favor. It would be his decision to come forward and seek revenge in some legal form, whatever that entails, if he chose to do so. It's shocking to me Bramwell would know who he was from all those years ago.

Bramwell paces the office again, tugging at his hair. "This has to come down." He turns to me, ordering, "Get it taken down, Dax. Whatever you must do, I need you to get it down."

I shrug my shoulders. "I don't know how to take it down. I'm not a tech person."

"You have resources. I know you know someone who can take it down," he accuses.

I put my hands in the air. "I don't."

"You do," he seethes.

His phone beeps, but he doesn't answer it, and we stare at it.

"You going to get that?" I question.

There's a knock on the door.

"Not now," he calls out, putting his hands on his desk. He leans over, stating, "I'm telling you—"

"Dean Bramwell," his assistant says from the doorway.

He glances up.

I turn to look at her.

She anxiously announces, "The police are here. They said they need to talk to you."

Bramwell's face turns fearful. "Just give me a minute."

"Okay," she replies, her eyes darting between us.

Bramwell begs, "Please, Dax, you have to do something."

I rise. "There's nothing I can do about this. I wish I could. Do you think I want a Carrington on there? Avery is a disgrace."

Bramwell's eyes widen. "She's your sister. You can pay for this to go away."

"How am I going to pay for this to go away? It's everywhere. It's in people's email boxes."

"Get it off the site," he demands.

I give him a final look. "I told you, I have nothing to do with this. I'm not a tech person. You have a whole department responsible for the university's website. Have them do their job. Figure out where your leak is, but it's not me." I exit his office and nod at the police officers, offering, "Gentlemen."

"Mr. Carrington," they say in unison.

I leave his office and get into my car. I speed away from campus feeling better than I have in years.

The end is near.

The cards are all on the table.

There's nowhere for them to hide.

But my glee is short-lived.

I still don't have Ivy, and none of this will be worth it if I don't end up with her.

I drive through town and arrive at the estate. I pull up to the cottage, hoping she's still here, but my Porsche is out front, so I assume she's home.

I slide out of my car, step up onto the porch, and knock on the door.

She doesn't answer, but I can see her sitting at the table inside.

I knock again, calling out, "Ivy."

She finally comes to the door and answers it. A red tinge of anger covers her face. Her hand's in a fist. Her phone's in her other one. She seethes, "Have you seen this?"

My gut drops. I glance at the phone and realize she's talking about the video. "Yeah, I've seen it."

"Did you do this?" she asks, her voice shaking.

I stay quiet, not admitting or denying it.

She snarls, "I asked you a question."

"Why are you upset? It was to hurt the people who have hurt you," I admit, confused. I know Ivy doesn't have any good feelings for Avery or Bobby. Or Professor Dyer, for that matter. She chose to go to him for some reason and have him bring her to the charity event last night, but it must have been to get under my skin.

Her voice shakes harder. Her lips quiver, and her breathing turns ragged. She shakes her head, blinking hard. She accuses, "Do you ever not create more destruction?"

I don't know what to say. I open my mouth and then shut it.

She adds, "You're trying to destroy him further, aren't you?"

"Bobby? I don't care about Bobby. I haven't in a long time. We haven't been friends since before you left. And I didn't know what he did to you until after that night, but I told you I would make him pay. This is part of me making him pay."

"I'm not talking about Bobby," she cries out.

I freeze. My gut churns and my mouth goes dry. I choke out, "Dyer? You actually care about him?"

"No, I don't care about Dyer!" she shrieks.

Relief fills me, but I'm still confused.

She glares at me. "Why can't you stop hurting people?"

"Ivy, I don't understand why you're upset."

She huffs. "You wouldn't, would you, Dax?"

"Why don't you fill me in, then? But I swear I did it for you."

She sarcastically laughs. "For me? How is that video for me?"

"Have you seen it? It's all the things Bobby, Avery, and Dyer have done to people. It's a lot of illegal stuff. I did it to hurt them because they hurt you."

"And you hurt other innocent people in the process," she states.

"Who? Everyone's faces are covered up. I made sure that people's identities were protected," I claim.

"But they aren't? Are they? What they did to Matt was horrible, and you just made him relive it," she accuses.

I gape at her and then recover. My chest tightens with jealousy, and I confess, "I didn't know you were still in contact with Matt or that you were ever good friends."

"I wouldn't say we're friends. I ran into him by sheer coincidence back in Georgia."

An unsettling feeling fills me. "Okay, and what did you and Matt discuss?"

"That's not your business," she snips.

I stare at her, feeling once again like a rug is being pulled out from underneath me. "Ivy—"

"Go away, Dax. I just want you to go away."

"I didn't mean to hurt anybody but Avery, Bobby, and Dyer. I thought because people's faces were covered—"

"You thought you'd share people's nightmares with the

world? How do you think he feels watching that and reliving those moments?"

It's something I never considered. My pulse skyrockets, and I reach for the doorjamb to steady myself. "I didn't mean—"

"Go away, Dax. You're toxic, and you're never going to be anything but toxic."

"I'm not the same person," I claim, but it sounds weak. *Maybe I still am?*

"This video isn't the same person you were?" she shouts, shaking her phone in my face.

"Ivy, please. I didn't mean to hurt Matt. I'll apologize if you want me to. I made sure that no one would be able to identify him."

"His father said Bramwell called him," she blurts out.

What?

She spouts, "How do you think his father felt when he saw it?"

My gut dives. Blood drains from my face to my toes.

"How do you think Matt felt learning his father watched that...that rape scene?"

Bile rises in my throat.

"What is it about you, Dax? Is it because your relationship with your father sucked so bad you have to make everyone's father ashamed of them?"

I close my eyes. "Ivy, that wasn't—"

"That wasn't the point? But you did it. You didn't think about the consequences and who you would hurt, did you?"

"I just wanted to destroy them for you!"

"I can destroy people on my own. I don't need your help."

"That's not who you are," I declare.

She stills and then a twisted smile curves her lips.

The hairs on my neck rise.

She declares, "You've always underestimated me, Dax."

"No, I haven't."

"Yeah, you have. And like I told you last night, I'm not that same girl you broke. You should be aware of it."

Ivy 17

SENATOR'S DAUGHTER

Sunlight streams over my face. I open my eyes and glance around the room.

I'm still at Dax's cottage.

The events from yesterday hit me once again. I squeeze my eyes shut, wishing the nightmares would stop—for everyone, all of their victims. It's as if I'm reliving ten years ago, and there's destruction all around me.

I grab my phone and text Matt.

> Me: Are you okay?

It's the first time I've reached out since he called me and told me it was him on the video. I had just gotten done watching it with horror, wondering who all the victims were. I was shocked at what Avery, Bobby, and Dyer had done. It was just more tragedy, more innocence stolen, more games played with unknowing pawns.

> Matt: I'll be fine.

>> Me: I'm sorry this happened to you. I feel like this is partly my fault.

> Matt: Why would it be your fault?

>> Me: I came back here. Maybe I opened a can of worms.

> Matt: Don't give yourself that much credit. They are who they are.

>> Me: I'm sorry your father saw the video.

> Matt: It's okay. I had ten years to prepare for this day.

>> Me: What do you mean?

> Matt: They always threaten to send it to him. At least now I can stop worrying about it.

My gut dives, and I feel sicker.

>> Me: I really am sorry. If there's anything I can do...

I don't finish the message and send it.

> Matt: It's fine. At least the whole world doesn't know it's me. My father can still hold his head high and walk around town and the country club.

I bite my lips, staring at the message.

Matt: Make sure you get out of there soon. Nothing good can come of that place or those people.

I don't respond, knowing he's right. Then I get up and get ready. I spend the day keeping to myself, ensuring I stay far away from the main house, ignoring any attempted communication from Dax.

When nighttime finally comes, I slide into his Porsche and take off. I pull up to the Harbor Inn.

The valet approaches me and opens the door. "Are you a guest or visiting?"

"Just visiting," I state.

He writes out a ticket and hands it to me. "No problem. Just call the number when you're on your way out."

"Okay, thank you," I reply, my stomach filling with nerves.

I'm just as clueless now as I was the day before. I don't know where Lilly stands in all this, but she seemed to have wanted to talk to me, and it makes me nervous. But I have to find out why she came back here after all these years and what her role was the night everything happened between us.

I get in the elevator and go up to the eighth floor. When the doors open, my stomach flips. I take a deep breath, step out, and find her room number. I knock on the door.

She opens it, wearing a black cocktail dress and holding a glass of champagne in her hand. She beams at me. "Ivy, come on in." She steps back.

I hesitate.

"Come in! I'm not going to bite you," she claims, then giggles.

I relax. It's the Lilly I know. The one I considered my friend, who I hope always was and still will be. And maybe I'm crazy even considering the thought that she's not as bad as the rest of them, but I want her not to be.

I step inside and shut the door.

She hands me a glass of champagne.

I reach for it and then stop.

She says in a sharp voice, "I didn't drug you. I would never do that now, nor would I have back then."

"Oh, I didn't mean—"

"It's okay. If I were in your position, I'd think the same thing, but I can assure you I didn't have any part of their twisted shit."

I don't know why I believe her, but I do. Maybe I'm being naive again. Perhaps I'm still gullible. But I take the glass of champagne and sip it.

"Let's go sit down," she says, leading me into her suite.

We sit on the couch and turn toward each other.

She puts her hand on mine. "How've you been all these years, Ivy?"

I shrug. "Surviving. I don't know. That's a loaded question." I take another sip of champagne, feeling my butterflies kicking off again.

"That's understandable," she states.

I decide there's no point in beating around the bush. "What happened to you after the video got posted in Dyer's classroom?"

She licks her lips, downs her bubbly, then gets up. She goes to the bar, brings the bottle over, and refills her flute. She sets the champagne on the table, answering, "That's a loaded question too. But I don't think it destroyed my life as badly as it probably did yours." She drinks more champagne.

I set my glass on the table. "What do you mean?"

"My father hated the video, of course. It embarrassed him, but he survived it. His people shut it down pretty quickly, and somehow, it never got out. I don't know how. You would think it'd be viral, me being a senator's daughter and all."

"Does he still talk to you?" I question.

She grunts. "It's more like I don't talk to him."

"Why?"

She takes another large mouthful, then answers, "Because I was always the senator's daughter. All that ever mattered was that I was the senator's daughter. I got tired of trying to be perfect, to fit into his precious little world where the only things that mattered were voters and his fake family image."

Sympathy fills me. "That must've been a lot of pressure."

She mumbles, "You have no idea," and drinks more of the champagne.

"So, your father got upset and took care of the video footage. Then what?" I question.

She leans back on the couch. "I stayed at Clifton. I tried not to get on any more videos, but I still had my fun. If anything, it just opened the door for more of it." She grins.

Confused, I ask, "More of it?"

She leans closer and puts her hand on my thigh. The spark ignites within me, and I inhale sharply.

She admits, "I like to have fun, Ivy. I like to have lots of fun involving sex. Women, men, I don't care. But I like sex. And after that video..." She leans back and laughs. "Well, I had my pick of the litter. People were coming out of the woodwork. All the work in my classes was done by other people, and I fucked my way through college. I got straight A's, by the way." She winks.

I gape at her.

She laughs again and finishes her champagne, then refills it once more. "Why do you look so shocked? I would've thought you, of all people, would understand what wanting sex is like." She grazes her thumb over my thigh.

I close my eyes, shuddering. "Lilly—"

She moves her hand. "I'm sorry. I didn't mean to make you uncomfortable."

I open my eyes and meet hers. "I'm a sex addict. When they drugged me—"

"I know all about that drug," she claims.

My heart beats faster.

"I didn't know they drugged you. I never would have agreed to that. All I did agree to was to have sex with you that night. It wasn't supposed to go down how it did." She blows out a breath of air, then looks away.

My pulse increases. "Go down how?"

She stays silent, continuing to look away.

My voice grows firmer. "Lilly, what did you have to do with that night?"

She shakes her head and then finally meets my eye. "Bobby approached me with Avery. They said they wanted me to seduce you, and we'd all have a fun night. And it was fun for me. I liked you, Ivy. Everybody did. The entire campus was into you and wanted to have you. Maybe it's because we knew we couldn't. But I wouldn't have done it if I had known they drugged you. I thought you were doing things of your own free will. I'm not into people doing things they don't want, and if I had known, I wouldn't have gone through with it. No matter what, I would not have gone through with it," she insists.

My insides churn. I stare at her, trying to decide if I believe her, and my gut says that I should.

"They told me it was fine if you didn't want to do it. They wanted me to seduce you in front of them, and they wanted to participate. Avery said everybody in Gamma Sigma Phi had to pass a test, and that was mine."

I stare at her.

She scoffs. "I didn't even care about the sorority. I just...

Well, I wanted to fuck you, but I wanted you to fuck me." She stares at me, and tension builds between us.

The ticking of the clock in the room sounds louder, and I open my mouth, but nothing comes out.

She scoots closer and puts her hand back on my thigh. I glance at it, and tingles explode down my spine.

"Are you not attracted to women at all? I mean, you've not been with anyone since our night together?" she questions.

My face fills with heat, and all the things I've done to get my hit when I was looking for the high that only Dax gives me hurts harder this time. I close my eyes, slowly shaking my head. "Lilly, if I told you the things I've done over the last ten years..." My voice trembles, and I stop.

She moves her hand from my leg to my shoulder, but it's more in a friendly way. "Ivy, what have you done that you're so ashamed of?"

I meet her eye. "I'm a sex addict. I've fucked way too many people I shouldn't have fucked. I've been in more orgies than I can recall, and every one of them leaves me empty. It leaves me wanting what I've only had with Dax and will never have again," I admit, my eyes filling with tears.

And I'm so tired of crying. I wish I could stop crying, but I can't control it.

A tear falls down my cheek, and I swipe at it. Sympathy fills Lilly's expression. She tugs me into her and puts her other hand over my head, pulling me to her chest. "Ivy, it's okay. There's nothing to be ashamed of."

"There is. I can't control my urges. Like right now...when you put your hand on my thigh, it... I shouldn't even say this because it wouldn't take a lot for you to convince me to fuck you right now," I admit.

Lilly strokes my head. "Oh, Ivy, don't tell me that."

I pull away. "I'm sorry. I didn't mean to embarrass you."

She arches her eyebrows. "No, what I meant was don't tell me that you'd fuck me. You know I'd love to fuck you again. Don't torture me." She smirks.

I sit there frozen for a minute and then I giggle. "Lilly, you've always been funny."

She shrugs. "Well, it's the truth. Don't tell a sex addict who embraces her addiction that you're a sex addict too."

"You're not a sex addict," I state.

She grunts. "Of course I am. I always have been."

"Because they drugged you too?"

"No, they didn't drug me. Even when I asked Bobby last night if he did, I knew he didn't."

"How? Have you taken the TimeMarker test? To be sure?"

She shakes her head. "I've been a sex addict since I was thirteen and lost my virginity after seducing my father's right-hand man."

My eyes widen.

"Well, don't be judgy," she says, taking another sip of champagne.

I laugh. "I didn't mean to be. I'm sorry."

She wags her finger at me, scolding, "Yeah, sex addicts shouldn't judge other sex addicts. Remember, everything's safe when we're in group mode."

My lips twitch. "You go to meetings as well?"

"I've been to a few, but you know what? I finally decided to embrace it. I've always loved having sex. I don't care who I fuck. If I'm attracted to someone, then I'm going to fuck them. If they can get me off, I'm going to fuck them. My daddy hates it. I love it," she says, finishing the rest of her champagne.

I release an emotional, relieved breath. I cautiously ask, "So our friendship was genuine?"

She nods and squeezes my hand. "Yeah, it was, and I'm sorry that I fucked you that night. If I had known you were drugged, honestly, I wouldn't have done it. Bobby's such a creep. So is Avery."

"Well, that's one thing we agree on," I add.

She wrinkles her nose, asking, "Why were you with Dyer?"

"To make Dax jealous."

We stare at each other, then start to laugh again.

When our laughter subsides, I inquire, "So why did you come back?"

"I don't know. I got the charity event invitation, and I had been avoiding coming back here for a while. I never really liked Clifton. California is so much better."

"So you're happy out there?"

"Yeah, I am. You should come visit. Soak up some sun with me!"

I smile. "I'd love that."

She adds, "I know L.A. like the back of my hand. We can have so much fun out there."

I smile bigger. "That sounds nice. I'd like that."

She claps. "Yay! Me too. I was hoping we could still be friends. I've missed you."

"I've missed you too. If I'm being honest, you were the last real friend I ever made. Well, except for my boss, Jaxon. But he's a different type of friend. After everything happened, I didn't trust anyone anymore."

"That's understandable." Her eyes narrow. "So, what will you do about Dax?"

"What do you mean?" I ask, my chest tightening.

She tilts her head. "You've seen the video, I'm assuming."

My stomach flips again, thinking about poor Matt and all those other victims Dax just broadcasted everywhere. "Yeah, I have."

"I'm assuming Dax leaked it?" She arches her eyebrows.

I don't say anything. For some reason, I feel like I need to protect Dax, even though he doesn't deserve any of it.

She smiles. "Well, I'm assuming that Dax leaked it."

"Why?"

She scoffs. "He hates Avery, Bobby, and Dyer. They all got what was coming to them, so I'm glad he did it."

I stay quiet.

She peers at me. "Why do you seem upset about this?"

"Because those people on the video have to relive things, just like you and I had to. Well, it sounds like it wasn't that bad for you."

She winces. "Sorry. I wish it were the same experience for you as it was for me, but it did perk up my social life even more, and I never thought that would be possible."

I stare at her like she's crazy.

She points to herself, stating, "Like I said, sex addict."

I laugh, confessing, "I love how you're so confident with yourself, Lilly. I wish I could be."

"But you are."

"No, I'm not," I claim.

"Yeah, you are, Ivy. You always have been. That's why everybody wanted you. Do you not understand that?"

I ponder her statement, still not understanding it. Everybody else around me seemed confident, unlike me.

"Okay, well, what are you going to do about Dax?"

"I don't know."

She cautiously asks, "Can I tell you something about him?"

"Sure."

She takes a deep breath and hesitates.

"What is it?" I push.

She bites her lip and then shrugs, declaring, "If you can't shake him out of your system, then I think maybe you should give him another chance."

I jerk my head backward. "Why would I do that?"

"He's not like the rest of them. Not anymore. And you two have something that nobody else has. It's clear, and it's always been clear," she voices.

I blurt out, "He used me. I was a pawn in his game and then he destroyed my life."

Lilly slowly nods. "Maybe so, but from where I'm standing, he's trying pretty hard to make up for it."

"How do you make up for that? He killed my father," I say.

Lilly's eyes widen. "How the hell did he kill your father?"

I open my mouth and then shut it. I take a deep breath, revealing, "My dad saw Dax and Avery on TV. When I walked in, he was having a heart attack, and they were on air. He died."

Lilly's expression falls. "I'm so sorry about your dad."

"Thanks."

"But why is that Avery and Dax's fault?"

"Let's just say Dax and Avery were throwing something in my father's face on TV that night."

Her eyes turn to slits. "Does this have something to do with Seducing Ivy?"

I can't help it. I admit, "Yeah, it does."

She stares out the window briefly and then turns back to me. "So your dad never had any heart issues, and he just dropped dead of a heart attack watching them?"

It sounds ridiculous coming from her. So I clarify. "No. He had heart issues for a long time."

"Soooo...he had previous issues?" she asks.

The conversation I had with Dax the other day fills my mind.

Maybe he's right.

No, he's not. He was trying to shift the blame off of himself.

Lilly tilts her head. "Ivy, what kind of heart problems did your dad experience?"

"He had several heart attacks over the last fifteen years. The last one was his seventh."

She gapes at me, then says, "Oh, wow. That's tough."

"Yeah."

"Well, I'm sorry to hear that. Are you sure it's Dax's fault though? That's a pretty big accusation to put on him."

I finish my glass of champagne and rise. "I don't know what to believe anymore. Coming back here, it's..." I look around the room and then stare at the ceiling.

"We're back in toxic city," she finishes for me.

I look at her. "Exactly."

"Well, life is what we make it, and sometimes things aren't always as they seem. I think you and I, of all people, know that, right?" she states.

I don't answer for a minute, then agree, "Yeah, you're right."

She shrugs. "Okay, well, maybe give Dax some leeway. After the video was released, he changed, just so you know."

"So he says," I mutter.

"He did," she insists.

"How?"

Lilly licks her lips and studies me. She finally says, "Dax was a wreck when you left. He stopped associating with Bobby. They were no longer friends, and it was very clear. His hatred for Avery came out at full throttle. He became a hermit and kept to himself."

"Really?" I bite my lip, thinking about Dax all by himself.

"Yes."

A moment passes and I ask, "Do you think Avery or Bobby released the video at Clifton?"

"Avery, definitely," she answers.

"Why do you think it's her and not Bobby?"

She snorts. "Bobby wanted to hold the video footage over my father's head. When it got released, he no longer could."

I gape at her.

She refills her champagne. "Don't look so shocked. We're talking about Bobby Winston."

I take a sip of my drink, asking, "How do you know he wanted to do that?"

"Avery blamed Bobby. Dax went off on him for releasing it. He reminded him that they wanted to use it to extort my father."

My pulse increases. "Dax was in on Bobby's plan?"

She winces. "Sorry. But yes, he was at the time."

Anger fills me.

"Don't look so pissed. In the end, Dax lost. I think he paid for it," she declares.

"How did he pay for it?"

She rolls her eyes. "By losing you, silly."

I can't even speak.

She adds, "He was the first man I'd ever seen with a broken heart, and it made me never want to see another one again."

Dax 18

I CAN'T HELP YOU

Avery seethes, narrowing her eyes further. "You know this hurts Carrington Enterprises. So the company needs to pay for my attorney and make this disappear."

I grunt. "Carrington Enterprises isn't paying for any of your legal fees. You made your own bed. You can sleep in it."

Her glare intensifies as she points at me. "If I go down, you're going down too, Dax. You are."

"Yeah, how's that?" I question arrogantly. My sister has always been smart and cunning, but she forgot that I taught her how to be that way. If she thinks I didn't dot my i's and cross my t's before putting everything in motion, she's wrong.

"You will. I'll make sure of it," she threatens.

I lean across the desk. "How are you going to do that, Avery? You have no proof I've done anything wrong. It's only you who's done despicable things."

"Don't sit on your high horse, dear brother! You've done just as horrible things as I have," she snarls.

Some of that's true, but she's crossed the line way further than I ever did. It doesn't make the things I did while playing the game right, but I'm not going to pretend like what I've done even comes close to what she's participated in.

I taunt, "I wonder what color the prison uniforms are nowadays."

The color in her face drains. She squeezes her eyes shut. "Dax, please. This has gotten out of control. We haven't always gotten along, but I'm your sister."

"Sorry, I can't do anything for you."

Her expression morphs back to one of rage. She hurls, "If Avery Carrington Scents goes down, it'll also take Carrington Enterprises with it."

I chuckle, and my amusement grows.

She snaps, "There's nothing funny about what I said."

I stop laughing. "No?" I arch my eyebrows. "I think it's funny you think that your company, the one you wanted under my brand, even matters."

She huffs. "Of course it matters. It's under Carrington Enterprises, so the company has to take care of my legal fees," she declares.

Once again, I can't help it, and my lips curl into a smile.

"It won't be funny when you lose billions," she spouts.

"I'm not losing any money, Avery. By the way, you're no longer part of your company."

She freezes then slowly shakes her head.

It's priceless. I wish I could take a video so I could put it on my TV to watch every day.

She asserts, "I don't know what you're talking about, but I will always be part of Avery Carrington Scents. There is no company without me."

Giddiness fills me. I open my desk drawer and pull out a file. I toss it in front of her, open it, and put a pen next to the first sticker that says "Sign here." I add, "You can either do this willingly or unwillingly. It doesn't matter. Either way, you don't belong with Avery Carrington Scents or Carrington Enterprises, so you might as well sign it over to me now. I'll put out a PR statement that you voluntarily resigned."

"You wish," she seethes.

I shrug. "Okay, that's fine. I'll take matters into my own hands."

"Meaning what?" she questions.

I grin at her. "You'll see."

Tense silence fills the air, with the flush of anger growing more on her cheeks. She turns away, and I press the pads of my fingers together, leaning back in my chair, enjoying this more than I ever thought I would.

She turns back to me and gives me the expression she's perfected over the years. It's the one where everyone's supposed to be sucked in and feel sorry for her. Her voice turns sweet. "Dax, we used to be friends. Remember when we played the first game together on that Rachel chick? You told me exactly how to make her cry, and she did."

"So what?"

"Please, you need to help me. And we need more money put into the company. There are orders to fill. We can't do that without cash, and you know it."

"So let the orders go unfulfilled."

"It's hundreds of millions of dollars' worth. Are you crazy?" she shouts.

I pin my gaze on hers. "Have you not learned anything by now, Avery?"

She doesn't say anything.

I let the silence settle between us for a bit. Then I add, "I don't care about your company as long as you're a part of it. I'm not giving it another cent."

"You stole my money! You had no right to that!"

"It's the corporation's money. And if you don't have enough for operations, then put more in," I tell her again, which is the same answer I always give her even though she'll soon be removed.

"You know all my money went to fund part of a retainer with my legal team, and even that's not enough. I need that money," she reiterates.

I've never seen my sister in this position, but it serves her right. I repeat, "Sorry, no can do."

She rises, puts her hands on my desk, and comes a foot from my face, threatening, "I'm warning you, Dax. You don't get to fuck me over like this. If you don't put an end to this, everything you've ever done will come to light."

"What do you think I'm scared of having come out, Avery?" I challenge.

Her lip quivers. She stares at me, her eyes red. The smell of stale alcohol oozes off her.

I add, "You might want to lay off the booze. It's only nine o'clock in the morning."

"Argh," she screams, shaking her head, and threatens one last time, "I will take you down."

"I welcome the opportunity to fight you."

"Dax, what the fuck's going on?" Cooper interjects as the door flies open.

I glance over at it.

He barges in, his blond hair a mess, wearing his designer clothes. He stomps across the room, a scowl on his face.

Avery spins toward him. "Cooper." She runs over to him and embraces him.

He returns her hug.

Avery begs, "Cooper, you have to get Dax to stop this."

"Avery, go outside. I'll meet you in a few minutes," he orders.

I chuckle inside. I don't know what my little brother thinks he's going to say to me that'll convince me to help Avery, but there's nothing he can do. And his days are numbered too. The more he tries, the more it'll accelerate his downward spiral.

I'll make sure of it.

Avery gives him her puppy dog look. "Cooper, this isn't good."

He nods with a solemn face. "Yes, I know. Now, go outside."

She reluctantly lets go of him, gives me a nasty glare, then stomps out of the office and slams the door.

Cooper turns his attention to me, shaking his head. "You really did it now, Dax."

"Yeah? What's that?"

"I know you released that video."

"Says who?" I ask, playing stupid just like I did with Bramwell.

Cooper comes over and sits, leaning back in the chair, similar to my position. We have many of the same physical features, but that's where it ends.

"Where did you just fly in from? France? Monte Carlo? Prague?"

He grinds his molars, staring at me.

"I have a lot of important things to do, so whatever it is you want to say, you might as well say it and get out of here."

He orders, "Stop this now, Dax."

"Next topic," I state.

Rage builds in his face. He announces, "I'm getting harassed on social media. I got black-listed at a club. This has to stop. Get your PR company to turn this around. Get Avery the legal representation she needs. And give her money back to her."

I laugh so hard, I tear up.

He slams his hand on the desk. "This isn't funny, Dax."

I stop laughing and give him a cocky look. "My PR company isn't doing shit for Avery. She can get her own legal representation because what she did was horrible."

"She's not getting away with it. You've ruined her reputation," Cooper declares.

I gape at him. "Jesus, you're just as sick as she is."

"Why? Because I don't want my sister in prison?"

"What about all the people she raped, whose lives she ruined? It's okay for them to go through life like that, as long as she's okay?" I question.

"She didn't rape them."

Rage fills me. "She drugged them. And she had others rape them! She deserves to burn in Hell!" I shout.

He clenches his jaw, glaring at me.

"The fact that you're sitting here and thinking it's okay for her to get away with what she's done only proves one thing."

"What's that?"

I accuse, "I'm sure you've added Trance to someone's drink or been part of their warped games."

"Shut up," he seethes.

"If there's nothing else you need to say, then get the fuck out of my office."

"Give her her money back, Dax," he orders.

I lose it and raise my voice. "That money belongs to Carrington Enterprises. Everything about her company is because of what Carrington Enterprises has given her or created. She didn't earn any of her money. Just like you didn't earn any of yours."

He scoffs. "Are we starting this again? Somehow, it's okay you got a trust fund, but it's not okay that we did?"

I snort, warning, "Go back to your life wherever it is, Cooper. It's not here, I assure you."

His eyes turn to slits. "Well, I would, but I can't. As I stated, I can't go on social media without being harassed or threatened. I can't get into any clubs."

"Oh, poor Cooper. You want to cry about it?" I taunt.

"You fucking bastard," he snarls.

"Do you think I give a shit about your social media?"

He declares, "I have sponsors. I'm an important influencer."

I groan and shake my head. "Whatever, Cooper. You go do you as long as you can."

"I can't do me when this is going on. When I can't get into a club—"

"Do you think I give a shit about your party schedule?" I blurt out.

He rises and slams his hand on my desk again. "It is important, Dax. It's part of my sponsorships."

"I don't care," I yell, trying to get through to him that I really don't give a fuck. All he's done is live off trust money. His sponsorships promote his lifestyle, but the money isn't enough for him to not run through his trust fund faster than he should. And that money should have lasted him, his kids, grandkids, and great-grandkids for the rest of their lives. It's irresponsible, and I'm tired of all my family members being so irresponsible in so many different ways.

He declares, "She's our sister. This is the lowest you've ever gone, Dax. But it's not too late to stop it and turn it around. Do the right thing."

I rise over this conversation. "I did do the right thing. I stopped helping Avery a long time ago. You should have too, along with Bobby. And I always wonder why you decided to get into bed with him. I warned you not to."

Cooper stands straighter and crosses his arms. "Ah, so that's what this is all about. You're still jealous that I'm better friends with Bobby than you are."

I huff. "I told you you could have him. He isn't a friend. He's just using you the way he uses everybody."

"Bullshit," Cooper claims.

"What does he have you doing nowadays? Are you going to be in the next video?"

My brother's expression changes, and I realize what I said affects him.

I taunt, "Ah, I see I hit the nail on the head, didn't I?" I shake my head in disgust. "So you're raping people too, being Bobby's little cohort in all of his games?"

My brother steps back and points at me. "You're making accusations that you shouldn't. Your days are numbered, Dax. Just be warned." He turns and starts to walk away.

I call after him, "Have fun going down with your sister."

He stops at the door and looks back at me. "You need to remember where your alliances lie. I can assure you it's not with that girl from West Virginia. We're your family, your blood. Bobby is more family than anyone as well. So clean up the mess you created and focus on somebody else."

My stomach turns, feeling sick that he can look at what Avery and Bobby have done and still try to protect them. I blurt out, "Guess that tells me everything I need to know."

"Yeah, what's that?" he questions.

"You stand here, fighting for them, okay with everything they've done. It tells me you're doing the same. I can only imagine the shit Bobby's gotten you into."

He grinds his molars and then shakes his head, muttering,

"You're not worth it." He opens the door and steps out, slamming it behind him.

I go to the window and stare out, looking across the lawn toward Ivy's cottage.

I'm trying to make things right, but I took a few steps backward with her. I didn't realize that people besides Avery, Bobby, and Dyer would be recognized. Now I know I've got a bigger hill to climb to get her back in my arms.

The cottage is too far away, and there are woods between us. It's why I picked it originally. I didn't want my father or anyone else in the house to be able to look out the window and see it. Now, it bothers me. I want to know what she's doing and can't.

I finally give up trying to see her, knowing I can't, and return to my desk. I text her.

Me: I want to see you.

Ivy: No, not right now.

Me: Okay, then later.

Ivy: I don't know, Dax.

Me: I'll pick you up at six for dinner.

Moments pass, and my heart beats faster. I check my desk, waiting for a response to come. It takes ten minutes for her to respond.

Me: Does seven work better?

More time passes, and I feel sick.

I have to get her back on my side.

> Me: Ivy, we need to talk.

> Ivy: Not today. I'm not having a good one.

Alarm bells ring in my ears.

> Me: What's wrong?

Dots appear on the screen, then disappear, then appear again, and disappear once more.

> Me: I'm coming over.

> Ivy: No, don't. I told you I'm not having a good day.

> Me: What does that mean?

She never answers. And then it hits me. It's been a couple of days since we had sex. She's probably jonesing for it.

My cock hardens thinking about our night together, but I also know that she has demons she's fighting.

> Me: I'm making a reservation at Finn's. It's the new seafood restaurant in town. I'll pick you up at six.

Ivy 31

PUNISH ME LATER!

Since I saw Lilly, my urges have gotten worse, to the point my body aches.

I should have done something with her.

I could have scratched my itch.

No, why am I thinking this way? I groan, pacing the cottage.

I need to get out of here.

I put on my shoes and step outside. I head toward the woods, jogging through the trees. The lake comes into view, and I pop out of the forest and stop in my tracks.

The barren lawn and lake make the boathouse loom larger. I pant hard, and sweat covers me despite a sharp chill in the air.

I stare at the building with the urges I'm trying to eliminate growing stronger.

The memories of what Dax and I did in there make everything worse. As much as I hate how the footage from that night got broadcast to all of Clifton University, it felt like we grew closer.

At least, it did that night.

I fell further into the world of Dax Carrington and all the things I never imagined I'd do. And the highs I experienced weren't only physical. His love wrapped around me, sinking deep into my soul until I could only foresee a future with him.

His love wasn't real.

He used me to destroy me.

I shake my head, remembering how Lilly made me promise her I wouldn't disregard Dax's current gestures to try and earn my forgiveness.

He killed my father.

Did he?

I lived in constant fear for over a decade, worrying about Dad's heart.

Is it fair to blame Dax?

I have to get past this either way, I tell myself. I tear my gaze off the boathouse and run back toward the cottage. During the entire trek through the woods, I continue the debate, never making any solid decisions.

The cottage appears, and I slow down, then walk the last few yards, deciding I feel better. I climb the porch, go inside, and shower. I dry my hair and then stare at the dresses in the closet, with a buzz in my veins growing stronger until I feel crazy again.

I should go to dinner with Dax. He can fuck me, and I'll get this out of my system until the next wave.

When will that be?

They're coming faster and stronger.

I need him.

I reach for a dress and set it on the bed.

Don't do this.

Be strong.

I force myself to return to the closet, select a pair of jeans, and tug them on. Then I pull a sweater over my head.

My phone dings.

What does he want now?

I'm not going with him, I reiterate, then reach for the phone and stare at the screen.

> Jaxon: I need to see you.

My stomach flips. I haven't thought about Jaxon since I got here. Part of me feels guilty. He's been a good friend to me. I should have checked in with him.

He doesn't know I'm here—in Connecticut or at the Carrington's estate. I told him I needed a few days to myself, then took some PTO days from work. He wouldn't approve of me being here. He would have tried to stop me. But once I saw the charity event online, I knew it was now or never.

I hate lying to Jaxon. My gut flips as I text him back.

> Me: I went out of town. I needed to get away for a bit to clear my head. I'll let you know when I'm back.

> Jaxon: I know where you're at.

My chest tightens, and the blood between my ears pounds harder. I stare at the screen.

How does he know I'm here?

> Jaxon: I need to meet you tonight. I'm in Greenwich.

The hairs on my neck rise.

Jaxon: Don't avoid me, Ivy.

Me: Where in town are you?

Jaxon: Downtown. There's a coffee shop a block from my hotel. It's called Steam. Do you know it?

I went to it often with Dax and some of the girls from the sorority. So I have good and bad memories of that place. It's no different from any other business in Greenwich. Everywhere I turn reminds me of how I thought I had everything, but it was only a farce.

Me: Yes, I know where it's at.

Jaxon: How quickly can you get here?

I glance at my watch. It's 5:45.

Me: I'll leave now.

I grab Dax's key fob and my purse off the table, then step outside. I get into his Porsche, drive through the estate, and out of the gates. I accelerate toward town.

My insides clench tighter. Jaxon's not going to be happy with me. I shouldn't have lied to him, but I feared he'd convince me not to pursue my plan.

I laugh out loud, thinking about the irony of how I thought I had a plan to get revenge on everyone, but in reality, it was too loosely put together. I still don't know how I'll ever do it, and wonder if I'm even capable.

The car goes over a pothole and tears me out of my thoughts. I rev the engine, and my blood buzzes again.

Not now.

Please, not now.

Maybe I could fuck Jaxon.

No. I have to stop doing that with him. He's not who I want.

I'm never going to have who I want. Dax will never truly love me.

By the time I arrive at the coffee shop, I feel sick. I'm guilty of so many things. There are too many people I've fucked who I shouldn't have, Jaxon included.

Now, I get to add lying to my list of sins. And of all the people in my life, Jaxon doesn't deserve dishonesty.

Who did I think I was, coming here and thinking I could hurt these people the same way they hurt me?

They're too twisted.

Dax is right. I'm not like them.

I am.

Ironically, Dax is taking them down for me. The thought makes my heart swell. It's just like when he used to protect me, but I remind myself he only did what he did to play the game. His protection never meant love. It was only a strategy to win whatever the sordid prize was between him and the others.

He hurt others in the process of revenge, including Matt.

What was the prize? What was so important to Dax that he had to win it?

I park the car a block away and get out. I put the key fob in my pocket and walk toward the coffee shop.

Not a lot has changed. The same stores are all still here, and they seem to be thriving. I pass the boutique where I lost my virginity and everyone in the store heard. A different security guard is outside the door, and I avoid looking at him. He doesn't know who I am, but it's like if I glance at him, he'll know my entire story. So I keep my head down, walking faster, and try to push the images of myself in the dressing room across Dyer's big screen out of my mind.

When I get to the coffee shop, I step inside and glance around.

Jaxon's seated at a table in the corner. There's no one else around him. He sees me and rises.

My nerves pick up. I walk over to him, and he embraces me. The mere feel of someone else's body against mine makes my core ache.

His hug gives me comfort. It's safe. But when I try to pull away, he keeps hugging me.

His voice is dark as he murmurs, "I've missed you, Ivy."

The urges I have, and the needs that never go away, spark hotter.

We could go into the bathroom.

I can't keep fucking Jaxon, I scold myself.

I push my hand against his chest, replying, "I missed you too."

He doesn't release me, glancing down like I'm his prey, stating, "You look good."

I squeeze my thighs together. "How did you know I was here?"

He studies me and then his eyes narrow. He releases me, admitting, "It didn't take a lot of thought, Ivy."

I arch my eyebrows. "No? Am I that predictable?"

He keeps his disapproving gaze on me. "Sit down," he orders and points to the chair.

I obey.

He takes a seat next to me and grabs my hand.

Tingles race up my arm, and I scold myself again, hating my demons I can never control.

"Are you okay?" he questions.

I can't help it and sarcastically laugh. "Am I okay? Yes. No. I don't know."

He studies me for a moment. "What have they done to you this time?" He strokes the back of my fingers.

I pull my hand away. His touch is too much. Anyone's touch, anywhere on my body, would be at this point. It's been too many days since someone's given me an orgasm.

I grip the edge of the table, trying to remind myself that Jaxon's my friend, and that's it. Just like Lilly had self-control and didn't push me the other day, I need to do the same with Jaxon because I see the look in his eye. He's jonesing as hard as I am.

His gaze darts down my chest and then back to my face. He slowly licks his lips.

A shiver runs down my spine. I lie. "They haven't done anything to me."

He tilts his head. "Then why are you here still?"

I breathe deeply and open my mouth, but nothing comes out.

He scolds, "This is dangerous and not the way to get your dad's patent back."

I sigh. "I told you I'm not dealing with lawyers. I know what I'm doing. I will get it back, but you don't use legal methods against the Carringtons."

He huffs. "It's a perfect time to hit them with my legal team. From what I can see on the news, their entire world's falling apart."

"That's because of Dax," I admit, then squeeze my eyes shut.

Why did I admit that to Jaxon?

He lowers his voice. He drags his fingers over my thigh, and tingles explode underneath it. "Ivy, what are you talking about?"

I open my eyes. "Nothing. I don't know what I'm talking about. Just forget I said that."

"No, I won't forget it, and stop lying to me. I've never known you to be a liar," he asserts.

My mouth is dry as dust. I swallow hard, declaring, "Things are complicated."

He grunts. "Of course they are. They're going to hurt you again."

Silence turns into thick tension.

He moves his hand higher up my thigh, and I shift in my seat.

"Jaxon, we can't do this," I mutter, but it's weak.

"Can't do what, Ivy?" he says, his thumb caressing my thigh an inch from my pussy.

Everything in me that needs what it needs lights up. But I fight it. "We can't." I put my hand on his to move it, but he flips his and traps my fingers.

He murmurs, "It's been too long for you, Ivy. Me too."

"I knew that's why you came."

"I didn't come here for that," he insists.

"Didn't you?" I accuse.

Guilt flashes in his eyes, but I also know he's my friend. I understand his demons as much as he does.

"No. I've been worried about you. And then when I saw that video... Jesus, Ivy, these people are horrible. It's way worse than I ever could have imagined. You don't belong anywhere near them."

I don't say anything. Part of me feels like he's right, but the other side still wants to be with Dax.

I'm fucked-up.

"Don't fall for him again," Jaxon warns.

"You don't know him," I say, realizing how stupid it sounds as it comes out of my mouth.

Jaxon's gaze darkens. He pins it on me. "Have you already slept with him?"

I turn my head, staring out the window. My heart beats so hard I feel like it'll explode out of my chest.

Jaxon leans close to my ear. "Whatever you've done, it's okay. Let's go back to my room." He puts his hand back on my thigh.

I take several breaths, fighting every part of me that wants to go fuck and forget about the world, even if it's for only a few minutes.

"Let's go," he repeats.

"We can't do this, Jaxon," I force out, meeting his gaze and moving his hand off my thigh.

He jerks his head backward, studying me.

My pulse creeps up higher and higher. "You're a really good friend, but you know we have to stop this."

"Just one more time, then we'll stop," he says.

I've heard it too many times. It's come out of my mouth. It's come out of his. Every time either of us say it, it's always a lie.

He adds, "I can't leave here without it. Please," he begs with desperation.

My insides quiver. My butterflies take off. My pussy clenches, wanting it, but I know it's the addiction.

I don't want Jaxon.

I want Dax.

Somehow, I find an untapped well of strength. I put my hand over his. "Jaxon, you know I love you as a friend. You've been such a good one to me, but we can't have sex anymore."

He leans closer to me. "That's what one of us always says. Maybe we should stop pretending we want that and admit what we are to each other."

I freeze and stutter, "Wh-what do you m-mean?"

He looks nervous. He licks his lips, confessing, "There's more than sex between us, and you know it."

I'm shocked at this. "Yes, friendship."

"It's more than that. Our connection's too strong, and we have what each other needs. I don't know why we've been fighting it, but we're more than friends."

"Yeah, we're fuck buddies," I state.

His face falls and he clenches his jaw.

Guilt and sympathy cause a pang in my chest. "I'm sorry. I didn't say that to upset you. But, Jaxon, you're just confused right now. How long has it been since you've had sex?"

"Since you left, but that's not why I'm here," he claims.

"Isn't it?"

"No. I love you, Ivy."

I gape at him, holding my breath.

"I do." He picks up my hand and kisses it. "I love you and your sexy body and that wet pussy of yours. It's time to come home with me."

I try to pull my hand from his, but he holds it too tight. "Jaxon, no."

He kisses it again, and more tingles explode under my skin, rushing down my spine.

Just this once.

That's what I always say, but there's always a next time.

It would feel so good.

No, I don't want him like that. It's just my addiction.

"Jaxon—"

"I need it, Ivy, and you need it too. You know you do."

I can't deny it. I do need it. I'm jonesing for a hit, even if it's not the high Dax gives me.

He puts his hand over my cheek. "Come on, Ivy, let's go to my hotel."

"She's not going anywhere with you," Dax barks.

My stomach dives. I glance up.

He curls his fists at his sides, his eyes dark with anger,

looming over us. He threatens, "I said to get your hands off her."

Jaxon scoots his chair back and rises, snarling, "It's you."

Dax scowls.

Jaxon says, "Don't worry, Ivy. I have this handled."

"Have it handled? You have what handled?" Dax questions.

Jaxon refocuses on him. "You. All you've done is destroy her life. You're never coming near her again."

Dax chuckles. "Is that what you think?"

"It's what I know. Come on, Ivy, let's go," Jaxon says, reaching down for me.

I shrug away from him. "No."

Jaxon's eyes widen. "What do you mean no? Come on, we're going."

"Don't go, Ivy," Dax orders.

I glance between the two of them, unsure what to do. I don't want to hurt Jaxon, but I don't want to leave Dax. As much as I hate myself for it, I have unfinished business with him. I'm not ready to part ways.

I haven't gotten my revenge.

It has nothing to do with revenge.

I love him.

No, I can't go there again.

"Ivy, now," Jaxon orders.

Dax reaches for his throat and lifts him up until he is on his tiptoes. "Don't ever talk to her like that again."

"Dax," I scream.

He doesn't take his eyes off Jaxon. Jaxon's cheeks turn red. He sputters.

"Dax, stop it," I order.

Dax glances at me. "He's not what you want, Ivy."

Guilt fills me, and I know Dax sees it on my face.

He turns back to Jaxon. "You have two seconds to get the fuck out of here." He releases him.

Jaxon grabs his throat, gasping.

"Jaxon, are you okay?" I ask, putting my hand on his back.

He recovers and looks at me, placing his hand on my arm, repeating, "Let's go, Ivy."

"I'm not going with you," I reiterate.

"You are."

"No, I'm not."

"Get your hand off her," Dax threatens again.

"Stay out of this," I warn him.

Jaxon takes his fist and slams it into Dax's face. His head jerks toward the wall.

"Jaxon, what the fuck?" I step between them.

Dax slowly glances back at Jaxon, with his hand on his cheek.

"Please. Don't," I beg Dax, afraid he'll retaliate.

Jaxon shakes his fist out, claiming, "We're leaving."

I put my hands in the air. "No. We. Aren't."

Dax steps closer to me. His face is already swelling. He points at Jaxon. "I'm giving you a final warning."

Jaxon steps closer.

I push at his chest, ordering, "Go."

He freezes, looking at me. "You don't mean that."

My eyes well up. I swallow hard, stating, "I do."

"You don't. You're coming with me," he insists.

A burst of anger blows through me. I'm tired of everyone telling me what to do. This is my life, and I get to make my own choices. I fume, "Did you not hear a word I said earlier?"

A look of hurt overtakes his features.

I feel horrible. Jaxon's been a good friend to me, but I don't love him, and I don't think he loves me either. He's just jonesing. Still, he's never said anything like that to me before.

So I soften my tone when I say, "You don't mean what you said."

"I do," he insists.

"You don't, and I am not going with you. You need to leave."

"You heard her," Dax warns.

I spin to face him. "Shut up!"

He opens his mouth and then shuts it, grinding his molars.

I turn back toward Jaxon.

Dax slides his arm around my waist, tugging me into him.

My core dances with endorphins. I inhale sharply and can't push away from him.

Shock and disappointment fills his voice, "You don't know what you're doing, Ivy."

"Please just go," I plead.

He hesitates another moment, then turns and leaves.

Dax doesn't say anything as he leads me out of the coffee shop and to his Hennessey Venom F5. He pushes me against it, leaning in close. "What do you think you're doing, Ivy? Did you think you were going to get your fix from him?"

My lips quiver. I lift my chin and square my shoulders. "You have nothing to say about it."

His eyes narrow. He presses his body to mine and pins me with a hot look.

It's the one I could never resist—the one that's haunted my dreams.

He seethes, "Oh, but I do. And if you need to use someone, there's only one person you use. Me."

Dax 20

IT'S ALWAYS GOING TO BE ME

THE RIDE to the estate is quiet. I barely feel the sting in my face or the swelling. I'm too enraged. *How dare he come here.*

Would she have had sex with him?

My gut churns at the thought. I knew from the moment I first saw him on the PI report there was more than friendship between them. But now that I know for sure, my jealousy flares out of control.

I pull through the gate and race to the cottage. I park and get out.

Ivy follows. "You don't need to stay."

"Yes, I do. Besides, we're going to dinner."

"I didn't say I would. In fact, I remember telling you I was having a bad day," she claims.

I put my arm around her waist, guide her up the steps, then open the door to the cottage. I wait for her to go first.

She glares at me, spouting, "You don't have any right to make decisions for me."

"Step inside, Ivy," I order.

She doesn't move.

"Okay, we'll stand here all night. If you want to do this out here so all the employees on the estate can hear, then fine."

She caves, sighing and shaking her head. She brushes past me.

I follow, then shut and lock the door.

She turns to me. "You can go now."

"Why? So you can run off to him?"

She glares at me, but there's guilt on her face.

I step forward, my insides shaking, asking the question I shouldn't, unsure I want to hear the answer. "How badly did you want to sleep with him?"

Her expression doesn't change, but her lip quivers.

My jealousy expands, making me feel crazy. I close the distance between us.

She takes a step back.

I follow her until she's against the wall.

"Dax, don't touch me right now," she warns, then closes her eyes, taking ragged breaths.

I don't listen. I put my hands on her cheeks and push my forehead against hers. "Isn't this what you want? What you need? What you're searching for, chasing all the time?"

She takes shallow breaths.

"It's *me*, baby girl. I know it's me, and it's always been me. It's always going to be me. Just like the only thing I'm chasing is you."

"You don't understand," she says, her voice quivering, eyes squeezed shut tight.

"No? Tell me what I don't understand."

She shakes her head, and a tear falls down her cheek.

I swipe at it with my thumb. "Don't cry."

She opens her glistening blues, swirling with guilt, shame, fear, and the craving she can't eliminate. "Do you think I want to? That I enjoy crying all the time, being emotional, not having any control of it, just like everything else I feel in my body?"

"I know the desire I have for you—and the one you have for me—has nothing to do with Trance."

She scrunches her face, looking away. Her voice cracks when she quietly says, "I'm fucked-up, Dax."

I pull her chin back toward me. "You're not. And I promise you, things are going to get better."

Hope lights in her eyes, but then she scoffs. "How, Dax? How are they going to get better?"

"They will. I promise you."

"They won't. You should go," she says.

"Why? So you can go back to him?" I snarl, still upset that he ever touched her.

But I'm angry at myself. My actions and the people I hung around caused her addiction. And that's what led her into Jaxon's arms.

Her eyes turn to slits. "What if I was, Dax? What business is it of yours?"

My chest tightens. I insist, "You don't want to be with him. I know you don't want to be with him."

She huffs. "Do you know how many times I've been with him? So many, I can't count."

Jealousy pummels me, attacking me down to my bones. I stay silent, trying to take deep breaths to stay calm.

She pushes my chest. "Just leave."

"So you can go back to him?" I repeat.

"Stop asking me that."

I don't move. I press my lips against hers, mumbling, "You don't want him, Ivy. You want me."

"You're so full of yourself," she says.

"So you don't want me?" I push closer.

Her hands relax against my chest. She asks, "Why are you doing this to me?"

"Doing what?"

"You know what," she accuses.

"Trying to get you back as mine once and for all? Forever?" I question.

Another tear falls down her cheek. Her lips shake harder. She spouts, "It's just another one of your lies. And I'm so tired of those, Dax. I refuse to be your pawn anymore."

"You're not my pawn, baby girl," I declare.

She sniffles. "Sure, I'm not. Everyone's your pawn. Your own family members are."

I clench my jaw, grinding my molars, knowing I can't deny what she said about the others. All I can do is kiss her, so I close any space between us and slide my tongue against hers.

She resists momentarily, then utters, "This isn't fair."

I freeze, then retreat an inch from her face. "What's not fair?"

"You. Here. Doing this to me. You know I'm weak," she admits.

Guilt fills me, battling with my raging erection that's pushing against her stomach. I stay silent, fighting too many demons of my own because I want her so much.

Tension builds between us to the point it feels electric.

I order, "Tell me that you really do want me to go, and I will."

She stares at me and whispers, "Go."

"If you want me to go, you're going to have to tell me a

little more convincingly than that," I declare, not moving, my blood pumping hotter through my veins.

"Why?" she questions.

I turn the tables on her. "If I leave, are you going back to him?"

She doesn't say anything, but her struggle is written on her face.

I hate Bobby and Avery even more. Jaxon and Ivy have a relationship—a history I'm not a part of—and it's all because they laced her drinks with Trance.

I insist, "You know you don't want him."

"How do you know what I want?"

"You don't. You would have gone with him," I state.

"That doesn't mean anything," she claims.

"Doesn't it?" I challenge.

She glances down at my lips, breathing harder.

I stay still except for my heart beating hard against her chest.

She finally caves. She pushes her head forward and kisses me.

I kiss her back until we're both breathless, but then guilt bubbles within me, and I retreat. "I don't want to take advantage of you, Ivy."

"I need to have sex. You don't understand. It...it hurts," she admits.

My erection throbs against her stomach.

She grips my shirt. "Don't make me beg."

"I don't want to take advantage of you."

"It's you or him."

"It's not him. It's never going to be him," I remind her, determined that she'll never touch him again.

"Then fuck me."

I still don't move.

"Don't suddenly become moral on me, Dax!"

I continue to grapple about whether I should have sex with her or not. We both want it, but I want her to want me more than just because of the urges tormenting her.

Does she still love me after everything I've done, or does every cell in her body only want me due to the effects of Trance?

She pushes on my chest. "Fine. Have it your way. I'll go back to Jaxon."

I grab her wrists. "Tell me you'll never go to him again."

She squeezes her eyes shut.

I desperately demand, "Tell me you don't want him."

She opens her eyes. "You know I don't want him."

Relief washes over me. "Then tell me you'll never go to him again."

She opens her mouth and then shuts it.

"You just told me you don't want him," I remind her.

She shuts her eyes again, shaking her head, her voice cracking. "You don't understand what this is like. I can't control myself. When things get bad..." She opens her eyes. "I'm at the breaking point right now, Dax. And when I get here, I do things that I hate...things I'm ashamed of...things you'll never understand."

My heart hurts, feeling the depths of her pain. I insist, "I understand. It's okay."

She sarcastically laughs. "No, it's not okay."

"I didn't mean it like that."

"Either you fuck me, or I'm going to go fuck him. Make a choice. I-I can't have you near me and not fuck me when I'm like this," she confesses.

"Baby girl—"

She reaches between my legs, grabbing my cock. "I know you want me."

"It's not about wanting you. I always have and always will."

Her voice grows louder. "Then what do you want from me? Tell me, because I'm over this guessing game!"

I don't hesitate. "Tell me you'll never use him again. You can use me as much as you need, but no one else. You and me only."

Her eyes fill with more water. She shakes her head. "You're asking for the impossible."

"No, I'm not."

"You are!"

My chest tightens. "Why is it so impossible? Hmm? Tell me, gorgeous."

She closes her eyes as if in pain.

"Tell me."

The agony never leaves her face. She confesses, "Everything's been getting worse. I can't promise you what you want me to, nor do I owe you my vow. You had it ten years ago and broke it. And now..." She opens her eyes. "Now I physically don't know if I can ever give it to you again."

It feels like I'm breaking. It's a statement I hate, but I can't argue with her. She's right, and it hits me hard.

I did have her.

It's my fault we're so broken.

She's never going to forgive me.

She slides her arms around my neck, one hand in my hair, pushing me toward her. "Do what you do and fuck me, Dax." She slides her tongue back in my mouth, and I give in.

I'm in a world between Heaven and Hell where I'm fighting to do the right thing, but I've lost all sense of what that entails. All I know is I need her as much as she needs me. But my reasons are different. And I want hers to be the same as mine, but I wonder if they ever will be again.

"Use me. Make me feel how only you can," she murmurs.

"I love you. I want you to know how much I love you," I declare, my stomach flipping. I'm not used to saying it and meaning it like I do now.

Her face softens for a moment, then hardens. She warns, "I'm not into love, Dax. I'm your filthy whore who you created exactly to your liking. So let me use you and get what I need, or I'm going to him."

WHO GIVES YOU WHAT YOU NEED?

MY THREAT HANGS in the air, building the tension between us to the point my veins buzz out of control. There's one thing I need, and nothing else matters until I get it.

I need him to fuck me.

Dax studies me; he's frozen, grappling with his decision, confusing me. This isn't the man I'm used to seeing. The old Dax took what he wanted and didn't care about anything or anyone else.

I threaten, "You or him?"

His internal debate ends. He tugs my head toward his, consuming my lips and tongue, propelling me into a world I never want to leave.

It's our place. Our secret existence that could burn to the ground, and we'd still never leave. And while the flames burned around us, our bodies would stay merged as one, fighting to own the other, dying to steal every last inch of the other's soul.

He moves me toward the kitchen, unbuttoning my jeans and shoving them down, then propping me up on the counter.

My legs curl around his waist. I reach for his belt, unfasten it and his pants, and shove them over his hips.

A loud clang sounds as he slides into me with full force.

My back arches. I moan with relief, clinging to him tighter.

He tugs on my hair, kisses my neck, and demands, "Is this what you want, baby girl?"

"No! I'm your dirty slut."

He slows his thrusts, raises my shirt over my head, and releases my bra, yanking it off my arms. "Is that what your greedy, slutty pussy wants, baby girl?"

"Harder," I order.

"Tell me who you are," he demands, dipping to my chest and sucking my tit.

I whimper.

"Tell me," he insists.

"I'm your dirty whore. Oh fuck, Dax. I'm your dirty whore," I breathe, tugging his hair and then sliding my tongue back into his mouth.

He mumbles through our kisses, "My gorgeous girl has a greedy cunt."

Adrenaline races through my veins. My pussy spasms, trying to get every bit of his cock and never let it go.

He tugs my hair and looms over me, pounding into me hard, his cheeks red and skin glistening. "Who gives you what you need, my little whore?"

"You do," I answer, a shiver rolling through my body.

"Don't you dare come and not say it!" he barks.

My eyes roll, and I cry out, "I love it when you fuck my slutty pussy!"

"Jesus, Ivy," he grits through his teeth.

Endorphins attack me, relieving me of my demons, giving me the one thing I constantly crave.

But I want more.

Fire blazes between us, and sweat pops out on our skin. I beg, my eyes welling, "Don't come! Please, don't come."

He groans, fighting through it, and my high begins to ebb. He lowers me onto my back, pulling out of me and moving my feet to the edge of the counter. He discards his shirt and cages his body over mine.

The cold quartz barely registers. His warm skin intoxicates me too much.

His eyes darken, and he demands, "Say it."

My butterflies attack me. I blurt out, "Fuck my slutty ass!"

He shoves his cock inside me, groaning so loud it overpowers my moan until his lips are once again on mine.

Incoherent sounds fill the air, mixing with hot arousal. The room closes in on us.

Dax never wavers, thrusting mercilessly and clenching his jaw while pinning his gaze on mine. He grits, "Say it."

I blurt out, "I'm your dirty whore!"

"What else, baby girl?"

"I love it when you fuck my slutty ass!" More relief fills me.

He thrusts a few more times, and his erection swells, taunting me further. "You're my little slut, gorgeous! Only mine!"

"Yours," I agree, then reach for his head, desperately pressing my lips to his.

His cock slides in and out of me, and he grunts. "Time to come, my filthy whore!"

A tidal wave of endorphins drowns me, dragging me down into a state of euphoria.

"Fucking perfect little slut," he cries out, then groans. His body fills me to the point I see white light, and he buries his face into the curve of my neck, thrusting relentlessly.

Our climax shoots higher and then slows. Our chests press against each other, fighting for air.

We stay locked together, covered in sweat, our blood starting to cool.

He kisses my neck and mumbles, "I love you, Ivy."

My heart soars and then a tree branch hits the window, tearing me out of my happy place and returning to my angry one.

Don't fall for it again.

I push him away, sitting up. "Don't you dare, Dax Carrington!"

Shocked, he says, "Don't look at me like that when I tell you I love you."

I scoff. "I know what you mean when you say you love me."

He leers at me. "Yeah? What exactly do you think I mean?"

My lips quiver. "It means you get exactly what you need for the minute. I give you my heart, and you slice it with a razor!"

He runs his hand through his hair, insisting, "I love you, baby girl. As fucked-up as it is, I loved you back then. And I'm not making excuses, but I'm no longer that guy."

"Sure, you aren't," I say, jumping off the counter.

"I've changed. And I won't stop telling you I love you, because I do."

I laugh, then shake my head. "I don't think you know what love is, Dax."

More hurt fills his expression. He declares, "I do. I'm going to prove it to you. Everything I'm doing is for you."

"For me? Hurting Matt and those other victims was for me?"

"Yes!"

I gape at him.

He shakes his head and scrubs his face. "I'm sorry Matt got hurt. Truly, I am. But I'm taking everyone down for *you*."

I lift my chin and square my shoulders. "I can get revenge on my own."

"No, you can't."

"I can!"

"No matter what you tell yourself, you aren't like us, Ivy."

The hurt eighteen-year-old who wanted to fit in and was told by Dax she never would, resurfaces. I seethe, "You don't know who I am anymore!"

"I do! And it's impossible for you to punish them. No matter how you try, you won't. You're not a bad seed, gorgeous. You don't have sharp thorns ready to prick all of them until they're bleeding to death. The only person you can do that to is me."

I stare at him, my mouth open, chest tightening.

He softens his tone. "You can't honestly tell me you believe I never loved you."

I stay silent, my heart and brain fighting against the other.

He steps closer, placing his hand on my cheek. "You do believe me. Deep down, you know I love you."

The pain is too real. I sigh. "I don't know what to believe, Dax. I thought I did, but I don't."

"I love you, baby girl." He kisses me.

It's all too intense. I retreat from him and grab up my pants. I go into the bedroom, sit on the mattress, and put them on.

Dax enters the room. He orders, "Tell me you're never going to see him or anyone else again."

My fears are a match to my anger. I rise and jab him in the chest. "You don't get to demand anything from me!"

He grinds his molars.

I don't flinch, determined not to let him intimidate me like he used to.

He steps forward, reaches behind me, and fists my hair. He positions my head so I can't avoid him.

I inhale sharply, my butterflies waking back up.

"We're going to get to the point where you have no qualms telling me you'll only have me."

My lips quiver, and more tears fill my eyes.

He looms over me, asserting, "You will. Now, promise me."

I can't. No matter how much I want only him, I know my demons. So I confess through tears, "It's never going to happen. I'm a sex addict, and it's only getting worse. I can't control who I fuck."

He keeps his gaze pinned on mine, declaring, "I want you to take CogniShift. It'll stop it from progressing."

My pulse creeps up and I stiffen.

"Why are you nervous? It's okay. Trust me."

"Trust you? You think because you just fucked me, you earned my trust again?"

"You can read all my research with all the lab tests we've done. It's safe and works," he says, disappointment lacing his tone.

Silence falls between us for a beat.

"Take it," he urges.

I blurt out, "Why aren't you telling me to take NeuroZap? Doesn't that reverse the addiction instead of only stopping it from getting worse?"

He releases my head and sighs. "There's a possible side effect to it. I'm trying to eliminate it."

"What's the side effect?" I ask.

He hesitates.

"Tell me," I demand.

"If you take NeuroZap, you might never want to have sex again."

I burst out laughing. "That would be a cold day in Hell."

"I'm not kidding, Ivy."

My heart beats harder. "Well, maybe that'd be a good thing."

"I don't think that's what you want."

"You don't live with this addiction. So, how do you know what I want?"

Hurt flashes in his eyes, but then his face turns firm again. "Take CogniShift. I have it in my safe at the house. We can go get it now."

"No."

He furrows his eyebrows. "Why not?"

I shake my head. "You've already drugged me once."

"I didn't drug you."

"You gave me birth control."

"You agreed to it."

"I agreed to everything, didn't I? Every manipulative, sordid thing you wanted, I agreed to!"

He clenches his jaw.

The tension ratchets up, and the air in my lungs grows thicker.

He asks, "Are you claiming you wanted to have a kid when we were in college?"

The statement he made all those years ago about wanting tons of babies with me when we were ready fills my head. It causes more pain over what we'll never have.

Dax lowers his voice. "Ivy, I need some clarification."

"No, I didn't want to have a kid in college," I snarl.

The silence returns.

He breaks it, saying, "Come to the main house with me and take CogniShift."

"No."

"Why? It'll stop things from getting worse."

"I don't trust anyone anymore, especially you. The last thing I'm going to do is take another drug."

"Ivy—"

"It's time for you to go, Dax."

Pain explodes in his expression. He pleads, "Ivy, please. I love you. I wouldn't tell you to take it if I weren't sure it would work."

The agony of the past is too fresh. I hurl it all at him, pointing toward the door, announcing, "No, Dax. There's no love between us. I've used you. If anyone should understand what that's like, it's you. I'm nothing but your dirty whore who got you off. Don't let the door hit your ass on the way out."

Ivy 22

IT'LL NEVER BE RIGHT BETWEEN US

All night, I've debated if I should take CogniShift or NeuroZap. If NeuroZap truly eliminates my addiction, even if I never have sex again, maybe I'm better off.

What would it be like to never want sex again?

I don't know what to do, but I also don't like the idea of taking another drug. It's a drug's fault that I ended up in this situation in the first place.

Yet, every day, my urges get worse. And I hated seeing how badly Dax wanted me to tell him I wouldn't sleep with anyone else. He doesn't have a right to ask me that. But even if I wanted to, I couldn't promise him. I know myself.

There's a knock on the door.

I answer it.

Kristen beams at me. "Good morning, Ivy."

"Hey, Kristen. How are you?"

"I'm fine." She holds out an envelope. "Dax wanted me to drop this off to you. He said it's important."

I glance at it. "What is it?"

She shrugs. "Your guess is as good as mine. I don't open his envelopes." She winks.

I laugh. "Of course you don't. Thanks, Kristen." I take it from her.

"No problem. If you need anything, you know how to reach me."

"Thank you," I repeat, and shut the door. I go over to the table, sit down, and put the envelope on it, staring at it with my pulse quickening.

What's inside?

Why is it so thick?

I'm almost scared to open it, but my curiosity has the best of me. So I pick up the yellow envelope, unclasp the gold metal toggles, then slide out a three-inch stack of paperwork.

There's a note on top. The letterhead reads Dax Carrington, and his handwriting is below it.

Ivy,

Here's all the research on CogniShift and also NeuroZap. I've highlighted important things. I assume there are words you won't understand. I didn't, so I left my notes on those pages.

Craig Pholer is the head scientist of our research and development department at Hybrid Pharmaceuticals. He's the best of the best and developed the drugs in addition to TimeMarker. I've already spoken with him. He knows at any time, if you call, he's to take it. Or if you want to meet with him, he'll sit down with you.

Please consider taking CogniShift. I don't think NeuroZap's for you until the side effects are eliminated. I don't think those are the consequences you're truly looking for.

I glance at the stack of paperwork and Craig Pohler's card, then back at the note.

I'm also giving you Vivian Armando's card. She's a PTSD and rape trauma therapist. She's worked with other victims of Trance. She's also the best of the best, and she's expecting your call as well.

My gut dives.

He told other people about me?

I stare at a black card with the name Vivian Armando embossed on it in gold, along with PTSD and rape trauma therapist underneath. There's also a bunch of credentials behind her name.

It's the first time I've seen the word rape since I found out I was drugged. My stomach turns. Shame fills me. I stare at the card for several minutes and then toss it across the table.

I turn back to the letter.

I love you. I always have. I always will. And I'll spend the rest of my life proving it to you if need be. I'm here when you need me. No matter what you want. Because all I want is you, Ivy.
You're all I've ever wanted.
I promise you, things will get better.
I love you,
Dax

My eyes fill with tears again, and I curse him. I'd give anything to have one day where I don't cry.

I blink hard and glance at the thick stack of paperwork in front of me. *Confidential* is stamped across it.

I find the courage to read it, but Dax is right. There are a lot of words and terms I don't understand. I couldn't even pronounce them if I tried.

As I go through some of the paperwork, I refer to the sticky notes in Dax's handwriting where he's explaining what certain things mean, and my heart soars.

He does care about me.

I shouldn't be thinking about Dax caring about me. It's dangerous.

I should. He's trying.

No, it'll never be right between us, I tell myself.

I'm lost in my thoughts again when my phone beeps. I go to the counter, pick it up, and my gut dives.

Jaxon: I need to see you.

My nerves pick up. I think about what to reply.

> Me: I don't think that's a good idea.

> Jaxon: I won't try to have sex with you, I promise. But we need to talk.

> Me: Did you have sex last night?

A few minutes pass.

> Jaxon: No.

> Me: Then you're still jonesing for it.

> Jaxon: We need to talk. I'll leave today, but not until we talk.

> Me: Why don't you go to a club? Or find someone online? I know it's what you need, so why don't you do it? I'm not going to change my mind.

He calls.

I sigh and reluctantly answer. "Hey."

His voice sounds desperate. "Ivy, I have to see you. I'm at the Harbor Inn. Please come. I'm in room 428."

"Jaxon, I can't."

"You can. Just come over. It'll be like it always has been between us. I'm sorry I said that about loving you. I won't do it again, I promise," he declares.

I'm relieved at hearing that. "Well, that's good because that was some crazy talk yesterday."

"Yes, it was, and I'm sorry. But, Ivy, I need you. You know what I'm going through."

I feel a pang of guilt, but I can't be Jaxon's go-to anymore. So I reply, "I know all too well what it's like, Jaxon. But you need someone else, not me. We can't do this anymore."

"Because of him?" he accuses.

I stay quiet, my heart beating faster.

"It is because of him, isn't it?" Jaxon pushes.

"Yes. I still have feelings for Dax."

Jaxon warns, "He's going to destroy you again."

"Maybe so, but I can't help it. I still love him," I confess.

"No, Ivy. You don't love him. You love what you think you had with him—what you've always wanted. He's just playing you again," he insists.

"He's not!" I interject, the words coming out of my mouth before I realize it.

Is it true? Do I no longer think that Dax is playing me?

Tense silence fills the line, and Jaxson begs, "Please, Ivy, just come over. We can talk about this."

"I can't."

"You can. I've never denied meeting you all the times you've needed me. Not once have I not been a good friend to you."

My guilt hits an all-time high. It's true. He's always been there for me.

"Please. I'm in room 428 at the Harbor Inn. Come now," he says and hangs up.

I put my phone down, staring out the window. My insides flip as I continue my guilt trip down memory lane.

Jaxon's been a good friend to me. There are times I've corrupted him. He tried so hard to abstain, but I pressured him until I got what I wanted. Now, I'm not being the same friend back to him.

I never had Dax around any of those times.

I need to at least talk to Jaxon. I can't leave him hanging like that, desperate.

I'll help him find another solution, I tell myself, then grab the keys and get in Dax's Porsche.

I take off, leaving the estate, driving slowly through town and attempting to figure out how I can convince Jaxon we can only be friends going forward. We can't have sex anymore, no matter how much either of us needs it.

What if I cave?

I won't. Dax and I had sex yesterday. It took the edge off. I'm stronger than I was when I met Jaxon at the cafe, I remind myself.

I pull up to the Harbor Inn, and the same valet who took the car when I met Lilly approaches me.

He grins. "You're back."

Nerves fill me. "How do you remember me?"

He points at the car. "This is a beauty. It doesn't come here every day, he declares.

"Oh." I glance back at the red Porsche, thinking about how much it looks like the whore-red lipstick and nail polish Dax loves me to wear. "I guess not."

"Nope." He starts writing a ticket. "Visiting again?"

"Yeah." I nod.

He hands me the green paper. "You know the drill."

"Thanks," I say, stepping away from the car.

I go inside, heading toward the elevator.

I pass the lobby desk and hear someone call my name.

I turn toward the voice.

Lilly chirps, "You're back! What are you here for?" Three designer suitcases and a garment bag sit next to her feet.

"Are you leaving?" I question.

She shrugs. "I woke up today and decided there's nothing keeping me here."

"No?"

"Nah."

"So you're going back to California?"

She shrugs again. "I'm not sure."

I arch my eyebrows. "Do you have a job, Lilly?"

She shakes her head. "No. My dad doesn't want me to work, so..."

I pin my eyebrows together, questioning, "No? Then why did he send you to Clifton University? What was the point of your education?"

She laughs. "So he can tell his voters his daughter got a college education."

"Oh, that's..." I pause, shaking my head. "Fucked-up."

She laughs, then rolls her eyes. "Another advantage of being a senator's daughter. Anyway, why are you here?"

My chest tightens. I glance at the people around us, then lower my voice. "My boss, Jaxon, is here."

Her eyes widen. "The one you told me about? Your only friend back home?"

I nod.

A suspicious yet devious expression lights up her face. She whispers, "Did you tell him to come visit you?"

I shake my head. "No."

"Then why's he here?" she asks.

I admit, "He's kind of jonesing."

Her lips twitch, and her eyebrow arches. "Really?"

"Yeah, really badly."

She cautiously suggests, "So... You're going to take care of him?"

"No, I can't," I blurt out, then look away.

Why am I feeling loyal to Dax?

Because he's who I want.

She puts her hand on my arm. "You can't because of Dax, can you?"

I meet her gaze again, admitting something I don't want to admit to myself. "No."

Her smile widens. "That's good, Ivy."

"Is it? I can't decide if it is or not," I admit.

She nods. "Yeah, it is. I told you, I really do think you and Dax have something."

"Something fucked-up," I toss out.

She giggles. "Maybe, but isn't everything fucked-up?"

I think about her statement. Maybe it's true.

She adds, "I don't know anyone who's in any relationship where something's not fucked-up."

"Really?"

"Do you?" she challenges.

I can't say I do, but I can't say I don't either. I don't know a lot of people in relationships. I've kept to myself, and the only people I really associate with are my sex addict friends, and that's mostly in our group sessions. And I know that's not normal life for most people.

"Well?" she pushes.

"No, I don't know anyone who isn't fucked-up."

She glances at her watch. "Let me have the front desk hold my bags. Maybe I can help you out."

"How?"

She gives me a look, and it hits me.

"Are you being serious right now?" I gape at her.

She leans into my ear. "I've not had sex since I got here. All I got to do that night was make out with Avery, and you know that wasn't fun with Ms. Drunky." She pulls her head back and gives me a bored look.

I stifle a laugh.

"Well, I mean, if Jaxon meets me, and he's okay with it, and I'm okay with it, then..." She shrugs and adds, "Maybe my bags will go into his room for a few more days. I feel a marathon coming on." She wiggles her eyebrows, beaming.

I laugh. "You're crazy, Lilly."

"Yep, I know it. So what do you think?"

I sigh. "I don't know. There are some things between Jaxon and me that we need to work out."

"Invite him down to the bar," she orders.

I hesitate.

"Do you think going to his room is a good idea?" She tilts her head.

"No, you're right. It's not."

"Text him to come to the bar."

I pick up my phone.

> Me: I'm here. Come to the bar.

> Jaxon: No, I gave you my room number. Come up to the room.

> Me: I'm not going to the room. Come to the bar.

> Jaxon: I want to talk in private.

I decide it's best to give him a heads-up.

> Me: Nobody's in the bar except my friend Lilly and me.

> Jaxon: Who's Lilly?

> Me: I'll fill you in when you meet us.

Several moments pass. I decide some transparency is needed.

> Me: Lilly's also a sex addict and jonesing as badly as you.

Silence follows.

Lilly asks, "What did he say?"

"He hasn't responded," I answer.

"I'm going to take my bags to the front desk," she states, and wheels her suitcases away.

Jaxon: Bring her to my room with you.

Me: Come down to the bar. I'm not going to your room. And that's the final decision.

Jaxon: You sound like you're on a game show now.

I smile. That's the Jaxon I know and love—but only as a friend.

Me: Glad your humor's back. Get your tight ass down to the bar.

Jaxon: Okay. I'll be there in a few.

Lilly returns. She links her arm through mine. "Bar's over here." She leads me into a dimly lit restaurant, and we grab two plush velvet seats at the bar.

I suggest, "Maybe I should talk to Jaxon first on my own."

"What's that going to do?" she questions.

"I don't know. Just... I mean, we've been through a lot."

She leans closer, giving me a knowing look. "He's jonesing. Do you really think he wants to talk right now?"

I contemplate her statement, deciding she's right.

She adds, "I'm jonesing too. So if you two really need to chatter, make it quick." She winks.

I laugh again.

"Ivy," Jaxon's voice calls out behind me.

I turn in my chair. "Hey."

He hugs me, and I hug him back. But this time, he only lingers a little bit. He pulls back and holds his hand out. "And you must be Lilly."

She ignores his hand and rises. She throws her arms around him. "I get a hug too."

He chuckles, returns her affection longer than he hugged me, and I hold in my laugh.

Is this really happening right now?

"Take a seat," I say, pointing to the one Lilly was in.

She takes the one next to it and pats the cushion. "Yeah, Jaxon, sit down."

He obeys.

She leans into him, dragging her finger over his forearm, cooing, "Tell me, Mr. Sexy. Has Ivy told you anything about me?"

Dax 23

MORAL CODE

MY OFFICE PHONE beeps and Michelle states, "Mr. Carrington, Richard Lyman Sr.'s office is on line two."

"Thanks," I reply and then pick up the phone. I hit the button and say in greeting, "Dick, where are we at?"

"You're good to go," he claims.

My adrenaline spikes. "You're sure? I don't have room for any mistakes on this," I remind him.

He grunts. "Since when do I make mistakes?"

I can't pinpoint any time he has, so I chuckle, adding, "That's why I pay you the big bucks."

He grunts. "That you do. I'll have my office send the bill over."

"I'm sure you will. Thanks." I hang up and get out of my chair. I walk over to the safe. I unlock it and pull out an accordion folder that's securely shut with an elastic string around it.

I relock the safe and set the folder on my desk, then pick up my phone.

> Me: We need to meet.

> Avery: Fuck off.

> Me: I've solidified something big with Avery Carrington Scents.

A few minutes pass. The dancing dots appear and disappear on the screen several times before a message finally comes across.

> Avery: Whatever you need to say, you can call or email me the details.

> Me: No, I can't. Now get your ass over here.

> Avery: Sorry, I'm at the spa.

I laugh out loud. Avery's running out of money and can't afford an attorney, yet she's at the spa. It's so very Avery of her.

Of course, she probably convinced some more-than-willing man to pay for her services.

> Me: All right, I'll come to you.

> Avery: Sorry, I'll be in my treatments. Maybe later we can talk.

My ass, we will.

I grab the package and leave my office.

Michelle asks, "Will you be back, Mr. Carrington?"

I shrug. "I'm not sure."

"What should I tell people when they call? Should I say you're out for the rest of the day or just busy?" she frets.

I huff. "Michelle, I've told you this. It doesn't matter if I'm here or not. I'm never available unless I tell you I'm available for somebody before they call. Do you understand?"

She nods. "Yes, Mr. Carrington," she says and then writes it down on her notepad for the eightieth time.

Jesus, she's an idiot.

I can't wait until my normal assistant is back. I offered Katrina a lot of money to return early from maternity leave, but she wouldn't budge.

But I'm not letting Michelle's stupidity steal my joy though. I step into the elevator and hold the envelope tight to me, whistling, feeling the giddiness that I've felt too often lately. I thought it was dead inside of me, but not anymore. Things are finally starting to turn around and go my way.

The elevator dings, and the doors open. I step out, nodding at security as I pass them.

My car is parked at the curb where it always is. I get in it, rev the engine, and take off.

The bumper-to-bumper traffic would normally irritate me, but not today. I've waited patiently for Dick's phone call and the confirmation I could deliver Avery another blow.

I pick up the phone and call Ivy. It rings three times.

She answers, "Hello?" There's a lot of noise in the background, as if she's in a restaurant.

My red flags go up. I question, "Where are you at?"

I hear a familiar giggle I can't quite place.

"I'm out," she replies.

"Who's with you?" I inquire.

"That's not your business," she declares.

My gut flips. "Don't play games with me, Ivy."

She groans. "You're so dramatic, Dax. I'm with Lilly."

Lilly.

The hairs on my neck rise. "What are you two doing?"

Ivy scoffs. "Not what you think we're doing."

I blow out a relieved breath. "Okay, so where are you at?"

"It's not your business. We can talk later tonight if you want. When I'm back."

It's a step forward for Ivy to permit me to see her, so I drop my inquisition for now. I state, "I'll pick you up at six, and we'll go out for dinner like we were supposed to the other night."

She hesitates, then says, "I don't know, Dax."

"Why not?" I ask, my chest tightening.

She lowers her voice. "I don't know. It sounds like a date."

"It is a date," I claim.

She inhales sharply.

"Ivy, let me take you to dinner, please," I beg, my giddiness completely zapping away.

"I don't know."

"Ivy, it's just dinner. You have to eat anyway, right?"

She caves. "Okay. I'll be ready by six."

My giddiness reignites.

"Great, baby girl, I'll see you then. And don't do anything with Lilly," I add.

She groans and hangs up.

My worries creep back in. I hate that I have to worry about her with other people, but I also know I quenched her urges last night. All I can do is hope it's enough for now.

She needs to take the drug.

Did she read over the information I told Kristen to deliver to her?

She has yet to reach out to Craig or Vivian.

I'll have to talk to her more about it at dinner.

I continue to the spa, fighting traffic. I pull up to the curb in the fire lane.

A young kid with zits on his face and a mohawk declares, "You can't park here."

"Fuck off," I say, and stroll past him, my happiness perking up again.

Avery is going to be livid.

I enter the building, going directly to the fourth floor, where the spa is located.

A woman behind the desk sees me as soon as I step out of the elevator. She bats her eyes at me, chirping, "Mr. Carrington, it's so good to see you."

I groan. She's always flirted with me, and I've always turned her down. She's the exact opposite of Ivy, so I wouldn't even consider her.

"I heard my sister is here," I state.

She nods and beams. "Yes, she's having the works today."

"Of course she is," I mutter.

"Um..." Her forehead furrows in confusion. "I don't see you on the schedule, but what service would you like today? We'll make sure we accommodate you, of course, Mr. Carrington," she quickly adds.

I hold up my hand. "I'm not here for a service. I need to meet with Avery."

She glances back at the schedule. "She's in her mud bath treatment right now."

"That's fine. Which room?"

Her eyes dart to the computer screen. "She's in room B on the east wing."

"Okay, thanks." I brush past her.

"Mr. Carrington, why don't we escort you back there?" she yells after me.

"No, that's fine. I know where I'm going," I call over my shoulder.

She relaxes and smiles. "Okay."

The last thing I need is an escort. I want Avery to be as shocked as possible.

I force myself not to whistle as I walk down the hall and find the east wing. I stroll through it and find room B.

I open the door, and a therapist I've never seen says, "Excuse me, this room's in use."

"Yeah, I know. Get out." I open the door wider.

"Dax!" Avery scolds.

The therapist frets, "Sir. You can't be in here."

"I'm Dax Carrington, and I told you to get out. Now, move."

Her eyes widen. She glances back at Avery.

"What the fuck, Dax? Get out of here," Avery protests.

"I told you I'd come to you. So that's fine, you can sit in your bath," I say, motioning toward the white tub full of mud that Avery's sunk into.

The therapist's eyes dart between us.

I open the door wider. "It's time for you to go."

She hesitates. "Um..."

"Go," I order again.

"No, stay," Avery argues.

"Go. Now," I warn.

"I said to stay," Avery states.

"Claire, it's okay. Step out," a woman's voice orders.

I turn my head. It's the manager, Celeste. I nod.

She smiles. "Mr. Carrington, it's good to see you." She refocuses on Claire and narrows her eyes, firmly repeating, "I said it's okay. Leave the room. Let them have their privacy."

"Thank you, Celeste," I say.

She steps closer. "No problem. I assume you'll keep your business quiet between you two so the other guests aren't bothered?" She smiles.

"You have my word," I assure her, but I don't mention I'm not responsible for my sister and her actions. Who knows what Avery is going to do when another bomb drops on her.

"Thank you, Mr. Carrington. As always, it's a pleasure to see you," Celeste declares.

"You too," I say, narrowing my gaze on the therapist who gapes at us.

"Now, Claire," Celeste firmly repeats.

Claire finally takes the hint and scuttles out of the room.

I shut the door and lean against it, crossing my arms.

Avery groans. "You're such a buzzkill."

"Well, be ready to have no buzz left at all," I taunt.

"Whatever you came here to say, get it over with, you traitor. If you can't tell, I'm busy."

I grab the chair and drag it across the room to the tub. I sit down, put my ankle over my knee, then press my fingertips together, staring at my sister.

She sits up straighter. She grabs two cucumbers on a plate next to the tub, puts them over her eyes, then sinks back into the tub. "On second thought, I've had enough of you. Get the fuck out of here."

I take the cucumbers off and toss them in the trash can several feet away, then wiggle my finger, chiding, "Uh-uh-uh. I haven't informed you of the latest developments with Avery Carrington Scents."

Avery's face turns beet red. She fumes, "I want my money, Dax. I'm not going to tell you again, or I'll—"

"You'll what?" I ask.

The question hangs in the air.

She snarls, "I know people."

"Yeah, so do I. What's your point?"

"You aren't going to get away with this," she warns.

"Away with what?"

"Everything."

I wave my hand in front of her. "Stop being so dramatic.

Now, I brought something for you." I tap the folder and set it on the table beside the bathtub.

She cautiously glances at it, asking, "What is it?"

"Well, when you need something for your reading enjoyment, feel free to go through it. But it's all the paperwork legally removing you from Avery Carrington Scents."

She sarcastically laughs. "I told you I'm not signing those. You'll never get me out of the company. It's my company, not yours!"

"Oh, how wrong you are, Avery."

She glares at me, insisting, "I'm not!"

"Don't worry. You don't have to sign any of them. I've taken care of all the legal details."

She freezes. Tension mounts.

I inhale a deep breath of lavender oil, feeling calmer than ever. I continue, "You've been removed from Avery Carrington Scents."

She huffs. "You can't just remove me. That's impossible."

"No, it's not. Once again, you didn't read the fine print anywhere," I point out.

Her eyes narrow further. "What fine print?"

I sit back in the chair, gloating, wishing once again I had a video of this moment. My lips twitch as I relay, "Well, all sorts of fine print."

"Like what?" she hisses.

I gladly state, "One example would be the fine print that said as a subsidiary, the CEO of Carrington Enterprises has full access to your funds."

"You stole my money! Give it back!" she demands, her voice rising.

"Shh! Respect your environment, dear sister," I taunt.

She tosses sharp daggers at me with a look.

I ask, "Have you ever read the bylaws for Carrington Enterprises?"

She glances at the paperwork, then back at me, then back at the paperwork.

I continue. "They state all sorts of rules in addition to the CEO of Carrington Enterprises having full control of the finances of any subsidiary."

"Spit out whatever you're trying to say, asshole," Avery spouts.

I wait a moment to piss her off further and add, "The CEO has the authority to override any CEO of a subsidiary under the corporation."

She swallows hard. "You're not getting away with stealing my money. And I'm not stepping down from the company."

I grin. "Ah, but that's the beauty of it, Avery. You don't even have to step down. You've been removed."

"You can't remove me, Dax. I'm Avery Carrington of Avery Carrington Scents. Do you not get this, or is your brain too thick to comprehend it?"

I chuckle. "See, that's where you're wrong again. It doesn't matter if your name is part of the company. Carrington Enterprises' bylaws have a moral code, and you violated it."

She jerks her head back. "Moral code?" She starts to laugh uncontrollably.

"I'm glad you find this funny. I thought you'd be taking it a little differently," I admit.

She stops laughing. "If there's a moral code in Carrington Enterprises, I can guarantee that you've violated it a thousand times over. So that's fine, I'll have you removed."

"Ah, but you can't. You've been caught on video for the whole world to see, doing things that are"—I pause a quick moment for a dramatic effect—"illegal. Things that will put you in jail."

"I'm not going to jail!" she claims.

"Sure, you aren't."

"I'm not!"

"Regardless, you've created a bad PR problem for your company, which is bad for Carrington Enterprises. Never mind what you've done is completely immoral. So, Carrington Enterprises had no option but to say goodbye to you. So bye-bye." I wave at her.

She shakes her head, pointing at me. "That's bullshit, Dax. You're lying."

I tap the envelope. "No, I'm not. It's all in here. Read it when you want, but it's all in here, and you no longer have anything to do with the company."

Her eyes widen. She sits up in the tub. "You're not going to do this to me, Dax."

"I didn't do it to you, Avery. You did it to yourself," I point out.

"You're not taking my company from me. And I want my money back!" she shouts.

I put my hands on both sides of the tub and lean toward her. "You're never getting that money back, and you never again will have anything to do with Carrington Enterprises or Seducing Ivy."

"We'll see about that!" she spouts.

"Grandpa was right. He knew you wouldn't be able to run the corporation. He had the wisdom to foresee that all you would do is run it into the ground. This is just another example of your incompetence," I say, rubbing it in.

Her face turns redder. She takes her hand and slings mud at me. It hits my face and drips down.

I wipe it off, laughing. "Sling all the mud you want at me, Avery. It'll never match the mud you've slung at yourself."

"You bastard!" she hurls.

I rise and go to the sink. I wash my face and hands and then glance in the mirror. I take my suit jacket off and start to take off my tie.

Avery calls out, "This isn't over, Dax! I'll get you back. If it's the last thing I do, I will get you back!"

I toss my tie in the garbage and unbutton my shirt, replying, "Think what you want. You can stew on it while you're in jail. But there's one more thing you should know." I take off my shirt and toss it in the trash next to my tie.

She stays quiet.

I pick up my suit jacket, button it over my undershirt, then look in the mirror to ensure I don't have any more mud anywhere.

When I'm satisfied, I spin back to face her and lean against the counter. I drop the final bomb. "You no longer are welcome in the house or on the estate."

"You can't do that either," she asserts.

"Ah, but I can. Jeez, Avery, you went to school and spent all that time learning to read. You really should have read the stipulations of our trusts in detail."

"I did read the trust in detail," she says through clenched teeth.

"Did you?"

"I have it memorized," she claims.

"Good. So do I. Clause 15, Part B." I stare at her and cross my arms, unable to help the grin widening on my face.

She thinks about it briefly, and the color drains from her face.

It's a priceless scenario, another one I wish I could capture forever.

"That's right, Avery. Any Carrington who ends up in jail is no longer welcome on the estate."

"I'm not incarcerated," she claims.

"Ah. But you will be, won't you?"

"No, I won't. And charges against me don't mean you get to kick me off the estate."

"Ah, but you're forgetting about Clause 15, Article F. I believe you violated it yesterday when you met with your attorney?"

She stills, and her cheeks take on a green tinge. Her lips tremble. She barely gets out, "Dax."

"Nope, it's over, Avery. Your shit's packed up. You can text me where you want me to send it," I assert.

"You can't do this!"

I insist, "I can. The trust clearly states anyone whose trust dips below the five million dollar mark is no longer welcome on the estate. I believe your last five million is with your attorney for your retainer fee?"

"Dax, you can't do this!" she repeats.

"Oh, but I didn't. You did. And you're over, dear sister."

"You can't do this!" she shrieks.

"Shoot me a text. You're lucky you're getting your shit," I say.

"Dax, you fucking bastard," she screams as I open the door, step out, and softly close it behind me, feeling like a million bucks.

Avery is going down. Piece by piece, her world's crashing around her, and I'll do everything I can to ensure nothing deters it.

Two down, one to go.

Bobby better watch out because I'm coming for him next.

Ivy 24

THE TIMELINE

THE DOORBELL RINGS. Kristen arrives with another envelope as thick as the last one.

"What's this?" I question.

She smiles wider, answering, "Once again, I don't know, but Dax wants you to have it."

"Oh, right," I say, taking it from her.

"Do you need anything?" she questions.

"No, I'm good, Kristen. Thank you."

"Sure." She nods and heads back to the main house.

I shut the door and stare at the envelope, muttering, "What is this?"

I take a deep breath and go to the table. I sit down, open it, and pull out a stack of papers.

There's a note from Dax on top of the pile, once again written on his personal stationery.

Ivy,

Please don't be mad at me, but I have to prove to you I didn't kill your father. I know we'll never get our forever together if I don't. Here is my full disclosure since I never want to lie to you again, and I promise you I never will going forward.

I had my investigator obtain your dad's medical records and the coroner's report. Here are the relevant files. The complete medical history is in my safe, and it's yours if you ever want to see it. I've highlighted the parts I hope will prove to you that I didn't kill him. While I don't claim stealing his patent and turning it into something profitable was ethically right, I maintain that I did it for you. I did what he refused to do, and I promise you, every development with Seducing Ivy has been for you. You'll soon see, I promise you.

Love always,
Dax

My hands shake, and tears well in my eyes. Shocked, I stare at the paperwork until I finally lift Dax's letter from the thick pile.

My father's name is all over the pages, and I slowly decipher the information. My eyes dart to phrases his doctor had written repeatedly and Dax highlighted.

•Patient still won't take his medication.

•Patient took medication for two weeks and stopped.

•Patient on medication for a month and stopped.

•Patient repeatedly won't take his medication.

•Patient still eating fried foods daily.

•Patient refusing to exercise.

•The patient claims medication is a way for the drug companies to get money, and he doesn't need it.

A timeline of my father's heart attacks weaves throughout the timeline of doctor notes. It's not as detailed as I'm sure the rest of the records Dax has in his safe are, but it's enough to hit me hard.

Why didn't my dad take his medication?

He lied to me.

Rage fills me. The only person besides Jaxon I trusted for years was my father. He guilted me for any lie I ever told him, claiming the devil is behind lies. Yet he repeatedly did the thing he shamed me for.

I blow my nose, then sniffle. I turn the page, and my stomach flips faster. I read it several times with horror sinking deeper every go around.

•Patient was given option to take home samples and refuses, claiming he isn't a charity case.

•Warned the patient again that his chances of having a catastrophic heart attack rise to 95% when not on medication.

My lips tremble harder, and my tears fall until everything's blurry.

Why was my father so cheap and stubborn? He had the money in his account. He had prescription insurance. When he did fill his heart medication, it was only thirty dollars a month. I remember because I picked it up a few times for him after he had his last heart attack before the one that killed him.

How could he have been so stubborn and foolish?

I pick up the coroner's report and read the highlighted marks.

•*Long-term coronary disease.*

•*No medication detected in bloodstream.*

The facts stare at me until they're too blurry to read.

He wasn't on any pills when he died.

Dax is right. He couldn't have caused my father's death. My father contributed to his own death. Sure, he might not have liked seeing Avery and Dax on TV, but he played Russian roulette with his health.

If he had been taking his medication, would he have had any of those heart attacks over the years?

I grapple with the what-ifs and facts. My grief mixes with anger. The blame I set at Dax's feet now moves toward my father.

One question never stops nagging me: What if...

Numbness sets in. I stare at the pages, unable to comprehend how my father could be so selfish.

A bird flies into the window, tearing me out of my dark thoughts, and something occurs me. I can't keep living like this. I can't keep wallowing in this sense of emotional grief day by day.

Determined to change things, I go into my bathroom and toss water over my face.

I stare at my reflection and order, "No more crying, Ivy. Enough's enough."

The doorbell rings again.

I pat my face dry and exit the bathroom. I go to the front door and open it.

Kristen stands there beaming, holding too many shopping bags in her hands to count at first glance.

Three women stand behind her, smiling just as wide.

Kristen chirps, "Surprise!"

"I, uh... W-what's going on?" I stutter.

A blonde woman pipes up, "We're here for your date."

My date.

I forgot about my date with Dax from the moment I sat down to read my father's medical records.

Kristen introduces the women. "This is Laura. She'll be doing your nails." She points to a brunette. "And Via is the makeup artist." Then she points to a redhead, announcing, "And Jackie's a hairstylist."

I admit, "I'm sorry, I'm confused."

Kristen answers, "Dax wanted to spoil you before your date. Are you going to let us in?"

"Oh, sorry." I step back and open the door wider.

They all shuffle in.

Kristen sets the shopping bags on the counter. The other women set their stuff on the table, filling it with items so nothing else will fit.

Overwhelmed and confused, I stare at everything. My phone beeps.

Lilly: Mr. Sexy doesn't disappoint.

I text her back.

Me: Glad you're getting along.

Lilly: He went down the road to get me a piece of pie I've been craving from Sugar Lover. He's so sweet, but I also told him he needs to feed me chocolate if we're going to go at it all night.

She sends three winky face emojis along with it.

Me: Jaxon's a good guy. That doesn't surprise me he went to get it for you.

Lilly: He fucks like a stallion.

My lips twitch.

Lilly: What are you up to?

Me: My house just got invaded.

My phone rings. I say to the others, "Excuse me. I'll be just a minute." I step into the bedroom and shut the door, answering, "Hey, Lilly."

She asks, "What do you mean your house got invaded?"

"I don't know. Kristen, one of the household staff, whom he assigned to me, showed up with a bunch of shopping bags and a team of professionals."

"What kind of professionals?"

"There's a manicurist, makeup artist, and hairstylist here. They said they're here to help me prepare for my date with Dax tonight."

"Ooh, date night with Dax! You didn't tell me about this," Lilly points out.

"Sorry. It all kind of happened quickly."

"Well, that's sweet of him. How fun," she offers.

I don't say anything.

She groans. "Ivy, stop pretending you don't want his gifts and the extra pampering. You're female, for goodness' sake. Go have fun."

I blurt out, "I don't want him to think he can buy me."

She scoffs. "Seriously? Come on. It's Dax Carrington. If he can't spoil you, he's just not going to be himself."

I ponder her statement and realize she's right; that's what Dax does.

He did it to trick me in the past.

As if Lilly can read my thoughts, she says, "He's doing it because he loves you. Now, go enjoy it. And tell me what's in those shopping bags, and send me a picture when you're all fancy!"

"Okay. You're right. Thanks!"

She adds, "But if I don't text back, you know why."

I laugh, and it feels good. "Gotcha."

"So, did you do anything earlier today while I was on the O train?" she questions.

I go quiet.

Concern fills Lilly's voice. "Did something bad happen?"

I admit to her what I haven't told anyone else yet. "I don't think Dax killed my father."

She cautiously asks, "Because..."

"He had a PI get my father's medical records and the coroner's report. He sent it to the cottage. I've been reading it all morning."

"That must've been hard for you," Lilly says sympathetically.

"Yeah, it was."

She lowers her voice. "What did you read that changed your mind about his death?"

I close my eyes and sit on the bed, shaking my head and releasing a stressed breath.

She waits for me to speak.

"My father didn't take his heart medication for years. He'd take it for a week or so and then stop. He told the doctor he wouldn't waste money on it. And I don't understand, Lilly. He had the money to pay for it. He had insurance. It was only thirty dollars a month."

She stays quiet.

"I'm sorry. I don't mean to sound angry toward you."

Gently, she says, "It's okay, Ivy. I didn't think you were mad at me. And you have a right to be upset, but at least you know the truth now. I think in your heart, you know Dax didn't kill him, right?"

I take another deep breath and slowly release it, finalizing my decision. "Yeah, he didn't kill him. My father was the reason his heart wasn't better."

"I really am sorry. Can I do anything for you?"

"No, just keep being my friend, okay? I don't really have any. Well, it's you and Jaxon, that's it. So, can you just keep being my friend?" I blurt out.

She laughs. "Don't be silly, Ivy. You're my friend as much as I'm yours, and I need you as much as you need me. So don't worry, we're going to stay friends, and we're not going to lose touch like last time. Okay?"

Her statement makes me happy. "Okay."

"Hey, Mr. Sexy just got back. I have to go, but enjoy Dax's gifts and your night, okay?"

"All right. I will."

"Tell me all about it tomorrow. Bye," she sings, then hangs up the phone.

I put my cell down and take a few minutes. Lilly's right, I need to enjoy my night.

My phone buzzes.

Lilly: Go open your gifts!!

I laugh, wondering how she knows I'm still sitting here.

Me: On it.

Curiosity gets me. The excitement I used to feel when Dax would give me gifts ignites inside me.

I leave the bedroom and step out into the other room.

"Ivy, are you going to open these boxes? I'm dying to see what's in them," Kristen says.

I laugh. "Sure."

I glance at the counter. She's taken all the boxes out of the bags. All of them are white with whore-red bows, and the same butterflies that took off when Dax gave me my first gift, flutter hard.

Kristen hands me a large box. "Here, open this."

I slowly pull the bow, trying to contain my excitement, and lift the lid. I gape.

"Holy crap," Laura exclaims.

I pull out a pair of whore-red leather boots. The heels have gold ivy leaves encrusted with diamonds on them. I touch the shaft, gaping. They're super soft. I finally declare, "Wow, these are beautiful."

"Yeah, they are," Kristen says and hands me another box.

I open it. There's a black satin minidress with a V-cut in the front, a low back that dips to right above where my ass would be, and long sleeves.

I hold it up and examine it. There's a built-in bra and a note in the box. I pull it out.

> Ivy,
> Don't wear panties.
> Love always,
> Dax

My butterflies go crazy. Via asks," What's the note say?"

"Nothing," I reply, refolding it and putting it in my pocket.

"Ooh, a little love note," she teases.

My face heats.

Jackie hands me another large box, ordering, "Open this."

I remove the bow and lid and pull out a soft-as-butter, black leather trench coat, matching gloves, and a whore-red cashmere scarf. There's another note in Dax's handwriting at the bottom.

Ivy,

It's going to be cold tonight. This will keep you warm when I'm not, but don't expect me to behave for long.

Love always,

Dax

My pussy clenches, and my cheeks grow hotter.

Laura exclaims, "Geez, I need a boyfriend like Dax Carrington."

Kristen hands me two jewelry boxes, and I might burst with excitement. I open the first box, and my endorphins spike higher.

A pair of oversized teardrop earrings, matching the color of my necklace, sits in the box. The whore-red, gold, and diamonds create an abstract design over a teardrop.

"They match your necklace," Laura points out.

"Another masterpiece," Kristen gushes.

Via raves, "Those are amazing."

"What's in the other one?" Jackie asks, pointing to the other jewelry box.

I open it.

Three thin ropes—one gold, one whore-red, and one in diamonds—twist together.

Laura whistles. "I didn't realize Dax knew how to give such good gifts. You're a lucky woman."

"There's one more," Kristen chirps.

A feeling of being overwhelmed hits me. She hands me a box bigger than what the jewelry came in but smaller than the others. I pull the bow and remove the lid. Then I stare at a whore-red leather evening bag. The chain has twisted gold ivy leaves encrusted with diamonds, similar to the boots.

"Damn, girl," Via exclaims.

"I want one of those bags! What brand is it?" Laura states.

Kristen chirps, "Sorry. Dax designed it himself."

I gape at her.

She nods. "He did, just like the jewelry."

"Wow. I need to step up my dating game," Via says.

Kristen claps, instructing, "All right, ladies, we have to get moving. If I don't keep you on schedule, Dax will be upset with me. You know how punctual he is."

The doorbell rings.

"Who's that?" I question.

Kristen answers, "Oh, that'll be Marcus."

I arch my eyebrows. "Who's Marcus?"

"He'll do your feet while Laura does your nails. He got stuck in traffic."

"Oh," I utter and shake my head. Then I admit, "This is all really nice, but I think Dax has gone a little overboard."

Jackie huffs. "I'd be okay if someone went overboard on me."

"Me too," Via says.

Marcus comes flying in and gushes over all the gifts and me.

Before I know it, I'm sitting in a chair with my feet in a pedicure tub full of water.

Marcus gives me a pedicure.

Laura works on my nails.

Via goes through makeup choices with me, and Jackie curls my hair.

My nails get painted whore-red, and my hair gets styled in long curls. Via contours my cheeks, gives me smoky eyes, and applies fake lashes. She holds up a whore-red lip stain and says, "Time to get you ready to pucker up."

I laugh.

She applies it, then holds up a mirror, claiming, "Perfection!"

I stare at my reflection. "Wow. I look..."

"Amazing!" Kristen gushes.

Laura states, "I was going to say glamorous."

"For sure," Via agrees, then hands me a tube of lipstick, stating, "Dax said for you to put this in your purse."

I glance at the familiar tube. The label says Whore Red.

I ask, "Why did he want you to give this to me? You just applied the stain."

She shrugs. "I don't know, but that's what he directed."

I stare at it and then get up. I go over to the table and open the purse.

A travel-size pouch of wipes is inside, along with another note. I carefully unfold it.

Ivy,
After dinner, go into the bathroom and apply your

*lipstick. I want your beautiful, slutty, whore-red
lips marking my dick before the night's over.
Love always,
Dax*

So much adrenaline pounds through me, I get dizzy. I hold on to the back of the chair.

"What does it say?" Jackie questions.

But once again, I don't disclose anything. I shove the note into the zippered pocket along with the lipstick, replying, "Nothing."

Kristen glances at her watch, directing, "You better get your clothes on."

I go into my room where she's put my outfit. I step into the dress, and she zips it up. Then I add the red boots and the jewelry.

"You look amazing! Go check yourself out," she says.

I go into the closet and stare at my reflection, feeling more beautiful than I've ever felt, but also sexy. My core lights up further. For the first time since arriving back in Greenwich, I'm looking forward to spending time with Dax. I permit myself to enjoy the moment and realize it surprises me.

The thought of revenge pops into my mind, but I push it away, wanting to have a fun night out and not deal with the stress.

And then the big question hits me.

If Dax didn't kill my father, where does that leave us?

"Come out and show us," Via calls out from the other room.

"Just a second," I yell back.

I snap a photo of myself and send it to Lilly.

She instantly replies.

> Lilly: So fuckable. Good thing we're only friends.

I giggle, feeling intoxicated from the good vibes even though I've not drunk anything but water today.

I take one final look, step out of the closet, then exit the bedroom.

Everyone gushes over me, clapping, telling me how amazing I look, and then they pack up. When I'm left on my own, it's ten minutes to six.

I pace the cottage, my belly filling with nerves, staring out into the darkness. The first snowflakes of the season begin to fall, and I smile, enjoying how beautiful it looks.

Dax's headlights appear from the direction of the main house.

My butterflies hit an all-time high. I brush my hands over my dress to ensure it's straight, then stand in front of the door. I bite my lip and tap my fingers against my hip, waiting for the only man I've ever loved, wondering if I'm finally ready to give him a second chance.

Dax 25

SINCE WHEN DO MY PALMS SWEAT

Once the forecast predicted snow, I decided it was best to take the Land Rover. It was a good call. The SUV headlights barely penetrate the flakes for me to see the cottage.

I strain to see Ivy's silhouette pacing before the window, and my stomach flips.

There's never been a date more important than this one. I can't screw anything up. I have to make sure everything goes perfectly.

I need my Ivy back in my bed, not at the cottage anymore. She's meant to be with me, in my house, forever.

I grab the Seducing Ivy bouquet with the matching whore-red bow I put together before I showered and changed. I exit the vehicle and fight my way up the slippery porch steps.

The butterflies in my gut take off, and I knock, shivering from the wet and cold.

Ivy opens the door and my blood turns to fire. My erection comes to life and my heart soars.

The minidress I picked out for her hugs her curves perfectly. The whore-red boots look sexier than I imagined, and all I want to do is bend her over and fuck her while she wears them. The jewelry I designed years ago finally hangs from her ears and over her wrist.

I whistle, stating, "You're going to turn everyone's heads tonight, gorgeous."

Nerves flutter over her expression, but she beams. "Thanks." She smiles bigger and shyly adds, "And thanks for today."

I grin. "I'm happy you enjoyed it."

She nods. "I did."

I step forward and kiss her, but I don't make it too deep. If I do, I'm unsure if I can stop, and I'm determined to take her to dinner. There are things I'm ready to reveal, and I hope she's happy about them.

So I muster all my willpower, retreat from her lips, and hold the flowers out. "These are for you."

She looks at the oversized bouquet, and her face lights up. "Thank you, they're beautiful."

I release a nervous breath. There's nothing I want more than for her to embrace the Seducing Ivy flower and all that's come from it. Yet I know it's been a hard pill for her to swallow.

She takes the bouquet and turns back inside, adding, "Let me go find a vase." She enters the kitchen, opens a top cabinet, and pulls one out. She fills it with water and sticks the blooms inside it.

I grab the coat hanging over the couch and hold it out to her.

She strolls over, slides her arms through each sleeve, then buttons it. She reaches for her evening bag and slings it over her shoulder. She gushes, "I can't believe you designed all this."

A giddy feeling comes over me, but my nerves increase too. "I'm glad you approve," I reply, and wipe my palms on my pants.

What the hell is happening to me?

Since when do my palms sweat?

She softly laughs. "I do. It's beautiful, and I'm sure you'd have some buyers if you wanted to make more. The other women were going gaga over it."

"Good. But they can't have it. It's only meant for you."

Her cheeks pinken, and I kiss her again, then grab the gloves off the couch. "Put these on, baby girl. It's freezing outside."

She obeys.

I lead her out of the house, carefully maneuvering down the steps and to the passenger door. I open it, and she slides in. I shut the door, go around the car, and get into the driver's seat.

The snow falls harder, and I double-check that the defroster is on.

"It's really coming down now," Ivy comments.

"Yeah."

The white flakes make driving difficult, so I grip the wheel, taking it slow and steady, unlike my usual aggressive way. I exit the estate, pass several streets, then veer to the left.

Ivy softly states, "I don't want to put a damper on tonight, but I need to ask you something."

My chest tightens. I don't take my eyes off the road, scared I might slide off it. "Go ahead. You can ask me whatever you want, baby girl."

She hesitates, then continues, "The reports you gave me on my father..."

My stomach dives. "What about them?"

"How long have you had those?"

I answer her honestly. "Two days."

She shifts in her seat. "And nothing's fabricated, correct?"

I look at her from the corner of my eye. "No, Ivy. I would never do that. Surely, you don't think I would do that after everything we've been through?" I ask, then focus back on the road, barely seeing past the blanket of white.

She sighs as if in relief. "Okay. Well, thank you for sharing them with me. What do the other documents in the safe say?"

I shake my head. "Nothing more important than what you saw, just more physicals, more in-depth information with medical terms about his heart. It's all yours to read whenever you want it. I didn't send it because I didn't want to overwhelm you. Was that not enough?" I question, but my real question lingers in the air with the silence.

Does she believe I didn't kill her father?

She remains silent for a few moments, the only noise the wipers scraping the ice on the windshield.

My nerves skyrocket. My gut churns. I cautiously ask, "Do you still think I was the reason your father had a heart attack?"

She slowly inhales and exhales, then puts her hand on my thigh.

Tingles race to my erection. I clench my jaw, stopping myself from pulling over and doing indecent things with her on the side of the road.

She answers, "No, I don't. I'm sorry I accused you."

Relief washes over me. I release the wheel with one of my hands and place it on top of hers. I declare, "It's okay. I understand why you did."

"You do?"

"Yes. And I'm sorry your father's dead. I wish he hadn't

been watching me on television when it happened. I can't imagine how horrible it was for you."

Tension fills the air.

"Ivy—"

"Thanks for your apology. Let's change the subject. I'd prefer not to cry all night," she admits.

My heart hurts over her grief. I hate I have a part in it. So I say, "Okay, gorgeous," and squeeze her hand, then grip the wheel with both hands again when the SUV slips on the pavement. I regain control and turn right on the next road.

She adds, "Thanks again for the gifts today. It was... Well, it was very Dax of you."

I chuckle. "Very Dax of me?"

"Yeah. Over the top."

"Is that a bad thing?" I question.

She takes a moment, then admits, "No, it's fun to be spoiled. I always liked that about you. Maybe I shouldn't admit that, but it's true."

I shake my head, declaring, "No, baby girl, you should admit it. And I'm glad you enjoy it. I promise you, I'm going to do more of it."

She softly laughs. "You're insane, Dax."

"Maybe," I agree, then pull up on the side of the pavement next to the newest restaurant in town.

Whore-red, gold, and bling mimicking the design of her necklace blur through the snow across the building. The logo could be sharper, but it's still recognizable through the flakes.

The hairs on my neck rise as I wait for her reaction.

She inhales sharply, and surprise fills her voice when she asks, "Ivy?"

"Yep," I cautiously state.

She tilts her head, squinting her eyes at it. "I thought we were going to a place called Finn's."

"I was hoping to surprise you. It's a soft opening tonight."

She pins her gaze on me. "This is your restaurant?"

I shake my head. "No."

She narrows her eyes. "What do you mean no? Please don't tell me it's Avery's."

I hate she would think such a thing. Avery should never have been associated with Seducing Ivy. I hope any memory of her attached to the brand will soon fade.

I assure her, "No, it's not Avery's. It's yours."

Her eyes widen. "Mine?"

"Yeah."

"Dax, I don't know anything about owning a restaurant."

I chuckle. "You don't have to, gorgeous. Everything's taken care of, but your name's on the business."

"With yours, right?"

I shake my head. "No. Only yours."

"I don't know how to run a business," she says.

"Don't worry. I have my people running it, and I'm overseeing it. But you can fire me if you want at any time."

She gapes at me.

I chuckle again. "It's true."

"There's no way you gave me control to fire you," she blurts out.

"I did, and it's yours. Now, let's go eat, I'm hungry." I open the door. The valet opens her side, and I bark, "Don't touch her."

He freezes, giving me a confused look, with snowflakes falling all around him.

I get around to the other side and then help Ivy out. I bypass the valet and go into the restaurant.

It's dimly lit and mimics the outside, with gold, whore-red, and diamond bling everywhere. Several walls have Seducing

Ivy climbing from the floor to the ceiling, with the blooms dancing across the vines.

Ivy gasps.

I tug her closer, murmuring in her ear, "Do you like it?"

She glances at me, her lips an inch from mine. "Dax, this is amazing."

Satisfaction and a hint of pride fill me. "Good. Let me show you around the rest of your restaurant."

"My restaurant," she mutters, as if she's still trying to believe it.

"I've been working on this for three years," I admit.

Her eyes widen in shock. "You have?"

"Yep. I'm relieved you like it."

She slides her hand on my cheek. "I don't like it, I love it. It's beautiful."

I'm so happy. My heart soars. It's a feeling I used to hate. It made me uncomfortable...vulnerable. But for the last ten years, I've been chasing it, trying to catch it once more.

The hostess, Melissa, pipes in, "Welcome, Mr. Carrington. And you're *the* Ivy?" She beams.

My baby girl nods. "Yes."

Another man I know well steps up next to Melissa. He holds out his hand. "Ms. Ford. I'm Ronaldo, the head manager. It's so nice to finally meet you. If anything is not up to your liking, please let me know, and we'll work on changing it immediately."

Ivy arches her eyebrows, softly laughing. "I'm sure everything is way above my liking. Thank you."

His shoulders drop in relief, but he quickly catches himself. He grins, offering, "Let me take you to your table and show you the rest of the restaurant."

He leads us through the building, and I continue to watch Ivy's shocked expression.

It's priceless. I wish I could take a photo and hang it on the ceiling over my bed. Then I could stare at it every night before I go to sleep and every morning when I wake up.

Ronaldo explains, "Besides the bar, every table's inside its own private room."

We get to the back of the restaurant, and he motions for us to go through the door.

"After you," I tell her.

Ivy steps inside and freezes. "Wow. This is incredible and very intimate."

All the walls have Seducing Ivy vines climbing up them with full blooms. A half-circle whore-red leather booth is the only piece of furniture. Real gold and diamonds fill the tufts on the seat back. A black candle is situated in the middle of the table in a metal and diamond holder. It matches the Seducing Ivy brand and flickers on the table. Next to it is a single Seducing Ivy bloom. The flower's aroma fills the air.

"I took the liberty to fill your water glasses only a moment ago. Would you like me to open the bottle of wine?" Ronaldo asks.

"No, I'll handle that," I tell him, wanting no one else to be in the room. Then to Ivy, I say, "Sit, baby girl."

She does.

I slide in next to her.

Ronaldo states, "Your server will be with you shortly. It's a pleasure to have you dine with us, Ms. Ford. You too, Mr. Carrington."

"Thank you," we reply in unison.

He holds his card out. "This is for you, Ms. Ford. If you need anything at any time, please let me know."

"Thank you," Ivy says, taking it and sliding it into her purse.

He leaves and shuts the door.

"Ready for your next surprise," I ask.

She bites on her lip.

"No?" I taunt.

She laughs and shakes her head. "Hit me with it."

I remove the bottle of wine from the chilled container and hold it in front of her.

Once again, the look on her face is priceless. I wait for her to speak.

She snaps her head toward me. "You created a Seducing Ivy wine?"

I can't help but grin. "Sure did." I grab the opener on the table and remove the cork. I hold it out to Ivy and ask, "Do you want to keep this? It's the first bottle ever opened."

"Wh-...how...? Dax!" she says.

I chuckle and pour an inch into the glass. "Let me know what you think."

She swirls the wine in the glass, holds it to her nose and breathes it in, and then takes a sip. She holds it in her mouth before swallowing, just like I taught her ten years ago, and pride fills me. She always picked up on everything quickly, and did it to perfection.

"Well?" I ask with anticipation.

She closes her eyes and moans. "This is delicious."

I fill my glass, and when she sets hers down, I fill hers and admit, "I bought a vineyard in Italy. It's in your name, as well as the winery that makes this wine."

Her blues go wide.

I lean closer, teasing, "If you want to fire me from that job too, you can."

She laughs.

A server enters the room. He sets a basket of warm bread and butter on the table.

"Hello, Mr. Carrington and Ms. Ford. It's so nice to meet you. My name's Daniel. It's my pleasure to serve you tonight."

"Hi, Daniel. It's nice to meet you too," Ivy replies.

He turns his focus on me. "Mr. Carrington, I just want to confirm you're still happy with the menu you already chose. I have on the list the burrata salad, cherry-braised grilled lamb chops, spicy lobster tail, and the carrot and squash puree?"

I turn to Ivy. "Does that sound good?"

She nods. "Sounds delicious."

"Great."

Daniel continues, "And Seducing Ivy pie is still good for dessert?"

She arches her eyebrows at me. "Pie?"

"Yep," I reply, then to Daniel, I say, "That sounds great, Daniel, thank you."

He nods and leaves.

"It's Seducing Ivy...a flower...but it's also pie?" she asks in confusion.

I nod. "Yep. The texture's like pumpkin pie, and it's phenomenal."

Her grin widens, but then it falls.

"Is something wrong?"

She opens her mouth, then shuts it. She picks up her glass and sips wine. I wait for her to speak.

She collects her thoughts and praises, "It's amazing how many ways you've used the hybrid."

"It's all been for you. Everything's been for you," I say, reinforcing what I've already told her.

"How—"

I put my finger over her lips. "It'll all come to light soon. You'll know everything. Just trust me." I search her eyes, expecting her to tell me she never will, that I've lost my privileges to her trust forever, but, for the first time since she's returned, I don't see it.

Her face relaxes, and she says, "Okay, Dax."

I cautiously question, "Are you saying you trust me?"

She leans over and softly kisses me. She retreats, answering, "I'm going to give you the benefit of the doubt."

Happiness fills me, and joy I haven't felt in a long time makes me dizzy. Still, I push, "You are?"

She nods. "Yes. But how are these things in my name?"

"Because I put you on the businesses."

"But how?" she questions.

I try not to laugh. "Baby girl, this is what I do. These are things up my alley."

She still looks skeptical.

"I can assure you that your name is on the restaurant, vineyard, and the winery. I'll show you the paperwork when we get to my place tonight. It's in my safe."

She arches her eyebrows. "Your place?"

My heart beats harder. "It's time you returned to my bed where you belong," I declare.

Her lips twitch, and I once again want to pump my fist in the air, feeling like I'm finally winning points with her, but then her face turns serious. "Dax, I want to trust you fully again. I'd love to move forward with you—with us—but I keep wondering how it's possible."

"It is possible," I assure her.

She hesitates and adds, "If it's possible, then you're going to have to give me honest answers to questions about subjects I doubt you want to discuss."

My stomach flips, but I don't blame her. "Ask me what you want. I promise you, I won't lie."

"You swear you won't?" she questions, and I wish she didn't have to ask me that, but once again, I can't blame her.

I pick up her hand and kiss the back of it. "Yeah, baby girl. I promise you, I won't lie."

"Okay, then." She takes another sip of wine and picks up a piece of bread. She butters it, sets it on my plate, and does the same with hers. She offers, "Why don't you have some bread first?"

"It's okay, we can talk first."

"No, you said you're hungry, so eat a piece." She takes a bite and groans. She chews, swallows, and declares, "This is so good."

I laugh, confessing, "I love that you still eat carbs."

She grins. "Well, you better eat your bread, or I'll eat yours too."

I take a bite and groan.

She laughs.

I wash it down with a sip of wine.

She says, "It is good, isn't it?"

"Mm-hmm," I hum in agreement.

She takes another bite. After swallowing it, she takes another sip of wine and then puts her glass down. She turns toward me, and her face once again goes serious. She blurts out, "What was the prize?"

The hairs on my neck rise. I hope she's referring to something else. So I cautiously ask, "The prize?"

She tilts her head, studying me. "Don't play dumb, Dax. What was the prize for the game you had me playing that I didn't even know I was in?"

Her words slap me in the face. Bile creeps up my throat, and I swallow it down.

She closes her eyes. "Please just tell me, no matter how bad it is. All these years, I just wanted to know. What was it you won?"

I shift in my seat, hating myself, trying to form the words, but there's no easy way to admit it. So I finally state the blunt truth. "It was just points on an imaginary scoreboard between Avery, Bobby, and me."

"That was it?" she questions, with a hint of anger mixing with hurt in her voice.

I put my hand on her thigh. "Yes. You said you wanted to know the truth. That's it, and I regret it. There's not a moment in my life since that I haven't regretted it."

She looks away.

I don't force her to look at me, wondering how she'll ever love me unconditionally again. What I did to her was horrible.

She stares at the bread, biting her lip.

"Ivy?"

She snaps her head back toward me. "Who leaked the video?"

"Avery."

"How do you know it was Avery?"

"It had to be her. It wouldn't have been Bobby," I assure her.

"And why is that?" she questions, tilting her head, her glare shooting into me like a laser I can't avoid.

I suddenly feel like I'm in a trap. *Does she somehow know?*

When I don't answer, she asserts, "I need to know the truth, Dax. Tell me now why you think Bobby didn't leak that video. Why are you so sure?"

My chest tightens. "You're not going to like this answer either."

"Just tell me," she orders.

"Okay. Bobby had the idea to blackmail Lilly's dad, Senator McBean, and I went along with it. Lilly was paired with you the night of the sorority party so we could get something to hold over her and her father's heads. Bobby wanted it so we could—"

"So you could extort him?" Ivy says, her voice dripping with displeasure.

I swallow hard. "Yes."

She looks away, stares at the wine, and taps the bottom of her glass.

I move my hand to her thigh. "Ivy, I know what I did was unforgivable. If I could do things over, I would. I hope you believe me."

She turns back toward me. "I do believe you."

Surprised, I arch my eyebrows. "You do?"

She nods. "Yeah, I do."

Real hope fills me for the first time since she's been back. But I'm cautious. It'll take a lot for her to forgive me and for us to be back where we were, and my gut tells me I'm more aware of that than Ivy is.

Dax 26

TALK TO ME, GORGEOUS

THE FOOD IS SERVED, and we eat, making small talk throughout dinner, avoiding demons of the past. Then Ivy sets her fork down and turns toward me.

I set my own fork down and wipe my mouth, then put my napkin on the table. I put my hand on her leg, grazing my thumb across her thigh, asking, "Something on your mind, baby girl?"

She stares at me momentarily, then questions, "Do you really want me to take CogniShift?"

My pulse creeps up. I nod decisively. "Yes."

"You think it will work? That it'll stop things from getting worse?"

I assure her, "I do. If administered correctly, it has a 99.8% chance of stopping the progression."

She mutters, "With my luck, I'd probably be in the 0.02% who it didn't help."

"Don't say that."

She sighs.

"I know it will help."

She blurts out, "But you don't think I should just take NeuroZap?"

I break in a sweat. I ask, "You read the research I sent you, correct?"

She nods. "Yes."

"Okay. Do you think the risk is worth that right now?"

She bites on her lip. I continue to caress her inner thigh, and she looks away.

"Talk to me, gorgeous."

She glances back. "Dax, you don't know what this is like living as an addict."

Guilt assails me. I didn't lace her drinks. That's on Bobby and Avery. But she never would have been in a room with them had I kept her away from them.

She adds, "Isn't it worth the risk? I mean, I'm tired of struggling with this."

"Ivy, do you want to take the risk that you'd never want to have sex again?" I question, unable to fathom that anybody would want to choose that. Then again, I don't live with her addiction.

She shrugs. "I don't know."

I see how much she's grappled with this.

"I think the risk is too big to take," I state.

"I don't know. It says it's a 20% chance, which means there's an 80% chance I won't have the side effect."

"Twenty percent is a high chance, baby girl."

"Is it?"

I arch my eyebrows. "You think you'll be in the 0.02% of cases where CogniShift doesn't work, but you're willing to risk a 20% chance with NeuroZap?"

"When you put it like that..." She bites on her lip, cringing.

I repeat, "It's not worth the risk right now."

"I just... Well, I don't know." She stares at the ceiling.

I shift closer and slide my arm around her. "You just what?"

She blinks hard, then confesses, "I do things, Dax. Things I'm not proud of. Things I hate myself for."

My stomach dives. I order, "Ivy, look at me."

She slowly shifts her gaze to me.

"Take CogniShift now. I know we're getting close to eliminating the side effects of NeuroZap. Let's take the first step and stop the progression before we do something that might not be reversible."

She releases an anxious breath. "Okay."

My adrenaline kicks in. "Okay, as in, you'll take CogniShift?"

"Yeah. Can we still do it tonight before I chicken out?"

"Why would you chicken out?"

She winces, then admits, "It's a drug. Drugs make me nervous after knowing I was given Trance."

I take a deep breath and then slowly release it. "I can understand that, but you're choosing to take this one. You've read all the research on it. This is your informed choice."

She's quiet for a minute, then nods. "Okay. But let's do it tonight, please."

"Sure. I have it in the safe in my room. I'm having you stay there anyway, so..." I grin.

She laughs. "Do you ever not get your way?"

I move my hand to her cheek and kiss her. I retreat and answer, "Yeah, I haven't had you for ten years."

Her smile stays on her face, and it's the only thing I want to see. I never want it to go away.

The server clears the plates. Then he sets a piece of Seducing Ivy pie on the table with two forks.

"Can I get you anything else?" Daniel asks.

"Ivy?" I ask, checking with her.

She shakes her head. "No, thank you."

"That'll be all, Daniel," I reply.

He leaves.

Ivy stares at the plate. Her lips twitch.

"What's amusing you, gorgeous?" I ask.

She points at the pie. "The gold crust has ivy leaves with diamonds sprinkled in it, and the filling is whore-red. Is nothing not on brand?"

I grin, informing her, "You can eat those diamonds. They aren't real."

She gapes at me and then laughs.

I take my fork, scoop up a bite of the pie, and hold it in front of her lips. "Try this, baby girl."

She cautiously does and then closes her eyes, moaning again.

I chuckle. "I told you you'd love it."

She nods and then pats her lips with her napkin. "It's delicious. And it's amazing how you created all these things from one hybrid."

I shift in my seat, confessing, "Your father knew what he was doing. He was talented. In all reality, he was the smartest man my father ever hired."

Sadness passes in her expression.

I squeeze her hand and confess, "I shouldn't have fired him. I shouldn't have ever let you walk off the estate. I should have never done what I did. And I promise you, everything I've done with the patent has been for you."

She breathes deeply a few times, and my nerves reappear.

"Dax, I don't want to talk about all that tonight. I'm tired of talking about it, thinking about it, and worrying about it."

I nod. "Me too."

"Okay, then." She smiles at me, grabs her purse, and slides out of the booth.

"Where are you going?" I question, worry filling me.

Her lips twitch. She seductively bats her lashes, puts her hand on the table, and leans across it so her face is an inch from mine.

I glance down at her cleavage, and her fucking C cups do the same thing they've always done to me—make my cock throb in pain.

She teases, "I'm going to the bathroom. I need to put on my lipstick."

Every cell in my body lights on fire. My voice comes out hoarse when I ask, "Is that so?"

Her lips curve higher and then she rises. "Yeah, that's so." She turns, then looks at me over her shoulder. "Dax?"

"Yeah?"

She warns, "Don't try to be someone you're not with me. I am who you made me into, and you are who you've always been. It's what makes us work. So don't try to fight it. I need you to be the Dax Carrington who takes what he wants and doesn't stop until he gets it." She purses her lips, then wiggles her ass as she leaves the room.

The blood in my veins boils. Her words replay in my mind.

I finish my wine and then slide out of the booth. I leave the room, go down the hall, and enter the ladies' room.

Ivy's standing against the wall with a smirk on her face.

She knew I'd come.

A woman washes her hands at the sink.

"Get out," I order.

She glances over at me. It's one of the old hag donors from Clifton University. She begged me for an invite to the opening, and I can't remember why I gave it to her.

"Dax, what are you doing in here? This is the ladies' room!" she reprimands.

I grunt. "I don't care, Corrine. Get out." I open the door.

"Well," she says on a huff, then grabs a handful of towels, dries her hands, and glares at me as she stomps past me.

I shut the door and lock it.

"Same old Dax Carrington," Ivy says, but there's approval in her expression.

I step over to her, feeling everything I felt years ago but so much more intensely. I'm not worried anymore about what I should or shouldn't say or do. Ivy's wiped my worry away, and she's right.

We are who we are, and this is Ivy and me. Wrongly or rightly, I've created this scenario, and she's chosen not to let it go, so there's no reason to try and stop it.

I give in to all my demons, all of the years of holding on to memories and chasing replays I thought would never happen. I drop my pants and lean against the counter.

She glances at my cock and smiles seductively at me. She coyly asks, "Dax Carrington, why is your dick out?"

I curl my finger toward her.

She slinks over to me, grazing her finger up my chest, and tilts her head. Her blues shine brighter, and it makes me want her more.

I tug her hair back, and she inhales sharply. I lean over her lips, staring at them, and then give her a quick kiss, but I don't let her tongue hit mine. She tries, and I pull back, ordering, "Be a good little whore and get on your knees. I want to see those beautiful, slutty whore-red lips mark my cock."

She gives me another heated look and slowly drops to the floor, dragging her palms down my torso until her face is in front of my dick. She looks up at me, and I grunt. She licks my shaft with long strokes until it's covered in her spit, then she takes all of my erection into her mouth, deep-throating me.

I groan, grab her hair, thrust into her mouth a few times, then pull back.

Her glistening blue eyes rise in question.

"Tell me," I order.

She licks the tip of my dick and breathes, "My slutty lips love your cock."

Fire ignites in my cells, raging through my body. "And?"

"Let me be your dirty whore, Dax. Please," she begs in a desperate voice, and pre-cum seeps out of my cock.

I let her suck me a few more minutes and then I pull her off me again.

She's breathing hard.

My chest rises and falls faster. I order, "Tell me again."

Her lips tremble. "I'm your dirty, filthy whore." She flicks her tongue, lapping up more pre-cum.

"And?" I bark out.

"And I'm going to be your dirty, little slut forever. Now, let my slutty lips suck you dry so you can recover. When we get home, you're feeding your cock into my greedy pussy."

I breath out a curse and push her back over me, thrusting into her mouth faster and faster, until I can't contain the buzzing within my veins.

I explode within her, shouting out, "I fucking love you, my fucking sexy little slut!"

She continues to suck me dry until I can barely stand and I'm gripping the edge of the counter with both hands. Her nails dig into my hips, and the pain has never felt so good.

When there's nothing left, I'm breathing hard, and she pulls back and rises. She grabs a tissue, pats her lips, and tosses it in the trash.

I blurt out, "You don't know how beautiful you are, baby girl."

Her lips twitch. She opens her purse and grabs a wet wipe. She hands one to me and then takes one out and wipes off the smeared lipstick around her mouth.

I clean myself up, being careful to leave some of the marks on me, focusing on just my cum. When I'm satisfied, I pull up my pants and secure them. I step behind her and slide my arms around her.

She stares at me in the mirror, a tiny smile dancing on her expression.

I admit, "Do you know that the only time I've ever been happy is with you?"

Her smile widens.

"It's true. I've only been happy with you."

She tosses the wet wipe in the trash and then spins into me. She throws her arms around my shoulders and pushes my head toward her, sliding her tongue into my mouth.

I palm her ass, thrashing my tongue against hers, and my arousal makes a comeback.

"Dax," she mumbles between kisses.

"Hmm?" I hum, not wanting to end our kisses.

"I want to go home."

My pulse pounds between my ears. I fist her hair and tug it, ensuring she's saying what I want her to say, "You mean my bed?"

She studies me quietly.

"Tell me you want to stay with me in my bed," I demand.

"Yes, Dax. I want to go home to your bed."

Nothing has ever sounded better to me. I don't waste time. I whisk her out of the bathroom, through the restaurant, and into the SUV. My veins feel like they might explode with adrenaline and endorphins as I drive home, but I concentrate on the road, trying to get through the snow as quickly and safely as possible. The entire way, she keeps her hand on my thigh, and we don't say much.

We get through the gates of the estate and into the main house. I steer her toward my bedroom, and as soon as we step inside, I shut the door and kiss her. I reach for her zipper, but she pushes against my chest.

"Dax, wait."

"What's wrong?"

She opens her mouth, then shuts it.

"Baby girl, what's wrong?" I ask again, the hairs on my neck rising, a chill running down my spine.

She releases an anxious breath. "Can I take CogniShift now?"

I blow out a breath of relief and stroke her cheek. "Of course. Let me go get it." I release her and go to the wall, removing a picture. I put the code in for my safe, then press my palm against it. It beeps and opens.

I grab the dose of CogniShift I've kept in there for her. There's also a dose of NeuroZap, but I don't want to use it on her, not until I can replace it with one without the side effects.

I grab a syringe, stab the needle in the vial, fill it, and set it on the table. I grab a rubbing alcohol pad, rip the packet open, and state, "It gets injected into your ass cheek."

Her lips twitch. She playfully wiggles her dress over her hips, spreads her legs, then leans over the bed, her arms wide.

"Jesus," I mutter, staring at her bare ass. My demon rises, and I rub my palm over her skin.

She whimpers.

I slap her ass.

"Dax," she yelps.

I slap it again several times and then lean over her, rubbing the sting. I murmur in her ear, "Did your pussy like that?"

The look she gives me is all the answer I need.

I kiss her neck, then down her spine. She shivers, and I get to the fading mark on her ass and press my lips against it.

She shivers harder.

I smack the spot again, wipe the alcohol pad on it, and quickly shove the needle in, injecting the medication. I pull the needle out and rub the spot with my hand. "Done."

"It's over?" she asks.

"Yep." I press my lips back to her body, moving back up her spine and neck until I'm next to her lobe. I inform her, "You have to drink thirty ounces of water within ten minutes."

She arches her eyebrows. "Seriously?"

"Yep." I kiss her on the cheek, rise, and pull her up. "Sit down, baby girl."

She does.

I go to the fridge, grab a few bottles of water, and sit next to her.

"Thirty ounces is a lot of water to drink," she claims.

"Yeah, it is, but you can do it," I encourage, opening a bottle.

"Why is this necessary?" she questions.

I hand the bottle to her and answer, "For CogniShift to penetrate the cells, it has to have water. If it gets anything less than thirty ounces, it won't work."

"Really? How did you figure that out?" she asks and then downs half the bottle.

"Good girl," I praise. "I told you, I have the best scientists in charge of the research and development team. That's why I know we'll find a way to reduce the side effects of NeuroZap."

She doesn't say anything and drinks more water. We stay quiet until she finishes and puts her hand over her belly. She groans. "I feel like a blimp right now."

I chuckle and kiss her, then state, "I can assure you that you aren't."

"That's a lot of water at once."

"It is, but you did good," I reiterate, happy she took the drug.

"I have to go pee. I'll be back." She rises and goes to the bathroom.

I pick up the water bottles and go to the trash can. I toss them in, and my door flies open.

"How the fuck could you do that, Dax?" Cooper shouts.

"Get the fuck out of my room," I reply.

He doesn't obey. He races toward me, his face red with anger, roaring, "You kicked Avery out of the house?"

"Damn right, I did," I confirm, crossing my arms.

"That's why you stole her money, isn't it?"

"That and a million other reasons, but I didn't steal it," I declare.

"You did," he seethes.

"No point in fighting over this. You have your opinion, and I have mine. Now, get out." I point toward the door.

He fumes, "No. I can't believe you did this. You're going to pay for this, Dax."

I scoff. "Yeah? How am I going to pay for this?"

He scowls. "You're sick, you know that?"

"So I've been told."

He sneers at me. "You can't kick Avery out."

"I can, and I did. Now, get out before you're next," I repeat.

"Where is she going to live? You can't just kick her out," Cooper protests again.

I step closer to him and jab his chest. "I can, and it's done. Now, get out before my fist connects with your pretty face," I threaten.

He doesn't move. He's as tall as me, and we stare at each other eye to eye.

He snarls, "I can't believe you chose that girl over your own blood."

Rage fills me. "I chose that girl?"

"Yeah, you chose that girl. And you know what? She's a fucking idiot."

"Don't you dare call Ivy an idiot."

"She is. I gave her a chance to escape you, and she was dumb enough to come running back," he hurls.

I freeze.

He stares at me, breathing hard, his fists curled at his side.

"What do you mean you gave her a chance to escape me?" I demand.

His eyes widen and the color drains from his face.

I grab his shirt. I grit between my teeth, "What the fuck do you mean, Cooper?"

"Just what I said," he answers, scowling deeper.

And then it hits me. My stomach churns, and rage fills me to the point I think I might kill my brother. "You were the one who leaked the video, weren't you?"

YOU RUINED IVY'S LIFE

A SHIVER RUNS down my spine as I halt in the doorway.

I couldn't have heard that right.

"Admit it," Dax seethes.

Cooper's eyes narrow. He pushes at Dax, roaring, "Get off me!"

Dax doesn't release him. "What did you do, Cooper?"

He pushes Dax again. "Let me go!"

Dax releases him. He demands, "I want to know right now what you did, Cooper."

Cooper shakes his head, pointing at Dax. "You've always thought you were better than me. Any chance you got, you threw it in my face that Grandpa put you in charge of the company."

Dax snarls, "So you destroyed Ivy's life?"

Cooper scoffs. "It was all going to eventually come out. And I only did what you would have done yourself."

"No, Cooper. I wasn't going to show anyone footage of Ivy. I loved her!"

He huffs. "Liar! You thought I was so stupid, but for the first time, I pulled one over on you."

The color drains from Dax's face and then it reappears, redder than ever. He steps close to Cooper, takes his fist, and slams it into his face.

"Dax!" I scream in horror.

Blood spurts everywhere. Cooper falls to the floor on his knees. "What the fuck, Dax," he spouts, putting his hand over his mouth and glancing up at him with hatred in his eyes.

Dax lunges at Cooper and punches him again. More blood spatters across the room.

"Dax, stop," I scream, stepping back away from the brawl.

Cooper recovers, flinging himself at Dax, and the two roll on the floor, hitting each other.

I scream several times, "Stop it," and realize they aren't going to. I run to the door and stand in the doorway, screaming, "Help, bring security! Quickly!"

It feels like they take forever.

Dax and Cooper continue to beat on each other while I yell for them to stop. Both men are around the same size, and it's an even match. I'm afraid they're going to kill each other.

By the time security finally comes in, there's blood everywhere. It takes five men to pull Dax and Cooper off each other.

Chad, the head of security, orders, "That's enough!"

Dax swipes blood off his face with his forearm, seething, "Get him out of here."

Cooper barks, "You can't! I have every right to be here."

Dax roars, "I said, get him out of here!"

"Everybody calm down," Chad demands.

"You bastard," Dax snarls at his brother.

"You're just pissed I did it before you could," Cooper claims.

I inhale sharply.

"I'll kill you," Dax threatens.

"Cooper, tell me it's not true," I blurt out, unable to fathom how he could have hurt me so badly. He was still in high school, and I didn't spend much time with him, but he was always kind to me whenever we were together.

The room goes silent.

He slowly turns to look at me. His face is already swelling and bruising. His hands and face are covered in blood. His lip is split and his nose busted. He's almost unrecognizable.

Still shocked, I beg, "Please, tell me I heard wrong and it wasn't you who released that video."

His silence tells me he did it, but there's no remorse in his expression.

My eyes fill with tears. I choke out, "How could you?"

Dax steps next to me and tugs me into him. "Get him the fuck out of our house."

Cooper's eyes light with outrage. "*Your* house? This isn't her house. And it's mine as much as yours."

"No. He doesn't get to leave yet!" I step closer and jab Cooper in the chest. "Tell me what I ever did to you for you to hate me so much!"

He lifts his chin higher. He glares down at me. "You're so naive, Ivy. I let you escape the game. You should thank me."

"Thank you?" I shout.

"Get him out of here!" Dax orders again.

Cooper turns back toward Dax, snickering. "He was destroying your life just like he destroys everyone's. I did you a favor. I got you far away from here, but you were too stupid and had to return."

The amount of shock filling me is overwhelming. My entire body trembles, and I go weak in the knees. I almost fall, but

Dax reaches for me, tugging me into him again. Tears spill out of my eyes. How did I never see it?

"I gave you your life back," Cooper insists.

"No, you didn't. You destroyed it," I hurl, still trying to come to grips with the fact Cooper did it and not Avery or Bobby.

"Get him out of here," Dax orders again.

"You aren't kicking me off the estate. I have every right to be here," Cooper claims.

Dax points at Chad and booms, "Carrington Enterprises pays your salary. I run Carrington Enterprises. Decisions I make are yours to implement. Now, I'm going to tell you one last time. Get him off the estate."

Chad still hesitates.

"You can't. I have every right to be here," Cooper smugly repeats.

"He doesn't. Get him off the property," Dax barks.

Cooper insists, "You can't, you—"

"Cooper, time to go," Chad interjects.

Cooper's head snaps toward him. "No, it's my right to be here. Same as Dax's. Same as Avery's. No one can kick me off the estate."

Dax scoffs. "Is that what you think? I can assure you, little brother, I can. Now get the fuck out of here before I kill you."

"No, you can't."

"Time to go," Chad repeats, and the security guards move him toward the door.

Cooper tries to fight but can't overpower them. He protests the entire way, screaming, "I'm going to kill you, Dax. I'll kill Ivy too, just to spite you."

I shiver, and Dax pulls me tighter against him, then leads me down the hall, following the guards.

Dax calls out, "You're finished, Cooper."

"You can't do this! I'll have you arrested! You're in breach of trust!" Cooper screams as the guards drag him down the stairs.

Dax grunts. "Just try it. Anything you want, Cooper, try it. I guarantee you the only place you'll end up is in a body bag. Now get the fuck out of my sight."

He continues protesting as they pull him out the door. It slams shut behind them.

Dax and I don't move, staring at the entryway for several minutes.

He turns to me. "I didn't know it was him! I swear I didn't know!"

"I know you didn't," I reply numbly.

He shakes his head, then leads me back into the bedroom. We step inside, and he shuts and locks the bedroom door. He slides his hands over my cheeks. "Baby girl, are you okay?"

I open my mouth, but no words come out. Then I stutter. "I-I-I..."

He tugs me into him, holding me close. "Shh. I'm so sorry. I don't know how I never figured it out."

I pull back. "I don't understand why Cooper would do that."

Dax squeezes his eyes shut, then opens them, revealing a pool of pain. He merely says, "He's a Carrington. He was playing a game as well."

The truth hangs in the air, reminding how naive I was.

Dax adds, "But he also has always wanted to take me down. I never took him seriously. I'm sorry, Ivy. This was about my brother getting back at me, not you. I'm so sorry that you were part of it."

I don't say anything. I'm too shocked to form any coherent sentences. I sit down on the bed.

Dax stares at me, his face swollen and covered in blood, just like Cooper's.

I blurt out, "You need to clean your face up. You're bleeding."

He glances down at himself and doesn't say anything. He turns and goes into the bathroom.

I continue to sit there, unsure what to think, wondering how Cooper, someone I never thought would hurt me, could have done something so damaging.

I can't fathom it, and I realize that the game played me more than I even knew. It makes me wonder what else is coming at me that I'm once again too naive and gullible to realize.

Dax 28

DOWNWARD SPIRAL

It was after five in the morning when Ivy and I stopped making love and she finally fell asleep in my arms.

I'm too charged up to get any rest. There's too much to do, and the sun has risen. So I kiss her on the forehead and try to slide out of bed, but she grabs my arm.

"Dax," she says sleepily.

I turn back and stroke her hair. "Hey, go back to sleep, gorgeous."

"Where are you going?"

"I have a lot of work to do today. I want to get into the office and get it done so I can come home at a decent hour. I thought we could stay in for dinner tonight."

She smiles. "Okay, but..." She stares at me.

"But what, baby girl?" I question, sliding closer to her.

She studies me and then states, "I forgot to ask you something last night, but we can discuss it at dinner."

I shake my head. "No, ask me now."

She chews her lip for a minute, then asks, "Whatever happened to Marcie and Cindy?"

I arch my eyebrows. "What made you bring them up?"

She shrugs. "I don't know. I just thought of them and was curious."

I inform her, "The last I heard, Cindy's been in and out of rehab. Avery showed me a video someone had sent her a few years ago. Cindy was in New York City, living on the street, addicted to heroin."

Ivy gapes at me in horror. She recovers and blurts out, "That's horrible."

"Yeah, it is, but Cindy always had a lot of issues with substance abuse, so I'm not surprised."

"Whoever took the video didn't try to help her?" Ivy asks.

I grunt. "Of course they didn't. They just took the video and sent it to anyone they knew so they could gossip."

She shakes her head. "Why are people so mean around here?"

"I don't know, baby girl. I assume it's because we all have too much money and there are too many bored people."

"Is that why you played your game? Because you were bored?"

Guilt fills me, but I realize she hit the nail on the head, so I don't deny it. "That and it was a competitive sport."

She stays quiet, staring at the quilt.

"You wanted the truth from me," I remind her, wondering if maybe I shouldn't be so candid. Perhaps my honesty does more harm than good?

As if she can read my mind, she nods, asserting, "I do want the truth. Always. Thank you for telling me."

I stare at her, hating how I can't erase my past.

She asks, "What happened to Marcie?"

"Marcie's been married several times. The last I heard, she was in Canada. She married some politician up there."

Amusement lights Ivy's eyes. "Really?"

"Yep. He's with the conservative party and wants to eliminate gay rights."

She gapes at me.

"It's the truth."

"She used to call me a homophobe!"

"Yeah. Now she's married to one and stands next to him proudly," I proclaim, "but we'll see how long this one lasts." I glance at the clock and add, "I really do have to get to the office if I'm going to eat dinner with you tonight. Is there anything else you forgot to ask me last night?"

Ivy ponders my question and then shakes her head. "No, that was it."

"Okay, baby girl." I give her another kiss on the lips and then retreat. "I'll do my best to finish work quickly so I can get home at a decent hour. Are you sure you're good staying in tonight?"

She smiles. "Of course. What do you want me to make?"

I chuckle. "You don't have to make anything. We have a kitchen staff who cooks."

Her face heats with embarrassment. She puts her hand over her face, groaning. "Oh, duh. I forgot."

I chuckle. "It's okay. The chef has a menu he creates every week. Look it over. If you don't like it, talk to Kristen. She can instruct the chef to make whatever you prefer."

She bites her lip.

"What?" I question.

"Just like that?"

I snap my fingers, grinning. "Just like that!"

She laughs. "Okay."

I force myself out of bed, then shower and get dressed. I

run through what I have planned for the day while putting on my socks and then I freeze.

She still hasn't called her.

I reach for my wallet, open it, and pull out a business card. I exit the closet, go to the bed, and set the card on the night table.

Ivy sits up, questioning, "What's that?"

I clench my jaw, staring at her.

She grabs the card, reads it, and her face hardens. She slowly meets my eyes.

"Just make an appointment with Vivian," I encourage. "She won't force you to talk about anything you're not ready to discuss."

Ivy snaps, "I don't need to talk to her."

My chest tightens. I argue, "Why not? What's the harm in meeting with her?"

Ivy glares at me. "I don't want to talk to her. Stop pushing her on me." She tosses the card back on the table, slides under the covers, and turns away from me.

I sigh and get back into bed, putting my arms around her. I kiss the back of her neck.

She turns her head, still glaring.

"Don't be mad at me. I only want to make sure you're okay."

"I am okay. If I need to see a therapist, I'll let you know."

"But—"

"It's my decision, Dax! Not yours," she spouts.

I sigh. "Okay."

"Don't bring it up again. I don't want to see her card or hear her name. Do you understand me?" she warns.

I mutter, "I'm sorry I upset you. I thought all women liked therapy."

She turns over and scoffs. "Is that a serious statement?"

"Yeah. Everyone around here goes. It's a bragging point who your therapist is if you're a woman," I declare.

She wrinkles her nose. "That's ridiculous."

I stare at her, then chuckle.

"What's so funny?" she asks.

"You're right. It is stupid."

"Glad we're on the same page. I expect you to voice your agreement with me," she asserts.

I kiss her on the lips. "I will, baby girl."

"Good." Her lips twitch. "Now, kiss me like you mean it."

I don't need to think twice. I kiss her with everything I have until we're both breathless and my cock is hard.

She retreats.

"Not fair. I'm going to have blue balls all day," I grumble.

She laughs.

I peck her on the lips and then leave the house. I slide into the Land Rover and drive toward the office. It takes longer because of the snow, so I make my first call of the day.

Craig Pohler answers. "Good morning, Mr. Carrington."

"Where are we at, Craig? Did you eliminate the side effects yet?"

He sighs. "Mr. Carrington, this takes time. You know how long it took to develop the drugs. I need your patience on this."

"Yeah, which is why you should be able to eliminate the side effects. You've had enough time," I press.

"It doesn't work that way. You can't rush science. We're doing everything we can."

"You're not working fast enough," I accuse.

"Would you rather we do something half-assed and then state it's not a side effect, but yet some people still experience it?" he warns.

I grip the wheel tighter.

I need to get it done for Ivy.

He adds, "We have to do it correctly."

"Just hurry up with it," I state and then hang up. I drive several more blocks, pull up to my office building, then get out of the SUV.

It takes another few minutes to get into my private office. I hang my coat in my closet and go to my desk.

Michelle's voice chimes over the intercom, "Richard Lyman, Sr.'s office is on the phone. Should I put him through?"

"Yes, Michelle."

"Okay, Mr. Carrington."

Line one blinks. I pick up the phone and sit back in my chair. I cross my ankle over my knee and tap the side of my armchair, answering, "Dick."

"What an interesting day, Dax," he states.

"Yeah? Why is that," I question.

"I received a call from Cooper this morning. Sounds like you had some issues at the estate last night?"

I groan. "Does my idiot brother think he's going to call you and you're going to solve his problems for him?"

Dick grunts. "Apparently, he does. I had to tell him I couldn't represent him and you simultaneously. Then, he tried to tell me he was coming after you, and it was in my best interest to side with him."

"When Hell freezes over," I mutter.

Dick continues, "He tried telling me that since I represent Carrington Enterprises, I represent him too."

I groan. "He gets stupider and stupider."

"I didn't have time to explain to him that a corporation isn't a person."

I chuckle. "Yeah, Cooper's not always been the smartest crayon in the box."

"Well, he was pissed. But you've got a fight on your hands.

Kicking him out of the house without consulting me was a bold move."

I admit, "It just happened. Regardless, what's my nail in his coffin? I know there's the incarceration thing and $5 million minimum in the trust, as well as the moral code for the corporation. But what are my other legal options to make sure he never steps foot on the estate again?"

Dick replies, "There isn't anything concrete. We went through this. Nothing's changed, Dax. He has to drop to less than $5 million in his trust fund or be sentenced to prison. In order to not receive any paid-out corporate dividend payments, he has to break a moral code. Has he done any of those things?"

I spin in my chair and stare out the window at the water, watching the waves crash on the shore. I admit, "He hasn't done anything concrete I can make stick."

We're both quiet for a minute.

Dick breaks the silence. "We can tie him up in some legal paperwork to keep him out of the house, but I'm pretty sure he's going to have another attorney contacting me today. At least, that's what he threatened, and I don't think he was bluffing."

"Okay. What about a restraining order," I question.

"On what grounds?"

"He threatened to kill me, as well as Ivy, last night. I had five security guards there who can all attest to it."

"I can work with that," Dick confirms.

"Good. Do it. And add one on Avery too. I'm not taking any chances with Ivy."

Dick asks, "Did Avery make threats as well?"

"Sure she did."

Dick chuckles. "Why do I not believe you?"

"She did," I insist.

"You have a witness who can corroborate?"

I grunt. "I'm sure the spa manager will be more than willing to say she heard it, in exchange for a college fund for her kid."

Dick's voice lowers. "Good. Grease her, and I'll do the rest."

"Tell me when it's done so I can make it public," I order and hang up, feeling giddy. My day's just begun, but it looks like it's going to be a really good one.

I open files on my computer, and, one by one, I go through all the subsidiaries of Carrington Enterprises. I log in to bank accounts and turn off all stock distributions. Nothing states I have to pay dividends. It only states who is entitled to any that are paid out. Then, I click on the main Carrington Enterprises account.

I stop all transfers into Avery's and Cooper's accounts. I press the intercom.

"What can I do for you, Mr. Carrington?" Michelle answers.

"I need a letter written stating there will be no more stock distributions from Carrington Enterprises until further notice. Address one to my sister and one to Cooper. Send it to me for my approval as soon as it's written," I instruct.

"Yes, Mr. Carrington," she replies.

I hang up, a huge grin on my face.

My siblings won't have any income coming in. They'll have whatever is left in their trust funds, but I already know Avery's is almost gone. Cooper's is just a matter of time.

My cell phone rings. I glance at it and smile. I let it ring several times and finally answer it, turning around to stare at the ocean again. "Mr. Winston, how are you doing this morning?"

Bobby's dad barks, "Who the fuck do you think you are? You need to reverse this!"

"I'm not sure what you're talking about," I say, claiming the same innocence I always have.

"We're meeting today," he demands.

"Sorry, my schedule's full."

"This isn't one of your games, Dax. I mean it. We're meeting today."

I wait a moment, then reply, "No, not today. I'll give you a few minutes when my schedule clears."

"Dax—"

I hang up and rise, standing in front of the glass and looking out at the waves. I pat myself on the back, ecstatic at how everything is finally unfolding after all these years.

The best part is the downward spiral has only begun. And I'm going to hold Ivy tight to me while everyone falls around us.

SEDUCING IVY

It's after ten a.m. when I wake up. I turn onto my side, and the card on the table catches my eye.

"Ugh," I mutter.

I pick it up, read Vivian Armando's name, then crumple it into a ball. I climb out of bed and toss it in the trash.

Time to make myself presentable.

I take a shower and dry off. I put the towel around me and then grab my phone.

I text Dax.

Me: I don't have any clothes in your room. How horrible would I be if I asked Kristen to go to the cottage and grab me an outfit?

Dax: Look in your closet.

Me: My closet?

Dax: There are two closets, baby girl. One of them is yours. It's the one on the right.

I exit the bathroom and find the closet. I peek into Dax's. All of his suits hang perfectly in a row. The other side is more casual clothes. His shoes are stacked neatly. I smile.

It's so Dax Carrington.

I open the door to the other closet and gasp.

There's a blingy chandelier and a beautiful plush rug with the Seducing Ivy logo and colors. The back wall mimics those in the restaurant.

Ivy crawls from the floor to the ceiling, and there are whore-red blossoms everywhere. Indoor lighting and a self-watering system keeps the plants alive.

The rest of the closet is perfectly designed with drawers, shelves, cabinets, and hanging areas. Designer clothes fill all of the spaces.

I step closer to the Seducing Ivy wall and deeply inhale. What would've upset me before, now makes me happy, so I grab my phone.

Me: I can't believe this room.

Dax: I was hoping you'd like it.

Me: When did you do this?

Dax: A couple of years ago.

I stare at the text.

Me: Why?

Dax: I told you I've always loved you and never stopped. That wasn't a lie.

My butterflies take off, and my heart soars. I realize I finally believe Dax. He does love me, and as fucked-up as all the stuff is that he did to me, I know in my heart that he always did.

> Me: It's beautiful. And thanks for all the clothes. You went overboard like always.

> Dax: No, I didn't. If there's anything you don't like, toss it on the bed. Kristen will get rid of it, and I can replace it.

> Me: You know that's not going to happen.

> Dax: You don't have to keep anything you don't like. Don't feel bad to eliminate things. Seriously.

> Me: Everything's beautiful. Thank you.

> Dax: You're welcome, baby girl. I'm going back to work now so I can hopefully be home sooner.

> Me: Okay. I love you.

Tingles race up my spine. I realize it's the first time I've said it to Dax and truly meant it since I've returned. And there aren't any harsh feelings attached to my words.

> Dax: You don't understand how happy I am to see that in writing.

> Me: Why don't you come home sooner, and I'll tell you it to your face. Maybe I'll wear...

I send the message. I search through the wardrobe, then open several dresser drawers until I find what I assumed would be in the closet.

A scandalous, whore-red lingerie outfit is folded inside. I

take it out, set it on the dresser, take a picture, and send it to Dax.

> Me: Maybe I'll wear this.

> Dax: I'll be home as soon as possible.

Three drooling emojis follow.

I laugh and set down the phone. I take my time exploring all the different items in the closet.

Another text comes in.

> Dax: There's one more thing, gorgeous.

> Me: What's that?

> Dax: If you're going to leave the house today, I want the driver to take you. The roads aren't great.

> Me: I'll be fine. I know how to drive through snow.

He calls me.

I pick it up, insisting, "Hey, I don't want to argue about this. It's not necessary for me to have a driver."

He replies, "I don't want to debate either, Ivy, but I need to know you're safe. After everything that happened with Cooper last night—"

"Did something else happen?" I interject.

"No, but I'd prefer to take precautions. He's angry and threatened to kill us, and I don't want to take any chances."

My heart beats faster. "Do you really think he's capable of physically harming us?"

"I don't know. I hope not, but like I said, I'd prefer to play it safe—especially with you, Ivy. So, can you please allow the driver to take you anywhere you want to go?"

Realizing that if Dax is worried, it may be best to do what he says, so I agree. "Okay."

I can hear the relief in his voice. "Thanks, gorgeous."

"Sure."

"I have to go. I'll see you tonight. Hopefully, in that sexy little number."

I softly laugh. "Better be a good boy," I tease.

He chuckles.

"See you tonight," I add and then hang up.

For the next hour, I try on several outfits, loving every article Dax chose for me.

My phone buzzes and I glance down it.

Lilly: Can you meet for lunch?

Me: Sure. Today, right?

Lilly: Duh.

I laugh.

Me: What time?

Lilly: Meet in an hour and a half?

Me: Sure. Is there a certain place you want to go?

Lilly: There's a great cafe downtown with good salads.

Me: Do they have anything besides salads? I'm hungry.

Lilly: You're just going to eat all those yummy carbs in front of me, aren't you?

I laugh again.

Me: Yep. I need some substance. Something gooey and delicious sounds good. Maybe a grilled cheese?

Lilly: They have those.

Me: Great. Send me the name and address of the cafe.

She does, and I continue to get ready. I select a pair of designer skinny jeans and an oversized cashmere sweater, and put it on the bed. I return to the closet and sit on the vanity's bench.

Makeup, hairbrushes, hairstyling products, hair tools, and anything I could need fill the drawers. I shake my head, amazed and touched at how thoughtful Dax can be.

I get ready and then I text him.

Me: I'm going to meet Lilly for lunch. Who's going to drive me?

Dax: I'll text Chad now. Just go outside, and there'll be an SUV waiting.

Me: I hope my carriage doesn't turn into a pumpkin before midnight.

Dax: Haha. Funny. I have to go into a meeting. I'll talk to you later tonight. Love you.

Me: Love you too.

I walk through the house and then out the front door. Sure enough, a black SUV's waiting. I don't know who the man is, but he opens the door for me. I slide in, and he shuts the door. I tell him the name of the cafe. He puts the SUV in drive, and we leave the estate.

It doesn't take long to arrive at the restaurant. I walk inside and glance around. Only four booths have guests.

Lilly jumps up from her table, singing, "Hey!" She beams at me.

"Hi!" I chirp back.

We hug each other and sit down. I cautiously ask, "Where's Jaxon?"

Her lips twitch. She reveals, "He had some video meetings he needed to take."

I wiggle my eyebrows. "And you're returning to his room after our lunch?"

She purses her lips, staring at me.

I laugh. "Of course you're going back."

Her eyes light up. She leans forward. "He's amazing, Ivy."

"Yes, Jaxon is a great person."

Lilly firmly states, "No. I mean he's an amazing man. For real."

"Aww. I thought you two would get along," I state.

She nervously stares at me and then licks her lips.

"What aren't you telling me?"

She swallows hard, opens her mouth, and shuts it.

I lower my voice, fretting, "What is it?"

She glances around again, but there's no one near us who I recognize. Lilly admits, "I think I like him."

I smile. "Well, that's good, right?"

"I mean *really* like him."

"And that isn't a good thing?"

She cringes and shrugs, confessing, "I don't know. What if I like him but he doesn't like me for anything more than a fuck buddy?"

"Did you ask him?" I question.

"No." She looks away.

"Well, why not? Just ask him. Tell him how you feel," I urge.

She furrows her eyebrows. "What if he doesn't feel that way?"

"You won't know if you don't ask him," I point out.

She sighs and looks out the window, twirling a lock of hair around her finger.

I reach over and grab her hand. "Lilly."

She turns back toward me, declaring, "I really like him, Ivy. Like, really, really, really! It's more than the hot sex. And it is hot sex! Oh my God, is it hot sex!" Her eyes widen.

I try to stifle my laugh, but I can't.

She lowers her voice again. "You know what I'm talking about, Ivy. I'm not sure how you can give him up."

I shake my head, insisting, "Jaxon and I were always just fuck buddies. It was just because of our addiction and friendship that we did what we did. You know how friends with benefits are. We didn't have the connection the same way Dax and I do."

"It's still ridiculously hot sex," she says.

"Eh." I shrug.

Her eyes widen in shock and she says, "Are you being serious right now? How can you say that it's not?"

My face heats. "Because that's what I have with Dax. I've never had it with anyone else, even Jaxon."

"Hmm." She studies me.

Anxiety fills my chest. I question, "What?"

"Have you finally admitted you're still in love with him?"

I stay quiet.

"Have you told Dax? I know you love him, and I think you should tell him."

"I did tell him," I admit.

"You did?"

"Yes."

She grins and claps her hands. "Yay!"

A server comes over. "Hi, I'm Shelby. I'm going to be your server today. Can I start you off with something to drink?"

"I'll have a mimosa," Lilly says.

"I'll have one too," I tell the server.

"Great. Two mimosas coming right up." Shelby leaves.

Lilly snaps her fingers. "Hey, did you see there's a Seducing Ivy restaurant in town? It opened last night."

My grin hurts my cheeks. I confess, "Yeah, Dax took me to it."

"He did?" she shrieks. "Oh my God. What was it like?"

"It's amazing. I've never seen anything like it. It's beautiful. The decor is stunning, Lilly. You have to see it."

She groans. "I tried to see it. They won't let me in. They said there's an eight month waitlist."

"Really?"

"Yeah. I'm assuming Dax owns it. Or does Avery?" She wrinkles her nose.

My stomach flips. I shake my head. "No, Avery doesn't own it." I pause, and a weird feeling hits me.

Should I tell her?

"Now you're holding something back," Lilly accuses.

I don't know why I want to keep the restaurant ownership a secret from others, but I decide Lilly is safe. Maybe it's because I'm still coming to terms with what Dax disclosed last night. But I glance around just as she did a few minutes prior, and lean closer. "If I tell you something, will you not tell anyone?"

"Your secret's safe with me," she declares, then pretends to lock her mouth and toss the key away.

I study her.

She squints, whispering, "Did you kill someone last night?"

I laugh. "Lilly!"

"Phew. I was worried you might've. Okay. What's the secret?" she asks, her eyes lighting up.

I admit, "I own it."

Her jaw drops toward the table.

"Well, say something," I order.

"Are you serious? When did you come up with it?" she squeals.

"Shh!"

"Oh, sorry!"

"I didn't, Dax did. He put it in my name, and he's overseeing it. But he told me I can fire him at any time."

Lilly's eyes widen, and she puts her hand over her mouth. She shakes her head and then says, "No way."

"Yeah, that's what I said, but he says it's all in writing."

She narrows her eyes. "Have you seen it in black and white?"

"No, but he said the paperwork's all in his safe. I can get it at any time."

She leans back. "Wow."

Shelby arrives with the mimosas. "Here you go, ladies. Were you ready to order?"

"We're going to need another minute," Lilly declares.

"Okay. Just motion me over when you're ready." Shelby disappears.

Lilly questions, "So if you own Seducing Ivy, can you get me in on Friday night? I want Jaxon to take me there. I heard it's super intimate and romantic."

"It's amazing! Perfect for a date."

"So, can you get me in?" she asks again.

"I can ask—"

She arches her eyebrows.

"On second thought, I can for sure." I go into my purse and

pull out the card Ronaldo gave me. I enter his digits into my cell and hit the call button.

He answers, "This is Ronaldo."

I reply, "Hi, Ronaldo. It's Ivy Ford."

"Oh, Ms. Ford. How are you doing today?" he asks.

"I'm good. And you?"

"Can't complain. To what do I owe the pleasure?" he questions nervously.

I take a sip of mimosa and smile, relaying, "My best friend is in town, and she needs a table for two on Friday night. She tried to make a reservation and was told that we're booked for eight months?"

"That's correct, Ms. Ford," he states.

"But you can make sure she gets the best table we have this upcoming Friday night, correct?"

A moment of silence occurs. I wait him out.

He answers, "Yes, Ms. Ford. I'll make that happen. What's her name?"

"Wonderful. Thank you, Ronaldo. It's Lilly—"

"Have him put it in Jaxon's name," Lilly interjects.

I clear my throat and instruct, "Actually, put it under Jaxon Savoia."

"Jaxon Savoia?"

"Yes. J-A-X-O-N S-A-V-O-I-A." I spell out the name for him.

"Okay, Ms. Ford. Is nine o'clock okay for them?"

"Hold on a minute." I put my hand over the phone and ask Lilly, "Is nine o'clock okay?"

Lilly nods. "Yeah."

I return to my call. "That's great, Ronaldo, thank you so much."

"No problem," he claims.

"Have a great day," I chirp.

"You too, Ms. Ford."

I hang up.

Lilly claps her hands. "Yay. You're amazing."

"No problem. So when do you think you're leaving town? Friday is several days away. I'm assuming Jaxon's staying longer too?"

"I sure am," Jaxon answers as he slides into the booth next to Lilly.

She turns and beams at him. "What are you doing here?"

He kisses her quickly, replying, "I finished my work early. I thought I'd meet you two for lunch."

He slips his arm around her, smiles at me, then his face turns serious. "Ivy, are you okay?"

"I am. Looks like you two are getting along?" I wiggle my eyebrows.

He chuckles and then glances at Lilly. His eyes dart to her lips. "We're getting along perfectly, right, Lilly?"

"We sure are," she agrees and then gives him another kiss.

I tease, "All right, you two, break it up."

He chuckles.

Lilly blurts out, "Hey, I have an idea. Why don't we have a double date tonight?"

Jaxon and I look at one another.

He narrows his eyes. "I don't think that's a good idea."

"Why not?" Lilly whines.

"Jaxon and Dax didn't exactly get off to a good start," I inform her.

Lilly rolls her eyes. "Okay, well, you two can get over it."

Jaxon's face hardens. Then he states, "I still don't agree with Ivy being around Dax."

Lilly elbows him.

"Ouch. What was that for?" he asks.

She declares, "Dax has changed. You can't hold stuff that

was in the past against him. We were all stupid kids back then."

"Can't I?" Jaxon asks.

"No, you can't. Ivy's in love with him, and he's in love with her. Plus, he's not the same Dax he was. So I think tonight's a great night for a double date," Lilly insists again and then smiles, nodding.

A tense silence ensues, with Jaxon and I studying each other.

Lilly grabs my hand. "Ivy, it'll be fun. There's no time like the present. We're your friends, and you love Dax, so these two need to get over their beef with each other."

I cave. "You're right. Okay."

"Yay," she claps.

Jaxon grinds his molars.

"Jaxon, how is work going?" I ask, eager to change the subject.

He groans and scrubs his face. "It's a nightmare. I didn't put enough of the Seducing Ivy orders in when they came to market. I was being cautious, and all my buyers are pissed. They're threatening to pull all their business if I don't produce the new blooms."

"Oh no. That's horrible," I say.

"Yeah, tell me about it. Let's change the subject," he says.

We spend the rest of the lunch talking and laughing. Jaxon and I tell Lilly things that have happened to us over the last few years. Lilly tells us more about California and her adventures.

Before we leave, we agree to meet at Dax's place at eight.

I return to the SUV and text Dax.

> Me: I need you home by eight tonight. We're having dinner guests.

Dax: Who?

Me: Lilly and Jaxon.

Dax calls me. "Is this a joke?"

"No, it's not."

"Ivy, I'm not eating dinner with Jaxon Savoia."

"Yes, you are," I firmly assert.

"No way!"

"Dax, Lilly's my best friend, and so is Jaxon. They're together now, and I want them to come for dinner. This issue between you and Jaxon needs to be resolved."

"What are you talking about? How are they together?" he questions.

"They're together. I hooked them up the other day. They like each other a lot."

"You're kidding me."

"No, I'm not. So I need you to do this for me. They're my only friends, and I don't want a bad relationship between you and Jaxon. Besides, it'll be fun," I insist.

Dax groans but gives in. "Fine. But if he tries to hit on you—"

"He won't. He's with Lilly, and they're happy," I reiterate.

"He better only have eyes for her," Dax warns.

"Don't worry. He does," I assure him.

"Lilly better not suggest an orgy," he adds.

"Dax! Stop! We're friends. That's all it is and will ever be. She knows that, so don't say things like that."

He groans louder. "Fine. See you later tonight."

"Yay! Bye!" I singsong. I hang up and smile. Happiness fills me. I finally feel like my life is starting to move forward.

Dax 30

YOU GET FIVE MINUTES

My day's flying by. It's four in the afternoon when I get another text.

Ivy: Turn on the TV.

Me: Why?

Ivy: Just turn it on.

I hit the button on the remote and sit back in my chair. There's a press conference, and Matt Montague is at the center of it. His pregnant wife stands beside him with her chin lifted, shoulders squared, and a solemn yet sympathetic expression.

Matt states, *"I decided to come forward with the support of my wife, Tori. I knew if I didn't speak out, Professor Dyer and Avery Carrington would get away with what they did to me."*

His wife puts her hand over his.

He glances at her, then continues, *"Since this happened, I've lived in fear of this coming out. The shame of what they did to me..."*

His wife steps closer.

Matt swallows hard and takes a deep breath. He declares, *"I don't want my children growing up as cowards. I want them to always be strong—stronger than I've been in the past. And it's my hope that other victims will come forward as well. I wasn't the only one on that video. There were dozens of us. And while I understand that it's hard to break the silence, if we don't, they get away with it. I refuse to live with the shame of this any longer."* He pauses.

Reporters scream out questions.

Matt puts his hand in the air. The noise dies down, and he adds, *"Professor Dyer and Avery Carrington are rapists. They raped me. And while there's a stigma behind men being raped, that's exactly what happened to me. And I won't sleep until I get justice."*

My phone beeps. I glance at it.

> Dean Bramwell: You could have stopped this. His father is sick.

My gut churns. I text back.

> Me: His father should be proud of him.

> Dean Bramwell: This is an atrocity. Do you know the shit that his father's going to get over this? He can't even show his face in the country club right now.

A ball of anger grows within me.

> Me: You just signed your resignation.

A moment passes.

Dean Bramwell: What the fuck are you talking about?

Me: You're used up, Bramwell. All this happened under your watch. You're done. Don't contact me again.

I put the TV on mute, then pull up my email and draft a new message. In the address line, I type in *Clifton Board*. The subject line states: *Dean Bramwell*. Then, I construct a letter.

To all board members,
The disgrace currently tarnishing Clifton University occurred under Dean Bramwell's watch. Dozens of events happened over the span of a decade, all while he was in charge.
Clearly, he doesn't know how to supervise his staff or students. I demand that he step down as dean, or I will no longer donate any funds to Clifton University.
This is nonnegotiable.
Sincerely,
Dax Carrington

I send the email and then sit back. I refocus on the TV and lean closer, turning the volume back on.

The view has switched to two photos, one of Avery and one of Dyer.

The news reporter states, *"While both parties' representation has stated no comment, it looks like the police aren't wasting any time."*

The screen splits into two videos. Avery's in one; Dyer's in the other. Both are in handcuffs and being escorted toward cop cars.

My phone rings, and more giddiness hits me. I mute the TV. Once again, I let the phone ring a few times before I pick it up. I rise and walk to the window, staring out at the ocean.

Bobby's father barks, "This is out of control, Dax. You caused this. I expect you to fix it."

"I'm not sure what you want me to do," I taunt.

He demands, "We need to meet. *Now*."

"Sorry. Can't do that."

"I'm not joking, son. We need to meet today," he repeats.

I state, "Sorry. I'm booked all day. It's not going to happen."

He roars, "I said I need a meeting with you!"

I wait a few extra seconds, staring at the waves. Then I finally offer, "We can meet tomorrow. I'll have my assistant let yours know what time." I hang up and then hit the intercom on my phone.

"What can I do for you, Mr. Carrington?" Michelle asks.

"Send a notice of an emergency meeting to our PR teams. I want a video conference in thirty minutes with all of them."

She replies, "Okay, Mr. Carrington. Do you want that on Zoom, or do you want that through Google Meetings?"

I groan, running my hand through my hair, snapping, "I don't give a fuck, Michelle. Just set it up and send the link."

"Yes, sir," she says.

I hit the button on the intercom and shake my head, wishing once again that my regular assistant was back.

The TV has the photos of Dyer and Avery back on the screen.

I pick my cell back up and text Ivy.

Me: I need Matt Montague's number.

Ivy: Why?

Me: Please don't ask me questions right now. Can I have it?

She sends it over to me.

Me: Thanks, baby girl. I need one more favor.

Ivy: What is it?

Me: Can you ask him to take my call?

A few moments pass.

Me: Please.

Ivy: I don't know if that's a good idea. Why are you contacting him anyway?

Me: You have to trust me. Please.

More minutes pass. I hate the dropping in my gut.

Me: You still don't trust me. I thought you told me you were going to.

Ivy: This isn't about trust. It's about Matt. I don't want to hurt him further.

Me: I promise you I'm not going to hurt him. Please just trust me. Tell him I need five minutes, and he won't regret it.

Ivy: Okay, I'll try.

Me: Thanks, baby girl.

I send a text to Matt.

> Me: It's Dax Carrington. I know I've been a dick to you in the past. I apologize. You don't owe me anything, but I hope you'll give me five minutes. I promise if you do, you won't regret it.

Twenty minutes pass, and I get another text.

> Ivy: I talked to Matt. I don't think he's going to call you.

I groan.

> Ivy: I'm sorry. I tried.

> Me: It's okay, gorgeous. I appreciate it. Can you send him another text for me?

> Ivy: What is it?

> Me: Can you tell him to please reconsider and take my call?

> Ivy: It would help if you told me what this is about.

> Me: I can't tell you right now. Please help me out and do it.

I wait for her reply.

> Me: Please.

> Ivy: Okay.

Over an hour passes. I keep my focus on other business matters, but it's hard. There's so much on the line right now.

Years of putting things together and being patient for everything to fall into place is finally occurring.

I finally get a text.

Matt: You get five minutes, maybe less.

Ivy 31

PUNISH ME LATER!

"Kristen, are there any bottles of the Seducing Ivy wine in the house?" I ask.

She grins. "There are several pallets in the wine cellar. Dax hasn't allowed anyone to drink it though."

My butterflies take off. He really did share the first bottle with me. It's another thing he's done that warms my heart.

Kristen arches her eyebrows.

I snap out of it and say, "Great. Can you bring a few bottles up and put them in the chiller? We're going to have some guests tonight."

She hesitates. "Do you think Dax will be upset?"

"No. But let me confirm," I say, not wanting Kristen to feel uncomfortable.

I pick up my phone and text him.

> Me: Can we take a few bottles of Seducing Ivy wine out of the cellar tonight for our dinner party?

> Dax: Sure, baby girl. Whatever you want.

I show Kristen the text messages, chirping, "All good!"

"Fantastic. I'll make sure a few bottles come up and go into the chiller."

"Thank you."

She leaves the room.

I study the dining room, loving how everything looks. There's a bouquet of Seducing Ivy on the table. Kristen found candles in the kitchen that match the ones in the restaurant.

I leave the dining room and overhear one of the workers in the hallway, whispering, "The press is everywhere. It took me ten minutes to get past the gate."

My gut sinks. Reporters have swarmed the gates of the estate ever since Matt's press conference and the breaking news about Avery's and Professor Dyer's arrests.

Why does Dax want to speak with Matt?

I've been dying to know what Dax is up to. Matt was annoyed that I asked him to talk with Dax. He was adamant he wouldn't speak with him. All of it makes me nervous. The last thing I want to do is hurt Matt worse, but Dax was just as adamant he needed to speak with him. So I've been on pins and needles, wondering what it's regarding.

I'd been glued to the TV until I realized I needed to figure out final details for our dinner date and get changed.

My phone beeps, and I glance at it.

> Lilly: Holy crap, it's a zoo out here!

> Me: I know. I'm sorry.

Lilly: It's okay. I should have anticipated it.

I pace the foyer until the doorbell rings. I open the door, and Lilly and Jaxon are on the doorstep. He has his arm around her waist, and she's carrying a bottle of champagne.

"Hi! Sorry about the paparazzi!" I say in greeting.

"That's crazy out there," Jaxon says with disapproval.

"I've never seen anything like it, and I live in L.A.," Lilly adds.

"I'm sorry," I repeat, feeling horrible.

Lilly waves her hand in front of her face. "No worries. It was kind of fun going through it. Maybe my father will see me on TV and freak out over my association with the Carringtons. Might give him a drop in voter approval this week." She winks.

I stifle a laugh, putting my hand over my mouth and shaking my head.

"Okay, you weren't lying. You do have daddy issues," Jaxon says, peering down at her.

She beams brighter and puts her hand on his chest, lowering her voice. She bats her lashes and coos, "Do you want to punish me later?"

Jaxon grunts, his expression darkening.

"Okay, why don't we go into the sitting room," I suggest.

Jaxon tears his lust-filled gaze off Lilly and shoots me a stern look. "I don't want you getting wrapped up in all this, Ivy. You don't deserve to be dragged through the mud by Dax again."

I put my hand on my hip. "Dax isn't dragging me through the mud."

"Not yet."

"Jaxon," Lilly reprimands.

"Are you going to have an attitude toward Dax all night?"

He clenches his jaw.

Lilly slides her hands up his chest. She laces her fingers around his neck, and he looks down at her. "Jaxon, we talked about this. Remember, you won't get your present at the end of the night if you don't behave and make peace with Dax." She smirks at him.

His heated eyes narrow.

I laugh. "Yeah, Jaxon, be a good boy so Lilly can give you her present."

He glances at me and then shakes his head once again in worry and disapproval.

I groan. "Come on, we're going to have fun tonight. Let's go."

I lead them down the hall and into the sitting room. I step inside and stumble to a stop.

Dax is on TV giving a press conference.

"Turn it up," Lilly orders.

I grab the remote and take the volume off mute.

Dax states, *"Avery illegally obtained the ability to use the patent for her perfume. She had already announced it and sent samples to all major buyers. I was trying not to bring any harm to the Seducing Ivy hybrid. Avery agreed to sign her company under Carrington Enterprises in exchange for me not pressing charges. Ultimately, her company has always had my full authority, and I was working with my legal team to take the steps needed to make the necessary changes."*

"What changes?" a male reporter shouts.

Dax continues, *"Yesterday, I officially removed Avery from Avery Carrington Scents. In addition, she no longer is welcome on the Carrington estate."*

A gasp goes through the crowd. Another female reporter yells, *"You kicked her out of her home?"*

Dax nods. *"Yes. She's in violation of the trust stipulations my grandfather put in place for my siblings and myself. He may be dead, but living on the estate he built is a privilege, not a right."*

More yelling fills the room.

Dax holds up his hand until there is silence.

"Let me make it clear. I do not, nor does Carrington Enterprises, condone any of Avery's actions. It's vile, illegal, and violates everything the corporation my grandfather built stands for and I continue to honor and build. At this time, Avery Carrington Scents has been dissolved."

"Damn," Lilly blurts out.

Dax announces, *"The perfume formula will be archived and all unfulfilled orders refunded. Any future perfume utilizing the Seducing Ivy brand will be a new creation. My hope is that Avery Carrington Scents will be a blip in your memory."*

"Will you stand by your sister and help her with her upcoming legal battles?" a male reporter asks.

Dax's face falls. He waits a moment and firmly asserts, *"No. Avery is on her own."*

Gasps fill the air.

A look of sympathy crosses his face and he declares, *"My sincerest condolences go out to her victims. Carrington Enterprises has set up a legal fund for any victim who wants to come forward and seek justice against my sister, Professor Dyer, or Bobby Winston."*

"Holy shit," Jaxon mutters.

My pulse pounds between my ears. I sit on the couch to steady myself, feeling light-headed.

Dax holds his hand up again until the room quiets, then adds, *"I'm also creating a therapy center. Victims can receive intensive counseling from the best professionals in the country. I've authorized my team to fast-track it. We hope the building is open within three months, but victims can receive immediate help via video therapy."*

A toll-free number pops up on the screen.

Reporters scream more questions, but Dax says, *"Thank you,"* and disappears through a door.

The news anchor appears, stating, *"And in the latest turn of events in the Clifton University scandal, Dax Carrington is stepping forward and making a blast of a statement."*

"He sure is, Trina," a male anchor agrees.

I turn off the TV.

Jaxon, Lilly, and I stare at each other.

My phone buzzes.

Dax: I'll be home in an hour. I'm sorry I'm running late.

Me: That was amazing what you just did.

Dax: You saw it?

Me: Yes.

Dax: I'm glad you approve.

Me: How could I not? Is there really a center opening?

Dax: Of course there is.

Me: That's really, really amazing. Thank you.

Dax: There's nothing for you to thank me for. I can't wait to see you.

Me: I can't wait to see you. Drive safely.

Dax: I will, baby girl.

I glance at the others and say, "Dax will be here in about an hour."

Lilly hands the bottle of champagne to Jaxon. "I think we should toast that announcement!"

Jaxon works on popping the cork while I grab three flutes from the bar.

Lilly holds up her glass and toasts, "To new beginnings."

"To new beginnings," I echo, feeling hopeful.

We clink our glasses and take a sip. Then we fall into comfortable conversation, discussing random things and laughing.

Dax finally appears, blurting out, "Sorry I'm late."

I rush over to him.

He pulls me into his arms and kisses me. He breaks the kiss and quietly says, "I missed you."

"I missed you too," I tell him, my butterflies fluttering hard.

He gives me another quick peck on the lips and turns toward the others. He tugs me into him, narrowing his eyes on Jaxon.

My butterflies disappear, and my chest tightens. In a calm voice, I say, "Dax, you remember Jaxon."

He utters, "Kind of hard to forget."

Jaxon's expression hardens.

Lilly steps up next to Jaxon and wags her finger. "Uh-uh-uh. You two need to kiss and make up."

They continue to glare at each other.

Lilly frowns at me.

I sigh.

"Seriously, are you two going to act like this all night? You both need to grow up," she reprimands.

"I agree. Come on." I pull Dax over to the others and add, "It's time to start over. Jaxon and Lilly are my best friends. And I'm in love with Dax. So you two are going to get along."

Lilly smirks. "Do you want pacifiers?"

Dax and Jaxon look at her in question.

"That's what babies get," she adds.

"Dax," I quietly beg.

The tension remains until Dax finally chuckles. "Okay. You're right." He holds his hand out to Jaxon. "Let's start over. I think we got off on the wrong foot. It's nice to properly meet you."

Jaxon softens. He shakes Dax's hand. "It's nice to finally meet you too. I've heard a lot of good things about you over the years. Well, before Ivy."

Dax's demeanor turns serious. "Yeah, I'm sure you've heard a lot of things. Most of them are probably true."

"But we're going to forget that stuff," I interject.

"Yeah. Come on. Here, have a drink," Lilly says, handing Dax a tumbler of scotch and then giving another one to Jaxon.

I hold up my flute, toasting, "To new friendships."

"Yeah. To new friendships," Lilly chimes in.

Everybody clinks glasses, and we take a drink and then sit down.

Dax asks, "How's business, Jaxon?"

I pipe up, "He has a supply chain issue. We need to help."

Dax snaps his head toward me, arching his eyebrows. "Oh?"

"Ivy, it's fine," Jaxon claims.

I glance at him and firmly assert, "No, it's not."

"It is," he says, and I forgot how he can be as stubborn as Dax.

"What's the issue?" Dax asks, his body relaxing as he slides his arm around me.

Jaxon doesn't answer.

I warn, "You tell him, or I'm going to."

Jaxon sighs and shakes his head. "Okay, fine. I didn't put enough orders in for Seducing Ivy when it came on the market. I wanted to be cautious. I've gotten burned before."

Dax nods. "That's a smart move, and understandable."

Jaxon adds, "I didn't realize it would be such a huge hit right out of the gate."

"His customers are threatening to move to a different wholesaler if he can't get them the Seducing Ivy supply they need," I say.

Dax nods, and his face turns solemn. "I'm hearing that from several wholesalers."

I slide my hand on Dax's thigh and tilt my head. "You're going to cancel other orders and send whatever Jaxon needs, even if it's the entire supply, right, Dax?"

He arches his eyebrows.

"Ivy, that's insane for him to do that," Jaxon claims.

Dax studies me a moment and then amusement flashes in his eyes. His lips curl.

My heart beats faster.

Dax states, "I guess a part of me is rubbing off on you."

Something changes in me. I can feel it. I can't describe it, except it's like a butterfly emerging from its cocoon. It gives me confidence. And I nod. "Yeah, I guess you have. So you'll do it tomorrow? You'll make sure Jaxon's set up?"

"You don't have to do that," Jaxon argues.

"Yes, he does," I assert.

Dax chuckles. He studies me for another moment.

"Well, you'll do it tomorrow?" I repeat.

He shakes his head.

"Really? You're not going to do it? For me?" I ask, disappointed.

He pulls out his phone. He types a text message and then tosses the phone on the table. "No, I just did it."

He turns his focus on Jaxon. "It's done. The supply coming out is limited, so I'm sure you'll do well, being the only supplier to offer it."

Dax 32

RAISE YOUR HAND

Dozens of women and men fill the conference room. Some attend via video due to the distance and the short notice. Their faces fill the screen at the front of the room. Two asked to listen only and weren't ready to reveal themselves to the others.

All are victims from the leaked tape. A few couldn't be contacted. One woman died from a drug overdose. Another died from cancer, and several couldn't be convinced to show up.

Zara, the woman who was only fourteen when Avery snorted cocaine off her pussy, was the hardest to convince to show up. Her father threatened to sue the college, but nothing's been done so far. She wouldn't confirm with the authorities it was her. But when Matt gave his press conference on TV, she called and said she would attend.

Getting the victims to show up was one battle. Convincing

them to do what I want is another, and the tension in the room mounts.

I state, "All of you need to be comfortable coming forward. It has to be of your own free will. And I hope all of you take the TimeMarker test. At least then, you'll know if you've been drugged or not, and you can pinpoint the time. Even if you're not ready to do something now, you can do it later."

More tension builds in the room.

Carla shakes her head. "You don't understand what it's going to be like for us to come forward the way you want us to."

Donnie agrees. "Yeah. We don't have the money you do. They'll bankrupt us."

"Even those of us who have money could be ruined. Anything that we've worked on in our careers could go down the drain," Leonardo frets.

"I understand—" I start but am cut off.

"Do you? How can you even begin to imagine?" Carla accuses, and shame fills her face. She looks away.

Brianna puts her hand on hers, and I am overcome with sympathy.

My gut flips. I take a few deep breaths and start again. "I won't claim to understand what you went through—are still going through. And I can only do what I can do."

"Which is what?" Zara asks.

I announce, "I have a fund for each of you with ten million dollars. It's only for you. You can use it for whatever you want, so you won't be any worse off, even if there is an initial financial blow or career roadblock. And I'll pay for the legal representation in a class action lawsuit against Winston Pharmaceuticals. We'll also personally go after Bobby Winston, Avery, and Professor Dyer."

"Sounds too good to be true," Leonardo mutters.

I reiterate, "I promise you, you won't be ruined by this financially."

"What about our reputations? How are you going to repair the damage?" Brianna calls out.

I sigh. "Look, I understand that this is going to be tough."

"Do you? Were you a victim? You weren't. So how can you even stand up here and pretend you understand what we went through?" Carla spouts.

My chest tightens. I nod. "You're right. I don't."

"You were just as bad as the rest of them," Theresa hurls, her eyes in slits.

My gut dives. I might have created the nickname Titty Teaser for Theresa. It stuck throughout high school and college. She had nipples so prominent, no matter what bra she wore, they were always visible. Even now, I have to avoid looking at her chest since they're still right there for the world to notice.

The room gets louder with accusations.

I hold my hand up. "Look, I told you at the beginning of this meeting that I was no saint. And I sincerely apologize for any pain I caused any of you. But what those three did is on a different level. It doesn't make me proud of my previous actions, but I am trying to do what I can to help get you justice."

"To clear your conscience," Leonardo hurls.

I shift on my feet, and the door opens. The hairs on my neck rise, and I go still.

Matt walks in with his wife and Ivy. The room goes silent.

Surprised, I blurt out, "Matt, you're here."

He grinds his molars, staring at me, and the hatred he feels for me is clear. I don't blame him, but if anyone can turn the room, it's him. I knew it when I reached out yesterday, but he refused to come.

Ivy steps next to me and grabs my hand.

Everyone gapes at her.

Theresa snarls, "Why are you holding Dax's hand?"

I tug her closer to me, unsure why she's here.

Ivy holds up her hand until the room quiets again. Then she says, "Some of you know me." She nods at familiar faces around the room. "And some of you were in school before or after me. For those of you who don't know, I was a victim as well. Bobby and Avery both gave me Trance at different times, and I'm a sex addict because of it. Is anyone else here a sex addict?" She raises her arm high.

Slowly, almost everyone in the room raises their hand. There are only three people who don't.

Understanding and sympathy fill Ivy's expression. I squeeze her hand tighter, and she looks at me, then back at the room. "The three of you who aren't... I'd say, consider yourselves lucky, but you're in this room for a reason. So I won't claim that you're any luckier than the rest of us. But those of you who did raise your hands, if you've ever sat there wondering why you are how you are, now you know the reason. It's 99% probable that you were given Trance. And Professor Dyer, Avery, or Bobby did it."

A new tension fills the air.

She continues. "I know it's not easy, and what Dax is asking you to do takes courage."

"Are you going to come forward?" Brianna calls out.

Ivy tenses.

My heart beats faster. I didn't invite Ivy to this meeting. She refused to see Vivian, and my protective instincts didn't want her to go through what I knew the others will if they step forward.

She lifts her chin and says, "Yes, I will come forward with the rest of you."

My insides quiver. I tug her tighter to me.

A collective sense of shock comes over the room.

I can do nothing but stare at her.

She avoids looking at me and nods, reiterating, "I will. I will come forward with all of you. If Matt could be brave enough to do what he did, then so can the rest of us." She looks at him.

He and his wife step forward. She keeps her arm around his waist, and he keeps his around hers. He declares, "That's right. If anyone understands how hard it is, it's me. But they're only going down if we all speak up."

The meeting takes a turn, and by the end, everyone agrees that they'll step forward. It's another win, except I'm not completely happy. I didn't consider that Ivy would come forward.

Everyone leaves, and I take her into my office. I ask, "Are you sure about this?"

Her eyes widen. "How can you ask everyone else to do it but not me?"

I put my hands on her cheeks. "I don't want the press coming after you."

She softly smiles. "I understand that, but I'm a victim as much as they are, and I need to do this as much as they do."

"Are you sure?"

She nods. "Yes. I'm sure. If TimeMarker can pinpoint when they drugged me, then I'm going after them too."

I study her momentarily and then admit, "You're one of the bravest people I know."

She laughs. "I don't know about that."

"You are," I insist.

The intercom buzzes and Michelle says, "Mr. Carrington, you need to look at the link I just sent you."

I release Ivy and go to my computer. I pull up my email and click the link.

Ivy steps next to me, muttering, "Holy crap."

Word of Cooper's restraining order is all over the news, and his sponsors are speaking out. All of them have issued statements about how they're dropping him. Several women have also come forward and accused him of drugging them with Trance.

"Oh my God," Ivy says, covering her mouth, the color draining from her face.

My stomach churns. I knew his relationship with Bobby and Avery couldn't be good, but I hoped he wouldn't have stooped to their level.

I turn to Ivy. "It's only a matter of time until everyone goes down."

She bites her lip and stares back at the computer screen.

I pick up my cell and call Dick Lyman.

"Dax. I assume you've seen the news on Cooper?"

"I have. How quickly do you assume before he's arrested?"

"Within a few hours," Dick states.

"Good. Set up trust funds for Cooper's victims. Tell them they'll have the full legal support to go after him as hard as possible. Same stipulations as the others," I instruct.

Dick whistles. "You are making a bold statement."

"Yeah, well, that's what I do. Let me know when he's arrested." I hang up the phone and turn to Ivy.

She shakes her head. "I never saw it coming with Cooper. I thought he was a good egg."

"I hoped he was smarter than to follow in their footsteps."

Silence builds between us.

My intercom beeps. Michelle states, "Mr. Carrington, your one o'clock is in conference room D."

"Thanks," I reply, then tell Ivy, "I have another meeting I

need to attend. It won't take long. Why don't you make yourself comfortable?"

"Okay."

I kiss her quickly, exit my office, and go down the hall. I step into the conference room.

Bobby's dad stands there, his back toward me, arms crossed, his gray hair perfectly groomed. His designer suit hangs looser than normal, and it appears he's lost weight. He stares at the crashing waves.

"Mr. Winston," I say.

He turns to me, scowling. "You're going to backtrack everything you've done, Dax."

"No, I'm not."

"You are."

"I'm not," I insist.

He points at me. "If you don't backtrack everything, undo all the stuff that you've done, I will haunt you until the day you die."

I grunt. "You're going to die way before me. Do you think that scares me? Besides, you're going to be tied up in legal battles for so long that you won't have time for anything else."

His eyes narrow, but I don't miss the fear in them. "What do you want for the drugs?"

I can't contain my grin. "Nothing. They aren't for sale."

"Everything's for sale, son. Now, tell me how much."

I let several minutes pass, which only infuriates him more.

His face turns redder. He snarls, "How much?"

"I'm not selling you the drugs so you can shelf them," I proclaim.

His face falls. He shakes his head, asserting, "I took you under my wing when you were a kid. You hated your old man, and I stepped in to guide you."

Part of me feels guilty. Bobby's father was more of a dad to me than my own. I spent countless hours at his house as a child, especially before I moved into the cottage. Whenever they went on trips, he would include me. And a lot of what I learned about business came from him.

Yet, it doesn't excuse his irresponsibility. He created Trance. It may have been for the meat industry, but he's fully aware of the damage it's causing on the streets. And he allowed Bobby access to it without thought of any consequences.

So I push my guilt aside and say, "That's why I gave you this meeting. To tell you to your face that this isn't going to go away, Robert. The best thing you can do is cut Bobby off. Don't defend him."

He steps closer. The scent of scotch flares in my nostrils. He declares, "You're not taking my business or my family down."

What's over is over, and it's clear my relationship with him has run its course. If he chooses to stand by Bobby after knowing what he's done, there's nothing else to discuss.

I step next to the door and hold it open, claiming, "You allowed your family and business to be vulnerable. That's on you, not me. And I'll be clear for you, Robert. I'm going to make sure nothing is left but ashes. Now get the fuck out of my office."

BAD GIRLS GET PUNISHED

T**HE WAVES** violently crash along the shore, keeping my adrenaline level high and not helping my growing unsettledness.

The meeting was intense. When Matt called me this morning, he told me what was happening and that he decided to attend.

I was bombarded by a slew of emotions. One of which was anger toward Dax for not telling me what was going on. Yet I loved that he was trying to protect me. I saw it the moment I walked into the room.

Now, though, my sexual urges are attacking me to the point I wonder if the CogniShift I took even works. How can it have stopped the progression when I feel so on edge?

Maybe my demons are awake due to the knowledge that after all these years, the predators who violated so many people, myself included, will finally pay the price. Perhaps they still need to fuck away all the years of pain. Whatever the root cause, my insides are quivering, needing a hit of Dax.

I discard my clothes, leaving on my crotchless, whore-red panties and cami. I keep on my four-inch matching stilettos with diamond-encrusted gold heels. I put them on this morning, wanting to feel confident.

But now I wonder if I semiconsciously knew I'd end up in Dax's office, waiting to surprise him when he returns.

I glance down at my body, again appreciating Dax's sense of fashion and how he spoils me. Then I stroll over to his couch and sit, crossing my legs.

The clock seems to tick louder, and my heart beats faster. I feel antsy, so I move onto my knees. I put one on each cushion and grip the back of the couch, wondering how I look and what Dax will think.

He flings open his office door, catching me by surprise.

I snap my head toward him.

He stops mid-stride in the doorway, and the sound of Michelle's nails clicking on the keyboard filter in behind him.

I drag my gaze down his body until it gets to his cock. Then I raise it slowly back up, pinning him with a challenging look and loudly stating, "What are you waiting for? Your dirty whore has needs."

The clicking sound ceases.

Dax's Adam's apple throbs in his neck. He clenches his fist at his side and studies me, his dark gaze lingering on my ass.

"Well? Is there a reason you're making my greedy pussy wait for you?" I ask saucily.

His lips twitch.

"Your filthy slut needs you to take care of her."

He shuts the door and locks it.

"Unlock it," I order.

He glances back at me, no longer able to hold back his grin.

"Unlock it," I repeat.

He obeys and walks over to me. He puts his palm on my ass, and to rile him up even more, I tell him, "I've been soaking wet all day just thinking about you."

He groans. "Fuck, you're perfect."

I laugh and then wiggle my ass.

He spanks me, and a sting erupts over my flesh from the strike.

"Yes!" I belt out.

He rubs the sting away, then spanks me several more times until my pussy spasms and my ass is numb. He murmurs in my ear, "You've been a bad little slut, wearing your stilettos and this outfit to my office, haven't you?"

"Yes!"

He demands, "I have a lot of work to do today. Who do you think you are coming in here and waving your bare ass cheeks in the air?"

"I'm your dripping-wet, greedy whore," I breathe, endorphins attacking me in full force.

He smacks me again, and I yelp. The sting resurfaces, and he rubs it out. "Louder!"

"I'm your dripping-wet, greedy whore!" I call out, my insides trembling with flutters. I'm sure everyone in the office can hear, but my demons love the risk of getting caught, and all I've thought about all day is how much I've missed Dax's public humiliation.

Maybe I'm a masochist. Perhaps the initiation into his world years ago entrenched me too deeply to ever return to anything vanilla. Yet I'm no longer ashamed of anything Dax or I say to each other during sex.

The world can know all of it. Every moment we're in our roles feeds my demons, and I won't hide them anymore. Not with Dax. Not with myself. This is who I am and who we are together, and I realize I don't want to change any part of us.

His mouth grazes my ear. He praises, "You fucking perfect, gorgeous baby girl. But what do you think you're doing, coming in here with your beautiful slutty lips when I'm in the middle of important stuff?"

Tingles burst throughout me. "Drop your pants," I order. "I don't have time to wait for it all day. My cunt's wet and ready for you. I need to be fucked, Dax. I need to be fucked now!"

The sound of his belt hitting the floor echoes in the room. He steps forward, puts his hands on my shoulders, and thrusts inside me, groaning loudly.

A sense of relief surges through my cells, deliciously tormenting me with the looming chaos I relentlessly crave.

Dax twists my hair around his hand, tugging so my head turns to face the wall. His palm curves around the back of my neck, securing my position. He thrusts slowly, taunting, "I should make you wait to come until I get home tonight."

"No! Faster!" I order.

He keeps his pace, warning, "I might do that, my little slut. I might make your pussy crave my cock the rest of the day."

"It already does. All day long! No matter what. Please! Fuck me harder!"

He doesn't. He leans closer, slowly sliding in and out of me, kissing my neck, then my cheek, then my lips.

I try to slide my tongue into his mouth, but he doesn't let me, moving his mouth to my lobe.

His breath teases me, mixing with the heat building in my blood.

"Dax, please," I beg.

"Bad girls get punished, baby girl."

"Please," I desperately whine, my insides clenching his cock as it taunts my walls.

"Your punishment has to fit the crime," he states.

"Dax—"

"Your greedy cunt needs to learn lessons," he adds, keeping his pace.

I try to move my hips, but he grips me tighter, not allowing me to increase the speed.

His lips curl against my skin. He asserts, "Whose slut are you, baby girl?"

"Yours!"

"Then you better declare it for the world to hear," he threatens.

I cry out, "I'm your dirty slut, Dax. My pussy needs it harder. Please! Fuck your filthy whore how only you can!"

He finally gives me what I want, thrusting his cock harder, gripping the back of my neck tighter.

"God, yes! Fuck me!" I scream, and sweat pops out on my skin.

He pounds into me, his pelvis hitting my ass over and over. He grits out, "Fuck, I love your wet pussy, my sexy little slut!"

"Harder!" I order, then my insides collapse, and a wave of endorphins hits me so hard I turn dizzy. My eyes roll.

"Say it," he demands.

"I love it when you fuck my slutty pussy!" I yell, violently trembling against the couch.

"Fuck I love you," he barks, his erection swelling against my walls.

"Dax!" I cry out, losing the ability to hold myself up and relying on the back of the couch.

"Fuuuck," he says on a groan, pumping me harder, filling me as I spasm against him. He thrusts through it until we're both spent, and he collapses over me.

My vision slowly returns to normal. My ragged breathing slows.

He releases my neck and turns me over, pinning his gaze on me.

I slide my arms around him, tugging his face to mine, urgently kissing him as if he might disappear.

He returns my affection as he sits and pulls me onto his lap.

We make out for a while, oblivious to anything except each other.

The intercom beeps, and Michelle tears us out of our trance, stuttering, "I-I-I'm sorry to interrupt, Mr. Carrington. Your next appointment is here."

Dax groans, shakes his head, then answers, "Put them in the conference room. I'll be there shortly."

"Y-yes, Mr. Carrington," she replies and hangs up.

I put my hand over my mouth and try to stifle my laugh.

Dax moves my hand, kisses me, and states, "I'm going to have to go back to work now."

"I know. Sorry I interrupted." I smirk.

He chuckles. "No, you aren't."

"Neither are you," I reply.

"Nope. You can bring your sexy body in here anytime, baby girl." He waggles his eyebrows.

I laugh, then move off him.

He rises and grabs my dress. He hands it to me, then pulls up his pants. He fastens them and pecks me on the lips. "I have a few more hours of work and then I'll be home. Okay?"

"Sure." I rise and tug my dress over my head.

He adds, "I have something for you before you go."

"What is it?"

He walks over to the safe and opens it. He pulls out three large accordion folders and holds them toward me. "These are for you."

I tilt my head, peering at them. "What are they?"

He studies me for a moment, and nerves fill my belly.

"Dax, why am I nervous about whatever is in those folders?"

He shakes his head, then answers, "Don't be. But I want you to take this information the right way."

"Meaning?"

He hands me the folders, and I take them. "When I obtained information on Seducing Ivy from your father's notebook, I also discovered these." He looks guilty, but I don't why.

The hairs on my arms rise. "I'm not following."

He briefly studies me, then says, "Your father created three more hybrids, but they weren't quite where they needed to be yet. My team has been working on continuing to develop what he started. After several tweaks, they're now winners."

I gape at him, speechless, my pulse skyrocketing.

He continues, "Read through these folders when you get home. We can discuss it over dinner, and it's up to you if you want to move forward with the patents."

I open my mouth, but nothing comes out.

Tension builds between us.

"Say something," he finally orders.

I swallow hard, my mouth dry. "I don't know what to say."

"Are you mad at me?" he asks.

I ponder his question. *Am I?* Dax has done so much with Seducing Ivy. His business acumen has given me businesses and income streams I never dreamed I would have. My father could have done anything with his hybrids, yet he did nothing. Now there are three more?

"Ivy, please don't be mad at me. I did it for you."

I shake my head. "I'm not mad."

"You're not?"

"No." I step forward, holding the folders close to my chest. "Thank you."

"You're happy about this?" he asks.

"If more of my father's work can be brought to market, yeah. He always dreamed about it, and I don't know why he never did anything with it. He had the money to get the patent."

Dax's eyes widen. "He did?"

I nod, admitting, "I didn't know until he was dead, but he did. He had a lot of money saved. I just..." I sigh. "I think he was too cheap to spend anything, and I don't understand why. But what you've done with the Seducing Ivy hybrid is amazing."

I can see the tension drain from his body. "I'm so happy you think so."

"I do," I reiterate. I rise on my tiptoes and kiss him, then state, "I'll let you work so you can come home sooner."

"Okay, baby girl." He slides his arm around my waist and escorts me through the building, then outside. The security guards create a wall, pushing us past the reporters until I'm safely inside the SUV.

The driver takes off, and when I get back to the estate, I go into the sitting room and open up the folders. I read through all of my father's original work. It's on a copy of a screenshot from his leather notebook.

Then, I read through all the tweaks Dax's research team has done and diligently documented. Everything is dated with the results of numerous modifications, some that worked and some that didn't.

When I reach the end of the pile, I lay the photographs across the desk.

The three new hybrids are gorgeous. The pictures show the new ivies climbing up walls. One bloom, marked *Tantalizing Ivy*, has sharp-edged, vibrant pink petals. A second photo, labeled *Teasing Ivy*, has dainty, striking purple blooms. A third photo, named *Conquering Ivy*, has huge, vivid flowers.

They all catch my breath, just like the Seducing Ivy hybrid. My phone buzzes. I glance at it.

Lilly: Turn on the news.

I grab the remote and click on it. Bobby's walking into a police station with his father. A team of attorneys sticks close to them, and security guards escort them through a crowd.

The news anchor announces, *"Dozens of women, as well as a handful of men, have come forward. The district attorneys stated multiple charges were filed against Robert Winston, III., known to most as Bobby, at five o'clock this evening."*

Dax 34

A MASTERPIECE

"Are you ready, baby girl?" I ask Ivy.

She arches her eyebrows, and her voice is laced with nerves when she says, "I'm not sure how to answer your question."

I grin. "It's okay, just come out with me. You don't have to pretend to know what's going on."

"No?" she questions.

I chuckle and shake my head. "Nope."

"Why can't you tell me whatever it is that you're announcing?"

I kiss her head. "You'll see. Come on."

We step through the doorway into the room full of reporters. Holding her hand, I lead Ivy to the stage with the podium and microphone.

Reporters scream in a deafening tone.

I release Ivy's hand and hold mine in the air, advising, "Quiet, please."

Since the scandals came to light, the reporters have become more aggressive at press conferences. They ignore my plea for silence.

Ivy steps closer to me.

I yell, "Quiet! Please!"

Slowly, the noise dies down.

I wait a moment to gather my thoughts.

A reporter calls out, "What's the newest Carrington scandal?"

A buzz fills the room, and I hold my hands in the air again, ordering, "Please. Let me speak."

It takes another moment for the room to return to silence.

I begin, "It's a shame my sister's and brother's actions tainted the Seducing Ivy hybrid. There's no doubt the Carrington name has been tarnished. I can't express the anger and disappointment I feel toward my siblings, but my heart aches for all their victims." I pause for a moment and glance at Ivy.

In the last few months, she's told her story, just like the others. She's been brave, and I've never felt so proud.

Flashes from cameras go off.

I blink and turn back to the reporters. "However, all of us have to move forward. There's more to the Carrington story and the future of my grandfather's legacy as well as Ivy's father's legacy."

Confusion is evident in the faces of the reporters. I glance at Ivy, and she has the same expression.

I declare, "The next thing you report regarding the Carrington name should be this. I'm not the rightful owner of the Seducing Ivy patent."

Gasps fill the air, and the reporters begin shouting.

"Did you say you're not the rightful owner of Seducing Ivy?"

"So you stole it?"

"Who does it belong to?"

I hold my hand in the air again, trying to calm the room.

Ivy smiles at me, and my heart soars. I still can't believe how lucky I am. She finally forgave me, and my life has never been better.

When the room quiets, I click on the remote. A screen behind me displays John Ford's face, and Ivy gasps.

I grab her hand and squeeze it. She blinks hard, and I sling my arm around her waist and tug her into me. I admit, "Seducing Ivy was a hybrid created by John Ford, Ivy's father. He was a hardworking man, and he put himself through college in West Virginia."

I hit the button on the remote, and a slideshow of pictures of John growing up in West Virginia, his time at school, and throughout his career, begins to play.

Ivy's eyes well with tears.

I hand her my handkerchief.

She dabs at her eyes, taking in the video.

I continue, "John Ford was the most creative, intelligent, and advanced botanist who's ever worked for Carrington Enterprises. He was the sole creator of Seducing Ivy. And he was also a wonderful father to his daughter."

I glance at Ivy, and a tear runs down her cheek. She swipes at it with the cloth.

I tug her closer into me and add, "In fact, he gave me a rightfully owed punch in the face one time, trying to protect his daughter from me. He knocked me right to the ground, so I can tell you he had a hell of a right hook too."

The crowd erupts in laughter.

Ivy laughs as well.

I pause for a moment and glance at the man on the screen whom I hated. He hated me just as much, maybe more. Yet he had something so brilliant in his hands.

He didn't know what to do with it. I'm unsure if it was from the fear of success or the fear of spending money. Either way, I'll always maintain he owed it to his daughter to get it out in the world. It's one thing I won't apologize for, but he's owed the credit, not me.

I lie to the reporters. "John wanted me to bring it to market so that Ivy would have the benefits. It was a shame he didn't see everything Seducing Ivy produced before he died. He created a masterpiece and knew we had the resources at Carrington Enterprises to develop his hybrid."

"Why did you claim it was yours?" a reporter shouts.

I continue to fib, knowing the press would be merciless if they ever knew the full truth. I state, "He didn't want his name on it at the time, but now there's no reason to hide it. I've added his name to the patent as well as Ivy's. The ownership has also been transferred to her, as she's the rightful owner."

Ivy's head snaps toward me, and I stare at her. She furrows her eyebrows.

I continue, "All profits from any Seducing Ivy product will fund a trust set up for his daughter, Ivy. Carrington Enterprises will license the patent unless the day comes when Ivy no longer permits us." I turn toward her. "I hope that never happens."

The crowd erupts with laughter again.

Ivy looks overwhelmed with everything she's just heard.

"Anyway, I appreciate all of you coming here, but it was time that the truth was told to the world. In the next year, Carrington Enterprises will license three new hybrids from Ivy Ford. They're all hybrids that John started creating and our researchers continued developing. We're excited about the future of Carrington Enterprises and these new hybrids under the supervision of his daughter Ivy. Thank you."

The room erupts with reporters shouting, and I steer Ivy back through the door.

As soon it shuts, she spins toward me. "Where did you get all the information on my father? And those pictures?"

"I told you I have a private investigator. People can find anything on anyone."

"I hadn't even seen some of those photos," she says, tearing up again.

"No?" I question.

She shakes her head. "No. Can I have them?"

"Of course you can. They're yours and in an envelope in the safe in our bedroom," I reveal.

"Thank you." She kisses me, then pulls back, asking, "Why didn't you tell me you were going to make that announcement?"

I shrug. "I thought it'd be better if you were surprised."

She arches an eyebrow. "Is that so?"

"Yep," I say, then chuckle. "I like it when you don't know what's coming, but it's a good thing."

Her smile widens. "Yeah, it's always better if it's a good thing." She reaches up and hugs me. "Thank you for doing that."

I nod. "You're welcome. And there's something else I want to tell you."

"What is it?" she questions.

My stomach dives. "My research team is telling me that they aren't any closer to eliminating the risks for NeuroZap. I've brought two other highly sought-after teams to work with our existing one, but they all confirm the same conclusion.

They can't give me an estimated time frame when or if it'll ever happen."

She tilts her head and puts her hand on my cheek. "I'm sorry. I know this is important to you."

I rarely feel anything but successful, but the issues with NeuroZap make me feel like I failed Ivy. I hate it.

She puts her hand on my cheek reassuringly. "Dax, it's okay. NeuroZap is still helping a lot of people."

"It's not okay. I've let you down," I insist.

She shakes her head. "No, you've not let me down, and I don't need NeuroZap. When you gave me the other drug, it stopped the progression. Besides, there's no one I want besides you."

"You don't?" I cautiously ask.

She studies me, then shakes her head. "No, Dax. I only want you. My addiction caused me to do things I was ashamed of for one reason." She pauses.

I wait, my heart racing faster.

She claims, "I did those things searching for you. But I have you now, and I'm okay. Unless you think we're having too much sex?"

I chuckle. "Is that even a real question?"

"Yes."

"How could you think I have any complaints?"

Her lips twitch. "Good. Then stop worrying about NeuroZap and the risks. I think it's great you're trying to eliminate it for other people, but I don't need it. As long as I have you, I'm fine. I can accept my addiction. You accept me and feed every urge I have. So I'm okay with it now. It's part of who I am, and I'm not ashamed anymore."

I study her, pondering her words, and I can't handle it anymore. I pull the box out of my pocket, that I meant to reveal later tonight, and kneel on the floor. I open the lid and hold it in front of her.

She puts her hand over her mouth and holds her breath.

Anxiety I don't usually experience attacks me. My mouth turns dry, and I swallow hard. I declare, "Ivy, I've wanted you since the moment I saw you. No matter what obstacle was in front of us, we've overcome it. Granted, most of those obstacles were my fault, but you're everything I've ever wanted. I can't comprehend ever living another second without you. And you're too good for me. You've always been too good for me. But I'm a selfish man, and the only way I'm letting you go is through death. Even then, I'll still have my soul entwined around yours, fighting to keep you with me through eternity. So I want you to be my wife. As much as I know you can do better, please say yes and become Mrs. Dax Carrington. Please, baby girl. Tell me you'll say yes and marry me."

Her glistening eyes dart between the ring and me. Her lips quiver and a tear rolls down her cheek.

"Please tell me you'll marry me," I say, my voice not as confident, afraid her silence means she won't.

She finally throws her arms around me and cries out, "Of course I'll marry you, you silly fool. All I've ever wanted to do is marry you."

I hold her tight, a surge of happiness pummeling me like never before, knowing I finally have it all.

I have her.

Forever.

Ivy 35

OUR LOVE STORY

Six Months Later

Lilly claps, squealing, "You look so beautiful!"

I'm overflowing with excitement. I stare at my reflection and pinch my arm.

"What was that for?" she asks.

"I wanted to make sure I'm not dreaming," I admit, dragging my eyes down the gown. Whore-red and gold flowers, mimicking Seducing Ivy, are stitched in lace over the white satin.

She slaps my ass.

I jerk forward and yelp, "Lilly!"

She giggles and smirks. "Sorry. Wanted to make sure you know this isn't a dream, future Mrs. Dax Carrington!"

Mrs. Dax Carrington.

My heart soars, and I tear up.

"Don't start that! You're going to smear your eyeliner and mascara," Lilly scolds, handing me a tissue.

I carefully dab my eyes and check that my makeup isn't running.

Lilly shoves a small box in front of me. She sings, "Time for you to open this!"

"What is it?" I ask, peering at the dark blue box secured with a fancy white ribbon.

She beams. "Something blue. Sit down."

I carefully lower myself onto the sofa, tug on the ribbon, and lift the lid. A matching blue envelope sits inside. I remove it, then open the flap. I pull out a glossy Seducing Ivy design. A blue arrow under it says, *Dax's*, with a squiggly arrow pointing down. Confused, I say, "Ummm, this is a nice picture. Thanks."

Lilly arches her eyebrows, her lips twitching.

"Am I missing something?"

She picks up a tissue, dabs it in her water glass, grabs the graphic, and points at me, ordering, "Lift your skirt."

"Why?"

"Just do what I say. Don't worry, I won't jeopardize our friendship and try to eat your pussy."

I cautiously say, "Okay." I pull my skirt to my hips, revealing everything since Dax didn't want me to wear panties today.

"Okay, stand up. This angle isn't going to work. And pull your dress to your belly button," she directs.

I rise, then pull my skirt higher, admitting, "I'm a bit confused about what's happening."

She laughs and states, "It's a tattoo, silly." She dabs the wet tissue on the back of the paper.

"Oh! Duh! That's super creative!" I say.

She steps closer. "Hold still," she advises, then presses the graphic an inch above my pussy.

"How long does this last?"

"It's the best quality I could find. They claim it can last up to two weeks."

"Wow."

She nods. "Dax is going to love it, which means you'll get even more tongue action."

I laugh, trying to contemplate receiving more attention from Dax than I already get. Sometimes, I wonder if he's the sex addict and not me. Or maybe I rubbed off on him, if that's possible.

"There! Don't let your skirt touch it for a few minutes," Lilly instructs and steps back.

I move in front of the mirror, check out the tattoo, and claim, "Dax is going to go nuts."

"That's the plan," she chirps.

I softly laugh. "You really are the bestie of all besties!"

"That I am," Lilly agrees, smiling wider. "Oh, hold on!" She grabs her purse off the table and pulls out a small fan. She turns it on and holds it in front of my body.

"Should we tease Dax?" I question.

Mischief fills her expression. "How?"

"One second." I grab my phone and step back in front of the mirror so she can continue drying the tattoo. "Can you hold my dress?"

"Sure." She takes the material in her hand while keeping the fan pointed at me.

I pull up my text chain to Dax.

> Me: Lilly got me a gift. She's staring at my pussy right now.

> Dax: What does that mean, baby girl?

Me: Sorry. I can't tell you until I'm Mrs. Dax Carrington.

Dax: You're going to leave me hanging like that?

Me: Yep. See you in a few.

I show Lilly the messages.

She laughs, then says, "There. All dry." She turns off the fan and lowers my dress.

There's a knock on the door.

She glances at the clock. "Time to go!"

My butterflies go crazy. I take a deep breath, staring at myself in the mirror.

"You ready?" she asks.

I lock eyes with her, lift my chin, and nod. "Yes."

"Great." She links her arm through mine and leads me to the door. She opens it.

Jaxon steps into the cottage. He glances at Lilly, his eyes darting with approval over her whore-red satin gown, and then at me. "Wow. You both look incredible." He kisses Lilly, then smiles at me, asking, "You ready?"

"Yeah."

"Okay, let's go." He holds his arms out, and Lilly and I link ours through his. He guides us to a golf cart.

Lilly sits in the back, and I slide in next to Jaxon. He drives across the estate and onto the trail through the woods.

My butterflies grow stronger, and Jaxon stops the cart a few feet before the trail ends and a whore-red carpet with gold and diamonds weaved over the edges begins.

Lilly grabs her Seducing Ivy bouquet, hands me mine, then steps to the edge of the woods.

Jaxon stays back with me. The music starts, and she disappears.

"Are you nervous?" Jaxon asks.

I smile and say, "No. Just excited."

He grins and hugs me. "I'm really happy for you. For both of you."

Over the last few months, Dax and Jaxon have grown closer, forming a strong friendship and business relationship. It's made me happy and relieved.

"Thank you."

He adds, "We've come a long way, haven't we?"

I chuckle. "We have."

The music changes, and the "Wedding March" blares through the trees.

He straightens and says, "Here we go." He leads me through the remainder of the forest, and the lake appears. Sailboats dot the background. The sun shines brightly, and sparkles leap off the water. The freshly painted boathouse has a wall of Seducing Ivy, Tantalizing Ivy, Teasing Ivy, and Conquering Ivy twisting all over it, creating a spectacular display of colorful blooms.

As stunning as everything is, there's only one thing I can focus on.

Dax.

He pins his dark gaze on me, intensifying all the flutters in my belly.

Jaxon steps in front of him and says something I don't even pay attention to.

Dax replies without unlocking his eyes from me.

Jaxon steps away.

Dax takes my hands and caresses them with his thumbs, his lips curving up.

My flutters calm. My heart swells so big I think it might burst out of my chest.

Once upon a time, I was a young girl who wished for Dax Carrington to be my love story. I wanted him to be my forever and for my father to love him too.

The scenario I dreamed of was far from the path we fumbled down. The story was doomed from the start, written with a perfect hero and a naive heroine who could do no wrong to the other.

My fantasy ignored reality. In the real world, people aren't perfect. They create pain for the ones they love, sometimes intentionally, sometimes by accident.

Maybe the agony is all part of true love. Perhaps those we can't live without need to test us, pushing us away until they realize they can't breathe without our love. Maybe there's no forever without the struggle to figure out how to unconditionally forgive the ones who hurt you so badly that, at times, you thought the grief might swallow you whole.

Either way, my reality is this: I fell in love with a villain. As much as he's grown, he'll always be one. Deep down, I know it, and so does he. Yet I wouldn't want him to change. The bad boy stole my heart, and he's not giving it back. Any chance he gets, he feeds me what I need. And once you've given in to a villain, you can't ever erase him from your heart.

But the villain also fell in love with a starry-eyed damsel who no longer exists. I'm fiercer, full of confidence, and no longer looking for anyone's approval but my own. Somehow, my newfound power didn't push him away. It pulled him closer, expanding his desire for me and giving me even more strength to step into my destiny.

My destiny is him.

Unfortunately, my father will never get to know the real man who stands before me, the one I know deep in my soul he'd be proud to call his son-in-law. I wish that chapter had been written differently. But some things you can't change, no matter how hard you wish.

As imperfect as Dax's and my love story is, it's ours. No one can change it or take it away. It's torn us apart and mended us back together, gluing the shattered pieces so our hearts became one instead of two.

So this is our real love story—flawed and stained, renewed by pain and laughter, smarter and wiser than the past. With every sin came the opportunity to bind us closer and start fresh with the knowledge you can't redesign the past. You can only create a brighter future, more aware of what will make the other person happy, even if it requires a sacrifice.

The naive girl I once was got one thing right.

Dax is my love story.

And as I stare at my love, the man who took me to Hell and then brought me back, I know I'd do it all over again. I'd relive every aching moment if I had to.

My villain's soul entwines with mine, over and over, so tightly wound there's no way it could ever come undone. I knew he was my forever then, and there's no way I could ever deny it now.

Epilogue

WRAPPED AROUND YOUR FINGER

DAX

Two Years Later

"No, Mommy!" Lilly pouts, tossing her peas into Ivy's face.

"Whoa! That's not what a good girl does," I reprimand, walking into the kitchen and grabbing a rag. I swipe green goop off Ivy's nose.

She tilts her head, scolding Lilly gently, "We don't throw food. Remember?"

Lilly holds her breath, her cheeks turning red, and scoops up another handful. She cocks her arm back.

I curl my fist gently around her fingers.

She defiantly glances at me.

I kiss her head and murmur, "Be nice to Mommy."

She releases a breath and wrinkles her nose. "Yucky."

I turn toward Ivy, stating, "Maybe we should grab another vegetable."

Ivy groans, rolling her eyes. "She has you wrapped around her finger."

"No, she doesn't."

Ivy scoffs. "Yeah, she does."

I glance back at Lilly.

She's the spitting image of Ivy. Her dark curls are extra frizzy today due to the summer heat. Her blue eyes well, and she exclaims, "Daddy! Yucky!"

My heart swells. I wipe her hand off and unbuckle her from the high chair. I pick her up, and she clings to me.

"Total sucker," Ivy chirps, smirking.

I kiss Lilly on the head and sit next to Ivy.

She leans closer to our daughter, tickles her stomach, and coos, "You grow moodier every day, don't you?"

Lilly giggles and holds me tighter.

"Not her fault. You named her after your bestie," I remind Ivy.

She grins. "Yep. And I hope Lilly's as happy-go-lucky and fearless as her aunt."

"I hope she's like her mom," I state and put Lilly on my knee. I bounce my leg and secure my hold on her back so she doesn't fall.

"You're home early," Ivy declares.

My chest tightens with a mix of excitement and nerves.

"What's wrong?" Ivy questions.

"Nothing."

"No?" She studies me.

I admit, "Craig Pohler called me about an hour ago."

"And?"

Goose bumps break out on my skin. I blurt out, "They found a way to eliminate the side effects of NeuroZap without compromising the drug's effectiveness."

Ivy gapes.

I take a deep breath and add, "He assures me it's ready to roll out to the masses."

"Wow! Dax, that's wonderful news!"

I nod.

Kristen enters the kitchen. "Sorry to interrupt, but it's someone's nap time."

"No nap!" Lilly spouts.

"Sorry, sweetie. Nap time is good for you." I tug her closer and hug her. I hand her to Ivy.

She hugs her as well, then passes her off to Kristen.

"No nap!" Lilly repeats, tears rolling down her cheeks.

"Aww, don't cry, Lilly," Kristen says.

"No nap!" Lilly screams, then sobs.

My heart hurts. I rise, stroke her back, and say, "Go lie down with Kristen. Daddy needs to talk to Mommy for a minute, then I'll come up and nap with you."

"You're spoiling her," Ivy mutters.

Lilly stills, except for the tears rolling down her chin.

"Be a good girl for Kristen. I'll be there soon."

"Now, Daddy," Lilly demands.

"Soon," I say, kissing her head.

"Now!" she screams, crying as Kristen carries her out of the room.

"You're creating a monster," Ivy adds.

"So you keep telling me. Anyway, what do you think?" I ask, sitting next to her again.

She peers at me. "About what?"

My stomach flips. "Do you want to take NeuroZap now that it's safe?"

Her eyes widen.

"Did I say something wrong?"

She reaches for my hand. "Dax, why would I want to take it?"

I stay quiet.

She adds, "I told you before. My addiction only gets to me when I don't have you. Do you plan on leaving me anytime soon?"

I jerk my head backward. "Of course not. Why would you even suggest that?"

Her lips twitch. "Then there's no reason for me to take NeuroZap. We have a very active, very fulfilling—at least on my part, it is—sex life. Why would I want to change anything?"

"Are you insinuating I'm not fulfilled?" I question.

"No, I just didn't want to speak for you."

"Well, don't say crazy things," I scold.

She laughs. "Okay. Fair enough."

I slide my hand over her cheek. "So you're sure you don't want to take it?"

"Yes. Nothing's changed from before. I love everything about our life. I'm happy you can roll it out to others, but I don't need it. I just need you."

Everything good inside me swells.

She leans forward and kisses me.

I return her affection, then retreat, holding her head in front of mine.

The fire in her eyes burns as brightly as it always does. My desire for her only grows stronger.

I study her, then suggest, "I think a nap would be better if you wore me out with those beautiful slutty lips first."

Thank you for reading The Wilted Kingdom Duet! I hope you loved their story.

Do you want one more spicy scene from Dax and Ivy? Flip the page :)

One More Spicy Scene

Find out what Dax and Ivy are up to in the future.

Can't get enough of Dax and Ivy? Want to read one last steamy scene?

If you are on a paperback go to:
https://dl.bookfunnel.com/n82jra14fn

If you are having any issues downloading this, please contact pa4maggie@gmail.com.

COERCION– American Scandal Book 1

A MORALLY GRAY STALKER AGE GAP ROMANCE

FROM INTERNATIONAL BESTSELLING author Maggie Cole comes a new morally gray, scandalous romance about the secret world of the President's daughter and the candidate she'll do anything to seduce.

The world says I can't have him, but he's the only thing I desire.

So I'll stop at nothing until every piece of his soul burns with the demented cravings he can't undo...the sins he can't unsee...the pieces of my mind and body he endlessly obsesses over.

I don't care if he's my father's Vice President, my best friend's dad, or married for political show.

Years ago, Drake Steele witnessed the dark crevices hidden within me.

He didn't run—he pulled me closer to him.

It was then I knew.

Our paths are intertwined for a reason.

My father didn't choose him to do a job. He unknowingly put him on his ticket for one purpose.

Me.

Coercion is book one of the American Scandal Duet. It's a stalker, morally gray, age gap romance about a political princess and her father's elected official. Drake and Virginia's story continues in Persecution, book two of the American Scandal Duet.

Ready for Drake and Virginia's morally gray, scandalous story?
Find it at your favorite retailer
OR
for DISCOUNTED paperbacks, audios, and ebooks go to Maggie's bookstore online!
https://maggiecolebookstore.com/

Can I ask you a huge favor?

Would you be willing to leave me a review?

I would be forever grateful as one positive review on Amazon is like buying the book a hundred times! Reader support is the lifeblood for Indie authors and provides us the feedback we need to give readers what they want in future stories!

Your positive review means the world to me! So thank you from the bottom of my heart! XOXO Maggie

Find Maggie's books at your favorite retailer
OR
for DISCOUNTED paperbacks, audios, and ebooks go to
Maggie's bookstore online!
https://maggiecolebookstore.com/

American Scandal (A Dark Stalker Age Gap Romance)
    Coercion (Book One) May 1, 2024
    Persecution (Book Two) TBD

Wilted Kingdom Duet (A Dark Bully College Billionaire Romance)
    Seeds of Malice (Book One)
    Thorns of Malice (Book Two)

Mafia Wars Ireland
    Illicit King (Brody)
    Illicit Captor (Aidan)
    Illicit Heir (Devin)
    Illicit Monster (Tynan)

Club Indulgence Duet (A Dark Billionaire Romance)
    The Auction (Book One)

The Vow (Book Two)

Standalone Holiday Novel
Holiday Hoax - A Fake Marriage Billionaire Romance (Standalone)

Mafia Wars New York - A Dark Mafia Series (Series Six)
Toxic (Dante's Story) - Book One
Immoral (Gianni's Story) - Book Two
Crazed (Massimo's Story) - Book Three
Carnal (Tristano's Story) - Book Four
Flawed (Luca's Story) - Book Five

Mafia Wars - A Dark Mafia Series (Series Five)
Ruthless Stranger (Maksim's Story) - Book One
Broken Fighter (Boris's Story) - Book Two
Cruel Enforcer (Sergey's Story) - Book Three
Vicious Protector (Adrian's Story) - Book Four
Savage Tracker (Obrecht's Story) - Book Five
Unchosen Ruler (Liam's Story) - Book Six
Perfect Sinner (Nolan's Story) - Book Seven
Brutal Defender (Killian's Story) - Book Eight
Deviant Hacker (Declan's Story) - Book Nine
Relentless Hunter (Finn's Story) - Book Ten

Behind Closed Doors (Series Four - Former Military Now International Rescue Alpha Studs)
Depths of Destruction - Book One
Marks of Rebellion - Book Two
Haze of Obedience - Book Three
Cavern of Silence - Book Four
Stains of Desire - Book Five
Risks of Temptation - Book Six

Together We Stand Series (Series Three - Family Saga)
    Kiss of Redemption- Book One
    Sins of Justice - Book Two
    Acts of Manipulation - Book Three
    Web of Betrayal - Book Four
    Masks of Devotion - Book Five
    Roots of Vengeance - Book Six

It's Complicated Series (Series Two - Chicago Billionaires)
    My Boss the Billionaire- Book One
    Forgotten by the Billionaire - Book Two
    My Friend the Billionaire - Book Three
    Forbidden Billionaire - Book Four
    The Groomsman Billionaire - Book Five
    Secret Mafia Billionaire - Book Six

All In Series (Series One - New York Billionaires)
    The Rule - Book One
    The Secret - Book Two
    The Crime - Book Three
    The Lie - Book Four
    The Trap - Book Five
    The Gamble - Book Six
    STAND ALONE NOVELLA
    JUDGE ME NOT - A Billionaire Single Mom Christmas Novella

About the Author

Maggie Cole is committed to bringing her readers alphalicious book boyfriends and fiercely strong heroines.

She's been called the literary master of steamy romance. Her books are full of raw emotion, suspense, and will always keep you wanting more. She is a masterful storyteller of contemporary romance and loves writing about broken people who rise above the ashes.

Maggie lives in Florida with her son. She loves tennis, yoga, paddleboarding, boating, other water activities, and everything naughty.

Her current series were written in the order below:

•All In (Stand Alone Billionaire Novels with Entwined Characters)

•It's Complicated (Stand Alone Billionaire Novels with Entwined Characters)

•Brooks Family Saga- A Dark Family Saga – Read In Order (Each book has different couples)

•Behind Closed Doors-A Dark Military Protector Romance – Read in Order (Each book has different couples))

•Mafia Wars (Stand Alone Novels with Interconnecting Plot and Entwined Characters)

•Mafia Wars New York (Stand Alone Novels with Interconnecting Plot and Entwined Characters)

•Club Indulgence Duet-A Dark Billionaire Duet – Read in Order (Same Couple)

•Mafia Wars Ireland (Stand Alone Novels with Interconnecting Plot and Entwined Characters)

•Wilted Kingdom Duet-A Dark Bully College Billionaire Duet-read in order (Same Couple)